A MOTHER'S DILEMMA

www.penguin.co.uk

Also by Emma Hornby

A SHILLING FOR A WIFE
MANCHESTER MOLL
THE ORPHANS OF ARDWICK

For more information on Emma Hornby and her
books, see her website at www.emmahornby.com

A MOTHER'S DILEMMA

Emma Hornby

BANTAM PRESS

LONDON · NEW YORK · TORONTO · SYDNEY · AUCKLAND

TRANSWORLD PUBLISHERS
61–63 Uxbridge Road, London W5 5SA
www.penguin.co.uk

Transworld is part of the Penguin Random House group of companies
whose addresses can be found at global.penguinrandomhouse.com

Penguin
Random House
UK

First published in Great Britain in 2019 by Bantam Press
an imprint of Transworld Publishers

A CIP catalogue record for this book
is available from the British Library.

ISBN 9780593080559

Typeset in 11/13.25 pt ITC New Baskerville by Jouve (UK), Milton Keynes
Printed and bound in Great Britain by Clays Ltd, Elcograf S.p.A.

Penguin Random House is committed to a sustainable
future for our business, our readers and our planet. This book
is made from Forest Stewardship Council® certified paper.

MIX
Paper from
responsible sources
FSC
www.fsc.org
FSC® C018179

1 3 5 7 9 10 8 6 4 2

For my readers – thanks to you all. Without you, it's simply words on a page. And my ABC, always x

About the experienced masters in the craft, there is the quiet canniness of the devil.

Benjamin Waugh, founder of the NSPCC, on baby farmers

Author's Note

It was whilst researching for something else that I first stumbled upon the subject of baby farming. Both horrified and fascinated, I was driven to find out more and the idea for this book was born.

Baby farming was a scourge of the Victorian era. The term referred to the act of accepting custody of an infant, usually illegitimate, in exchange for money. Social conditions of the time forced desperate mothers to use such services in their droves. However, though most baby farmers were paid with the understanding that care would be provided, not all were as trustworthy as they seemed. Once the fee had disappeared, the child quickly followed suit.

The heinous practice was widespread and vast numbers of children were disposed of by so-called 'angel makers'. Rising numbers of convictions for murder and neglect finally forced Parliament to confront the epidemic, and proper fostering and adoption regulations were introduced. The last baby farmer to be hanged was in 1907.

Research for *A Mother's Dilemma* made for grim reading, but immersing myself in a subject matter is vital to bring the reader an authentic portrayal. Bygone times were hard for the people that lived them and I always strive to weave the fact into my stories. I do hope you enjoy Jewel's journey.

Emma Hornby

Chapter 1

1856

THE BABY'S GUSTY yell filled the kitchen again and Minnie Maddox chuckled. A healthy pair of lungs on the tiniest scraps of life always brought warm happiness to her. It was the quiet ones you had to keep an eye to, for Death's cold claws never hovered too far away. Were it to catch you unawares, the shadowed fiend would spirit a body away in half a heartbeat. She should know. Hadn't she borne witness to such, time and again?

Abandoning her baking and wiping her floury hands on her apron, she then lifted the lid of a small saucepan. Before dipping a fingertip inside and wiggling it around to check the temperature, she glanced to the damp-stained wall to her left. Muffled shouts could be heard from next door and, though Minnie wasn't one to eavesdrop on other folks' business, how could you close your ears to such goings-on when the dividing bricks were as thin as theirs were and the voices so loud with the passion of their disagreement?

'Please. Oh, won't tha reconsider?'

'I'll not waste another breath on this, woman.'

'But Fred, we could make it work, aye, if only you'd give it half a chance—'

A thud, sounding like a fist meeting a tabletop in

angry frustration, smothered the pleas. 'Nay, I said! That's an end to it.'

Minnie lowered her stare with a small, sorry sigh. As she knew it would, seconds later, her good friend and neighbour Flora Nightingale's harsh weeping pushed next through the crumbling plaster: 'Husband, please, please . . .'

'I'll not – cannot – fetch up another fella's babby.' Fred's words had lost a little of their hardness but still, his tone was firm. 'It's a child of our own or none at all.'

'I'm fifty-one years of age, Fred. There's been norra glimpse of a monthly bleed from me this past year or more – it's over for me that way, can't you see? Yet there's babbies aplenty needing homes still and always shall be; we could give such a thing to one. A poor mite without a mam or father to call their own could be ours, if only you'd—'

'It's not to be for us and that's that. The Lord has made His decision loud and clear and it's not for us to question His design.' He paused. Then he took a loud, shuddering breath that relayed locked up inside himself a mountain of disappointment and pain. 'Now, we'll speak on this no more. That's an order, Flora.'

Gulping sobs were the only sound as his wife struggled to stem her heartache in compliance, then silence fell. Minnie wiped away a tear for the couple next door and returned her attention to her task.

When the child yelled out once more, this time, it brought no laughter to Minnie. Instead, she bit her lip, for if she heard as easily as she did business from the Nightingales' dwelling, so they must hear well enough the noises in here, and how much worse must Flora's emptiness stab to hear what she craved more than anything else in the world? Minnie was heartsore for her – for the pair of them.

She craned her neck to glance to the staircase, calling, 'Eliza, lass? Cradle the new mite, will thee, whilst I prepare its grub? Poor divil shall waken the rest, else, and that's the last thing we need.'

A girl around ten years of age, a floral-patterned scarf tied around her head, emerged at the top step. Her face, hands and apron were grubby with coal dirt and her equally dark brows drew together as she clattered down to the kitchen. 'Thought tha told me to see to the fire up yonder?' She flicked her eyes in the direction from which she'd just come. 'I can't be in two places at once, you know. If we're to make the bedroom presentable for the next what calls with a full belly, you can't keep yelling for me to aid you in this and t' other—'

'Shurrup blathering and see to him, will thee?' Minnie cut in mildly. 'He just wants a cuddle. Reassuring, like. He's likely fretting for his mam.'

With an exaggerated sigh and a roll of her eyes, the girl crossed to the sagging bed wedged into the alcove by the fire. Arranged in a neat line the length of it and wrapped in an assortment of clean but ragged coverings were half a dozen bundles – babies of varying ages. Eliza reached for the smallest one snuggled between two others and held him against her chest, making clucking sounds of comfort.

The mixture in the pan Minnie was occupied with, which had been warming by the fire for most of the day, still held some heat; she nodded, satisfied. She poured the pap – a creamy concoction made up of water, flour and animal milk, sweetened sufficiently – into a glass nursing bottle. Checking that the fine twine that attached the sparkling white calf's teat to the bottle's neck was secure, she too now crossed to the bed. Before relieving Eliza of her burden, she drew a little of the food through to warm the teat, thus heightening the chance of the baby not rejecting it. Some children required gentle manipulation for them to believe it was what nature intended and not the artificial but adequate thing it was. She prayed this child would be easy to hoodwink.

'There, now. That's right. Ay, you're not fussy, are thee? Good lad,' Minnie cooed with approval as the scrawny fingers clamped around the feeding vessel, drawing it closer. Grasping the teat between his lips, he drank heartily, eyes too large for his monkey-like face at once growing drowsy with satisfaction.

Her own misted at the sight. Poor young devil – and oh, his poor young mother, too. Hadn't she wept something awful this morning when she'd deposited him here? She'd loved him, that much was plain. But what was an unfortunate of this city, with nothing in life, to do? She couldn't very well have kept him with her in the one room she shared with two other women of her trade, could she? Customers wouldn't much like that, nay, and besides, it was no life for a child, his mother had insisted, and Minnie had agreed. Best he was given half a chance, eh, at this struggle most called life?

As she had then, filled with pity watching the street-walker count out the necessary coins, Minnie silently swore again she'd do her best for him. And she would. She did, for them all. Every child who entered her home would only leave it for one better than anything its mam could have dreamed to offer it. That was her mission. As far as she knew, she'd failed none yet.

'Min?' Eliza's whisper sounded behind her, pulling her from her musings.

'Aye, lass?'

'This one's dead.'

She swallowed in cold dread. 'What?'

'This one's dead,' the girl repeated.

Slowly, Minnie forced herself to turn. In the crook of Eliza's arm, the grey-white face and colourless lips outlined with their ring of blue confirmed it. Minnie deposited the feeding child into the girl's free arm and lifted the still-warm body of the other, larger child. But for his bloodless features, he appeared to be resting. Just sleeping the deep slumber of the innocent, not dead, gone . . . Her voice was hollow. 'All right, poor angel. Aunt Min is here.'

'Seems to have slipped away, quiet like, whilst you were about your baking. He'd not have suffered none, Min,' the girl offered gently as reassurance.

Though Minnie knew her words to be right, still the truth did little to dampen the hurt, the guilt. *One baby departs this earth, another arrives to take its place in the world* . . . She released a pain-filled sigh.

'Don't be for blaming yourself,' continued Eliza, as though reading her thoughts. 'He weren't for settling from the off, was he?'

She shook her head. 'Mind, it's not only that he were sickly in health and strength, nay. He's pined away, that's what. Watched him wither before my eyes, I have, these past weeks. What was there for me to do? Feed, bathe, clothe – love even, aye – I can do that. Mend a broken heart, I can't. That's what's finished him off. Being parted from his mam proved too much for the poor soul, I reckon.' She looked to Eliza for confirmation and, receiving it in way of a nod, breathed deeply again in an attempt to pull herself together. She couldn't afford the luxury of a good weep; besides, what good would that do? She had the scant burial to plan, the others to care for, her home, her baking to see to. Babies came and babies went. One way or another.

Throughout the following hours, necessary arrangements were conducted and life in general behind the door of number six Kirby Street continued, as it must. Now, the departed soul, washed and wrapped in a white blanket, lay in a tiny, rough wood coffin, which the undertaker's boy had carried upstairs shortly before to the bedroom Minnie and Eliza shared. The remaining infants, as though sensing his departure and the heaviness in air wrought by the loss, had been quieter than usual – Minnie was thankful for it. She couldn't wait to get into bed later and allow herself that cry. Aye, that's what she needed: a cup of tea and a good bawl. The latter would have to wait a few more hours, but the former, she could do.

Eliza, one eye on the bed and the sleeping babies within, the other on the ancient blanket she was darning, glanced up as Minnie passed her fireside chair en route to the teapot. 'All right?'

'Aye. I'll grab some air forra minute, lass. Just yell should one of the babbies stir, I'll hear thee.'

The early June sun barely touched the dying afternoon. Sitting like a dull white disc in the smoke-choked sky, it acknowledged the inhabitants of this grey industrial city with little more than a passing glance. The daily struggle of its rays to pierce the sulphurous fog from an army of cotton-mill, factory and domestic chimneys, whose numbers had astronomically increased throughout the century, had left its mark – it had given up the fight long ago. Even in the height of summer, the haphazard maze of cobbled streets, lanes and narrow courts remained imprisoned in impenetrable gloom. Unsurprisingly, it mirrored the mood of an already suffering populace entirely.

Glancing to her left, Minnie eyed the mass of sooty

red bricks that was the Manchester Flint Glass Works. The main works building of the ever-expanding premises, nestled at the south side of Kirby Street and adjoining Canal Street, loomed like a guard overseeing its workforce. Indeed, a large fraction of those who laboured hard beyond its doors resided in the surrounding streets. Situated strategically along the bank of the head of the Islington Branch Canal, which fed into the main line of nearby Ashton Canal, it transported its raw materials and finished products through the short body of water continually. Canals fostered the growth of industry with their ability to carry bulky goods long distances cheaply and efficiently – like many other businesses, the glass works took full advantage of the fact.

Aye well, thought Minnie with a bitter shake of her head. So long as the labour was completed in as short a space of time as possible and the profits were healthy, the masters were happy. Mind, much of their workforce were not afforded the luxury of those descriptions – healthy, happy – were they?

Her long-departed husband had been employed there most of his life – today, along with hundreds more men, women and children, Fred Nightingale next door still was. He and her Walter had been firm friends since they were kiddies and, when Fred secured the neighbouring house shortly after his marriage, she and new bride Flora had instantly grown just as close. A grand couple, they were, and a great comfort to her when Walter succumbed to the harsh conditions of his trade.

The life of a glass blower was not for the meek of heart. The majority died young. The long, irregular hours were hardship enough. Yet it was the great heat that proved the crux for many. Temperatures reached such hellish heights that it was not unheard of for the very boards on which the workers stood to catch fire beneath their feet.

Besides the obvious susceptibility to burns, as well as violent bouts of nausea and rheumatic disorders, their sight and lungs were also affected – her beloved's red eyes and rattling wheeze were what she remembered most about him now. The chest affliction that carried him off had taken a piece of her, too. But for the now-grown children born from her womb and those she cared for today with as much attentiveness and affection – none more than Eliza – she'd have followed him to the soil many a long year before this one, she was sure.

And what had she to show for an early widowhood and the torment that came with it? Her gaze flicked behind her indoors, to linger on the sideboard against the back wall. Winking atop it in the fire's glow stood an eight-inch-tall, thick glass candlestick of cut prisms, presented to her after Walter's death as a token of acknowledgement for services rendered. Quite exquisite; a fine example of industrial art. However, a poor comparison to a blood-and-bone companion.

Yet despite it all, he'd had work, and that wasn't something to sniff at. Brass to pay the rent, keep the cold from their marrow and hunger from their bellies. The unemployed of this city would give their right arm and leg, as well as eventually their life, she'd bet, for the chance to earn an honest crust. It was how it was. Aye, she'd known loss, but who hadn't?

Again, Minnie's eyes travelled inside, only this time towards the stairs and the chilled body of the poor dead babe now free of this life of want. Fresh tears stung. She hugged herself.

'Hello, Minnie.'

Lost in thought, she jumped at the quiet greeting

8

and fingers squeezing her shoulder. 'Flora, love. All right?'

The slightly built woman rested her back against the bricks by her own front door. 'Catching some air, Minnie.'

'Aye, and me.' She stole a sidelong look at her friend. 'And how's Fred?' she asked carefully, not wanting to give away that she'd heard their ruckus earlier and embarrass the woman.

Her response was barely above a whisper. 'Abed. He's on night work the night.'

Minnie turned now and eyed Flora properly. She looked terrible, all pale cheeks and purple-rimmed eyes. 'You sure you're well, wench?'

'Nay, if I'm honest. That pain's nagging me again. Feel queasy summat awful, an' all.'

Minnie frowned worriedly. For many months now, her friend had been blighted by internal complaints and sickness. She also seemed to have a permanent headache – stress, Flora reckoned, but coupled with her other symptoms, Minnie wasn't so sure. She'd attempted several times to coax her into getting the doctor out, but Flora wouldn't hear of it. His services cost money they could ill afford; she'd be right as rain soon, she'd insist, yet her ailments showed no signs of abating. She looked to be getting worse, if anything.

'Fred said nay again.' Flora shrugged miserably. 'I don't know why I keep going on about it. Does no good at all. He'll not consider another fella's offspring.'

Minnie's voice was soft. 'Some men can be funny about things like that, that's all. He's not denying thee to hurt thee, wench.'

'I know. He's a good husband to me. I just can't understand . . . It matters norra single bit to me. I just want . . . any would do, any.'

9

'Eeh, love.'

Tears had thickened Flora's words, but she cleared her throat and a wistful smile appeared. 'Remember when me and my Fred were wed, Minnie, and came to live here?'

'I do. I were just thinking on that a minute since, as it happens.'

'Ay, we had all our lives before us. So hopeful, we were, for the future. Never did we think that the Almighty would turn His back on us and deny us the one thing we both yearned for more than owt else.'

Minnie had heard such lamentations hundreds of times over the years and now, as always, she simply listened. It was what Flora needed: a frequent, open ear to which she could unburden her heartache. Minnie, unable to imagine what a motherless existence must be like, offered it always, willingly.

'Fred says it's His will we weren't blessed,' Flora continued. 'I don't know. It just don't seem fair to me. I'd have made a good mam, Minnie.'

''Ere, course tha would.' She reached across and squeezed her hand. 'By, the best, I reckon. I'd not let these babbies I care for go to just anyone, now would I? And ain't I allus said, you and Fred could have had any one of the poor blighters what's come to me. For I know you'd provide the love and care they deserve, no doubt about that, nay. But Flora, lovey . . .' Minnie broke off to sigh.

As much as it would pain her, and likely the woman beside her, to say this, it needed voicing. It was doing her friend's health – not to mention her marriage – no good. No good at all. 'I think it might be time to . . . you know. Accept things as they are, like. Fred'll not be swayed and, well, husbands are the ones what have the final say.

I'm that sorry, oh I am, to be saying this. But for your own wellness of mind and heart . . . you need to accept how it must be, wench. It'll make you iller still, else.'

Flora didn't respond, simply heaved a long, slow breath that seemed to come from her very soul. 'Can I come in and see them, the babbies? Give them a bit of a cuddle, like?'

'Course you can.' Minnie nodded, smiling. 'You do most days, don't you? Have I ever turned you away afore now?'

'I'll not be in your road? You're not busy?'

'Nay, nay.'

Eliza had dozed off and, likewise, in the bed facing her chair, the line of babies slept on peacefully. Flora's eyes shone as she approached them, and Minnie had to swallow down her pity. Her words to Flora about putting aside her wish of becoming a mother herself had fallen on deaf ears. Flora wouldn't – couldn't – ever accept it, it was obvious.

'Ah, the new angel. A tiny thing, he is.' Flora brushed a finger across the cheek of the child Minnie had fed earlier. Suddenly, she turned, eyebrows knotted. 'Where's t' other one?'

'Upstairs.' Immediately, her eyes were wet, and she had to gulp her next words out. 'The precious thing passed away, Flora love, earlier on.'

Despite her own upset at the news, Flora came to put her arm around her friend's shoulders. 'You're not to blame yourself.'

'I do all the same. Babbies come and babbies go, I know it, but it never gets easier.'

It was the other woman's turn to offer some sage advice. 'You did your best for the poor mite, I'm sure.' She motioned to the girl by the fire. 'Look at the lass akip, there. And where would she be, I'd like to know, but for your kindness? You kept her on with you when no one wanted the sorry, half-lame soul. Fed, clothed and kept a roof over her head, you have, when many a body would've left it to the workhouse to provide.'

'Aye, well. I weren't aware of Eliza's bad legs at the time. She were but a few hours old the day her mam dropped her off here – it weren't 'til later, after her mam had long scarpered, that I noticed her affliction. And well, when couple after couple turned their noses up at adopting her because of it, what were I to do?'

Flora inclined her head again, this time to the rag rug and the animals snoring softly there before the leaping flames. The ancient one-eyed dog lifted its head, yawned and returned to its dreams. The contented three-legged cat with only half a tail, however, didn't stir. 'And them two – not to mention countless other strays you've took in afore them?'

Minnie shrugged. 'Couldn't very well leave the buggers to starve or freeze to death on the streets, now could I?'

'Nay, and shall I tell thee why? For you're the keeper of the waifs and unwanted of this city, and honest as the day is long. For you've a golden heart, allus have had. But your ways, you play them down. Truth is, you love that girl there as if she were one of your own. The animals, an' all. As for the babbies you find new lives for, well, just what would they do without you? Be at the mercy of others pretending to ply a similar trade to yours, that's what. Now, admit it.'

'I do, aye. I grow to love every one of them, be it beast or child, what passes over yon threshold, however long I have them for,' Minnie admitted, smiling.

'Don't ever doubt your goodness. Promise me.'

'Aye, wench.'

'And you'll cease blaming yourself over that poor dead babby up yonder?'

Minnie held Flora close. 'I will.'

'Good. Good.'

'There's some tea not long since brewed if you're for wanting a sup?' Minnie asked softly, filled with love for this small woman she didn't know what she'd do without. However, her friend didn't answer and, when Minnie pulled back to look at her, her lips bunched together. Flora was ashen and was gritting her teeth in obvious discomfort. 'Flora? What is it, what's to do?'

'That pain, it's back again.' She pressed her palm to her ribs. 'Don't fret none, it'll pass in a minute,' she gasped out.

'For the love of God, wench, will you see the doctor? Please, for me? This has gone on long enough, you can't keep putting it off and—'

'I'll be off home, now, Minnie,' Flora cut in quietly.

'Wench—'

'I'll be seeing thee, love.'

Insides churning with frustration and worry, Minnie could only watch as her friend slunk away. The front door shut and she lowered herself into the chair facing Eliza's. However, her gaze remained on the door and, despite the passing minutes, her anxiety refused to leave her. Possible causes affecting her friend's health flitted through her mind, each more fearsome than the last. What if it was this illness, that disease . . .

'Stop it,' she told herself firmly, though it did no good. Her friend needed medical attention, there were no two ways about it.

Suddenly, another thought struck and the worry lines faded from her brow. Flora wouldn't listen to her, that much was clear. Fred, on the other hand, was another matter.

Her eyes strayed to the clock and she quickly calculated the time yet to pass until the night shift began at the glass works. Mind made up, she folded her arms with a determined nod.

*

Eliza's frightened yell, swiftly followed by the fretful cries of several of the babies, hauled Minnie from her dreams in a heartbeat. A crick in her neck jarred as she bolted up; wincing, she rubbed the spot and blinked around the room, senses muggy with sleep.

The fire had burned low and she had to squint through the gathering gloom at the girl. 'What's all this? What's to do with you? Set the babbies off, you have, with your noise—'

'Never mind my noise,' Eliza cut in, jabbing a finger to the street outside. 'Some mad swine hammered hell out of yon door; frickened me half to death, it did— Eeh!' she added when, sure enough, on cue, another heavy thump sounded. 'Ay, Min, what's afoot? I'm scared.'

'Now then, no need for all that.' She tried to sound more nonchalant than she felt. Moments like this, when it could be anyone out there in this impoverished, crime-riddled city trying to gain entry, made her wish all the more that she still had a man about the place. But she didn't. She must be the protector, always. Squaring her shoulders, she headed for the door.

The knocking struck up again as she reached it, more insistent than before. When she opened it wide, an admonishment ready on her tongue for whoever was causing the disturbance, she found herself almost barged to the ground as the visitor rushed inside. Gazing up, her anger instantly gave way to dread. He wore no shirt and his dark red hair stood up in all directions, as though he'd rushed straight from his bed to here. Though his eyes sparked with emotion, the rest of him was expressionless, as if frozen in panic.

'Fred? Lad, speak to me.'

His mouth flapped open and closed but no words emerged. He shook his head.

'Flora . . .' The name trembled from Minnie's lips and in the next moment she'd pushed past Fred and was running outside, through the Nightingales' open door and into the kitchen. She stopped dead in her tracks.

'Mi— Minnie. Mother of God, the pain . . .'

'Wench!' She hurried towards the table and her friend beside it in a heap on the hard floor. Next to her, a chair lay on its side – likely its falling over the sound which had awoken Fred. 'What happened?'

Having followed Minnie home, Fred answered for his wife. 'I heard a crash and her cry out like a beast in pain. When I ran downstairs she were lying there like this. She couldn't speak, then, with the shock, like. I came straight to yours, didn't know what to do.' He crouched beside her to stroke his wife's head. 'Flora? You well now, lass?'

'Course she ain't ruddy well.' Minnie spoke more harshly than she'd intended, worry and not a little anger bursting out before she could stop it. 'The poor love's been unwell for months and months – why didn't you notice, Fred? Why didn't you drag that doctor round here to attend to her? And now see what's happened, look at the state she's in—'

'It's not . . . not Fred's fault. I've hid it from him, Minnie. He knew nowt . . . nowt about it.'

Fred's face creased with hurt. 'Why, Flora?'

'I didn't want you fretting is all. I thought it'd . . . pass soon enough.'

15

'Eeh, lass, you should have told me!'

'I know, I'm sorry, I—' A wail ripped from Flora's throat, killing her speech. 'Merciful God, my insides . . . the pain . . . !'

As though absorbing all he'd heard, Fred released a low gasp. His face had turned corpse grey and he grasped Minnie's arm with such force she winced. 'Fred?'

'Flora's father, and her grandfather afore him . . .'

'What? What?'

'They both died from the stomach cancer. God above, it can't be. My Flora can't . . . She can't . . .'

Minnie tried desperately to swallow down the shock and horror clogging her throat, but it was useless; she burst into tears. Her friend had stated only a few short hours ago her belief that God had turned His back on them. For reasons she'd never fathom, it really did seem He had. She fumbled for Fred's hand and squeezed. By now, Flora was slipping in and out of consciousness. Minnie shook her by the shoulders to rouse her. 'Love, stay awake. Please. You're going to be just fine, you'll see. Fred's off to fetch the doctor.' To him, she added, 'Quickly, lad. Go now.'

'Why didn't I give consent to taking on one of them babbies of yourn?' he murmured, eyes fixed on his wife's face, as though he hadn't heard Minnie. 'It's all she ever wanted. All she wanted her life through. Had I, she'd have told me she were ill sooner. A child would have given her summat to want to go on for.' Gruff sobs bent him double. 'I could have fixed her broken heart and never did, were too hung up on my own feelings to think of hers and all. Lord forgive me!'

'You mustn't think like that. Now, the doctor, Fred,' Minnie told him, more firmly this time. 'Fetch him, go on.'

When he'd stumbled off she placed her palm on

Flora's stomach and, gently, felt about. The woman didn't stir and nothing, as far as Minnie could ascertain, seemed out of the ordinary. Then she shifted it around to Flora's side and immediately her fingers brushed a large, hard lump behind her ribs. Her mouth ran dry. Hand trembling, she retraced the area. She pressed it lightly. To her astonishment, the mass pushed back – she felt it clearly against her skin. She snatched her arm away with a cry.

It had almost felt for a moment there that something, some living thing . . . Minnie's lips parted and her mouth fell open. Her eyes followed suit; wide with incredulity, they studied the prone woman, now, in a fresh light. The months and months of sickness and lack of bleeds, the clear swell of Flora's normally flat breasts . . . 'Good God, it cannot be,' she murmured to the empty room. Her banging heart threatened to spring from her chest in euphoric realisation. Given her years of experience, the countless expectant mothers whose babies she'd helped bring into the world . . . How had she not noticed? She hadn't suspected a thing, never considered for a single moment . . . 'Wench? Wake up, please, wake up. Does tha hear me?'

'Mm?'

'Oh, Flora, love.' Minnie could barely give life to her words and her vision was blurry with tears. 'I think . . . Mother of God, I do actually believe— Eeh!' she exclaimed on broken laughter when, suddenly, like a river bursting its banks, water gushed from between Flora's legs.

'Minnie?' With a small frown, the woman blinked up at her drowsily. 'What's occurring? I'm . . . wet. Wet and . . . Why are you laughing? Where's my Fred? Where is he?'

'Oh, wench.' Tears of joy streamed down Minnie's cheeks unchecked. 'By, you daft bloody bugger, yer.' She reached for Flora's hand and kissed it soundly. 'Fancy you frightening the livers out of us like that and all the time . . . Flora, you're with ruddy child!' She bobbed her head in confirmation when her friend simply gazed at her. 'And said child is set to make its appearance – right now!'

Flora hadn't the chance to respond; her face contorted and she let out an agonised scream. 'Down below, it feels . . . I want to push!'

'Then you do it.' Gathering back control from sheer instinct, Minnie rolled up her sleeves with a firm nod. 'Listen to your body, wench. Do as it's telling thee and you'll not go far wrong. Now don't you fret none, for I'm here. I'll not let nowt happen to thee, you have my word on that.' Positioning herself between Flora's legs, she lifted her friend's skirts, whipped down her undergarments and examined her, murmuring soothingly all the while. From what she could tell, this miracle child would be here in a matter of minutes, if not sooner. Swallowing down her excitement, she instructed quietly but firmly, 'At the next pain, I want you to bear down with all your might. You understand, wench? Nice deep breaths and a strong, steady push.'

'I can't . . . don't know what's happening . . . A cruel trick, that's what this is! There's no baby, there's not, it's a mistake—!'

Minnie cut off her high-pitched shouts with a chuckle. 'No mistake, Flora, oh nay. Now, remember what I said. At the next pain—'

'Oh Lord, oh, it's coming back.' Flora writhed to her hands and knees, grunting and groaning. 'God above, the pain's too much, I can't, can't . . .'

'Tha can and tha shall. Deep breaths, wench.' Minnie crouched behind her and now, taking another look between her legs, she gasped. The child's head was crowning. She was overcome with emotion at the sight – quickly, she swiped an arm across her eyes. There would be time for all that later. Right now, her friend needed her to remain composed and aid her through this. 'Harder!' she urged, when Flora, panting on all fours, began to push. 'More, wench, that's it, go on, a last big strong 'un . . . ! Ah! Good girl, you've done it!' she cried, catching the slippery body in her firm grasp as it emerged into the world. 'Eeh, Flora! Oh, wench. Would you look at that – oh, beautiful!'

Flora sank to the floor, sobbing loudly. 'How can this be?' she repeated, over and over, dumb with shock. However, when Minnie placed her child into her arms, the words melted on her lips and she gazed, awestruck, her breaths coming in short bursts.

'It's a girl, love.'

'Minnie, I never knew. I thought I were long past my time for it to ever be possible. I thought I had the cancer, were dying. How could I not know?' She burst into tears again, only now her weeping held snatches of wild, ecstatic laughter. 'I've gorra babby. I'm a mam!'

Minnie giggled through her own tears. 'Aye, you are. Babby must have been lying more towards your back behind your ribs; that's why you've not showed none at the front. It ain't uncommon – I've heard of such happening over the years. Hiding from your mam and father, were you, eh?' she added tenderly to the child. She shook her head. 'Eeh, I just can't . . . I'm lost for words, I am, really.'

'Fred! Lad, can you believe . . . ?'

Her husband, who had entered breathlessly, the doctor in tow – he bumped nose-first into Fred's back as he juddered to a halt – gawped at the incredible scene. Flora repeated herself but still he stood mutely, as though set in stone.

Rubbing his nose, the young medical man stepped around him. He nodded down at mother and babe and smiled. 'Well. This is a grand sight to behold. From Mr Nightingale's explanation, I was prepared for something else entirely.'

'It's a certain miracle, Doctor!'

'Indeed.' He grinned at Flora then turned his attention to Minnie. 'The child was delivered by your capable hands, Mrs Maddox?'

'Aye, Doctor.'

'No complications?'

'Nay, none.'

Relief passed over his face. He rolled up his sleeves. 'Excellent. I'll take it from here, Mrs Maddox. I'm sure your girl . . . Eliza, is it?'

'That's right.'

'Her legs are well?'

'Well as they can be. We've not been in need of you of late, as you'll have noticed, anyroad. They don't bother her so much as she gets older, glory be to God.'

'Good. Well, I'm sure she will agree you've earned a cup of tea for your work here today. Instruct her to put in a drop of brandy for your nerves.'

It was her turn to grin. 'I shall, Doctor. And aye, aye – it give me quite the shock!'

'And me, though I'll not hold it against her. My precious jewel.' Flora lifted her head and her eyes were bright with tears. 'Jewel . . . Suits her that, I reckon. My Jewel. Aye.'

'A bonny name for a bonny lass,' Minnie wholeheartedly agreed. 'I'll be away, now, let you grab some rest. Eeh, wench.' She caressed her friend's cheek then the baby's. 'I'm that happy for thee.'

'Ta, love, ta for everything. Minnie?' she added as her friend rose to her feet.

'Aye?'

'I'm complete.'

The two words, spoken with such raw simplicity, such truth, brought a lump to her throat. 'Bye for now, wench.'

Patting Fred's shoulder with a chuckle as she passed him, Minnie stepped into the cobbled street. And as she closed the Nightingales' door behind her, she was just in time to hear the new father rouse from his shock and his tearful laughter and heavy clogged steps as he rushed to his family's side.

*

'Eeh, lass.' Having filled Eliza in on the incredible occurrence, Minnie dropped into a chair at the table. 'I'm in need of a strong sup after that, I am. Nay, bugger the tea, just fetch the brandy.'

The girl obeyed, bringing down from a shelf the ready supply kept for rubbing on to the swollen gums of teething babies. She pulled out the stopper and pushed the bottle across. 'A rum do is that. I ain't never heard the like. Aw, bet the pair are fair daft with joy.'

'They are that.'

'Lord bless them.'

Minnie took a draught of the fiery drink and her eyes flickered towards the stairs. What a day. One soul departs this mortal realm, another enters it. Such was the world over, every second of the day. It was a queer old doing, this thing called life.

Her gaze moved to where Eliza limped around the fire, dragging her twisted leg behind her, busy at a fat-bellied cooking pot – preparing their evening meal of mutton broth by the smell of it. On impulse, she crossed the room and hugged the girl close. Eliza didn't question it, simply returned the embrace. And Minnie breathed a slow sigh.

21

It might have come late but those good people next door had got their happy ending. Not many did, that was for sure.

This day, right now, all was well with the world.

If she could have held on to the moment, kept it safe in her bunched fist and never let it go, she would have. Because for reasons she couldn't fathom, a quiet panic had settled in her breast and she was powerless to shake it.

Chapter 2

'MADDOX, IS IT?'

Minnie opened the door wider. The surly-faced woman before her whose harsh knocking had pulled her from her chores offered not a glimmer of a smile, and her next words were as hard as the first:

'Well? Are you deaf or summat, or do I have the wrong dwelling?'

'I'm Mrs Maddox, aye.' And who the devil was this? she wondered. Certainly not the sweet young lass she'd been expecting, had the room upstairs all ready for, that was for sure. She eyed the shabby, squirming bundle in her visitor's arms. 'And what can I do for thee?'

'What d'you think?' Without waiting to be invited, she brushed past Minnie into the house. Here, in the kitchen's glow, her features were more visible – Minnie saw instantly that she'd been crying, though she was doing her utmost to appear stony, unfeeling. Minnie felt herself soften towards her.

She'd seen this stance a hundred times over. Some women wailed and wept the moment they entered and were still doing so upon leaving. Some ranted and railed, puce with rage, against life in general, while some were meek or as silent as the grave. Others adopted this one here's approach, believed that in quelling the

23

emotions the stab in their hearts at what was to come would be less and the wrench easier to bear. One did what one must, what suited each best, was right for them. Minnie neither assumed nor judged. But she felt, oh she did, for all of them, every last one. And their babes, too. Poor devils.

'How much?'

Minnie paused in her task of checking the teapot's contents to glance over her shoulder. Hopping restlessly from one foot to the other, the woman was biting her lip. Minnie gave her a soft smile. 'Sit thee down, lass, and take a sup. Let's discuss matters proper, like.'

'Nay, I ain't got time for all that bother.' Despite her thick, dun-coloured shawl and the room's good fire, the woman shivered. 'Just name your sum, then I can be away from here.'

Minnie sat anyway and, before lifting her cup to her lips, enquired, 'How did you come by my name?'

'Friend of mine. You took her burden off her hands a fortnight past.'

The slight but robust, monkey-featured mite who had taken so well to the bottle . . . Realisation brought a nod from Minnie. Only this morning she'd waved him on his way to a new life with a well-to-do childless couple from neighbouring Salford. If she remembered rightly, his birth mam had been an unfortunate of this city – one of many lost souls who plied what was between their legs on these mean streets. Was this acquaintance of the same trade? she wondered fleetingly, then cast her musings aside. It mattered not, at least to her. The well-being of the children was her concern, not how their mothers chose to survive this life. Her place was not to judge but to help. As usual, she would ask no questions. Not part of the deal, not her concern. Only the welfare of the child.

24

'Look 'ere, I've places to be. Now will you take this in or won't yer—?'

'All right, all right, calm thee down,' Minnie interrupted the outburst. 'If you've not the time for tea, you've surely some to spare to hear my terms.'

The woman's face relaxed a fraction. 'You mean you'll have it?'

Her choice of the term 'it' brought a disapproving frown to Minnie's brow. Nonetheless, she held her tongue and nodded. 'Aye. Now, let's iron out the details.' She motioned to a chair and, this time, the woman accepted, perching on the very edge as though prepared for flight at the earliest opportunity.

'I will start by saying I don't normally, as a rule, deal with folk turning up at yon door as you yourself have the day. I solicit infants through proper and above-board means: adoption advertisements in newspapers, through nurses, midwives, keepers of lying-in houses, that sort of thing.'

Though she had a single room upstairs, Minnie didn't class hers as a lying-in establishment. Such places – private houses where poor, unwed women could pay to give birth and arrange for the transfer of their infants to women such as herself – were generally a saviour to those in need of them. She'd only take in a woman with whom she'd some connection: a family member of a friend, that sort of thing. Her main business was in finding new homes, new lives, for children. And she was proud of that fact.

'I'm a respectable procurer,' she continued. 'Don't turn no babby over to anyone else, unlike some of my trade I could mention. Pocket the initial fee, some do, then if they can't find parents or are too impatient to look, dump the young angels on anyone with the promise of a cut of the brass – they've earned money for nowt, then, you see, and to hell with the child. Aye, it's to them a quick and easy way to make a few bob. And the one what took it off their hands . . . Well, once their sum has run out . . .'

She paused and lifted her shoulders in a small shrug. Raising a child cost money. Disposing of the millstone round their neck, in whatever way their conscience saw fit, was soon to follow. She shuddered to dwell on the evil of humans. 'Nay. Babbies comes to me from their mams and they stops with me until such a time as they are found new – permanent – homes with fresh parents. Good parents, to boot, aye. The best.'

'How much?'

The cold tone of the woman before her brought Minnie's brows together again in a frown. It was as though she hadn't heard a word she'd said. Such utter indifference, and at such a thing – on one so young, too – was unnerving. She'd be glad to rescue the infant from her, she admitted to herself, hoping God would forgive her for thinking such a thing. Mothers being separated from their babies . . . well, it wasn't the natural way of things, was it? Yet with this one . . .

'Well? Are you for bleedin' telling me or have I to take the thing elsewhere?'

Minnie was struggling to cling on to the last shred of her patience. If this unfeeling piece referred to the mite just once more in the way she kept doing, she'd be powerless to stop herself giving her a whipping from her tongue. 'Depends,' she forced out through gritted teeth.

'On what?'

'Whether it's weekly or monthly fostering you're after, or a permanent adoption. I'll require two shillings a week, or eight shillings per month – and at least with these options the child would stop with me and you'd maintain contact, get to visit, like, when you dropped off payment—'

'Nay, none of that. I want shot. Permanently.'

'The cost will be greater, you understand?'

'Aye, and worth every copper coin. The sooner I'm rid, and for good, the better.'

Minnie nodded. 'Then adoption it'll be. I'll find someone decent, no need to fret on that. A respectable couple what can give the precious mite a sound future.'

For the first time a flicker of something flashed across the woman's face, softening her features. She blinked twice, cleared her throat. Then the stony look returned and she nodded stiffly. 'How much?' she barked again.

'Four pounds.'

Eliza had been hovering nearby, and the woman thrust the child into her arms and extracted a cloth pouch from the folds of her skirts. She counted out the relevant coins and placed them on the table. Then without another word or glance to anyone, including her offspring, she swung on her heel for the door.

'Wait.'

Though she paused at the threshold, she didn't turn.

Shaking her head – Minnie had never encountered anything quite like this, like her, in all her days – she crossed the space towards her. 'I'd like some details: your name – the child's, too, and age,' she added. 'And Lord in heaven, besides owt else, won't you be wanting to say your farewells, like?'

'Nay.'

'Lass, listen to me. Don't come to regret your haste. Once new parents have been found, you'll not—'

'No goodbyes.' Still she had her back to her, and Minnie could gauge nothing from her tone. 'My name's Webster. Miss Webster, if you'd not already guessed.'

'My place is not to judge—'

'Huh! You'd be the first, then, let me tell thee.'

Pity stirred within her. Whatever the woman's attitude – and to all intents and purposes, it could very well be a front to hide how she really felt; though, by God, if so, she was a fine pretender – she didn't know her story, did she? Neither did she know what had driven her to this point in her life, this day, here. Nor who was to blame. After all, unless she was the reincarnate of the Holy Mother, women didn't get a bellyful of baby by themselves. 'And the child?' she asked quietly.

'I gave birth three weeks ago.'

'A name?'

She shook her head.

'But . . . surely you've been calling the mite by summat these past—'

The slamming of the door at the woman's sharp exit was the only answer. Minnie and Eliza shared a shocked and saddened look.

'A queer 'un, she were, and no mistake.' Eliza moved to the window to pull aside the length of faded curtain. She flicked her gaze left and right along the street. 'She's gone.'

'Aye well. Pass the child to me, lass. Let's take a look at what we've got here.'

'Reet cold, weren't she?' the girl continued as she handed the grubby bundle over. 'Nowt beating in that breast of hers at all, I'd say.'

However, Minnie wasn't so sure. Why, if she cared nought for the infant, take the trouble to seek her – a respectable, trustworthy minder – out? Her friend had clearly told her that Minnie was clean-living, God-fearing, honest, and the woman just now had sought her out on the strength of that reassurance to offload her child. And paid a small fortune to do so.

There were a hundred and one other avenues she could have chosen to dispose of the child if she'd a mind to; plenty that wouldn't have cost her a penny. Countless others did, in the most heinous of ways. And if you hadn't the nerve or stomach to do it yourself, this city and beyond were teeming with unscrupulous characters who would willingly take the task on for a lot less than four pounds. The canal, not an arrow's flight away, which she'd likely passed on her way here, was another example. Lord only knew how many people, desperate or otherwise, had taken advantage of its dark, watery belly to rid themselves of unwanted life.

Yet she hadn't. And though still it told nothing of her decision, her choice to come here instead said it all. Spoke a thousand words, it did, aye.

'Now then. Who've we got here? Oh, would you look at that.' Having laid the child in the centre of the table and drawn aside the swaddling, Minnie stood back to fully assess her latest charge. Eliza shuffled to her side and Minnie smiled down at her. 'What d'you reckon?'

'Bonny as the day is long, Min.'

'I'll say.'

The child was a picture of health, despite its somewhat grubby appearance. The nose and eyes were clear of discharge and crust free – good signs that illness wasn't present – and the cheeks held a soft bloom. Breathing sounded steady, no rattling in the chest indicating bad lungs. Minnie counted the little fingers and toes – all present and correct.

She nodded, satisfied. 'A fair size, an' all. Looks to have entered the world near full term. Good, good.'

''Ere, is it a lass or a lad? I don't recall the mam saying, do you?'

Minnie blinked, surprised to realise she'd allowed the

29

oversight and that Eliza was right. She peeled back the child's clothing. 'We have a girl. Mind you . . .' She motioned downwards and Eliza nodded understanding.

The tender flesh was raised in shiny red pimpled patches, and caked powder in the creases of her thighs and groin had hardened, causing further irritation. However, it wasn't the worst case of napkin rash she'd seen. The skin wasn't broken; there was no spotting of blood on the sopping material. This could be put down more to lack of parental experience than neglect. The infant was well fed and free of injury. All in all, the waspish woman from before had provided adequate care, despite her stance that she worried not for her daughter's welfare.

'Poor love. Looks sore, that does,' stated Eliza.

'Aye. Sour smelling, an' all, she is, but we'll soon remedy that.' Minnie rolled up her sleeves before filling a large, chipped ceramic bowl with water still warm from the kettle. 'Go on, lass,' she told Eliza, 'give her a good soaking whilst I sort her with a fresh rig-out. Gentle, mind, as I've shown thee. And be mindful of supporting her head.'

As the girl softly splashed water over the baby's body with a clean rag, cooing and smiling, Minnie lowered herself to her knees and opened the deep bottom drawer of the dresser. This was filled to capacity with woollen clothing in various sizes, each piece knitted by her own hands and which had served countless nurslings to have passed through her care. After selecting what she needed and leaving them by the fire to warm, she went to fetch the bottle of olive oil for use on the angry rash. Then she went to stand beside Eliza.

The baby, rosebud mouth pursed in mild interest at the proceedings, offered no resistance. Her violet eyes flicked about, taking in everything. In turn, Minnie watched her keenly. She seemed to possess an intelligent, almost wise air; Minnie was charmed.

'Look see at this.'

'What, lass?'

Eliza tilted the child with a jerk of her head. 'The shoulder, there.'

Minnie stooped to finger what she'd indicated – a neat, coffee-coloured stain the size of a farthing coin. She smiled. 'Only a simple birthmark, nothing to fret about. I think it's fair becoming, actually. It has the uncanny shape of a sycamore leaf, you see?'

Eliza nodded, though no doubt she couldn't rightly say she'd ever seen one, never mind the trees whence they sprung. Industry had swallowed up their city's green spaces long ago.

'Right, let's be having her. You clear away her old clothes and her blanket – oh, and put that soiled napkin in the pail of cold water ready for washing and boiling at the day's end. Good lass.' She wrapped the wet body Eliza held up in a scrap of towel and, sitting in a fireside chair, dried the baby before the heat of the flames. All the while, that cut-glass gaze remained locked to her face, beautiful and bright with implicit trust. Minnie softened towards her further.

She'd find this one an extra-special home, she determined. Not that she let her charges go anywhere but the best she could find. She always made sure she'd selected the right parents before setting a child loose from her fold. However, this one deserved that extra bit more care, she reckoned.

Returning to the table, Minnie dried the infant's sore skin thoroughly and applied olive oil to the affected area. She'd just folded around her a clean napkin and was securing it in place with a pin when a knock came at the door. 'That'll be the lass we're expecting, come to make use of yon room upstairs,' she said, indicating for Eliza to admit the visitor. 'She's a bit late, mind— Oh, it's thee, hello wench,' she added, face spreading into a smile, when instead Flora entered the room.

'Hello, Minnie, love. Glorious day, in't it?'

Her smile spread into a grin to see that, though Flora's greeting had been meant for her, she'd directed it instead to baby Jewel, cradled tenderly in her arms – her friend had eyes only for her daughter these days. The change in the new mother was nothing short of a miracle. Minnie knew she wasn't exaggerating – her friend looked to have shed at least two decades in appearance; every worry line, every grey hair seemed to have faded, the dark circles gone from beneath her eyes just as sure as the pain of want within them had. Radiant, that's what she was – there was no other word to describe it. She shone from the inside out with happy light. It was lovely to see.

Minnie left the new baby to Eliza to dress and crossed to the fire, saying over her shoulder, 'Sit yourself down whilst I brew a fresh pot, wench.'

'Oh, no tea for me, ta, Minnie. I can't stop. I've my purchases to make if I'm to have summat on the table for Fred's evening meal. I just nipped in to say hello, like, on the way.'

And show off the precious being in her arms, no doubt, thought Minnie with warm amusement. Flora did so any opportunity she got and Minnie neither blamed nor begrudged her it one bit, bonny babby that she was. 'Now don't talk daft – sure, you've time for a quick sup,' she told her on a chuckle. 'Take the weight off, go on, and I'll see to the kettle.'

'Aye. All right, love. Ta, Minnie.'

They had their teas in their hands and had been con-
versing for all of half a minute when a gust of rain assaulted
the draughty window, sending the thin glass rattling in the
frame. They turned as one, Flora's face falling at the sight
of the rapid droplets bouncing off the panes. 'Bugger.'

'I'll go and fetch your foodstuffs, Flora,' offered Eliza.
'Save you and the babby trudging out in that foulness.'

'Ay, good thinking, good lass.' Minnie nodded in agreement. 'You'd both be soaked to the bone in moments,
Flora, wench, else. That'll not do, nay it'll not, Jewel as
young as she is.'

'I were for calling in at my mam's, though, on t' way.
She ain't been too well these few days past, as you know.'
Flora gnawed her lip. 'Mind, I'd not want the babby
here to develop a chill . . .'

'Course you don't. 'Ere, you leave Jewel with myself
and Eliza, how about that? That way, you can check in
on your mam still.'

'Oh, I don't know, Minnie . . .'

'Now come on, wench. Now you know she'll be in safe
hands with me. God above, the number of babbies that
have been in my care—!'

'I know, I know, love,' Flora cut in quickly. 'Eeh, there's
norra soul more experienced than thee where infants
are concerned in all the land, I'm certain. She couldn't
be in safer hands, nay. It's just . . .' She swivelled her gaze
to drink in her daughter's delicate features. 'Well, happen the weather will brighten in a minute, eh? Mebbe
we should wait it out.'

'Aye, and yon shops will be closed and bolted by then,
an' all. And what will your Fred say to that, coming home
famished after a day's graft to an empty table? He'd be
for taking his belt to you, missis, and you'd not blame
him for it.'

33

Eyes still on the child in her arms, Flora chewed her lip again. 'Eeh, I don't know . . .'

'Wench, she'll be fine. I'll not take my eyes off her bonny face forra second, you have my word. Anyroad, I reckon the break will do you good. Not been from her side since birthing her, you've not, and it ain't healthy. You need space to breathe, an' all.'

'She's precious to me is all.'

'Well, of course she is. By, you waited for her long enough. But it's me what will be minding her, remember? Besides, you'll not be away long, eh? Tha can be there and back again in less than ten and twenty minutes.'

Flora nodded, albeit reluctantly. 'Aye, all right then. Ta-ra, you,' she told her child, planting a tender kiss on her brow. 'I'll see thee soon and ay, you be good, now, for your Aunt Minnie.'

'Course she will.' Minnie lifted the girl and waved her friend off. 'No need to rush back, neither, wench. Take a sup of tea with your poorly mam and be sure to send her my love whilst you're about it.'

The woman dithered by the door. Minnie flicked her hand, shooing her on her way, and, chuckling, Flora drew her shawl over her head against the elements and left the house.

'Eeh, I don't know,' said Eliza, crossing to the bed to lay the new, freshly bathed and clothed baby with the others. 'Protective ain't in it.'

'And who can blame her?' Minnie motioned to Jewel, asleep in the crook of her arm. 'Waited half a lifetime for this angel, she did.'

'Suppose so. Oh!' Eliza looked to the door as knocking came and, at Minnie's nod, went to answer it.

Their visitor was the pregnant young woman they had been expecting; Minnie waved aside her apologies for her lateness and ushered her inside. 'Bedroom's all made up ready for thee, lass. Eliza here will show you up and get you settled in whilst I brew us a fresh pot.'

'Ta thanks, Mrs Maddox.'

'Plain owd Minnie will do, lass. Go on now, go and get yourself out of them wet things and we'll speak in a minute over a sup of tea.'

They disappeared upstairs and Minnie released a small, sad sigh. Worried witless, the poor thing had looked. A full belly, no ring on her finger, and with the same old sorry tale to tell. The fellow she believed loved her had had his way with her then reneged on his promise of marriage, denying any involvement in her predicament into the bargain. At her horrified parents' insistence, here she was, sent before her belly began to grow so as not to arouse their neighbours' suspicions – gone away working or nursing some sick relative or other, they would no doubt be told in explanation of her absence.

When the time came, Minnie would deliver the child and see to its adoption whilst the lass returned home, taking no baby and therefore no shame on to the family with her. Likely a gaping hole in her heart that would never be filled, too.

Aye well. Hers wasn't to question the rights and wrongs, was it? she reminded herself, placing Jewel on the bed and heading off to refill the kettle. She'd just begun pouring out tea into three cups when Eliza's thin figure appeared at the top of the stairs:

'Min?'

'Aye, lass?'

The girl's voice dropped further. 'Come up, will thee? She's overcome with upset up here; I don't know what to do.'

Minnie gave a sad nod. 'Poor thing; it's likely just hit

35

her what being here means. Hang about, I'm coming.'
She abandoned the teapot and, flashing the babies a
look to check they were all right and wouldn't miss her,
made for the bedroom.

Ten minutes later, after much tears and talk, the
woman was undressed and in bed. Quieter now she'd
finally unburdened her worries to someone, and that
Minnie had put her mind at ease as to her child's future,
she settled down for a well-needed sleep.

'You rest easy, child,' Minnie told her softly. 'The lass,
here, shall stay with you awhile whilst I get back to my
duties.'

Holding Eliza's hand, eyes drooping, the woman murmured a thank-you, and Minnie headed back downstairs.

What alerted her to the fact that something was
wrong she couldn't say. She felt it the instant she entered
the kitchen. She scanned the space, frowning – all
appeared as it should be. Then her eyes settled on the
bed and, for reasons she couldn't fathom, her heart
tripped a few beats in quick succession. She swallowed
hard and made her way across.

One by one, she peered at the slumbering babies. All
the while, she knew, she just knew . . .

She touched a trembling hand to the last infant's
cheek. Still warm. So perfect, peaceful . . . She fixed her
gaze on the tiny chest anyway, watched intently for its
rise and fall. It never came.

As though observing the scene from afar, Minnie
watched herself cover the purple-tinged mouth. Then,
with the tip of a finger, she compressed one nostril; into
the other she blew steady puffs of air, inflating the
lungs, all the while praying silently, fervently, the words
falling over each other in her mind. And yet she knew –
knew – her pleas were landing on deaf ears.

Again, as if witnessing everything from outside of her body, her hands loosened the clothing then turned the child's body on to its right side. She saw herself reach for the brandy, dip her fingers inside the bottle. Starting at the head, she quickly, sharply, rubbed the spirit the length of the spine to evoke heat in it – a tried-and-tested method that had worked more than once over the years. But not now. Not this time. Once more, her lamentations filled her brain. Still, she knew she'd hear no gasp, no cry – faint or otherwise.

Nothing could alter the truth that Jewel Nightingale was dead.

A sudden clap of thunder broke through the rain, momentarily dazzling the room with light – and Minnie stilled. Like herself, many believed thunder following a death to be a sign that the recently departed had entered into heaven. She didn't much go for the idea that children who passed from this life before they had a chance to be baptised were set to languish in some form of infant limbo for eternity. What God would allow such an awful thing? No. The Lord she knew and worshipped received every lost soul into His arms, she was certain.

Gently, Minnie laid the girl down and on limbs that felt attached to someone else's body crossed to the window. The chimney-stack sky held its usual factory tint – a red sheen that cast the city in a haunting light. A numbness had seized her brain in its grasp and she could neither feel nor think. A strand of sound tapped at the mind fog. She heard in her memories the decades of bitter tears telling of Flora's painful yearning. And she heard the joyous cries as she'd held her so-longed-for child in her arms. Then she imagined the unearthly ones to come at her friend's return to discover she'd had the priceless title of motherhood snatched away from her.

Flora would die, too. There wasn't a single doubt of that. She would follow her daughter into the black ground, would make sure of it, for she could never function, never exist, now, without her.

As with the child Eliza had found in this very bed, deceased for no apparent reason, who had lain cold in his box in Minnie's bedroom until she'd watched him be buried only last week, the dreaded cradle death was commonplace. Small babies were spirited away in their sleep sometimes, everyone knew it; though why was another matter.

Neither rhyme nor reason could explain either case, here. The children in her care had suffered no injury, their little faces hadn't been accidentally covered by the bedclothes, nothing like that. It was just something that happened, with no explanation or means of prevention. It didn't make it any less heart-rending. Nor did it make the truth easier to accept. And Flora wouldn't, not at all. She'd do whatever it took to be with her daughter, whether that meant in life or death. She'd do it, all right.

Minnie's breaths came in short gasps. She glanced up and down the street then behind her towards the stairs. Then she hurried to the bed.

Her gaze went not to Jewel but the female child with the violet eyes who had been thrust into her care not half an hour ago. She was virtually the same size and stature as the dead girl. They shared the same colouring, the same button nose and rosebud mouth, both no more than a dusting of downy hair. They even had the same features, as far as she could see. The passage of time hadn't yet begun to define their individuality – babies at the beginning of life did, by and large, look the same. Aye, they did . . .

Tongues would wag for certain, questions would be raised. The demise of two of her charges in as many weeks – whom she'd received money for, no less? The possibility of her coming under suspicion by the authorities was a very real one. Her good name, her spotless character, would be tarnished. She'd be ruined. And she didn't care. Flora mattered more to her. Much more.

Now, Minnie was in full control of her actions. Swiftly, deftly, she stripped the new girl of her clothing. Then she did the same with Jewel.

The beautiful garments Flora had lovingly knitted, she now dressed the new girl in. Seconds later Jewel was wearing the items from the dresser's bottom drawer. After switching their blankets and wrapping both children up, Minnie stepped back and surveyed them through eyes blurry with tears. She swallowed at the panic threatening to choke her.

They really did look one and the same. To her, at least. But what of a mother? Would Flora . . . ? God above, what was she doing?

'I don't know.' Minnie answered her own thought in a small whimper. 'Don't know what I were . . . were thinking . . .' With a cry, she rushed forward to right the madness of her actions. She'd begun removing the babies' blankets when the sound of rainfall filling the room as the door was opened, then Flora's cheery welcome, halted her in her tracks. On jerky legs, she turned.

'Eeh, it's foul out there!' Flora jiggled on the spot, shaking the outside from her wet shawl. 'Ta ever so, Minnie, love, for minding my angel. How's she been?' Her hungry gaze looked beyond her to the bed, seeking out her child. 'Not fretting over me, were she?'

Minnie couldn't breathe. Speaking was an impossibility. She shook her head.

'Oh, I am glad. Been worried summat sick, I have.' Flora flashed a sheepish grin. 'What am I like, eh? I knew she'd be gradely, course I did. I'm a daft beggar, that's what.' When Minnie didn't answer, she cocked her head. 'You all right, love?'

'Aye.' Her voice sounded off to her own ears. Short, high-pitched. Guilty. She tried to smile but failed. She watched Flora's own smile slip from her lips, watched unable to do anything, wide-eyed and frozen, as her friend crossed the space towards her. Towards the bed. Towards the children. Again, that sensation of being out of her body had returned and, like the rest of her, her tongue acted without her say-so: 'The lass . . . The new lass entrusted to me earlier has passed away, wench, in her sleep.' She waited. Nothing. Flora was staring intently at the sleeping infant adorned in her daughter's clothes. 'Love? Love, I—'

'I'll be off home, now, Minnie.'

Minnie's brow creased in a frown. She exhaled slowly. Flora was still stooped over the children and her eyes swivelled continually from one girl to the other. Her expression was unreadable. After a last, lingering look at her dead daughter, she lifted the other girl and turned for the door. Close to tears, Minnie stumbled after her.

'Ta again, love, for minding my Jewel. I'll be seeing thee.'

Before she could say or do anything – grasp at Flora's arm, pour out her guilt, cry, beg her forgiveness – her neighbour was gone. The door clicked shut and Minnie sagged against the wall.

She knew. Minnie had heard it in her flat tone when she'd bid her goodbye, had seen it in her eyes before she'd turned dazedly for home. She knew. She knew and had done nothing. God in heaven above. Horror and panic swamped her – she gripped the mantel for support as her legs threatened to buckle. She knew.

But did she really? Surely any mother would have said something – anything. Surely she would have? And yet . . . Minnie shook her head. She felt dizzy and sickness was swooping through her guts in waves.

It was only then that she remembered the birthmark.

Like that of little Jewel lying feet away, her own heart ceased its beating. Stare fixed on the fire's hypnotic flames, she felt behind her blindly until her fingers brushed the shelf and the brandy atop. *One baby departs this earth, another arrives to take its place in the world* . . .

With tears coursing down her lined face, Minnie lifted the bottle to her lips.

Chapter 3

'BY GUM! WHAT a sight. I ain't never seen the like.'

Esther Powell shoved her niece aside with an ample hip. Resting her arms on the windowsill, she squinted through the driving rain to the square below. 'Well, what do you expect?' she asked in her usual withering tone. 'It's Bolton's first royal visit. A bit of bad weather weren't about to put the townspeople off catching a glimpse of the Prince and Princess of Wales, now, were it?'

Biting down on her tongue to stem a retort, as she was frequently forced to in the prickly woman's presence – Esther had a knack of making a body feel as thick as a brick with her caustic remarks – Jewel returned her attention to the heaving crowds. As well as a strong police presence, there had to be thousands of people down there, she reckoned. By, but it was a gradely sight to behold.

'Anyroad, lady.' Her aunt speaking again scattered the smile from her face. 'Why you up here, like? You finished your duties downstairs? Nay, I'll bet. Skiving as per usual. Take yourself away and get back to it. That shop floor won't scrub itself, you know.'

Jewel felt her cheeks flame with indignant colour that matched that of her hair – a sure sign her temper was about to show itself, whether she wanted it to or not. Fortunately, her uncle intervened:

'Let her be, Esther. Sure, the cleaning ain't going nowhere. The day's an important one, after all, and should be marked as such; by everyone, aye. Besides, don't it also happen to be the lass's birthday an' all, to boot? A few hours away from the grind won't hurt none.'

Jewel flashed him a grateful look and he gave a discreet nod back. Esther merely sniffed. What she'd do without Bernard Powell on her side, Jewel dreaded to think. She wouldn't stay, that much she knew. She'd turn stark staring mad without him here to buffer her from the worst of his wife's nastiness, she was certain. Or finish up in a prison cell for bashing Esther's podgy face to a pulp, which most of the time she'd really like to do.

That last wicked thought – oh, if only her aunt could hear them! – brought a bubble of laughter, and she chewed her bottom lip to stop it escaping.

The electrifying atmosphere outside carried through once more and her smile returned. Despite the inclement weather, the scene was mesmerising. The Market Square, or the Town Hall Square, as most now called it – a proper market hadn't been held here for years since the nearby constructions of the impressive Market Hall and Fish Market – had been transformed. So, too, had the carriageways and streets forming the route of the procession, which had been barricaded since ten o'clock that morning and would remain so until after the event. People and horses alike, scrubbed and groomed, stood proudly in their best, waiting patiently. Building fronts and gas lamps were garlanded with large, swaying flags, banners and bunting, which reflected in the glistening-wet cobbled setts, adding splashes of welcome colour.

To the north side of the square, where the Powells' umbrella shop stood, a battlemented archway as tall and wide as the abutting buildings had been erected. Through this, the royal carriage would emerge from Oxford Street, containing their long-awaited visitors. Nose almost touching the pane, Jewel craned her neck left towards the decorated wooden structure, checking for their imminent arrival, but there was no sign yet. Instead, she trained her gaze on the centrepiece facing and the purpose of this auspicious occasion: the new Town Hall, towering over the town.

Neoclassical in style, the vast sandstone edifice was majestically designed. On both sides ran a high basement storey, above which sat two floors dotted with arched and rectangular windows and broad columns. At the centre was a six-columned portico and pediment adorned with sculptures. Bolton's elephant-and-castle emblem, human and lion heads and figures by the doors holding date stones into which were carved this year, 1873, were included in the embellishments.

The entrance itself was reached by a bold flight of over two dozen wide steps. Either side of these near to the top stood a pedestal, intended to hold a large stone lion. Alas, the beasts had not been completed in time for today's grand opening and so potted shrubs were positioned in their place.

The finishing touch was the tower, boasting four clock faces and stretching two hundred feet into the sky. The overall impact was, in a word, magnificent.

Inside consisted of a large meeting hall, council chamber and committee rooms, mayor's parlour, reception and banqueting rooms as well as numerous offices. Little Bolton town hall, the modest building that held the county sessions court, constabulary station and lock-up and was situated at the nearby junction of St George's Street and All Saints' Street, which had served them until now, paled dramatically in comparison.

Bernard had followed Jewel's gaze. He puffed out his chest, face holding pride; smiling, she did likewise. Everybody in the town was inordinately proud of their new structure, which had taken seven years to construct, and deservedly so.

'Not long to wait, now,' her uncle announced, glancing from the clocktower to his pocket watch then adjusting the latter to run at 'town hall time', as did Bolton's inhabitants and industries alike. 'It's a pity Wigan town had His Royal Highness before us – I read in the paper he's just opened the new infirmary there. But no matter, no matter. Better late than never, eh?'

Jewel nodded in agreement. Then she, too, glanced at the hour, and frowned. Her mother should have been here by now. She'd hate for her to miss something as momentous as this.

Here, from the Powells' private quarters above their shop, they had the best view possible. For weeks, they and the owners of surrounding premises had been inundated with offers from people desperate for a clear vantage point to rent out their rooms – some even prepared to brave the rooftops – and willing to pay handsomely for the privilege. Fortunately, her aunt and uncle, not wanting to miss the proceedings themselves, had flatly refused.

She'd just told herself she'd give her mother another five minutes then go and collect her when she heard the door opening. She turned expectantly but, to her dismay, it wasn't Flora but a pimply, overweight youth who entered the room – her cousin, Benji. He smiled at her and she forced one back.

45

'All right, my lad?' Esther's tone was sickly sweet. 'Come on over here next to your mam. I've saved the best spot for thee.'

Benji crossed the space. As he normally did any opportunity he got, he stood as close to Jewel as he could, their hips touching, his arm pressed against hers. His hot breath fanned her bare neck and, after making sure her aunt wasn't watching, she shoved him away with a narrow-eyed look. Mild hurt flitted across his face then the corners of his mouth lifted. He resumed his position and she swallowed a sigh of irritation.

His unwelcome attentions had begun out of the blue several months ago. They had never really been close – even as children, they did nothing but bicker – but lately, he wouldn't leave her alone. Of course, her aunt wouldn't believe a word of it, so what was the point in complaining? Whether her uncle would, she couldn't say. Not that it would matter either way. His wife would turn his thinking, had the final say with their lad, always did. Her precious son could do no wrong in her eyes – sunbeams shone from his earholes, as far as she was concerned, aye. She'd defend him to the death, no matter the issue. Besides, Jewel was no tell-tale. She could handle this – him. She'd show him if he dared push his advances. If he went too far with her, he'd bloody well regret it.

'I don't know where Mam could be,' she announced now, catching sight of the time again. 'I'd best run home and fetch her; she'll miss the royal pair, else.'

'I'll walk with thee, shall I?' offered Benji.

Jewel shook her head. 'There's no need. It'll not take long.'

'You reckon?' He jerked his head at the crowds outside. 'You'll have a job getting through that lot. I'm bigger than you; I'll get us past the mob in half the time.'

As he'd spoken his arm had moved without her noticing; discreetly, he fondled her buttock. Incensed, she dug her nails into the back of his hand then gave it a thump for good measure. She stalked to the door, saying over her shoulder, 'I'll manage, I'm sure.' And when her aunt mumbled something about her being an ungrateful piece for turning down her son's generous offer, Jewel quickened her step before her temper boiled over.

Outside the room, she paused to take some deep breaths. Swine! She'd give him a tongue-lashing later, all right. He was growing up, she understood this – most lads were beginning to get certain urges, such as he clearly was, at his age – but still, he had no right to mess with her like that. She frowned as a sudden thought occurred: was he in love with her? Was it possible that he knew what love was at fifteen? Even she didn't, today at seventeen. Did she? She was very fond of Jem Wicks, a handsome lad who dwelled in the next street whom she'd been courting for several months, it was true – but love? She honestly couldn't say.

Smoothing her long, red plait, as thick as a man's wrist, over one shoulder, she donned her shawl and left the shop. The very air buzzed with feverish anticipation; all thoughts of Benji and lads in general melted from her mind as, once more, the atmosphere of the day swept her up and made her giddy with excitement. With smiles and apologies, she fought her way through the throng. Then, reaching the edge of the square, she picked up her skirts and ran, past the mouth of Exchange Street and the Grapes Hotel pub on the corner and on down the narrow, cobbled road adjoining it.

47

Her clogged footsteps rebounded off the buildings' sooty bricks as she continued at a sprint for the two rooms she and her mother occupied in a tumbledown dwelling at Back Cheapside. When she burst inside, breathless and laughing, her mother whipped around with a gasp from where she stood by the fire.

Jewel grinned. 'Sorry to make you jump, but we must hurry. The time . . .' Her words petered out as, on closer inspection, she saw that Flora's face was wet with tears. 'Mam? Mam, what is it, what's to do?'

The older woman quickly scrubbed at her eyes with her sleeve. 'Ah, nowt to fret over, my lass. Smoke from yon fire is all it were. Sets my eyes astreaming, it does.' She flashed a bright smile. 'Now, what is it that had you tearing in here and frickening me half to death?'

'Lord, Mam, surely you ain't forgot? The royal visit!'

'Oh, that. Course I've not forgot. I were just about to join youse at the shop when you came careering in.'

It hadn't looked that way – she'd seemed in a world all of her own, Jewel thought, but nodded nonetheless. Then her mother moved to fetch her shawl from the nail in the wall by the door, and that's when Jewel saw it: a small, cream-coloured heap on the hearth. Mam must have dropped it when she'd startled her. She went to retrieve it and discovered it was a baby's woollen vest. Frowning, she held it up. 'Mam?'

'I'll take that.' Hurrying over, Flora almost snatched it from her grasp. She folded it carefully and placed it in a cupboard against the far wall. 'Right then, let's get going afore we miss the event altogether,' she said, heading for the door.

'Mam.' Jewel's voice had softened; she took her mother's hands in hers and squeezed. 'That were my vest from when I were a babby. You were looking at it, reminiscing, afore I came in, weren't you? Is it because it's my birthday? Eeh, Mam.' She chuckled, then kissed the lined brow. 'Whatever my age, I'll allus need thee. You know that, don't yer?'

'My baby. My daughter.' A single tear accompanied Flora's whisper and splashed to her cheek. Then, blinking, she reached out to stroke her hair with a loving touch. 'My precious Jewel.'

'And you're my precious mam. And there ain't none better in the land than thee. And now we must hurry – come on!' she finished on a laugh, shooing a now-smiling Flora into the street.

The crowd's furore had intensified further still – the air crackled with expectancy. Glancing at the clock-tower, Jewel gasped. It was just a few minutes to the appointed hour. 'Quick, Mam!'

Pulling Flora behind her, she shoved and elbowed her way through the mass of bodies to finally fall, puffing for breath, through the shop door. With no time to waste on catching their composure, they rushed upstairs.

'Well, youse are cutting it fine! Come on, they'll be here any moment.' Esther shuffled closer to Bernard and Benji, Jewel and her mother squeezed in close, and they waited in charged silence.

When the clock chimed, releasing three long bongs into the grey afternoon, they and every other spectator craned their neck towards the man-made arch. Then there it was. Flanked by an entourage of dragoons and territorial volunteers, the royal carriage glided into the square. The crowd broke into warm cheers, waving hats and handkerchiefs, beaming from ear to ear, and the family following the proceedings from the umbrella-shop window matched their vigour entirely.

What made Jewel look past the regal scene, she

49

couldn't say. Some fifty years earlier, when the square was created, a striking ornate gas lamp had been donated to mark the occasion – and there, leaning against the circular water trough surrounding its base, stood Jem Wicks. However, her usual smile of delight upon seeing him didn't appear now. For by his side was a lass she vaguely knew from their cluster of streets – a loose piece, to boot, if rumours were correct. Of all the . . . !

Anger rose up in her and she swallowed hard. She saw him laugh at something the girl had said and slip an arm around her waist. To her utter shock, they then kissed, right there in public – on the lips!

Before she knew what she was doing Jewel was leaning out of the window: 'Jem!' But he was too far away to hear her – though several others certainly did, and had turned to gawp up at her. 'Jeremiah Wicks, you rotten dog, yer! I'll tear you limb from limb, just you see if I don't!' she yelled across the square, her burning fury overriding thought and reason, until:

'Mother of God. Oh, the shame of it!'

Her aunt's horrified squawk brought her back to the present. Following the quivering finger as Esther pointed outside, Jewel slapped a hand to her mouth.

Whilst her attention had been on the cavorting couple, the carriage had pulled up by the broad town hall steps and the royal pair had alighted. And it was evident that the prince had heard – he was looking over his shoulder towards the shop! A terrible thought occurred: what if His Highness had caught only part of her outburst, believed her insult and threat were meant for him? Her aunt was right: Lord, the shame!

With a squeak, she ducked out of sight, face ablaze. She'd never been so embarrassed in her whole life.

Damn and blast Jem Wicks – and so, too, this infernal tongue of hers!

As if Jewel didn't feel bad enough, Esther shook her roughly, hissing, 'Why, you devil-tempered article – look what you've done! Sullied our name and reputation to royalty, you have. God above, future monarch King Edward VII at that! Oh, I'll never forgive you for this, never!'

'All right, woman, don't fret so.' Bernard spoke placatingly, though definite laughter danced behind his eyes. He motioned to the square. 'See, look. The Prince and Princess have forgot the incident already.'

Jewel braved a peek over the lip of the window ledge – sure enough, the pair had ascended the steps, their attention once more on the task in hand. 'Terrible sorry, truly,' she murmured. 'D'you think the Prince can forgive me?'

'Now, lass, enough of that.' Flora didn't try to mask her amusement; she chuckled quietly, much to her sister-in-law's annoyance. 'What's done is done; and it's that young bugger Jem's loss, aye. Come on, ruddy hiding down there, up you get.'

Jewel allowed her mother to help her stand. She tried her best to enjoy the proceedings but, for her, the day was ruined. Esther's sly, angry glances didn't help none. Jem Wicks, the low-down dog – she'd believed him to be fond of her. She'd been a fool. He'd bloody pay for this!

The grand opening of the new civic building, constructed for the needs of present and future generations, had brought out high and distinguished guests. The town's leading gentry and political and industrial dignitaries joined, amongst other important people, the town clerk, councillors and Mayor. Even the building's talented architects were in attendance, on the steps. Men, impeccably dressed in dark frock coats and top hats, predominated but several ladies, in colourful bustled dresses heavily adorned in pleats and ruffles and wearing magnificent hats, were included in the smiling party circling the royal couple.

Jewel couldn't help stealing a glance at her own clean but heavily patched skirts in comparison. Though the dream of owning clothing like these ladies flitted into her thoughts, it quickly vanished again – a reality such as that would never be. She accepted this without a flicker of resentment. Your station in life was determined at birth and no one got a say in it, to choose. It was how it was.

After being welcomed by the Recorder of Bolton, who read an address on behalf of the Mayor, the Prince offered his and his wife's gratitude for their visit to the town today. He touched upon its importance as a manufacturing centre and announced it gave him and the Princess very great pleasure to be present on such an important occasion as the opening of the new town hall of Bolton. Jewel tried to listen but ignoring her embarrassment was difficult. And at one point, when thanking everyone for the beautiful appearance of the streets – and the order that was kept – she was certain the Prince looked her way. She ducked out of sight amidst her family's laughter – all but Esther's, in any case.

Nevertheless, the Prince couldn't fail to lift her spirits – his effusiveness held the inhabitants in the palm of his hand – and she was soon smiling, along with the rest. When he praised the townsfolk's declaration to the throne and his high gratification with the very sunny, gladsome reception he'd received, she cheered with everyone else – which reached a crescendo when he stated that he wouldn't fail to inform the Queen of the truly loyal manner in which they had been welcomed. He finished by saying he would not very easily forget his visit to Bolton – this time, there could be no denying his twinkling glance in the shop's direction – but now, though her cheeks again flamed brick-red, Jewel couldn't contain a giggle. His affable nature was a treasure and she loved him for it.

The crowd erupted in rapturous applause – even her aunt managed to crack a smile. The vicar of Bolton then opened with prayers and, when he'd concluded, there came the moment they had all been waiting for: stepping forward, the Mayor presented a silver key and asked the Prince if he would be kind enough to accept it. The spectators held a collective breath as he unlocked the door. When he turned to the assembly and formally declared the town hall open for public services, every man, woman and child cheered for all they were worth.

The double doors were thrown wide open and the Prince and Princess were escorted inside to the Great Hall for the banquet. Not quite sure what to do with themselves now, and unwilling to bring an end to the event, the townsfolk milled around the square in their soggy boots.

Tomorrow, the newspapers would be singing with details of the bill of fare those dignitaries had enjoyed – most of the foodstuffs listed, the poor of this smoggy little town wouldn't ever have heard of, never mind be able to imagine how they tasted – and all the while, most folk found it a daily struggle to keep body and soul together. And yet the lower orders flocked to events such as this, marvelled at the evident wealth of their betters, their clothing and carriages, acknowledged their lofty demeanour and superior station with easy acceptance. It was as normal to them as breathing, this strict hierarchy. Such was life, and most never thought to question it at all.

Jewel and Flora went to make a pot of tea whilst Esther, still carrying a definite air of annoyance, took herself downstairs to the shop. Bernard, with a slight roll of his eyes to his sister and niece, who smiled, followed his wife to attempt to calm the waters.

'Jeremiah Wicks don't deserve thee. Tha knows that, aye?'

Her mother's words, calm but warm with love, brought tears to Jewel's eyes. She blinked them back. 'Aye.'

'Young swine. He'll think so when our paths next cross.'

'It's all right, Mam. He ain't worth the aggravation.' She didn't want Flora involved. She'd be the one to dole out the tongue-lashing he had due to him.

'Aye well. He'll rue his folly the day. You're worth a dozen of him.'

Benji had been hovering nearby; at this from the older woman, he nodded, saying, 'Aunt Flora's right. By, he wants his brain looking at snubbing thee.' *I'd not*, his gaze added, boring into Jewel's. Frowning, she looked away.

'You off soon to continue the festivities at Bolton Park, lad?' Flora asked him, oblivious to the tension between the two. She smiled when he confirmed he was. 'Take our Jewel along with thee, eh? She could do with cheering up – and her that's had this rotten fortune on her birthday, to boot! What says thee?'

'I say it's a gradely idea, Aunt Flora.' He beamed. 'Jewel?'

She shrugged. She may as well go. Better that than moping around here for the rest of the day with Esther's acid presence.

'Right, well, you leave them cups, lass, and fetch your shawl. Youse take a slow walk there, enjoy the air. I'll see thee later.'

Many were still present in the square, whilst others, hoping for a last glimpse of the Prince and Princess, had walked the short distance to Trinity Street Station, where, soon, the royal train would depart for London, bringing an end to the brief visit. Others of a similar mind to Jewel and Benji were heading in the direction of the park situated on the west side of town by Chorley New Road; at a leisurely pace, they joined the throng.

Created from meadow and pastureland following the Bolton Improvement Act of 1864 and officially opened two years later, the beautiful pleasure grounds were a favourite amongst the townsfolk. Some fifty acres, surrounded by lakes and woodland, it featured grassy slopes and curving paths generously planted with shrubbery, trees and immaculate flowerbeds. By the time the cousins reached the pavilion in the centre of the park, thousands of spectators were already gathered in readiness. By five o'clock, the heaving mass of bodies, swelling in number by the minute, spread as far as the eye could see.

Jewel began to wonder if she'd made a mistake in venturing here. Jem's betrayal still stung and the beginnings of a headache throbbed dully behind her eyes. However, at least the weather had brightened and Benji's roving hands were behaving themselves. Best she tried to enjoy the evening here than be alone with her thoughts at home.

A band had struck up a song to please the townsfolk whilst the entertainment prepared to get under way and there was much jollity from young and old alike. Then the huge balloons, one of which had been named Alexandra in honour of the Princess, began their ascent into the white-grey clouds amidst the crowd's collective 'Ooh!' and 'Ahh!' – Jewel herself was entranced. The daring fliers grew smaller and smaller until the balloons' baskets were nothing more than brown smudges in the sky. The impressed audience cheered and stamped their feet with gusto.

'I'll fetch us both a penny pie and a pot of ale, shall I?' Benji shouted above the medley, inclining his head towards a gathering of hawkers beyond the park's enclosure.

She nodded. 'Aye, all right.'

'I'll not be long.' Elbows at the ready, he set off to fight his way through the crush.

Jigging couples bumped Jewel this way and that with grins and breathless apologies; laughing, she looked about. A group of children playing catch in a less crowded spot nearby drew her attention, and she watched them with a smile. Seemingly out of nowhere, a toddler with tight blond curls suddenly appeared amongst them, screeching in delight, and attempted to join in the fun in a wobbling run. The children fell over themselves, giggling, and Jewel chuckled along. Then a tall, well-dressed man with dancing brown eyes was striding towards them. He wagged a finger at the toddler, who was clearly his daughter – grinning, she attempted to dash off again, but he gathered her up in his arms and smothered her in kisses.

As he made to carry her off, as though sensing he was being watched, he glanced in Jewel's direction. She smiled. With a slight incline of his head, he returned the smile. Moments later, he and the child were gone, lost amongst the crowd.

Longing stirred in Jewel's breast; she turned away with a small sigh. She'd have loved to have known her own father. Fred Nightingale, from what her mother had told her, sounded like a very nice man, fair and hard-working. He'd passed away before she was old enough to retain any solid memories of him and, for that, she felt cheated. This day seventeen years ago was the happiest of his life, Mam told her often. If only he could be here now to share it with her, wrap his arms around her as that man had just done with the girl, tell her he loved her . . .

''Ere, grab yours. Eeh, that's good.' Dragging Jewel from her musings, Benji dumped her meat pie and ale into her hands before taking another long draught of his own drink. 'Eeh,' he said again, wiping his mouth on his sleeve. Then he nodded down. 'Eat up then afore it grows cowd.'

Before she did, she scanned the area where the children had been playing but, again, the father and daughter were nowhere to be seen. Swallowing another sigh, she turned her attention to her food.

'What's to do with thee?' asked Benji after some time. 'Still wasting your thoughts on Wicks?'

'Am I hell. He can rot there, an' all, for me.'

Benji smiled, pleased at this, and inched closer to her. Jewel hadn't the energy to scold him. At least he was keeping his hands to himself.

'Well, you're quieter than normal,' he continued after some moments. 'Summat's up.'

Once more, the toddler and the man with the dancing eyes crept into her mind. She shrugged. 'Bit tired is all. Anyroad, will tha pack it in with the questions? You're getting on my nerves.'

He did, and she was free to forget her thoughts in the entertainment. The festivities continued for hours and, by the time they set off back to town, her mind was more at ease. Entering the square, she smiled. Gas illuminations had been lit throughout in celebration; the scene was dazzling.

'Don't know why you couldn't of stayed with me longer at the park – at least 'til the fireworks,' Benji grumbled, thrusting his hands into his pockets as they reached his parents' shop door. 'Your mam's not expecting you yet, so what? I thought you were enjoying yerself.'

'I were.' She meant it. The day hadn't been a complete nightmare, on the whole. 'I'm ready for my bed, though, now.'

'Aye well. Do what tha likes, then. I ain't mithered.'

His pouting face made him look like a three-year-old who couldn't get his own way rather than the overgrown young man that he was. 'You could of stayed, didn't have to miss the fun,' she told him. 'I'm big enough and ugly enough to see myself home.'

'You're ugly all right.'

She rolled her eyes. 'Grow up, Benji. 'Ere, anyroad,' she added in a hiss, anger sparking, 'I can't be that foul-looking, going by your behaviour – you're bloody fortunate I agreed to accompany you at all after your antics earlier at the window up yonder. And I'll tell you this for nowt: should them hands of yourn stray in my direction again, I'll chop them off – and summat else, an' all, if you're not careful. You hear?'

He released a snort of laughter then opened the door. 'If tha says so.'

58

'I bleedin' do.'

'Night night, Jewel.'

'Sod off, Benji!' she shouted after him as, still chort-ling, he disappeared, slamming the door in her face. 'Bloody lads, I've had a bellyful for one day,' she told the darkening sky. Just who did they think they were, anyway? They thought they could treat lasses as they liked and to hell with their feelings. Swines. They could go and rot for all she cared, every last one! Turning on her heel, she headed for home.

She'd almost passed the town hall when she saw him. Leaning against the corner premises on Newport Street, Jem stepped forward as their eyes locked. He held out his hands. 'Jewel . . . I can explain . . .'

'I'll bet tha can.' Surprisingly – she'd thought she would struggle to stop herself clawing the flesh from his face when their paths next crossed – she felt little anger.

'I called in at your dwelling earlier but your mam said as how you'd gone to Bolton Park with your cousin.'

'That's right.' Jewel's glance swivelled towards the umbrella shop. Benji was watching them in the distance from his upstairs window. 'Had a gradely time, we did, an' all. What?' she asked when Jem's face fell. 'Did tha think I'd be wallowing at home instead? You think too much of yourself, Jeremiah Wicks. That loose piece you were slobbering over is welcome to thee. Now, if you don't mind . . .' She made to step around him but he caught her wrist. She stared at his hand for a moment then brought her gaze, now burning with fury, to his. He had the sense to release her. 'Now shift out of my way,' she growled.

'Jewel, please. I made a mistake, a terrible one, and . . . We weren't that serious, me and thee – least I didn't think so – but now . . . I want us to make a go of things, proper like. We'll . . . we'll . . .' His eyes narrowed as he searched around inside his head for something to win her around. Suddenly, he clicked his fingers. 'We'll get wed. Aye, yeah.' He nodded, smiling. 'What d'you reckon?'

She could only stare at him with incredulousness.

'We're meant to be, you know it. Remember, I'm the gem to your jewel—'

Seeing his hand reaching for her again, her temper reached its peak – throwing out her own, she delivered a slap to his cheek. 'You're no gem – a mucky lump of coal, more like!' To her chagrin, tears were threatening; she blinked them back furiously. 'I'll take the head from your neck for you if yer don't get lost, I mean it—'

'You heard her.'

Spinning around, she saw Benji standing behind her, arms folded. Despite herself, she was touched by his support. When Jem, admitting defeat, sloped off with a shrug, she cast the lad a wry smile. 'Ta. Though you know there were no need for you to involve yourself. I can fight my own battles, thank you very much.' Her tone softened. 'I'll tell you what, how's about we have a walk back to the park? We might still be in time to catch the fireworks?'

His face lit up. 'Aye?'

'Yeah, sod it. Come on.'

The display was already under way when they arrived. Clutching pots of ale, they grinned and cheered with everyone else as one firework followed the next, bursts of light whizzing through the night sky like a shower of golden rain.

'May Bolton prosper!' The cousins added their voices

to the thousands ringing out across the park. 'Long live the Prince!'

'I'll fetch us another ale,' Benji shouted above the high-spirited noise some time later, but Jewel only half heard him. Her attention was on the faces to her right – she could have sworn she'd just spotted a familiar one: the toddler's father from earlier. However, if she had, he wasn't there now; shrugging, she continued with the merriment.

When less than ten minutes later Benji made to go and replenish their drinks yet again, she shook her head. 'Nay, no more, lad. Your mam will have a blue fit were you to roll home skenning drunk.'

'A few pots ain't doing no harm. Well, d'you want one or don't yer?' He wiggled his eyebrows and she chuckled.

'Well, I suppose it is a celebration . . .'

'Your birthday, to boot.'

'Aye. Aye, all right. Last one, mind.'

Watching him walk off, she sighed happily. It felt good to throw caution to the wind for once. Work and want were forgotten for the moment; this day had turned into the best she'd known for many a long year. Picking up her skirts, she danced along to the fiddler's lively song with the rest of the townspeople.

By the time Benji rejoined her she was helpless with laughter and having the time of her life. Through smiling eyes, he watched her as he drank. The ditties were thirsty work; before she knew it, her pot was empty yet again and, this time, when her cousin held out a hand, she gave it to him without protest. What did it matter so long as they were enjoying themselves? A day like this didn't happen often – royalty, in their town! And how handsome the Prince of Wales had been! By, it had been a grand experience and one none of them would ever forget.

'You all right?' Benji asked her some time later, grinning. 'Happen you should take a sit down forra while.'

'Aye. Aye, yeah.' Squinting through one eye, Jewel allowed him to guide her through the throng. She felt queer; her head felt light yet heavy as lead at the same time. 'Oh 'eck, lad. How much have I supped?'

'A fair bit. Come on.' Taking her elbow, he led her to a more secluded spot. 'Here, rest yourself on the steps here. You'll feel reet in a handful of minutes.'

Jewel plopped down on to the edge of the cool stone. Her surroundings had started to spin – she rested her head in her hands. 'Benji?'

'Aye?'

'I think I'm going to be . . .' Slapping a hand to her mouth as the contents of her stomach rose, she jumped to her feet. Fancy her getting herself into this state. In public, too. Lord, the shame . . .

'Over here.' Supporting her, he headed for a cluster of trees nearby. Whether accidental – though she very much doubted it, given his previous conduct – the hand of his right arm, draped over her shoulder, brushed against her breast with each step. However, she hadn't the sense nor the strength to scold. Sickness, rising by the second, was washing over her in dizzying waves.

When they reached the seclusion of the canopy of thick-leaved branches, she leaned her hip against a trunk and bent forward. 'God, I feel awful.'

Benji didn't respond. He moved her long plait away from her face and rubbed her back.

'Mam'll give me a dressing-down good and proper to see me like this.'

'Nay.' His voice was a murmur and his hand moved

62

up, down, up, down, in firm but steady strokes. 'We'll stop here 'til you feel well enough. She need never know. That's it, now sit down here,' he told her when her retching subsided. He helped her to the damp grass.

Lying back and closing her eyes, she instantly regretted it as nausea swooped again. Groaning, she tried to haul herself up.

'You're all right. It'll pass in a minute.' Ignoring her meek protests, Benji pressed her back. 'You're all right,' he repeated. 'Close your eyes, rest.'

'What . . . ?' Was he? she asked herself, the thought jumbled. He was. He was touching her thigh. She knew a moment of confused panic but her lids were weighty and her eyes wouldn't open properly. 'What are you doing?' she croaked.

His only answer was his heavy breathing. He lifted her hand and closed her fingers around something warm and hard. She tried to pull away but his hold tightened around hers; he moved her hand up and down in rapid jerks. What was . . . ? What was he . . . ?

His other hand had risen to the sheltered place between her legs. Feeling his fingertips play at the down there lent her a burst of fight – eyes widening in horror, she opened her mouth to scream. Lightning fast, he clamped a hand over it before the scream could escape.

Her heart was beating so fast she could barely feel it. Peering up, her bleary gaze picked out parts of his face. Dappled moonlight filtering through the leaves distorted his shimmering features. She could only stare, mind and body locked in hazy fog as he exposed her breasts. His breathing grew to heavy pants as he fumbled at them with his hands and mouth, and still she was powerless to do a thing, too numb with confusion and shock and terror to even squeak. Neither did she cry out when once

63

more her skirts lifted and now, his fingers probed roughly. Her screams remained deep within; not for anything could she push them past her lips.

The last thing she was aware of before blackness claimed her was the hot breath on her face and the crushing weight as her cousin climbed on top of her.

Chapter 4

'JEWEL? CUSTOMER! WAKE up, for the love of God.'

'Oh. Aye. Sorry.'

Esther threw her a look of disdain. 'You need a fire-work up your backside this morning, lady.'

Fireworks.

Dancing, ale. Trees. Wet grass, *pain* . . .

She swallowed hard; once, twice.

'I knew – didn't I tell Bernard it were a mistake having thee out front?' Esther continued, through the side of her mouth so the man perusing canes across the shop couldn't hear. As well as their staple of umbrellas, items such as walking sticks, cigars and pipes could also be purchased at Powell & Son's. 'Useless, you are, that's what.'

'And didn't I tell him I'd be just that: no use? I'd much rather have stopped out of the way out back or upstairs with my scrubbing. It were him what wouldn't take nay for an answer.'

A meeting at the bank had pulled her uncle from his duties and, though her mother helped out with the serving of customers in such an event, Flora was at this minute tucked up in bed with a chest cold caught from yesterday's damp weather. Esther, of course, wouldn't dream of soiling her hands in the shop. Besides, it was

Friday: the day she regularly partook of refreshments and gossip with several other traders' wives in the front parlour of the bonnet-makers' shop across town. As for Benji, where he'd disappeared to was anyone's guess.

Disgust, fast becoming a familiar foe, slithered through her guts at the thought of her cousin. Disgust at him. Disgust at herself . . .

'Look lively.' Esther's hiss, accompanied by a swift elbow jab to Jewel's ribs, sliced through her thoughts. 'Good morning, sir,' she continued, tone now sickly sweet, face bright in smile, to the gentleman customer who had approached the counter. 'I'm afraid I've been called away on an important engagement but my very competent niece, here, will see to your needs. Have a pleasant day.' She straightened her bonnet, flashed another smile then crossed to the door – but not before shooting Jewel a warning look over her shoulder. Then she was gone, leaving a faint scent of musky perfume and the unspoken threat of what would befall her niece should she put a foot wrong in her wake.

Resisting the urge to sigh deeply, Jewel turned her attention to the customer's purchases. When, minutes later, the bell above the door tinkled, signalling his exit, she leaned her arms on the countertop and, dipping her head, closed her eyes.

She had to confront him.

Waking earlier in her own bed at Back Cheapside with an ache in her head that felt like a dozen cantering horses had taken up residence there, she'd been at a loss to remember the tail end of the previous night. She'd had to ask her mam when she'd come to rouse her with a cup of tea and slice of bread and pork dripping. Benji had brought her back, Flora had told her, with a tut-tut of disapproval at her inebriated state on their arrival.

Good lad, he was, seeing her right home – anything could have occurred in her condition. And what would Esther say should she hear, and her good enough to give her time off yesterday to enjoy the festivities? Best that she get up and swill with cold water, dash the drink pallor from her face, and quick sharp before she made matters worse by rolling into work late. The last thing they needed was her – or the pair of them – losing their positions, for coal and rent and grub didn't fall freely from the sky, did they? Then where would they be? Rapping at the workhouse doors, that's what. And on . . .

But Flora's words had stopped meaning anything. Slivers of memories had begun to trickle through the fog. Yet wispy as a spider's web, they broke just as easily when she dug into them too much, leaving nothing but cold blankness.

Something had happened, she knew instinctively. Squeezing her eyes shut hard in concentration, she'd tried again to remember . . . something, anything. Slowly, Benji's face had appeared through the mugginess. If the jumble of emotions she was experiencing, a mixture of confused shame and simmering panic, couldn't shed light on events then the tenderness between her legs told her all she needed to know.

She'd risen, dressed and broken her fast with numb calmness, though her remembrance of this was now hazy. She couldn't even recall arriving at the shop. Yet here she was, as though nothing had occurred, nothing was out of the ordinary. In reality, the world as she knew it had shattered to dust. Half her mind was vaguely aware of this, but the rest, including her body, didn't seem to have caught up, was suspended in some frozen, unfeeling state that she neither understood nor could attempt to understand. She'd turned in on herself, closed down, this she knew. And here she'd prefer to remain. For the alternative, the truth . . .

'Jewel.' Now, Benji paused on the threshold, blinked twice, then closed the shop door. 'All right? Has Mam already left?'

Outside, rain pelted the windows, its steady drum filling the silence. Her head moved of its own accord in a nod.

'Bad again out there.' He shook the water from his cap and tucked it under his arm. 'All right?' he asked again.

'Last night.' Once more, her actions were not her own – she felt her lips move but hadn't commanded them to. 'At the park.'

'Aye?'

'You . . .'

He broke their stare. 'We did, aye.'

We . . . ?

'Does tha regret it?' he added quietly.

We. Him and her. The two of them? But . . . This couldn't, couldn't be . . .

'I don't,' he continued. 'It were gradely. Christ, the feel of thee . . .' He cleared his throat. 'I'll not tell no one.'

She'd consented. She'd allowed him? Never, she'd never . . . And yet doubt pierced like hot knives inside her chest. She felt breathless, light-headed. She had to say it: 'I lay with you willingly?'

Again, his gaze flicked away. He looked at his feet. 'So tha does regret it.'

God in heaven above . . . 'I need . . . need some air.' She stumbled past him and out of the shop.

Jewel's feet took her in the direction of Deansgate. Grinding to a halt at the corner, she viewed the bustling street through a film of tears.

She'd consented to relations with her cousin – he but a boy at that. Though unable to grasp why, she knew she would bear his child, could almost feel his seed inside her.

And if she should, would he deny all involvement? The Powells would take his word; would Mam? Would she blame her for allowing herself to get drunk, letting it happen? And if Benji did hold his hands up, what of it? The lad was fifteen years old, for God's sake. They *couldn't* wed – not that his parents, particularly Esther, would consent in a month of Sundays to such a notion anyway.

Covering her face with her hands, Jewel gave the bitter sobs life. There was no way out of this. Everything was ruined, everything. She'd be shunned by all she knew and loved, cast out with nothing, no one. Her life was in tatters, over . . .

The scrape of iron-rimmed wheels caught her attention and she paused. Peering through her fingers at an approaching cart, a thought entered her mind. What if she was to step into the road? The horse's large hooves would have power enough to trample her skull to pieces, and then she'd be dead and all this would be over with. Swept away by her emotions, her heartbeat quickened in relief at the prospect.

Putting out a foot, she took a step. Her other foot followed.

She moved forwards again. By now, the sound of the clomping hooves was deafening. The toes of her clogs brushed the road's edge – this was it. She took a deep breath, closed her eyes and stepped out.

Hot air from the beast's frightened snort fanned her face. Coming up against solid muscle, intense pain shot through her right hip and the cobblestones swept away from beneath her feet. Muffled yells faded to nothing.

69

'Lass?'

Splintered light filtered through her lids. Grey figures hovered above her.

'God in heaven above . . . Help me get her up, will thee, Mr Birch?'

'Yes, of course.'

Jewel felt hands go underneath her. Her cheek rested against a firm chest and she wanted to take her fists to it, beat it with all her might, for she was alive. No, no! Why couldn't they have left her be, to die in the gutter as she'd planned, as she deserved? Bastards! But it was useless – she seemed to have left her strength by the roadside and could do nothing but lie mutely in these unfamiliar arms, though inside she was screaming.

When the shop bell rang above her head, followed by Benji's shocked enquiry as to what had happened, her heart sank further and, now, she was glad of the sanctuary afforded by the man carrying her – she hid her face in his chest. He smelled of soap and fine cigars. She breathed the scent of him in, finding it pleasant despite herself. Anything to distract her mind from the lad speaking. The lad she'd . . . Fat, silent tears dripped down her cheeks and soaked into his crisp white shirt.

'Lay her down there, Mr Birch. That's it.'

'Uncle?' Jewel croaked as she was lowered on to a bed, brows knotting to realise it was Bernard speaking, had been from the start. He'd instructed this Mr Birch to aid him in getting her up. He'd found her in the road. Had he seen what she'd done? Lord, what must he be thinking? How would she explain this away?

'Don't try to talk,' Bernard murmured, covering her with a blanket and tucking it beneath her chin. 'You rest. Doctor's on his way. Fetch Flora, lad,' he added, to, she assumed, Benji – she still couldn't open her eyes, let alone move. Every ounce of energy seemed to have deserted her. She just wanted to sleep. Sleep and never, ever wake up . . .

'I'm afraid I must get back to the bank, Mr Powell. Unless you still need my assistance . . . ?'

'Nay, nay, you go. My thanks to you, Mr Birch, for your help. I – my niece here, too, I'm sure – appreciate it, sir.'

Jewel felt pressure on her fingers as they were squeezed lightly, then Mr Birch spoke again: 'I wish you a speedy recovery, Miss . . .'

'Nightingale,' said Bernard.

'Miss Nightingale. Indeed. Yes, well, I'll be on my way. Do not hesitate to send word should you need me for anything further, Mr Powell. Good day.'

'Ta, thank you, sir. Good day to thee.'

His footsteps died away then all was still. Though Bernard didn't make a sound, Jewel felt his presence beside her; it was comforting, safe. Sighing, she slipped into a heavy slumber.

*

What could only have been minutes later Flora was chafing her hands with soothing words. Now, when Jewel tried to open her eyes, they obeyed without resistance. Surprisingly, she felt alert, refreshed, as though she'd rested the day away. 'Mam. Oh, Mam.' The worry in the older woman's eyes tore at her. 'I'm sorry, I—'

'Hush now. Don't fret so. You're going to be just fine.' There was a break in Flora's voice. 'Doctor, here, shall fix you up, lass.'

A large, frowning man loomed above her and began prodding her stomach and examining her head with clipped instructions to say so if an area hurt. She winced

71

once or twice – more from his harsh handling than possible harm inflicted by the cart – but otherwise, she felt fine.

God above, why? she raged inwardly, bunching her hands into fists until her nails bit into her palms. Why couldn't I have died and taken my problems with me to the grave, then no one need ever have known . . .

'Remarkably, you don't appear to have sustained any obvious injuries,' the medical man announced finally. He turned to Bernard. 'I shall return to check on her tomorrow in case of delayed damage. For now, see she gets plenty of rest. If her condition should change, send for me immediately.'

'Aye, Doctor. Ta, we will.'

Her uncle left to show him out; alone with her mother, Jewel avoided her gaze, certain she would see the truth burning in her own, that this wasn't an accident, as they all seemed to be assuming, that she'd . . . Her hands clenched tighter. That she'd wanted to die and did still.

'What happened, lovey? Weren't tha watching where tha were going? Or happen it were the driver's fault? Is that it?'

Outside, rain was pattering steadily once more. Jewel closed her eyes and listened for a while. Then: 'It were my fault. I stepped out without thinking, judged yon cart to be further away than it were. That I've worried thee so . . . I never meant to . . . Eeh, I'm that sorry, Mam.' And she was. For this, at least. Not that she'd done it, though. Not that. Yet how utterly selfish she'd been; she hadn't given a thought to Flora, to how she would have borne the loss, had her actions had the desired effect. She was a terrible daughter, she was. A terrible, foul rotten person . . .

'I don't know what I'd ever do without thee, you

72

know?' Her mother gripped her hand tightly and her usually tired eyes burned with no purer love. 'Never leave me, my lass. You must promise me.'

In that moment Jewel knew there was no escaping this. She couldn't flee from her problems, from what was to follow. She'd been foolish to think she could. She must face this, however difficult, whatever the outcome, the loss. 'I promise,' she whispered thickly.

'What's all this Bernard's just informed me of? What am I hearing, lady?' Esther's heavy tread on the stairs accompanied the questions – mother and daughter shared simultaneous sighs. As if matters were not bad enough, *she* was home.

'Here we go,' muttered Jewel.

'Well!' Her bulk filled the doorway as she paused, hands on hips, and took in the scene. 'What on earth has occurred here the day in my absence? Answer me.'

'Jewel took a tumble at the road's edge and was knocked down by a horse.' Flora spoke for her. Rising from the chair by the bed, she added, 'A terrible shock, she's had, and it's rest she needs now.' She moved towards the door but, clearly, her sister-in-law was deaf to the hint of leaving Jewel be.

'Well, of all the dim-witted, brainless . . .' Esther shook her bonneted head with a snort of disdain. 'And what, pray, were you doing, taking leisurely strolls around the town when you were meant to be working?'

'I . . . felt bad of a sudden, needed some air.'

Her aunt's eyes narrowed. 'You sickening for summat? That Wicks boy on your mind, was he, instead of your duties? Pining for him, were thee?' she finished spite-fully, mouth lifting at the corners, as though thoughts of Jewel heartsore brought her pleasure.

'I care naught for Jem Wicks.'

'Hm. And what of the shop? Did you leave the place unattended, lady?'

'Course not. Benji were here.'

'Thanks be to God for that. Poor lad, burdened with the running of the business all afternoon and at his age.'

A simmering rage was building in Jewel – with effort, loath to make matters worse, she bit her tongue. *Poor lad?* Huh! This blinkered fool didn't know her precious son as well as she believed; nay, not a bit. And anyway, what about her? There was no thought of poor Jewel, who had toiled in this rotten shop since she was knee high. No poor Jewel, with the chapped and mottled hands since the age of seven from daily scrubbing this family's living quarters for a pittance. She'd broken her back in this shop almost her whole life to ease the financial burden on her mother's shoulders, and had done so without ever a word of complaint. Poor lad, my left eye . . .

'You'll work the doctor's fee off, lady, let me tell you that as well. Oh yes. Why must we be expected to fork out for your stupidity? Then there's your poor mam, here. Tearing her from her sickbed and frickening her half to death, I'll bet. By, I just don't know what's the matter with you at times, I don't, really—'

'That's enough, Esther.' Flora's tone was firm. 'The lass has suffered enough for one day.'

'Oh, Flora.' Esther addressed her with exaggerated patience, as though talking to a child. 'When will tha stop making allowances for her daftness?'

'When I'm snug in my grave beneath the clay, that's when! Jewel's sorry, so why don't you just leave her be and—?'

'Now then, wenches.' Bernard had appeared behind his wife and, as always, his quiet tone had the desired effect; they fell silent and he nodded. 'Flora, would you brew a pot of tea?' To his wife, he said, 'Come, let our niece rest up. Sleep is what she needs, aye.'

He led the women from the room and, before disappearing, turned to give Jewel a soft wink. She smiled gratefully. The door clicked shut and she trained her gaze on the ceiling.

How could life as she knew it change so rapidly in so short a space of time? The question swirled around her mind for a moment as though searching every nook for the answer. Of course, it wouldn't find it; there was no explanation, no sense or reason. What she wouldn't give to turn back the hands of time, be the carefree girl from a day ago, before the park and Benji, before the town hall, the Prince, Jem. For that's the point at which things had started to spiral into trouble, she understood this now.

'*That Wicks boy on your mind, was he, instead of your duties?*' Esther's assumption, so far removed from the truth of things, came back to Jewel and she almost laughed. If only that was what troubled her! Jem, the past months, their misguided feelings for one another, seemed embarrassingly childlike now. So, too, did his scratching at an excuse when he realised he'd been caught out, his wild suggestion that they wed . . .

Her brow cleared. She sat up in bed. Somewhere deep within her, a spark of hope smouldered and spread. She swallowed hard, her heart beginning to bang.

'Aye,' she whispered to the empty room. Beneath the bedclothes, her hand travelled to her flat stomach. 'Aye, yes.'

Chapter 5

LOOKING BACK, JEWEL couldn't say how she bore the following days.

Flora had been reluctant to see her go back to work, suggesting that returning the very next day following her 'accident' was too soon, that she must have time to recuperate. Jewel had dismissed her worries with quiet resolution. Not only was remaining at home impractical – the rent was due and they required her wages to supplement it – she also desperately needed the distraction. She'd lose her mind entirely were she to waste away the hours fretting in bed.

Besides, what impression would it give to Benji if she stopped away? He'd believe she was avoiding the place – him. She wouldn't give him the satisfaction of that. Never one to wallow for long, she'd always had a steady outlook, refused to let life knock her down for too long. She wasn't about to change now.

Lifting a figurine from a side table in the Powells' parlour, she ran the duster over it in swift, efficient flicks. She'd definitely made the right decision in coming back to work. For the very first time she was glad of Esther's slave-driver ways – the hours marched steadily by when she was engrossed in her duties and she was thankful of it. Fortunately, too, it looked like Benji was giving her a wide berth. Now, if only matters could stay the same until the end of the week . . . If she could just get through these next few days drama free . . .

Pausing in her task, she sneaked a hand to her midriff. Brows knitting in a frown, she stroked it slowly. Would her monthly bleed come? she asked herself, though she knew almost with certainty that it wouldn't. And yet . . . yet . . . The prospect of what that meant no longer filled her with all-consuming terror. Not since the solution had presented itself.

In odd moments of reflection – she did her best to quell memories of the incident with the cart, though, sometimes, they stole to her mind unsummoned – she still marvelled that she'd escaped unscathed. It truly was a miracle she hadn't been at all hurt; even the doctor said as much during his final obligatory visit the following day. It was as if it was somehow . . . meant to be . . .

Instantly, her hand sprang from her stomach to retrieve the duster and she resumed her cleaning with gusto. Don't harbour such thoughts, remember? she told herself firmly, mouth set. What shall be shall be – in no way, though, is this a positive thing. Stepping in front of that oncoming beast as she had – well, her mind hadn't been her own, had it? It was a flash of madness, she knew this now. Yet though she was grateful she was still here to ponder on such things, that her life had been spared, the fact that her stomach hadn't received at least a hard knock from the cart or cobbles, or a kick from a hoof, was something to be regretted.

Although, would it have made a difference so soon after . . . the deed, with Benji? Surely the child to come couldn't yet be removed from her body, by brute force or otherwise? Surely it needed to grow some for that to be possible? Oh, she'd been so foolish to think . . . to risk everything . . . If only she could speak to her mother. Of course, that was a cavernous impossibility. Flora knowing – God above, the thought made her want to be sick. She could never discover that her own daughter had lifted her skirts for a lad willingly. The shame would surely kill her.

No. She'd remedy this mess. She'd got herself into it; she and she alone would drag herself out of it, somehow, God willing. And there was but one person who could make that possible.

She'd put off seeking him out long enough – time she spoke to him, saw how matters stood, for this wasn't going away. The sooner she put her plan into action, the better.

Even as Jewel made these resolutions, she knew it was wrong. Desperate she might be, but this cruel streak she saw emerging in herself was new to her – could she really go through with this? Jem Wicks had hurt her, yes, it was true, but he didn't deserve this, did he? Hers would be a whole other level of betrayal.

'But do I have a choice?' she whispered to the empty room. Tears welled. She gulped them back and with an angry flick of her wrist flung the duster into her cleaning box. This she then returned to the cupboard on the landing before heading downstairs.

Bernard glanced around as she entered the shop. 'Finished for the day, lass?'

'Aye. I'll be away home now, Uncle Bernard, unless there's owt else . . . ?'

'Nay, nowt.' He flapped a hand. 'You go, I'll see thee the morrow.'

'Ta, thanks.' Jewel retrieved her shawl, draped it around her shoulders and left the shop. Outside, her gaze went in the direction of Jem's home and she took some deep breaths. She felt sick with nerves. Guilt, too, but she wouldn't dwell on that – couldn't. Sucking in a last lungful of air, she headed across the square.

After knocking at his door and being told by his mother that he wasn't yet back from work, Jewel went to wait for him at the corner. The passing minutes felt like hours and with each one that crawled by her nervousness steadily grew. Eventually, hooters from the surrounding cluster of mills and factories sounded and the town began to tremble quietly with the thud of clogs. They grew louder by the second and workers appeared, trudging through the grey streets like living corpses. Some chatted amongst themselves but, mostly, the exhausted crowd passed along mutely, minds on hearth and home and, if they were lucky, a meal of sorts awaiting them on the table.

By the time she saw him appear, empty bait tin swinging in one hand and flat cap in the other, his dark hair and clothes flecked with cotton spores, her heart threatened to smash through her chest. She stepped forward as he neared the ginnel's entrance and he slowed, his face showing his surprise.

'Jewel.'

'Hello, Jem.'

They stared at one another for some seconds until, his brow creased slightly, he asked cautiously, 'All right?'

She nodded. 'Aye, you?'

'Aye.'

Again, silence fell between them. In the past, he'd told her a little of his work as a mule spinner, that cotton pieces clung to the air in the mills like thick snow – it had made her glad she was employed in clean and respectable shop work. Now, a white wisp bobbed on his

79

eyelashes as he blinked; without thinking, she reached out and brushed it away with her fingertip.

He smiled. 'Was tha waiting here for me?'

Again, she moved her head up and down. Stabbing guilt returned, twisting her guts into knots, when his mouth spread further in pleasure. 'Can I talk with thee?' she forced herself to ask.

He led her through the cobbled entry to the familiar nook between two houses. Here, until not too long ago, they had shared innocent clandestine kisses. She was glad of the bad lighting that helped to conceal her flush at the memories and regret at what must come. 'Jem, I—'

'Please, let me say summat first.' He stared at his feet. 'I've been daft, Jewel. I miss thee, you know?'

'I know,' she murmured. And she knew he told the truth. It was clear in his tone. She couldn't, however, return the sentiment in either feeling or speech. If she was true to herself, she hadn't missed him, had she? Once the initial sting of betrayal had worn off, she'd found herself over him relatively quickly – proof their relationship hadn't meant that much, really. Nor would she now say she had. The lies to come, the ones she must force herself to see through, would be enough. She wouldn't add to them if she could help it and so she remained silent.

'She, she meant – means – nowt to me.'

'Happen I were hasty in ending things. Between us, like.'

Jem's eyes widened. 'Tha means that?'

'Aye, I do.' The words tasted bitter on her tongue and she had to swallow several times before continuing. 'Mebbe we . . . well, we could begin afresh. What d'you say?'

'I say aye, Jewel. Eeh, lass, you'll not regret it.' He took her hand in his. 'I'll do nowt to hurt thee again, you have my word on it.'

She blinked rapidly, nodded twice. 'Right then. That's sorted. I'd best get on home afore Mam gets worried.'

Jem walked with her. At the turning to her street he planted a loud kiss on her cheek. 'Ay, I'm that happy.'

'Aye,' was all she could muster.

'Bye for now, then.' Whistling a cheery tune, he turned and sauntered back towards his house.

She watched him go through a film of tears. That was that, then. And how easy it had been. He hadn't a single inkling of what she was about, the scheme she'd hatched, of just what he'd let himself in for.

She'd hoodwinked him without any effort at all.

She was the most despicable being in the world.

With effort, she suppressed her emotions. Where did feelings ever get you, anyway? she told herself bitterly. She squared her shoulders, lifted her chin and continued home.

*

Focusing on the here and now worked best for Jewel, she found. Were she to let her mind wander even a day into the future, she'd begin to shake all over and her brow and palms broke out in a cold sweat.

How her mother didn't guess that something was amiss with her, she struggled to think. Of course, Bernard was too busy to notice. Esther wouldn't have cared even if she had. As for Benji, she barely set eyes on him. Life was seemingly continuing just the same as it ever had for him. He made no other mention of what had taken place between them. She could have almost imagined the whole thing had never occurred – if the reality wasn't embedded like a cancer in her mind, that was.

Then came the day that she'd been awaiting with a

mixture of frantic hope and heavy dread. It brought with it sickening, world-shattering truth, and she knew life as she'd known it would never be the same, for any of them, again.

Despite her having already accepted it from the start, still she found herself slipping out to the privy hourly. There, she would offer up a silent prayer before checking her underwear. Every time, the longed-for crimson staining was absent. And she just knew – knew – that what she'd feared all along had happened. Mother of God, how would she bear this?

She'd told herself that should, by some miracle, her bleed arrive, she'd make her excuses and call the whole thing off with Jem Wicks. After all, she'd have no use for him then, would she, and everything could return to some semblance of normality. How could she be so utterly deceitful? She avoided asking herself that, for her terror and self-loathing that it had come to this, that she had sunk to such a low, was like a physical pain.

But survival, self-preservation, were much stronger forces. Desperate folk did desperate things. Now, she had no option but to see her plan through. None.

She wouldn't – couldn't – bear the world knowing the real circumstances. Judged, disowned, loathed . . . The stigma of bastard clinging not only to herself but to the child, for ever more . . . She really would sooner die than that.

And no one did need to know, did they? If she played this right . . .

'I'll be a fair wife to you, Jem, I promise. I'll devote my life to making it up to you, making you happy, I swear it,' she whispered now through trembling lips to the cloud-filled sky, arms wrapped tightly around herself. 'Forgive me. I'm sorry but I must do this.'

82

'Lass, are you all right? Your grub's growing cowd, here.'

'Coming, Mam.' Scrubbing at her wet cheeks with the back of her hand, she pushed herself away from the outside privy wall she'd been sagged against and dragged herself back indoors.

'Good potato pie, that is, and you've barely touched it.' Flora pointed at Jewel's plate with her fork. 'You sickening for summat? You've been back and fro to that privy the whole day long.'

Jewel forced down a morsel of pastry. 'I reckon I'm sick, aye, Mam. My guts are off, must be summat I've ate.'

'Coming out of both ends, is it?' asked her mother sympathetically, adding, 'Well, you get yourself an early night the night. There's nowt cures a body better than sleep.'

Jewel nodded, though she had no intention of upholding the agreement. Tonight, the deed with Jem must be done – the sooner the better. Her entire future depended on it.

The following hours crawled by agonisingly slowly. Sitting at opposite sides of the fire, she and her mother darned in companionable silence. Finally, through the flames' cosy rose-gold light, she spied her mother's eyelids drooping. Jewel's heart gave a few heavy thumps in response. Not long now. Almost time . . .

'Ready for bed, lass?' Dropping her sewing into the wicker basket on the table, Flora rose and stretched. 'Go on up, my love. I'll join thee in a minute once I've banked down the fire.'

'I'll do that, Mam.'

Her mother made to protest but tiredness won through: 'You sure?'

'Aye, go on. I'll not be long.'

'A good lass, that's what you are,' her mother said as she climbed the stairs, and Jewel could have cried.

Oh, Mam. Good I ain't. Nay, not now. It's foul and wicked I've become and there's worse still to come. I'm sorry . . .

'You asleep?' she asked minutes later as she entered the tiny bedroom. It was clear Flora was; her steady, rhythmic snores proved it but still she pressed closer to the bed they shared, had to be certain: 'Mam?'

Nothing. Watching her sleep, Jewel's eyes filled with shameful tears. She reached out a hand to stroke her mother's hair then, fearful of waking her and her plan being ruined, let it fall back to her side. She straightened and tiptoed from the room.

Avoiding the stairs she knew creaked, she reached the kitchen again with barely a sound. The ill-fitting door refused to cooperate and released a low groan as she opened it – cursing it under her breath, she squeezed her head through the gap and peered through the cool, indigo night. A full moon threw its cream-coloured beam along the cobbled expanse and after some moments she picked out a familiar figure through the shadows. A sigh of relief escaped her that he'd received word and had showed. She'd paid an urchin boy to call on Jem with the message earlier, but they couldn't always be trusted to deliver; sometimes, they would simply scarper with the brass, never to be seen again. She beckoned Jem across with a flap of her hand.

'All right, Jewel—?'

'Sshhh.'

'Sorry,' he whispered back.

'Come on in. Hurry, in case we're seen.' She pulled him inside and closed the door.

'So.' He removed his cap and placed it on the back of a chair. 'Tha wanted to see me? All's well, ain't it?'

'Aye, aye.'

'Then what . . . ?'

'I just wanted to see thee is all. Here, sit down.'

Looking pleased – which tore at Jewel – Jem did as she said. He smiled in surprise when, instead of taking the seat opposite, she perched on the arm of his. He took her hand in his. 'By, I've missed thee.'

She motioned to the ceiling and held a finger to her lips. 'Quiet, lad. We don't want to waken Mam.'

He nodded agreement. But something behind his eyes told her he wasn't altogether comfortable with this – Jewel was quick to reassure him.

'Don't fret, it's all right, really. She's a fair heavy sleeper.'

'I just don't . . . Why did you ask me here at this hour, lass? You ain't ever afore now.'

He was on to her, knew she was up to something. Paranoia stole through her, bringing heat to her cheeks. Her behaviour had made him suspicious – he was right, she'd never initiated anything like this in all the time she'd known him. She must take this slow or else all her carefully made plans would be ruined . . . 'Like I said, I just wanted to see thee. I wanted to be alone with thee. Proper, like. We never really have time to ourselves. Do we?'

'I . . . suppose not, nay.' Understanding had finally filled his eyes. His licked his lips in a nervous yet excited motion. 'Jewel?'

'Aye, Jem?'

He wetted his lips once more. 'When you say "time to ourselves", do you mean like . . . well, you know?'

What if I do the deed with Jem and my bleed comes after all? The thought crashed through her brain. What

85

if I'm wrong, if I'm not carrying Benji's child? I'd have given myself – chained myself – to this lad here for nothing. Yet didn't it arrive right on time every month? When had she ever been even a day late before? Never, that's when – she could usually set the clock by it. Besides, hadn't she just known that this would be the outcome of her shameful behaviour with her cousin? Instinctively, she'd felt the truth of it from the very start.

There was no mistaking it, however much she wanted to. She was with child. The sooner she had Jem's seed inside her, the better for all concerned. For once he discovered her condition – which he would believe to be his doing – he'd wed her just as he'd suggested when hoping to win her back, she was certain of it. He'd be none the wiser to the real truth of things, she'd do her utmost to create a happy marriage and home for him in return and her reputation would remain unblemished. More importantly, the child would be spared the stigma of illegitimacy. After all, when all was said and done, none of this was the poor blighter's fault, was it?

She was confident that Benji hadn't the sense to put two and two together. He was too young, too immature, to understand the female body and its workings, surely? He couldn't yet have any real knowledge of bleeds and dates and suchlike. Even if he was to suggest anything, she'd deny it to the hilt. He'd have no choice but to take her word as truth. It wasn't as if he'd ever be able to prove otherwise.

Nothing stood in her way but her conscience. Could she really see this through? Did she have it in her to trick this lad like this, in the worst way possible?

'Why don't you come and sit here?' Jem mumbled, hauling her mind back to the present. His cheeks had taken on a cherry hue – it was clear, despite his behaviour with that other girl, that he'd never before gone further with a female than kissing. He was as awkward as a young boy. 'That's if you want to, I mean,' he hastened to add, flushing further. 'If you'd rather not, if you're comfy enough where you are, then . . . well, I just thought . . .'

Jewel snaked an arm around his neck. Then avoiding his gaze, she slid into his lap. Immediately, she felt his arousal straining through the coarse material of his trousers. Panic swamped her; she shifted instinctively but the motion proved only to stoke the flames to an inferno – he grew harder, groaning low in his throat.

'Jewel . . . Oh, love.' Wrapping his arms around her, he covered her mouth with his.

She matched his passion but, inside, her every sinew screamed at her to leap up and run as fast and as far away from him as she could. For his touch had awakened memories she'd thought the drink had killed for ever. She remembered. Benji's podgy fingers probing painfully where they shouldn't . . . His hot palms on her thighs, drawing them wide . . . Lord, no, don't make me live it, not again . . .

Jem broke their kiss to fumble at his belt buckle and it took everything she had not to shriek and cry and slap his face again and again and again . . . She must allow him, must see this through. Jesus, give me strength.

'Are you certain about this?' Jem whispered through his panting.

Jewel doubted he'd be able to contain himself much longer but the fact that he'd even asked . . . Tears sprang to her throat and her guilt reached fever pitch. The enormity of what her answer would be was crushing her like a ten-ton weight.

'We don't have to, Jewel. Not if you ain't ready.'

Oh Jem, Jem . . . Her heart was hammering so fast she thought she was going to pass out. Then, 'I can't. I'm sorry.' She disentangled herself and scrambled to her feet. 'I'm sorry, Jem.'

He closed his eyes and nodded. 'No bother.'

'You . . . don't mind?'

'Nay, course not. Just . . . give me a minute to cool down.' He flashed a self-conscious grin then closed his eyes once more as he strove to steady his breathing.

She'd worked him up to such a level and yet . . . At least now she knew some males could control their urges if they wanted to. His understanding tore at her heart. How had she considered manipulating this decent lad for her own selfish gains? God, she was rotten through and through . . .

He deserved better. Oh, he did that. And she deserved everything she had coming to her, and more. She'd never forgive herself for what she'd almost done tonight. 'Happen you should leave,' she murmured.

He turned to look at her and frowned. 'Aye. If you're sure?'

'I'm sure.'

'Jewel, are we all right?' Putting on his cap, he took her hand.

For the briefest moment, she squeezed back. Then, biting back tears, she slid out her fingers from his hold. He made to reach for her again but she stepped away, shaking her head.

'You seeking me out the other day; was you acting through spite all along? Was tonight, all of it, about revenge for what I did to thee?'

Nay. Oh, nay. God above, she couldn't bear this . . .

'Jewel?'

'Goodbye, Jem.'

He stared at her for a long moment. His shoulders slumped and, sighing, he turned and left the house.

'It's for your own good, lad,' Jewel mouthed to the closed door. 'You'll see that one day.'

Pressing a fist to her mouth, she crumpled, sobbing, into the chair.

Chapter 6

THE FLASH OF colour from the mass of bedding plants on the sloped bank captured hints of the sun's gold. Sat on a set of steps at the south end of the park, Jewel hugged her knees and watched the delicate petals bobbing in the breeze.

Oddly, being here aroused no feelings of fear or disgust within her – in fact, she found that the park still evoked the same emotions it always had: calm and quiet enjoyment. For this, she was more grateful than she could express. Her drunken wickedness hadn't tainted at least this one aspect of her life.

She heaved a sigh. She was due in work in half an hour and each passing second felt like a step closer to the gallows. She might as well find a rope and put it around her neck herself now, save her family the trouble.

Cotton manufacturing being the staple trade of the borough, a body could never escape the fact, whichever direction in the town they took – in the distance, mills and chimneys hovered on the skyline like silver-black bricked ghosts. Up and beyond, rising stately, proud, stood the tower of the new town hall. The sight made her want to weep. She could scarcely believe how different things were since that opening day. Had it really been but a few short weeks ago?

'Sod them, all of them,' she whispered fiercely. 'To hell with their judgement. I'm past caring.'

Nonetheless, prickly heat flooded her face at the unavoidable confession to come. All was lost with Jem. Hiding her condition for long was impossible. There was nothing else for it – she had to come clean.

In desperation, she focused her concentration on the flowers once more; following tradition since the park opened, they formed the name of Bolton's current mayor. But her distracted stare refused to linger on the letters for too long and, all too soon, her mind strayed to thoughts of the abhorrent words she must soon speak. That terrible, existence-shattering truth . . .

'Hello. Miss Nightingale, isn't it?'

The easy tone from close by had her whipping her head around as though the speaker had yelled the greeting into her ear.

'Forgive me. I didn't mean to startle you.'

Jewel squinted up in surprise. She glanced to the man's side but the mischievous toddler she'd first seen him with in this park was absent.

'How are you?'

'I . . . I'm well, ta.' She nodded in confusion when he indicated if he could sit. He lowered himself on to the step beside her and her brow creased. 'You called me Miss Nightingale. How do you know my name?'

'You don't remember?'

Her frown deepened. 'Remember . . . ? But we've never passed words.'

'Yes, indeed, that much is true.'

'Sorry, I don't under—'

'No need to apologise; after all, you'd had quite the shock that day, when you . . .' He paused to clear his throat.

Realisation brought embarrassment to her eyes and

heat to her cheeks. She recognised his voice now all right. 'The day I walked in front of a passing cart?' she finished for him quietly.

'Yes, well.' He shrugged matter-of-factly. 'We all make mistakes.'

Was that a hint of amusement pulling at the corners of his mouth? she asked herself. Anger rose within her. He was mocking her? Just who the hell did he believe himself to be to even think of taking such a liberty with someone he barely knew? As far as she could see, it was no bloody laughing matter. Sod him, too. Sod them all! She rose abruptly.

'Oh. I do hope you're not leaving on my account?' he asked, almost disappointedly.

She released a soft snort. This one didn't half think a lot of himself. 'I'm due in work.'

'You're employed at Mr Powell's premises in the square, is that so?'

'That's right.' She rearranged her shawl, nodded a stiff farewell and set off across the grounds.

However, after only a few steps, Jewel found herself reluctantly turning back towards him. He was her uncle's acquaintance – and a gentleman, to boot. Bernard wouldn't be best pleased to learn she'd acted rudely towards him. And when all was said and done, he *had* come to her aid that day, had carried her back to the umbrella shop. 'I . . . well, your assistance after my accident . . . Thank you.'

The man stared at her for a moment. Then, smiling, he held out a hand. 'Maxwell Birch.'

She felt her hand slip into his. 'Jewel.'

'What an interesting name.'

'So I'm told.' Surprising herself further, she resumed her seat beside him.

'You have some time to spare after all?'

'Aye, mebbe. Well, a little.' Colour touched her cheeks again. She shot a sidelong glance to see him smiling wryly and, this time, her own lips twitched in response.

She would have guessed him to be in his middle fifties. A slight dusting of grey at his temples correlated with her assumption, although this only added agreeably to his looks. His broad upper arms and shoulders and firm-looking thighs showed her he took care of his physical fitness – no doubt chasing around after his live-wire daughter helped with that. Besides the laughter creases around his deep brown eyes, his open face was unlined. Perhaps his nose was a little too large and his lips a little too thin but, nonetheless, he cut an attractive figure.

Bringing her gaze back to the flowerbed before he noticed her staring, she said, 'Sorry, Mr Birch, for being short with thee earlier. It's just—'

'You believed I was poking fun at you,' he observed mildly. 'I wasn't, you know. It was simply my attempt to lighten the mood but, evidently, it failed miserably.' His smile broadened. 'You see? We *do* all make mistakes from time to time.'

'Aye.' *But God above, me more than most,* she added in her mind.

'Your uncle is most fond of you.'

A stirring of pleasure chased away Jewel's misery. She smiled. 'He told you that?'

'He didn't have to. It was clear to see upon him realising that the girl lying by the roadside was his niece.' Maxwell turned fully to look at her now and all traces of laughter had left his face. 'I'm senior clerk at the Bank of Bolton, and it was during my meeting with Mr Powell that the incident occurred.'

She nodded. Puzzlement had brought her brows together at the sudden seriousness of his tone. 'It was fortunate that he was close by, that he spotted me, aye.'

'Miss Nightingale ...' He paused to run a hand through his thick hair.

'Yes?'

'It was I who alerted your uncle. I saw it happen from the window.' His voice dropped. 'I saw it *all.*'

'You did?' She swallowed hard when he nodded. Further words deserted her. She could only stare at him dumbly. Then was he aware it had been no accident, that she'd intended for that horse to hit her ...?

'Why did you do it?'

Oh, he was aware all right. His quiet question hung between them. She closed her eyes.

'Miss Nightingale?'

'Yes?' she whispered.

'What on earth prompts a young woman such as yourself, with her whole life ahead of her, to attempt ... Why?' he repeated.

'I don't know.'

'You don't know?'

'Nay.'

'However, you don't deny it?'

Jewel opened her eyes. They were blurry with tears. 'I did intend it, you're right. It were a mistake, mind; I see it now and I regret it. It were nowt but a second of madness.' What was she doing? Why in the world was she admitting this to him? He had a way of putting you at your ease, making you comfortable in his presence ... Sudden panic gripped her. She turned wide eyes to him. 'You'll not tell anyone – not the police?' Suicide was, after all, a criminal offence. 'Surely not my uncle? Please, I ... I were wrong, I know it now. I'll never do it again, nay, never.'

'I rather think you should be the one to tell—'

'Nay. I can't!'

'Miss Nightingale.' Maxwell's voice was low, gentle. 'Your family would be only too willing to help with whatever it is that troubles you, I'm certain.'

'Please . . .'

'You must understand my predicament. If you were to attempt something similar and the results next time proved disastrous, I would never forgive myself for keeping my silence—'

'I shan't. Mr Birch, I told thee, it were but a daft, brainless mistake.'

'Be honest with them. I'm sure—'

'I'll be going now.' On shaky legs, she rose and backed off towards the park gates. Scalding tears clogging her throat threatened to choke her. To think she'd believed that things couldn't get any worse. Here was just another of her sins set to be exposed. Her mother would die from the shame of it all, she would, without doubt.

Maxwell called her name but, shaking her head, she turned and hurried away.

He thought her insane. Of course he did, and who could blame him? Perhaps she was. She didn't even know herself any more.

Troubles ran on in her mind, unrelenting as she trudged through the dank-coloured streets. The gentleman she'd just fled from believed her capable of attempting self-murder again, at any given time, and was worried that he was privy to the fact. That she'd dragged yet another innocent being into this putrid mess! Just how many decent people's lives would she taint or ruin completely before all this was over?

Right now, she didn't class Benji as being half to blame. She'd been the one to agree to lie with him,

95

after all. She was the elder, supposedly had more common sense. Hadn't he been after her for months? She'd been well aware of it; his hungry eyes and hands when he was around her made it impossible not to be. She should never have let herself get into the inebriated state she had, shouldn't have let herself – let the two of them – get into the situation they had.

Without question, fault lay with her. However much people would hate her once the truth got out, it wouldn't even begin to touch the level of black loathing she carried for herself.

*

Benji was lounging behind the counter looking bored when Jewel entered. She glanced around. 'You here alone?'

'Aye. I ain't sure when Mam and Father will be back – they've gone calling on a sick friend or summat – but Aunt Flora should be here shortly, thank God.' He released a theatrical sigh. 'It ain't half dull in here.'

He looked like a spoilt youngster who had been told he couldn't go out to play. God above, to think she was to have a child with him ... He was nowhere near mature enough for this – well, obviously he wasn't, he was fif-bloody-teen! she reminded herself, angry tears threatening. Just what the *hell* was she going to *do*?

'Make a fresh sup, eh, Jewel?'

Nodding distractedly, she made for the door that led to the Powells' living quarters. As she collected cups and spooned tea from the caddy into the small teapot, she rehearsed in a whisper the conversation she must have with her cousin: 'Benji, listen, our night together ...' She paused to close her eyes, grimacing. Just uttering those words made her feel sick.

However, she must. There was no putting this off any

longer. Best she made him aware of the circumstances before the rest of the family heard it. At least then, she'd be a little better prepared, would know his feelings on the matter. He might even come up with some sort of solution . . . She dismissed the last notion immediately. What in God's name *could* he think up? There *was* nothing that would remedy this, was there?

The spoon clattered noisily as she threw it inside the cup with a cry of frustration. Splaying her hands on the table, she closed her eyes again, her breathing ragged. Hearing footsteps behind her, she forced herself to regain her composure, though her chest burned with unshed anguish. She rescued the spoon and reached for the caddy once more, saying over her shoulder, 'Benji, you shouldn't leave the shop; I'll fetch the tea down.'

'Well, when? I'm parched.'

'When it's bloody ready,' she snapped, turning towards him, hands on hips. 'You'll think so, should your mam and father return and catch you leaving the business unattended. Go on, get back down, will thee?'

'Customers are slow this time of day.'

'Even so—'

'We'll be all right for a few minutes.'

She'd returned her attention to the teapot – now, at his last quiet statement, she swivelled around again. 'What's that meant to mean?' She frowned when he didn't answer. 'Well?'

Benji moved so quickly that Jewel didn't have time to process what was happening until it was too late. His chubby hand groped clumsily at her breast and, after initial shock, blistering fury gushed through her veins. She staggered back against the table. Then she struck out with all her might, landing a deafening backhander

97

across his stunned face. She moved in for a second time, sending his head swinging in the opposite direction as she slapped his other cheek, the sound like the cracking of a whip.

'Listen to me, you foul little divil,' she hissed through gritted teeth, shaking him by the front of his jacket as he whimpered and twisted, trying to break free. 'Touch me one more time and I'll cut them sweaty hands of yourn clean off. You understand?'

'But I thought . . . after last time . . .'

'Don't speak of that, just you don't! You thought wrong, by God you did.' She flung him from her, then to her horror promptly burst into tears.

Benji stood scowling before asking after some moments, 'What you upset for? It's me should be bawling.' He reached up to touch his tender face. 'Bitch. I've a good mind to tell Mam you put your hands on me.'

'Is that so?' Though tears still streamed down Jewel's cheeks, her voice was now void of emotion. 'Not before I do, lad. Aye, it's me what's to do the telling – about *you* putting your hands on *me*.' She nodded when his face paled. 'Consensual it might have been, God help and forgive me, but it's gone beyond a drunken fumble now. I'm with child. Do you hear me? I'm growing your bloody babby. There's no getting out of this – not even for thee. We're done for, lad.'

Whatever response she'd expected, it certainly wasn't what she received – her cousin folded his arms, expression calm. 'Happen it's Jem Wicks tha should be spouting this to, not me.'

'You what?'

'You heard. Word has it you offered yourself to him, an' all, not a week since. Not for the first time, I'll bet.'

She couldn't breathe. Though she tried to brazen it

out, she knew the guilt in her voice gave her away: 'I don't know what you're talking about, Benjamin Powell.'

'Aye, you do. Sneaking him in your rooms, eh, whilst your mam were abed above youse . . . ?' Shaking his head, he clicked his tongue several times.

'Nay. Nay, that's not . . . not right, I . . . !'

'Aye, it is. Jem's told all the lads at the mill. I overheard a few laughing and discussing it in t' square.'

Jem . . . Lord, how could you? Jewel thought her heart would break in two. Could things get any worse than this?

'I'm surprised Aunt Flora's not got wind of it yet . . .'

'Don't you dare try to threaten me,' she choked out, disgusted at the smug look Benji now wore. 'You've no idea what you're saying. Despite what you've heard, me and Jem Wicks have never . . . *You're* the only one I've ever . . . I'm telling our family the truth of things, whether you like it or not. Them believing me is another matter, but I have to—'

'I'll deny it, Jewel. Just so you know.' Unnervingly, there was no malice in his words, only certainty. 'And once you've finished with the telling, I'll be the one informing them of a thing or two – that Jem Wicks is the father of the child you reckon you're carrying.'

Helpless rage made her hands, hanging loosely by her sides, shake. She bunched them into tight fists. What she wouldn't give to thump the pockmarked face before her to dust. She'd underestimated him, thought him but a simple kid, when all along . . . He'd likely planned this from the off.

Yet surely there was a way around it? she thought desperately. Jem would confirm what she was saying was the truth: they hadn't lain together, had they? But how could she trust him now? She'd hurt him – humiliated

99

him, even – it was true. Still, she'd have never believed him capable of such cruelty, never. Thanks to him, her name was dirt enough before the reality of her condition had even emerged. Could she rely on him to back her up? Did she even know him at all? It certainly didn't feel like it now. Though Jem wouldn't want folk assuming he'd fathered her child, that didn't mean to say he'd help her expose Benji as the culprit. Jem might very well put it about that she'd had other lovers besides, or some other such fabrication – who knew what? As far as she could see, the lad she thought she knew was a stranger capable of saying anything.

Benji had outwitted her. They both knew it. Taking in his self-assured expression, a familiar emotion washed through her and she shivered: she really did want to die. Anything was preferable at the minute to this hell called her life.

'What will you do, then?'

'I'm telling them the truth, have to,' she whispered.

'You're daft, that's what. Everyone else will think it, too, for I'll deny everything. Not that it'll take much effort, mind – I mean, come on, who will believe at all that we . . . you know?'

Incredulous, she shook her head. 'Why are you doing this?' He didn't answer and her voice broke as she added, 'You'll ruin me.'

'Well . . .'

'Well, what?'

Burying his hands in his pockets, Benji shrugged. 'Say you were attacked by some unknown man. Tell folk you don't know who it were and that, afterwards, you were too frickened and ashamed to speak up.' He lifted then dropped his shoulders again. 'Most won't hold you to blame for bearing a bastard child in that way, will they? Not if you have them think it were no fault of yours.'

Despite her anguish and fury, she knew a trickle of relief at his suggestion. Why hadn't she thought of something like that? Could it work? Some in the town would doubt her, it was guaranteed. Nevertheless . . . However, a thought struck her and her building hope dimmed. 'And if the child should look like you? What then?'

Silence thickened the air between them. Benji broke their stare to look at the floor.

'Hello? *Hello?*' Flora's puzzled voice drifted upstairs from the shop, slicing through the charged atmosphere like a hot knife through butter. 'What the divil . . . ? Where is everyone?'

'What then?' Jewel repeated in a whisper to her cousin.

Finally, he lifted his eyes. Neither fear nor worry, arrogance nor anger were reflected in their grey depths – there was nothing. They bore blankly into hers like those of a dead kipper.

'Well?' Jewel hissed.

As though he hadn't heard her, he turned his head slightly towards the door. 'Coming, Aunt Flora!' he called downstairs. He continued staring at his cousin for some moments before walking from the room.

Jewel dropped into a chair at the table. She had to call on all the restraint she could muster to stop herself from grabbing the teapot and hurling it at the wall in a pique of anguish. Bernard's newspaper, neatly folded, lay by her elbow and, instead, she gripped this in her two hands, squeezing with all her might, teeth gritted, which eased her bubbling temper a little.

She had a good mind to storm the shop and reveal all to her mother this instant. Yet where might that get her? It would cause a holy hell of trouble; should Mam believe her, she would understandably kick up war with Esther and Bernard – maybe even give Benji a well-deserved clout in the process. The family would be ripped apart and no one would suffer more than Flora as a consequence.

They were the poor relations, always had been; they relied on the Powells' support significantly. Not only would the truth mean inevitable unemployment for the pair of them – if Esther didn't throw them out on their ears, then Flora would certainly insist they were finished with the shop – it would also mean losing the only kin they had left. Jewel couldn't deny that her uncle and aunt had been there for her mother both financially and emotionally throughout the years since Fred Nightingale's death. This would fracture beyond repair a relationship that her mam not only held dear but depended upon.

Concocting a tale of a mystery attacker was becoming more appealing by the second. Could she pull it off convincingly? Would her family believe her? Could her tongue really allow her to see her cousin walk away scot-free from this mess he'd helped create?

Crushing powerlessness swamped her and her shoulders sagged. She took some deep breaths to steady her frayed nerves. She must get up and see to her chores, couldn't let her mother see her like this, had to go on as normal without arousing suspicion until she had a concrete version of events devised in her head. She couldn't afford to slip up, had to get this right if she was to do it at all.

She rose from the table, then, catching sight of the scrunched pages of Bernard's newspaper, clicked her tongue in contrition. With care, she smoothed it out as best she could and placed it back where she'd found it. She was about to make for the fire when her eyes, straying to a particular piece of smudged text, picked out a few words. She paused.

Thanks to her uncle's patient teachings, Jewel had learned to read sufficiently well alongside her cousin at a young age. Though she hadn't revelled in it quite as much as Benji did, she had still grasped enough to be able to read at an adequate level. Now, lifting the paper once more, she scanned the short advertisement:

NURSE CHILD WANTED, OR TO ADOPT.
Widow with moderate allowance would be glad to accept
the charge of a child. Age no object. If sickly, would receive
a parent's care. Terms 15 shilling a month or would
adopt entirely for small sum of £10.

Jewel re-read the words a half-dozen times or more. Her heartbeat had quickened and her hands felt clammy. This sort of thing really happened? There were folk out there willing to take a child off your hands, no questions asked? For what purpose? A married couple unable to bear a baby of their own, she could understand, but a widow? *Dear God, what did the ins and outs matter?* her mind yelled. This could be the answer to her prayers . . .

Just as quickly as it had risen, the rush of hope drained away and disappointment replaced it – ten whole *pounds*? How in heaven could she ever dream of having such an amount at her disposal? Even the monthly fee this widow was asking was beyond her means. Jewel handed over her wages to her mother each week, and the little that Flora gave back for her to treat herself with didn't amount to anywhere close.

Looking down, she was surprised to see that her hand had travelled to her midriff. It had done so of its own free will, almost as if to shield the life lying within from the article, from its mother's contemplations . . .

'Shut up,' she told herself firmly. 'Daft imaginings like that will get you nowhere but the asylum, for you'll bring on the madness with such thoughts.' And yet . . .

Her gaze once more swivelled to the paper. But again, the impossibility of it was undeniable. She shrugged, sighed and gave the advertisement underneath it a cursory glance. Again, the word 'Wanted' leapt out at her, only this one was followed by something else – something that brought heat to her veins and excitement to her breast more than the first had done.

Bringing the newspaper closer to her face, she read on quickly:

WANTED, IMMEDIATELY, GENERAL SERVANT.
A gentleman's family seeks respectable girl to attend a young child as well as regular household duties. Good wages. Character reference required. Apply to Mrs Kirkwood after 6 p.m. at the following residence . . .

Scanning the address, Jewel's face lit up to see it was no distance from her own home. Then surely this instead was the answer, albeit a temporary one, to her prayers: escape.

Anything could happen over the course of the next few months: she could lose the child naturally – it happened to women all too often, she knew. Should that occur, she'd be all right, could continue with her life afresh. And if the child didn't break from her before its time . . . well, then she'd just have to try to hide her condition from these potential new employers for as long as she could.

It would be a while yet before her belly began to grow.

Time in which, mercifully, she wouldn't have to be in Benji's presence, wouldn't have to look at the hard-faced swine, nor be forced to resist smacking him in the teeth . . . Also, being so close to home, this family might just be persuaded to let her stay on at Back Cheapside with Mam.

She was aware that general servants – a glorified title for maids-of-all-work – normally lived in, but there was no harm in asking, was there?

But the ad stated that her duties would involve caring for a child. She had no experience of such a thing. However, how hard could it be? If the family asked, she'd say she'd cared for little 'uns before – surely this would arouse no suspicion and she'd learn as she went along? Besides, if it came to it, it would be much-needed practice for when her own baby came along, God help her.

She nodded to herself, her enthusiasm mounting. Her mother and, undoubtedly, Esther would want to know why she'd decided to leave the shop but, for now, explanations could wait. At this moment, she could think of nothing but doing all in her power to secure this position. The fact that the prospect evoked this level of pleasure proved to her she was doing the right thing.

It could be said she was approaching such a career relatively late. Most girls began at thirteen, often younger – how they coped with such responsibility at that tender age, Jewel didn't know. Not only was it a solitary situation but a gruelling one. Arising with the lark and to bed barely shy of midnight, general servitude was not for the faint of heart. A maid-of-all-work was just that: a sole servant with an endless list of tasks that were seemingly never done. Housemaid, kitchen maid, cook, washerwoman, seamstress – and at this residence, nursemaid, too – rolled into one.

105

To make matters worse, vast numbers of girls received rough treatment from their employers and endured a miserable existence with next to no thanks. She just prayed the gentleman and his family were kindly and didn't use her too hard.

After memorising the house number and returning the newspaper with a determined nod, Jewel set to her chores with gusto. The hours flew by, and before she knew it Flora appeared in the doorway informing her it was time to come home. She smiled, nodded and went to collect her shawl, then she and her mother set off on the short distance across the square.

Jewel had spoken to her mam at odd intervals throughout the day but to her cousin she'd uttered nothing more. Likewise, Benji hadn't spoken to her – what, after all, was there left to say to each other? He'd made his feelings known and she, unable to see a way forward in that respect, had kept the truth locked within.

She wouldn't, as she'd sworn she must, tell their family anything just yet. One matter at a time – securing the servant's job should take priority. When she did eventually break the monumental news, a faceless attacker being the culprit, as Benji had suggested, would be the explanation she'd go with. This she'd decided during her work, and the more she'd mulled it over the more sensible the idea had become. Though she was loath to let that swine off the hook like this, she could see no other option for a quiet life. He'd get his comeuppance some day, somehow, she was certain. Past wrongs had a funny way of catching up with you like that and she looked forward to the time Benji was called to answer for his. Oh, she did.

'More bread, lass?'

Reasoning that she might as well learn the outcome of

her interview before revealing to her mother her decision to leave the shop, Jewel had done her best to act naturally whilst helping Flora prepare their evening meal. Inside was another matter; anxiety coupled with hopeful anticipation had churned her stomach throughout – she'd struggled to get the food down. Now, as Flora lifted the knife to the stale loaf, Jewel shook her head quickly.

'Not for me, ta, Mam.'

'You sure? Another sup of tea, then?'

She shook her head once more. Avoiding her mother's gaze and forcing herself not to gawp at the cheap tin clock yet again – she'd barely taken her eyes from it since they arrived home – she pushed back her chair. 'D'you know, I fancy a walk.'

'Now?' Frowning, Flora glanced to the window and the pale grey sky beyond. 'It favours we're due rain.'

'Nay, it's brightened up a bit, I reckon,' she responded mildly; inside, however, her heart was thumping like a drum. 'Anyroad, I'll not roam far and I've got my shawl.'

'Aye, all right. Thinking on it, the air will do thee good after being holed up in that stuffy shop the day through. Mind, you never bemoan it. You're a good lass, aye.'

The soft pride in her mother's tone brought a sting of guilt. They had never kept secrets from each other and she hated the fact that she'd started now. Before leaving, Jewel bent over her and pressed her cheek to hers. She closed her eyes. 'I love thee,' she murmured against the warm, lined skin.

Flora stroked her daughter's long plait which lay between them. 'I know, lass. And I thee. Now, go on, enjoy your walk. I'm for putting my trotters up awhile by the fire.'

The town hall clock struck five thirty as Jewel stepped outside, and excitement stirred in her. Positioning her shawl to drape loosely around her shoulders against the midsummer breeze, she turned her clogged feet towards the square.

She'd take a wander around, after all, until the appointed time; hopefully, it would help to calm her racing heart and mind.

Chapter 7

HERE, MERE YARDS from the slum dwelling Jewel had always called home, was like stepping into another district altogether. Lined with fine, mainly three-storey late-Georgian town houses and institutional buildings, Mawdsley Street was an attractive spot.

Naturally, the very best places to be were the villas in areas away from the belching chimneys of industry; by Bolton Park, for example. That was where the wealthiest and most important – the cotton merchants and their ilk – made their homes. They wouldn't dream of polluting their own lungs with the noxious smoke their businesses created. They left that to their workers, who could afford rent only on the crumbling rooms clustered around their mills and factories. Money didn't just talk here, it bellowed for the world to hear. Such was life.

Nevertheless, despite its central location, Mawdsley Street was certainly not to be sniffed at. You could quite easily forget the truth that its residents lived cheek by jowl with the less fortunate packed into the tight grid of lanes surrounding it once you turned the corner into this straight and narrow, well-kempt road.

Jewel paused outside the address and looked about. Some of the mixed stone and brick edifices were more elaborate and imposing than others, but each seemed like a royal palace compared to what she and everyone she knew was used to. And to think she might shortly be living amongst this, too, she thought excitedly, eyes drinking in the clean and quiet surroundings.

The private residence before her boasted a pedimented entrance and a tall, shiny dark-wood door with a brass knob and knocker – these, she spied, were dull and in need of a good polish. In fact, looking more closely, she saw that one or two other things showed subtle signs of neglect. The sash window panes appeared a little dirty and the front step looked as if it hadn't seen a scrubbing brush in months. She frowned. Then the corners of her mouth lifted and she nodded. It seemed she'd come at just the right time.

After quickly tidying her hair and smoothing down her skirts and shawl, she took a deep breath and knocked. The door opened almost immediately and she stepped back in surprise. 'Oh. He–hello.'

'Yes?'

'My name's Jewel Nightingale. I'm here about the general servant's position advertised in the *Bolton Evening News*.'

A tall, well-dressed woman with greying brown hair secured in a neat bun who she assumed was the mistress, Mrs Kirkwood, lifted an eyebrow with evident interest. 'I see. Follow me, please.'

She led the way to a good-sized drawing room in dusky blue. Like the curtains, the sofa was a shade darker and complemented the space beautifully – to this, the lady motioned and, tentatively, Jewel sat.

'It is not quite six yet. The advertisement did stipulate that all applicants were to apply here after that time.'

'I'm sorry . . . Should I come back later?' Jewel had

110

half risen as she spoke, but the lady brushed her suggestion aside.

'No need, you're here now. You're able to wait?'

'Aye, yes, Mrs Kirkwood.'

'Good. He's normally home a few minutes after six, then we can get down to business.'

Jewel smiled and nodded instead of letting her frown show. He? Husbands never usually involved themselves in such matters – the taking on of staff was left to the mistress of the house to deal with. Something else didn't quite add up: the terms mentioned she'd have to care for a young child, yet Mrs Kirkwood appeared a little long in the tooth to have recently borne one. She was fifty if she was a day. It *was* possible at such an age, it was true – Mam was proof of that – but still . . .

'Have you experience of domestic servitude, Miss Nightingale?'

Snapping out of her reverie, Jewel chose her answer carefully. Though she'd cleaned at the umbrella shop and helped with the cooking for her and her mother for just as long, she hadn't ever actually held the title of servant . . . 'I can scrub and cook with the best of them, Mrs Kirkwood,' she announced with what she hoped was confidence.

'Good, good. And children?'

Again, Jewel thought her response through. 'I have a younger cousin.' That Benji was barely two years her junior, she didn't mention. To her relief, the lady took from this what Jewel had hoped she would – Mrs Kirkwood nodded, satisfied.

'Well, so far so good.'

The ticking of the clock on the ornate mantel filled the silence for a minute or two until, finally, there was the sound of the front door opening and closing.

Mrs Kirkwood disappeared into the hall and Jewel

111

took the time alone to prepare herself for the interview proper, checking again that her hair and clothing were neat and taking some slow, deep breaths. She'd just fixed a small, polite smile to her lips when the drawing-room door opened and the couple stepped inside.

'Oh.'

'*Oh.*' Jewel echoed the man's surprised greeting. Blinking in confusion, she could lay her tongue to nothing more: what on earth was going on?

'The two of you have already made one another's acquaintance?'

Maxwell Birch nodded to the equally puzzled-looking lady. 'You could say that.' A definite smile lingered behind his eyes. 'Her uncle is a client of mine at the bank.' To Jewel, he added, 'Miss Nightingale, may I introduce Mrs Kirkwood, my sister.'

Sister? But she'd assumed . . . God above, how could this be? Her shoulders drooped and disappointment pained her chest. That was her dream of employment here dashed right away. Given what he knew of her, that he believed her to be of unsound mind, there was no chance he'd want her beneath his roof, and especially tending to his child . . .

'Shall we begin?' Maxwell removed his dark jacket, which his sister took from him and left the room to hang up, then loosened his stiff collar. Then he motioned to the sofa and when Jewel, after a long hesitation, resumed her seat, he sat in a chair facing her. Resting his elbows on his knees, he steepled his fingers and stared at her.

She dropped her eyes to her feet. 'Mr Birch—'

'How are you?'

Their encounter at the park that morning played in her mind and her cheeks grew redder. 'I'm well, ta. Look, Mr Birch, I shouldn't have come—'

'You've changed your mind about the position?' he interrupted again. 'So soon?'

'You mean . . . ?' She lifted her gaze to his. 'You don't want me to leave your house? You're prepared to interview me, sir?'

A quiet smile appeared at Maxwell's mouth. 'Why ever would I not be? Is there a reason why you deem yourself as undeserving of a fair trial, same as everyone else?'

'You know there is.' She spoke in a dull whisper. 'You believe me to be mad. To be honest, I don't blame thee. Often question it myself of late.'

For a full minute, he was silent, then: 'I think you are unhappy, and deeply so. Something troubles you which you feel unable to disclose, even to those nearest to you. However, I don't think you are mad. Not at all, Miss Nightingale.'

Jewel's eyes filled with tears at the sincerity of his tone. To hell with the job – she just needed someone to talk to. She opened her mouth, fully intending to spill her secret, for that's how this man affected you. He made you feel . . . *safe* was the only word she could summon to mind. Aye, secure in the knowledge that he would listen without judgement. That he'd understand, maybe even offer a solution. That it was just you and him, here in this moment, in the whole world . . . Until, the door opened and Mrs Kirkwood breezed back in, snapping Jewel back to her senses.

God above, what was she playing at? That she'd almost . . . had actually considered . . . To *him*?

Her mind was racing; she needed to leave, must get away from this house and Maxwell Birch. She watched in dismay as, before she had a chance to make her escape, the lady took a seat in the chair facing her brother as though to continue the interview.

113

'So, Miss Nightingale.' Mrs Kirkwood raised her brows encouragingly. 'You were saying earlier about your experience in tending to children?'

'I . . . Well, I . . .' Jewel's face burned brighter still. She licked her lips. 'Aye, yes. Well, what I, I mean, is—'

'Blast, there is the door,' Mrs Kirkwood cut in as a knock sounded. Flashing an apologetic smile, she rose and disappeared from the room once more, unaware that Jewel was secretly thanking God for the diversion.

Now is your chance – think of an excuse, quickly! her mind yelled. She jumped a little too suddenly to her feet, as if she'd been bitten on the backside or some such; her embarrassment heightened yet further at Maxwell's surprised frown. *Damn it, I have to get out of here!* 'Mr Birch, I'm afraid I must go.'

'Oh?'

She nodded. 'Aye, I've just remembered there's summat I need to . . . there's somewhere I have to be, like, so I'll take my leave of thee now and—'

'Brother.' Yet again, Mrs Kirkwood had re-entered to shatter Jewel's train of thought.

She cursed under her breath, forgetting what it was she'd been saying; *please, just let me leave . . .*

'There is another girl arrived interested in the servant's job,' continued the lady. 'I've left her waiting in the hall.'

Maxwell nodded, though his stare was still on Jewel, who was now standing uncertainly in the centre of the room. He released a long, quiet breath. Then he turned his head towards his sister. 'Please inform the newcomer that the position has been filled.'

'Oh, you mean . . . ?' Mrs Kirkwood inclined her head to Jewel. At her brother's nod, she smiled brightly. 'Wonderful. Miss Nightingale appears a clean, tolerable, respectable young woman.'

Jewel almost baulked at the last description. *Respectable*. If they only knew . . . She dropped her gaze quickly lest her sin gave her away.

'Indeed, a sound choice,' added the lady, blind to Jewel's shame. 'I'll tell the other girl right away.'

'Thank you,' Maxwell responded, his eyes now back on Jewel.

Before leaving, Mrs Kirkwood placed a friendly hand on her shoulder. 'Welcome to the family, Miss Nightingale. You're just what my brother has been searching for, I'm sure.'

The drawing-room door shut behind her and Jewel and Maxwell Birch were alone once more. She simply gazed at him, lost for words. What the hell had he gone and said that for? She didn't want the wretched job any more, did she? She just wanted to leave this house and never have to see it or its master again. Well, she'd tell him so, she would—!

'You're angry?'

Queerly, him bringing light to the fact in that calming voice of his caused her temper to rapidly diminish. 'What makes you think that?' she asked quietly.

'Your eyes, they give you away. Right now, they're spitting steel. You don't desire to work here? Is that it?'

Despite herself, she shook her head, found it impossible to lie. 'Nay, that's not it, sir. Toiling here would be gradely, I'm sure.'

'Then . . . ?'

'Are you certain it's me tha wants?' He didn't answer. Sighing, she continued. 'I haven't even fetched a character reference—'

'Don't worry about that. It shan't be necessary, given that I know your uncle.'

'That's not all. I must be honest with thee, I bent the

115

truth to Mrs Kirkwood. I've no experience of minding youngsters—'

'But you can clean?'

'Aye, but—'

'And cook?'

She nodded. 'Aye, I can, but Mr Birch, sir—'

'Then that is all that matters. The rest will come naturally to you, I'm sure. Constance is a happy child; albeit a little mischievous, perhaps, as you saw some weeks ago at the park . . .'

At this, a smile lifted Jewel's mouth. The lively toddler with the golden curls who had excitedly stormed the children's games, wanting to play, flashed into her mind. Then a sudden thought struck her and she frowned. She glanced at the door. Why was Mrs Kirkwood presiding over this household and not the mistress? Where was the infant's mother, Mrs Birch?

'Mary, my wife, passed away last September,' Maxwell murmured, as though seeing into her thoughts. 'She was always one to flout convention, insisted upon us not having servants, was a very involved wife and mother.' A wistful look, tinged with pain, appeared in his eyes. 'She was certainly one of a kind. Alas, the cancer cares not about such things, nor who it strikes.'

'Eeh, I'm sorry, sir.'

He nodded. 'My sister has proven to me that guardian angels do exist. What Constance and I – Roland, too – would have done without her these past months, I shudder to imagine.'

'Roland, sir?'

'My son from my first marriage. I shall introduce you to him later.'

Then this was really happening. She was here to stay. The reality quickened Jewel's heartbeat but, oddly, the feeling of trepidation had left her now and only a pleasing sense of readiness remained.

'My sister and I have both agreed that the time for her to return to her own family permanently has come. It has taken some persuading, however; she has been loath to leave me—' He broke off, then smiled. 'Mary's passing was very difficult for me to accept. But, by the grace of God, each day gets a little easier. And, of course, having a piece of her in Constance helps.'

Jewel didn't know what to say. His plight had touched her deeply. His daughter's, too; motherless at such a tender age. Life could be so cruel at times.

'Yes, indeed, my brother-in-law will certainly be glad to have my sister home,' Maxwell added. 'Her dividing her time between him and me cannot have been easy for him; his patience throughout has been nothing short of remarkable. Now you're here, she will return with an easy mind, I'm sure.'

Now you're here . . . Jewel's shoulders involuntarily straightened. She lifted her chin, the sense of responsibility leaving a warmness inside that both surprised her yet felt natural, almost comforting.

'There is just one thing I feel I must ask.'

Dread trickled back, for she knew what he was about to say. He wanted to know her secret, what troubled her to the point she'd attempted self-murder. *Dear Lord, he'd know soon enough once her belly expanded, but she couldn't tell him here, not now.* 'Aye?' she finally forced herself to respond.

'Your uncle and aunt won't miss you?'

Releasing her breath slowly, she swallowed her relief. 'Nay, sir.'

'You didn't leave on bad terms, I trust?'

Only now did she remember that she was yet to inform

them of her decision to terminate her employment. Esther would probably have a blue fit, rail at her for what she'd deem her ungratefulness, which would likely upset her mother into the bargain ... She drew in a deep breath of determination. That, she would worry about later. Whatever resulted, she wouldn't be swayed, *couldn't* remain in that shop another day with that cousin of hers.

'Nay, sir,' she repeated. 'I fancy a change of work is all.'

His face spread in a slow smile. 'Well, I'm glad you happened upon here.'

'As am I, sir. Ta ever so for taking me on.'

After a long moment, Maxwell shook his head. 'No, Miss Nightingale. Thank *you*.'

*

The kitchen, which Mrs Kirkwood led Jewel to minutes later, was reached by a set of narrow stone steps that were in need of a scrubbing – Jewel discreetly pulled a face.

Maxwell's sister might well have done a good job of looking after her brother and his children's immediate needs over the months, but it was plain that she wasn't used to the more menial aspects of running a home. Likely she had maids in her own residence so hadn't the experience of keeping house. How nice it must be to not have the need to sully your own hands!

They emerged into a fair-sized room, though what a contrast to the scrumptious house proper above. The space was stark, serviceable, fit entirely for purpose. The design of homes such as this was no accident – the sole purpose was to keep 'uppers' and 'lowers' apart. Down here, in these lonely holes in the ground, the work was completed out of sight by unseen hands, thus not impinging in any way upon the lives of the genteel whom they served. Sights, sounds and smells were contained, as the families desired them to be. Their needs were pandered to without attention being drawn to this, such were the rules of this complex world.

Houses, particularly larger establishments, wouldn't have been able to function without an army of staff to see to their smooth running. However, a vast number of the underclass would likewise be lost without the call for domestic positions. Masters and the staff they employed needed each other, perhaps equally. So long as respect was shown on both sides, thus avoiding the inevitable ripples of contention, relationships between the two glided without a hitch.

If lucky to find a decent household, domestics were happy to devote their whole lives to service. A true testimony to their loyalty. Many even grew to love the families they served, regarding them almost as their own kin. In turn, it wasn't unknown for their rulers to grow fond of these people they paid to see to their every whim. Proof that, if done right, and with continued effort from each party, these agreements could and did work well.

Pay and treatment differed widely from residence to residence but, nonetheless, the career was a respectable one. That servants were fed, housed and in most cases provided with uniform, all without costing them a copper coin, was a desirable proposition and highly sought after.

Though the choice wasn't hers to make – once the baby made an appearance, even before then, she'd be forced to leave here – Jewel couldn't see this as *her* life for ever. She wanted to marry one day, aye. She didn't want to be a spinster, toiling for someone else's family for all her days – a family of her own was what she desired.

Huh! And what make of man will take you on, now? a small voice inside her head mocked.

119

The stinging truth crushed her heart. Blinking back tears, she forced her attention back to the kitchen.

A cooking range, shiny pots and pans hanging from long hooks either side, dominated the left-hand wall. A large cupboard stood beneath the high, thin strip of window facing her and in the centre of the room a scrubbed, light-wood table and one chair took up most of the floor. There was a scullery-like area to the opposite side of her for washing dishes and vegetables, and this concluded the furnishings. Or so she thought. Turning, she spied in a dim far corner behind her a small, iron-framed bed. Neatly made with thin pillow and plain sheet and counterpane, it looked neither warm nor comfortable. *Well, hopefully, she wouldn't be in need of that . . .*

To think that most girls would barely leave their kitchens – day, week, month, year following year – was a depressing notion. They had no cause to, after all; everything they needed was right there in their one stuffy, solitary little room.

'Mrs Kirkwood, I wanted to ask.' Jewel pointed to the sleeping area. 'Could I please be permitted to stop on at home rather than dwell here? Mine and Mam's house is but a stone's throw away in Back Cheapside—'

'I'm afraid that would not be practical, Miss Nightingale,' cut in the lady, though not unkindly. 'Has it been just yourself and your mother?' she asked when Jewel's face fell.

'Aye, Mrs Kirkwood.'

'This will be your first time away from home?'

'Aye,' Jewel murmured again, with a terrible feeling of regret. She should never have come here, had naively assumed she'd be permitted to stay on at home. How could she leave her mam all on her own? How would *she* cope without Flora?

'You would have to be here to light the fires and so forth for when my brother and his children awaken. It really wouldn't do if you had to knock them up of a morning to admit you into the house, now would it?'

She shook her head; she hadn't thought of that. 'Nay. I suppose not.'

The lady stepped back and surveyed the space. 'It isn't awfully inviting in here,' she admitted. 'However, once you've made it your own, I'm sure it will feel more like home. Yes, yes,' she added thoughtfully. 'A few pictures, perhaps, to brighten the walls . . . Leave it with me, I'll see what I can do,' she finished with a nod.

'Eeh, you don't have to trouble yourself with that, Mrs Kirkwood.' Though surprised and not a little grateful for the offer, Jewel didn't want to appear to be taking liberties. However, the woman brushed her worries aside and Jewel thanked her warmly for her kindness.

'Now. You will rise each morning at six o'clock. My brother breakfasts early, you see; this should give you ample time to complete your early duties before seeing to his meal.'

Jewel nodded then listened intently as the lady proceeded to rhyme off the complete list of chores that would be required of her, not wanting to miss anything, for she was eager to make a good job of this. Maxwell Birch had been generous enough to take her on, despite everything; the least she could do in return was serve his household with the respect and efficiency it deserved. Its smooth running was vital.

'The doors are locked and bolted at ten o'clock each night – a duty my brother undertakes himself – and you are then free to retire to your bed,' the lady finished.

'Aye, Mrs Kirkwood.'

121

'Is there anything you would like me to go over with you again?'

'Nay, I think I've got it all, ta.'

'Sunday afternoons are yours to spend as you wish – resting in preparation for the week ahead would be wise.'

The lady had a point. Such multifarious occupations could easily become overwhelming. 'I'm sure if I divide my time successfully, I'll not wear myself thin and make myself ill, Mrs Kirkwood. I'm sure to be fatigued at the day's end, aye, but not completely fagged, so long as I plan accordingly. A thorough clean of different rooms on different days, with regular duties in between, of course, would work well, I reckon.'

'Oh?'

'Like, say, I tackled the drawing room on a Monday, the dining room and hall on Tuesday, stairs and nursery on Wednesday, the master's bedroom on Thursday and his son's on Friday. Saves running myself ragged trying to see to it all in one day at the week's end. This will leave me with Saturday to scour and scrub the kitchen and get everything in nice neat order.'

She appeared impressed with this, maybe even somewhat regretful that she hadn't come up with the scheme during her stay here. 'A sensible approach. You will receive twelve pounds per annum, although this may be increased later on, should you prove satisfactory. Which I'm sure you will,' she added, smiling. 'I can see you're an industrious girl.'

'Aye, Mrs Kirkwood. Hard and honest toil is in my blood,' Jewel stated proudly.

'Yes, I can see that. Well, I think that's everything,' she added, crossing to the stairs. Before ascending, she looked at Jewel over her shoulder. 'Leaving this family in the morning shall be a wrench, indeed. However, I'm most reassured knowing they are in your capable hands.'

'I'll do my very best, Mrs Kirkwood.' And she meant it.

Midway upstairs, the lady paused again. Her tone was thick as she murmured, 'You will look after him, Miss Nightingale?'

Jewel's response held just as much sincerity as before. 'I will. You have my word.'

*

'Leave the shop? Why?'

The hour was approaching nine. A curve of the frigid moon, visible through the ill-fitting curtains, lent its light to the small kitchen Jewel had called home for as long as she could remember. Her mother had slowly lowered her darning into her lap at her announcement and was gazing at her in shocked puzzlement.

Doing her best to appear nonchalant, she shrugged. 'I fancy a change is all, Mam.' The false explanation she'd given to Maxwell Birch tasted acrid on her tongue when she used it with her mother.

'Nowt's occurred? That Esther ain't done you wrong, has she?'

'Nay, nay.' Jewel gave her an easy smile. 'It ain't so big a deal really, Mam. I'll be no great distance away, eh? Besides, I'll have Sunday afternoons off, which we can spend together. *And* the brass is better.'

'But . . .' Flora plucked at her lip. 'I'll miss thee, lass.'

Christ, she was going to cry. Hell's damnation to that swine Benji and all he'd helped create! She wished to God he'd never been born, wished they were not related so they never would have met. And all the while, he'd slithered his way out of blame completely, leaving her to deal with the muck storm alone.

'We've not spent a single sun without each other since the day tha arrived to brighten my world. Norra one. But ay, I'm being selfish. You must do what you want to do, never mind my ramblings. You're a sound worker, lass, and don't often get what credit for it you deserve. Anyroad, I'll have to let you go some day, won't I, for you'll soon have scores of lads queueing at yon door, vying to wed thee.' She flashed a wobbly smile. 'Aye. Now's as good a time as any. You've my support and more. I only ever want thee to be happy.'

Jewel was speechless with emotion. *Oh, Mam. My hand has been forced in this, and I ache to tell you why, tell you everything, but I can't. As for getting wed . . . Never that. Not now.*

'Go on, lass,' Flora added. 'You take yourself up and get a healthy sleep for the morn. Start as you mean to go on, bright-eyed and bushy-tailed. I'll follow shortly. 'Ere, and don't go fretting over that wife of our Bernard's, neither. I'll inform her of you leaving when next I see her.'

'Aye?'

Her mother nodded. 'She'll like it or lump it, an' all, and I'll tell her so.'

Again, Jewel was overcome with a host of painful emotions. 'Ta, Mam,' she managed to croak before quickly escaping upstairs.

Savouring the room, its feel, its smell, she was afforded some comfort, but still her breast throbbed with the devastation of it all. For the last time, she snuggled beneath the coverings. Sleep wouldn't come, Jewel knew that, but simply being here, beside her mother shortly, was enough. She'd wait until Mam dropped off to sleep then hold her plump body so tightly, more than she ever had before, and she'd tell her in her mind how much she regretted that things had come to this and how sorry she was to have to leave her. She'd tell her how much she loved her, more than any other single being on this earth. And she'd vow to her that she'd never forgive herself for it all.

When muffled weeping seeped through to her from downstairs, Jewel's heart finally broke. That she'd brought about such suffering to the selfless woman undoubtedly now feeling adrift, dreading the loss of her and fearful of being alone, was simply too much to bear; she curled in on herself like pummelled wax.

An image of her mother huddled in her fireside chair, face wreathed in sorrow, burned itself in her mind. Jewel just knew she'd be holding to her breast the glass candlestick, as she was wont to in times of woe. It had been a last token of love from her father – all, besides her memories, that she had of him now. But Jewel couldn't trust herself to go to her. She'd end up blurting the truth, she would, then all would be completely lost.

This night, another plane of hatred was born.

Foul and black towards Benjamin Powell.

More so for herself.

Chapter 8

'HM. IT'S RATHER a large fit.'

Stretching out the full, ankle-length apron then letting the voluptuous material fall back to her sides, Jewel chuckled. 'Mrs Kirkwood did her best at such short notice, sir, I'm sure.' She gave the matching white cap, which had slipped over one eye, a shove to the back of her head. 'This, too, shall be right as rain once I've secured it well with some pins,' she assured him.

Maxwell covered his twitching lips with his fingers. 'You're certain?'

'I am. Now, sir, you pass the little lady to me and take yourself off to the bank afore you're late. She'll be just fine. Won't you, Miss Constance?' she added smilingly to the flaxen-haired beauty, holding out her arms.

'Lizzie will be here at eleven,' he told Jewel yet again, almost apologetically – though she couldn't think why. Hadn't the position advertised in the newspaper stated clearly that part of her work would include tending to his daughter?

The lass Lizzie he referred to was Constance's nurse-maid but, with an ailing mother, she'd had to cut her starting hour to when her married sister was free to call to share the daughterly duty of care. Jewel was certain she'd manage the child well enough until Lizzie arrived.

So long as she kept her occupied she should be free to get most of her chores done as planned.

The morning had been an emotional one – and, she suspected, not just for herself. Despite her best efforts, her mother had been unable to hold back her tears when kissing her goodbye. And afterwards, clutching her small bundle of possessions, Jewel had stood for an age outside her house, desperately wishing she didn't have to leave it or the woman within. Finally, biting back heartache of her own, she'd turned her clogged feet in the direction of the new place she would from now on call her home.

What would Esther say later – Benji, too – when Mam revealed this new development? she'd asked herself repeatedly. Flora had assured her she'd give it to them straight and they could deal with it, and not to fret, but Jewel couldn't help it. What if her aunt grew suspicious of her motives? Yet how could she? she would remind herself. She was being paranoid, that's all. There wasn't a chance in a hundred lifetimes that Esther could ever guess the real reason behind her sudden move. As for her cousin, well, he wasn't about to reveal anything, was he? He'd likely be glad to have her out of the way now, given what he knew. Rotten young swine that he was . . .

When she'd arrived at Mawdsley Street, Maxwell had answered her knock with a definite look of strain on his face. His sister had left shortly before, he'd informed her quietly; that the parting had been a wrench, for all involved, had been clear to see. Jewel had felt the urge to offer him comfort but couldn't think of anything to say or do that wouldn't seem like she was overstepping her station.

Instead, she'd followed him down to the kitchen in silence, where he'd shown her where to put her things and pointed out the neatly folded pile of material on her bed – her uniform, which Mrs Kirkwood had procured for her before her departure. That wasn't all. True to her word, she had indeed found her several cheap pictures, and the calming woodland scenes broke up the blank expanse of wall beautifully. That lady was a kind and thoughtful soul, and no mistake.

Now, as Maxwell headed off for work and when his footsteps had died away on the stairs, Jewel glanced down again at the apron and allowed herself a relieved smile. Thank the Lord he hadn't insisted she had the thing altered. With any luck, it would conceal her sin once her belly began to swell for a little longer than she'd anticipated. God, but she hated all this deception. He, not to mention Mam, didn't deserve this. *She* didn't deserve their trust and kindness.

'Down! Down!'

Bringing her mind back to the kitchen and the child now doing her utmost to wriggle from her hold, Jewel nodded with quiet resolution. Time to stop these destructive thoughts. She must simply make the best of a bad situation – it was all she could do for now – and suffer the consequences of her wickedness later.

'*Down!*' the youngster demanded again; chuckling, Jewel lowered her to the flagged floor.

'You're not one for doing nowt, are thee, lass? Like a cat on hot bricks, you are. Oh, 'ere, missy, don't do that!' she added on a gasp as, lightning fast, Constance, having dragged up the rag rug from in front of the fire, made to toss it on to the leaping flames. 'Eeh, young imp!' Jewel gathered her back up into her arms, much to the toddler's disgust. 'I can see I'm to have my hands full with thee.'

'No! Down!'

'Now then, less of that. Come on, let's find you summat to do. I've my chores to see to.' Had she bitten off more than she could chew here? Jewel was beginning to think so. She'd no experience with children, had she, and it was starting to show. Would she be able to manage? Time would soon tell. She'd give it her best, in any case.

She stuffed a few rags and a tin of polish from the shelf by the fire into her apron pocket. Then, collecting her brushes box from the large cupboard and the broom propped in the corner on the way, she took the child upstairs to the main part of the house.

Upon reaching the hall, she sat her on the black-and-white, diamond-shaped tiles and opened out the box. Constance's eyes lit up at the array of items she'd never seen before, and Jewel smiled. That should keep her busy for a few minutes whilst she swept the floor.

Working deftly, figuring it was worth leaving the patch that the child occupied so as to get the rest cleaned, she had the space done in no time. Nodding in satisfaction, she now turned her attention to the mats and gave them a vigorous shake outside.

She glanced to the child, still happily playing with the brushes, and smiled. Maybe she wasn't all that bad with children as she'd feared. Now, if she could just get through the next few hours until Lizzie arrived . . .

Minutes later, Jewel's arms ached terribly, but the results of her efforts had been worth it – she'd polished the brass knocker and door handle to within an inch of their lives and they dazzled like stars in a midnight sky.

By this time, Constance had grown bored of the play-things; not trusting her to be left alone, Jewel lifted her up and carried her down to the kitchen. The large pan of water she'd left heating on the fire was bubbling nicely – after filling a pail, she lugged it and the girl back to the hall. Now, already, her back hurt as well as her arms. Lucky for her she was no stranger to hard toil and had grown accustomed over the years to pushing through the fatigue. No wonder the house had slowly fallen into disarray under kind but privileged Mrs Kirkwood's watch. It required a dogged worker unafraid to get their hands dirty to keep a place ship-shape.

After carrying the pail outside, Jewel took Constance's small podgy hand and helped her into the street. She handed her the smallest brush from her box. 'Watch me, lass. Like this.' She dipped her own brush into the water and nodded when the child copied her. 'That's it. Eeh, you are clever.'

'Clever?' Constance beamed.

'Oh aye. Now, give the stone here a good scrub. Look, I'll show thee.' Kneeling on the flagstones, Jewel moved her brush in circular motions across the surface of the doorstep. 'That's it,' she encouraged at the child's attempt to imitate her. 'Good girl.'

'By gum, did you ever see the like!' The statement rang out across the street and was followed by a hearty guffaw. 'You're a bolder one than me, lass. That you are!'

Jewel looked over her shoulder towards the source of the voice and was surprised to see that the young woman who had spoken was addressing her. 'Sorry, what?'

Similarly dressed in apron and white cap, knelt with pail and brush outside her own door, the woman bobbed her dark head towards Constance. 'I were saying, you've got pluck, setting the young miss to such a task – in full public view, an' all, by all accounts. Who ever heard of a servant turning their master's daughter into a skivvy? Not I, nay.'

Jewel glanced down at Constance. As the woman's words sank in, her cheeks reddened in horror. She hadn't thought about her actions at all, had merely been trying to keep the toddler occupied. Lord, but the servant was right. What on earth would Maxwell say to see such a thing? He'd likely be furious, maybe even throw her out on her ear, and who could blame him? This would be seen not so much as overstepping her station but leaping over it headlong.

Quickly, she took the brush from the child and shot the woman across the road a grateful look. 'Ta ever so. I don't know what I were thinking.'

'Ay, don't fret on it, lass. This your first day?' At Jewel's nod, she tossed her own scrubbing brush into her pail and sauntered across the street. She had a pleasing face with what Mam would describe as 'eyes in love with each other' – a heavy squint that gave the impression she was staring at the tip of her nose. Smiling down, she held out a hand. 'Maria. Pleased to meet thee, I'm sure.'

Jewel shook it warmly. 'Aye, you too. I'm Jewel.'

'Bonny name.'

'Ta, thanks. Yours, too. So, you're employed at that residence there?' she asked, motioning to the attractive house opposite.

Maria snorted. 'Oh no, I were just passing and spotted their step were a bit on t' grubby side, thought I'd do them a favour ... Course I'm bloomin' employed there!' she burst out good-naturedly. 'By, you're a bit daft, ain't yer?'

Jewel couldn't help grinning. 'Suppose it were a silly question. Well, I'd best get on. Nice talking to thee, Maria.'

But the woman had stopped listening, was peering past Jewel along the street. 'Eeh, you are a lucky divil to have the excuse of being under the same roof as him, lass,' she whispered out of the side of her mouth. 'Tending to his wants ... well, that's summat I *would* willingly do for nowt, aye.'

Frowning, Jewel followed Maria's gaze. Thirty-something, tall and broad-shouldered with wavy brown hair and smoke-grey eyes, she could see why the gentleman approaching them had Maria in such a tizzy. But what had she meant about her being lucky to be under the same roof . . . ?

Roland. It had to be. Maxwell had said the previous evening that he'd introduce her to his son, but he hadn't returned home in time. Neither had she caught sight of him this morning. Mind you, judging by his rather crumpled clothing and fresh stubble, it was little wonder – he'd clearly spent the night elsewhere. What were his father's feelings on such behaviour? Didn't Roland have a job to go to?

'And how are you on this fine morning, Maria?'

The young woman blushed to the roots of her hair. She smothered a giggle with her hand. 'Gradely, sir, ta for asking. And yourself?'

'Oh, all the better for seeing you.' He flashed a dazzling smile then turned to enter his house – and almost toppled on to Jewel, still knelt by the step. 'God alive! I didn't see you there!'

She scrambled to her feet and attempted a clumsy curtsey. 'I'm Jewel Nightingale, sir, Mr Birch's new maid.'

Roland lifted his eyebrows. 'Ah, I see. Yes, I recall my aunt mentioning she was to put an advertisement in the *Bolton Evening News*. Well, welcome to our abode, little nightingale. Seems my father has been most astute in his selection.' His let his stare linger over her for a moment before touching his hat and brushing past her into the house.

'You've snared his eye all right,' Maria announced with not a little envy. 'Eeh, you are lucky.'

Jewel pulled a face. She had to admit, he'd seemed

132

pleasant enough and she'd take that any day over the poor treatment some domestics faced. Nevertheless, just let him try anything with her and he'd know about it. It was common knowledge that many young men of privileged households saw their female staff as fair game – it was almost like a rite of passage to bed the family's maids. God help him if he was of the same mind. She'd had a bellyful – literally – of the male species, enough to last her a lifetime already.

There was no denying Roland Birch was devilishly handsome, but boy did he know it. His easy-charm talk with Maria was proof he enjoyed flirting with anything in skirts. Though, unlike the swooning maid, such an attitude did nothing for her. She much preferred his father's subtle confidence and maturity.

The observation halted in its tracks, stopping further musing. Why on earth had that entered her mind? What a thing to be thinking – about her master, to boot. She just hoped her blush didn't show.

'I'd best get back to that ruddy step. My mistress would have a blue fit were she to spot me gossiping here with thee. Not that she's likely to, mind, what with her hard at work whiling her day away on the pianoforte, eating cakes and drinking tea . . .' Maria gave Jewel a wry grin. 'I'll be seeing thee, lass. Bye for now.'

She watched her go with a smile. Maria was a rum 'un all right. Hopefully, they would become friends. The woman was nice in a mildly brash sort of way. Besides, right now, Jewel needed every ally she could find.

*

By the time Lizzie arrived to take over Constance's care Jewel was mentally exhausted. Who knew caring for a child could be so fatiguing? Keeping the boisterous girl

133

from becoming bored, and therefore wreaking havoc in the kitchen, had taken every ounce of energy her brain possessed. No sooner had she invented some game or other to occupy her than Constance was up and toddling off in search of mischief again.

No wonder Maxwell had appeared apologetic earlier over Lizzie's changed hours. Could she really cope with this particular duty? Jewel asked herself as she lay, spreadeagled on the bed, eyes closed, savouring a few precious minutes of peace. *More to the point, how would she manage her own child when it arrived – not only full time but alone?*

The prospect made her feel ill. There would be no palming the life growing inside her on to a nursemaid when she needed a break, would there? No time to spare lounging on the bed with a child to care for as well as money to earn to support them both. Christ, how would she manage? Just what the hell was she going to do?

'Nay,' she whispered to herself fiercely, swinging her legs off the bed and dragging herself up as panic threatened to swamp her. 'Don't dwell on it, any of it. It'll do thee no good.'

Expelling her worries temporarily on a deep sigh – aye, for she knew they'd be back soon enough, were always lurking close by – Jewel crossed to the fire to heat some water, tackling the mucky upstairs windows she'd spied yesterday, now at the forefront of her mind. *Anything* so long as it offered a much-needed distraction.

*

'Will that be all, sir?'

Placing his newspaper on the table, Maxwell nodded. 'Yes, thank you.'

Before leaving him to his meal, Jewel watched him

lift the serviette she'd spent ages shaping into a fan and shake it out without seeming to notice.

In fact, she pondered upon reaching the kitchen, he'd seemed somewhat distracted since this morning. Clearly, his sister returning home had affected him more deeply than she'd realised. Her heart contracted a little for him and she vowed to do her utmost to see he overcame the loss in whatever way she could. After all, hadn't she given Mrs Kirkwood her word that she'd look after him?

As she washed up the dirty pots and pans, she smiled, pleased with herself that she'd chosen lamb stew as her first meal to cook for him. It was one of her specialities and her mam's favourite. She hoped Maxwell liked it as much. It was important to her that she made a good impression. Though whether his son would enjoy it, dried up as it would be by the time he got to it, remained to be seen.

She hadn't seen Roland again following their meeting with Maria outside. He must have taken himself up to his room, though she hadn't heard a thing from inside when crossing the landing on occasion. Likely he'd gone to bed to catch up on sleep he'd missed last night elsewhere. Neither was he present in the dining room just now. Maxwell hadn't seemed too concerned at this, had asked her to leave his son's meal to warm by the fire.

Her thoughts switched to her mother, who, for the first time, would also be eating alone at this moment. Guilt pierced her and she closed her eyes. She was missing her terribly and she knew Flora would be feeling the same. Jewel just prayed her venomous aunt hadn't kicked up much of a fuss about her leaving and taken it out on Mam. That poor woman would be suffering enough.

Flora was still on Jewel's mind later when she climbed

the stairs to draw the curtains and extinguish the lights before retiring to bed. She'd been up earlier to clear the dining room – like his son, Maxwell was nowhere to be seen – and she'd finished up her chores with a heavy heart. Already she had begun to see that life as a general servant was indeed a lonely one.

Reaching the drawing-room window, Jewel's gaze immediately went left up the street. Again, she pictured her mother at Back Cheapside, this time alone in their bed, the pillow soaked with her tears ... As she struggled to swallow the lump in her throat, a movement across the street caught her eye. There, looking back at her from her own residence as she carried out the same late-night task as herself, stood Maria, flapping her hand wildly. The friendly sight was like a balm.

Smiling, Jewel waved back. And as she returned to the kitchen, she did so a little lighter of heart.

Chapter 9

TONGUE PEEKING OUT in concentration, Jewel raked out the dead ashes as quietly as she could manage. The early-dawn lighting of the bedroom fires without waking the family was a real skill that all maids had to master – thankfully, she seemed to have got the hang of it quickly, hadn't disturbed any of the Birch members up to now.

In the four-poster bed behind her, Maxwell lay on his back, one arm resting above his head on the pillow. The new sun trickling through the gaps in the curtains, which lent Jewel the only light whilst she went about her task, fell in straight, silver rays along the bedclothes and up across his bare chest, picking out the thatch of dark curls there. But it was his face when she glanced over her shoulder to check his sleeping, worried she was creating too much noise, that caught her attention and kept it there.

Turning fully to face him, she sat back on her haunches. He wore a look deep in forlornness. His brows were together in a slight frown, the corners of his mouth down. He put her in mind of a youngster having a bad dream, and this she would have believed and given it no more thought had she not glimpsed now and then since arriving, when he let his gladsome mask slip, him wearing the same expression in his waking hours, too.

Did his sister's absence trouble him still? After all, he hadn't been his usual self since – Jewel had noticed his withdrawal. However, she sensed something more now, that he couldn't conceal fully in this state of unconsciousness: raw grief. She recognised it unquestioningly; she'd seen her mam wear it often enough.

Lowering her gaze, guilty to be secretly intruding on his inner feelings, she returned her attention to her work. She'd just finished black-leading the fire and was wiping her soiled hands on a scrap of rag when, again, her attention was drawn to the man. She hesitated then crossed to the bedside. His frown was still in place and now his lips were moving – tilting her head, she listened but no words emerged. Only a moan, low with sorrow, escaped on his breath. His pain was tangible.

Jewel's heart contracted for him. What made her do it, she couldn't say – perhaps it was the promise she'd made to Mrs Kirkwood – as ever so gently, she laid her palm on his slick forehead. Instantly, the skin-on-skin contact seemed to comfort him; his brow smoothed out on a soft sigh.

She removed her hand but continued watching him for some seconds. Satisfied he was calmer, she gathered up her box of cleaning brushes and slipped from the room.

Later, Maxwell entered the dining room wearing the easy smile Jewel hadn't seen since their earlier meetings. He seemed fresher, brighter somehow, and she was glad of it.

'Good morning, Jewel.'

'Morning, sir.' She stole another look at him as he sat. 'You're . . . well today, Mr Birch?'

He appeared to consider his answer. His smile returned. He nodded. 'Yes. Yes, I think I am.'

With a happy smile of her own, she finished setting the table then left him reading his paper to collect breakfast from the kitchen.

Today was her first Sunday off. Thoughts of spending the whole afternoon with her mother brought excited flutters to her stomach and she quickened her pace. However, midway down the stairs, cooking smells reached her nostrils and a sudden bout of nausea whacked her full across the face. Her guts changed direction, somersaulting worryingly, and she bolted down the remaining steps. She reached the kitchen just in time to heave up what felt like her soul into the stone sink.

Sweating and shaking, she took some deep breaths – realising too late her error when the broiled mackerel gripped her insides again as though with invisible hands. She swallowed quickly, this time managing to stem the sickness, but was still forced to drop into a seat for a minute to regain her composure.

Slowly, clarity reached her – her eyes swivelled to her midriff. She could have cried, for this had made her terrible predicament all the more real. The seed inside her was growing by the minute into a real person; it was as if her body had realised and had decided to begin reminding her of the fact. As if she could forget. It was with her every waking moment. *God, help me.*

With great effort, she forced herself back to her duties. Holding her breath, she dished out the meal and hurried as fast as the tray would allow her back to the house. The sooner she had delivered this disgusting fare upstairs, the faster she could escape from here for a few hours.

When she re-entered the dining room, she saw that Roland had joined his father in her absence. Lounging in a chair at the table, he watched her approach with lazy interest. She placed his breakfast in front of him and he cocked his head for a better view of her face.

'Are you feeling well, little nightingale?'

Embarrassment brought heat to her cheeks. Stemming her anxiety, she nodded. 'Aye, Mr Roland.'

'You're rather pale. I hope my father isn't working you too hard,' he added with mock-sternness to the older man.

'Nay, sir.'

Maxwell had lowered his paper, was regarding her with something akin to concern. Her face flushed a deeper red; cursing it, she averted her head, saying, 'Will that be all, sir? Mr Roland? Only I planned to visit Mam . . .'

'Of course.' Maxwell looked as if he'd say more but, after glancing towards his son, changed his mind. 'Off you go, enjoy your afternoon.'

'Ta, thanks. I will, sir.'

In less than a minute, she'd donned her shawl and was stepping into the street with a thankful heart. High clouds framed a pleasant sky and a slight breeze took the edge off the humid air. Drawing in a long, slow breath, she turned her back on the house and set off for Back Cheapside.

'Mam?' Jewel burst through the door at a half-run, giddy with anticipation, but her happiness was soon dashed. She halted and took in the scene before her. Two figures were seated by the fire drinking tea and eating slices of bread and dripping. Her mother turned with a joyful cry at her entrance – the other simply stared and didn't utter a word.

'Eeh, lass. By, but it's good to see thee.' Flora fussed around her daughter, removing her shawl and stroking her hair, before pulling her close in a quick hug. 'Sit yourself down, I'll pour thee a sup,' she told her, unable to keep the smile from her face as she crossed to the table.

All the while, Jewel's gaze never strayed from her cousin's. Just what the hell was *he* doing here? What she wouldn't give to dash across and slap *his* face daft for him until the flagged floor ran red. Was there no escaping him at all? Hadn't she a constant reminder burrowed in her womb without this? Today of all days – but, of course, he'd have known she had the afternoon off from work, must have planned this. All she'd wanted was to enjoy a few precious hours in her mam's company, but he'd spoiled it, like he had everything else. Lord, how she loathed him.

'Does tha want a refill, Benji, love?' asked her mother, busy with the teapot, her back to them. 'Ay, lass, he's been an angel hisself this past week,' she informed her daughter. 'Reet looked after me, he has, running errands and the like. He's just this minute finished fixing that sideboard door we've had trouble with for ages. Shuts perfect now, it does, thanks to him. Well, lad? Will tha stop for another sup?' she asked him again.

He broke Jewel's stare to glance inside his cup. When he brought his eyes back to hers, she sent him a look that held both pleading and warning. *Don't you bloody dare accept, just you get gone from here*, she silently screamed at him.

Benji's gaze swivelled to her breasts, much to Jewel's disgust, then he trained it towards his aunt. 'Ta. I will, aye. 'Ere and after, I'll take a look at that shelf up there; seems a bit lopsided to me.'

Anger shook Jewel's very bones. By God, he'd pay for this.

Groping behind her to where her mother had hung up her shawl, she plucked it down and dragged it across her shoulders.

'Lass? What—?'

'I meant to explain right away but hadn't the chance . . .' Wincing at the confusion in Flora's wide eyes, Jewel busied herself with securing the garment. 'Mr Birch asked me to work this afternoon, you see. I said aye, for he's stuck without a nurse for the child, and . . . He needs me, so I'll have to go. He said I could dash home to inform thee but I've to be right back. Sorry, Mam.'

Flora was crushed. 'Oh, lass . . . Well, if you must, then you must. Eeh, but I were so looking forward to having thee by yon hearth forra few hours.'

'Sorry, Mam,' Jewel repeated, before rushing from the house, sure she'd explode into violent sobs – or blurt out the truth behind her need to make a speedy exit – were she to remain here a second longer.

Her tears flowed freely as she pelted, shawl flapping behind her and her long, swinging plait whipping her back, towards the park. There was nowhere else to go. She certainly couldn't return to Mawdsley Street so soon; what would the Birch men make of that? Questions would be asked as to why she wasn't using her free afternoon as it was intended, and she really hadn't the energy to spin off a convincing untruth. Besides, she must look a state. They wouldn't fail to notice something was amiss. One show of kindness or concern and her resolve would crumble. She couldn't risk that.

Today, the serene grounds did little to ease her worries. She walked aimlessly, mind going over the scene, her anger slowly building into the familiar rage now with the passing seconds. Her mam, praising *him* . . . But, of course, she wasn't to know. None of this was her fault. He was at wrong here. He was up to something, must be. He'd never shown much interest in his aunt or her home before now. And the way he'd looked at her with that lustful glint in his eye she'd come to loathe. Did he honestly think she'd let him . . . a *second* time? Perhaps having claimed her once, he now believed he could have her whenever he chose.

Her mouth moved of its own accord into a grimace. God above, just let those foul hands of his come anywhere near her again! She'd kill him. She would.

A familiar giggle drifted through the swaying branches of a cluster of trees to her left. Now, her spirits did lift somewhat and she stepped closer to peek through the shiny leaves. Maxwell was sat cross-legged by a flowerbed in the distance. His sleeves were rolled to his elbows, his dark coat and hat lying in an untidy heap beside him where he'd tossed them on to the grass. He pretended to pounce and his daughter let out another squeal of laughter, her small, chubby legs tripping over themselves in escape.

Despite her earlier concerns regarding him seeing her and guessing all wasn't well, Jewel's feet itched to go to them. Mind made up, she quickly tidied her hair and rearranged her shawl – then turned sharply as, again, a voice she recognised rang out in the opposite direction, this time calling her name:

'Over here, lass! Jewel, it's me!'

Maria's grinning face came into view and Jewel forced down her disappointment. 'Hello.'

'What you standing there for on your ruddy own?' The maid beckoned her across. 'Come on, take a walk with me, lass.'

Maria would think her stark, staring mad were she to turn down her offer to instead spend her free time with the master and miss. Didn't Jewel see enough of them the rest of the week? she was sure to ask. And what answer she'd give Maria, she didn't know, couldn't explain the desire to be with them even to herself.

'Well? Is tha coming or no?'

Glancing back through the foliage, Jewel swallowed a sigh then ran to catch her up.

'So.' Maria linked her arm through Jewel's. 'What *were* you about just now, hiding in yon trees?'

'I weren't hiding, just resting is all.'

'Don't you have a home to go to?'

'Don't you?' shot back Jewel, her irritation rising. However, at Maria's grin, she couldn't help chuckling. 'You're annoying, you, d'you know that?'

'Aye, I do know.' The servant shrugged good-naturedly. 'It's just my way. We all have our crosses to bear.' She spread her hands wide. 'I'm annoying, you're a moody cow. You see?'

Again, Jewel laughed. Despite her disappointment when the woman had appeared, she was now glad she had. Maria was a tonic for the soul, there was no denying it.

'Mam died when I were little but I've a father and two sisters, if you must know. Called in on them earlier, I did, but father was skenning drunk, as per usual. His nastiness had driven the others from the house afore I arrived; I didn't see the point in sticking around myself. He'd have only started on me had I stayed. Sod. I only drag myself there of a Sunday for the lasses' sakes.'

'Sorry to hear that.'

Again, Maria shrugged. 'It's all right.'

144

Turning right, they wandered along the grassy expanse in companionable silence. Overhead, a flock of small birds glided and swooped. Bees hovered around the colourful flowers dotted about and their hum mingled with that of conversation from others out taking advantage of the weather and pleasant surroundings. Jewel felt she could have remained here for ever.

'What's your story, then, lass?'

'I've a mam. I called in earlier but . . . Well, I didn't want to stay. It's nowt, really,' she continued carefully when her friend frowned curiously. 'My cousin were there and I don't much like his company.'

'Tries messing with thee, does he?'

Jewel was too shocked to respond to the accurate assumption spoken so matter-of-factly. She simply gazed straight ahead, wide-eyed. Her silence spoke volumes; Maria nodded.

'Aye, thought so. My brother were the same afore I got my position. Always trying to get at me, he was, touching and what not where he shouldn't. I were glad when he wed and buggered off out of it.'

'Maria, that's terrible.' Jewel was wholly sorry for her. 'Didn't your father do anything?'

'I never told him. Doubt he'd have done much anyroad if I had.'

'But why? You should have gone to him, lass.'

The servant cocked an eyebrow. 'Like you, yer mean? I take it your mam's not aware of your cousin's antics, eh?'

Maria was right. How could she, in her position, stand here and spout hypocritical advice? She nodded, shamefaced. 'I'm sorry. I just can't tell her, Maria. The trouble it would create . . . Aye well. Least I'm away from him now, at any rate. Mind, he'd best not be hanging around

145

Mam's next Sunday, let me tell thee. He'll bloody know about it if he is. No way will he stop me and Mam seeing each other. Never.'

'What will you do?'

But Jewel hadn't an answer. Talk was cheap; reality was an entirely different matter. She banished Benji from her thoughts and the women continued on their walk.

*

'Here, sir, let me.'

'Ah! Thank you, Jewel.'

Abandoning her chore of dusting the mantel, she held out her arms to the weary father with a smile. Constance, grisly with tiredness, wriggled to be set loose again but Jewel hushed her soothingly. 'All right. Let's take you forra little lie-down, eh? You'll feel the better for it, aye.'

'Thank you,' Maxwell said again when she re-entered the drawing room to resume her duties, the child now napping peacefully upstairs. 'You're good with her, you know.'

'Aye?' Surprised pleasure brought a pink glow to Jewel's cheeks. She'd doubted herself constantly since arriving here because of her inexperience with caring for youngsters and fretted herself sick over how she'd cope with her own. To hear this from him was a precious boost to her confidence.

'I mean it. She's taxing, I understand, but you manage her admirably.'

Though he spoke the truth – the girl in the nursery was an exhausting whirlwind of energy – still, she felt the urge to defend her. 'She's but a babby, sir. The world and everything in it is so much more interesting

146

and exciting to her; she can't help but want to explore it. She'll settle down, no doubt, as she grows.'

Maxwell nodded slowly. 'Do you know, I've never thought of it that way. Of course, everything is new to her young senses. Here am I accusing her of making mischief. I feel ashamed.'

'Oh, don't. You're a wonderful father. It can't be easy for you, raising her by yourself—' She broke off and cleared her throat, regretting her bold overfamiliarity. It wasn't proper to put voice to her observations. It wasn't a servant's place. 'What I mean is,' she added quietly, 'well . . . you're doing just gradely, sir.'

Maxwell's eyes creased. When he spoke, his words held a deeper meaning: 'As are you, Jewel.'

Thanks to thee. In a way, you've saved me, Maxwell Birch. Saved me from myself. And you don't even know it. The response swirled safely inside her mind. Though she could never voice it out loud, it didn't make it any less true.

For a long moment, they stared at one another silently, gratitude in their eyes.

'I'd best get on with my work, sir,' Jewel said finally. 'You put your feet up awhile, enjoy the peace afore the evening meal.' She smiled, turned and made back towards the fire. She heard the door click shut behind her, telling her that Maxwell had heeded her advice and had taken himself to his room. With another small smile, she got on with her dusting.

As she worked, her mind switched to her afternoon with Maria. She was seeing a different side to her new friend and felt guilty that she'd judged her as brash on their first encounter. She wasn't at all, no, just lively of spirit. Despite her harsh beginnings, she was generous and caring and fun. She was also desperate to be liked, it was clear to see.

147

Well, Jewel *did* like her, a lot. A connection had been formed when they had revealed their shared experiences with rotten family members of the opposite sex. For the first time, she felt she had an ally, and it brought her comfort. They understood in a world where it seemed no one else did. Perhaps they could be there for one another now, when either needed it, with a listening ear and a hand to hold. Hope made her heart warm.

The front door opening and closing heralded Roland's return and, again, Jewel's musings went back to the domestic across the street. Maria had revealed that he worked at the bank with his father. A few weeks before Jewel had begun her position here, Roland's intended had broken off their betrothal after discovering he'd been romantically liaising with another woman. Servants talked – Maria was friendly with a maid who knew a maid employed by the betrayed fiancée.

'Mr Roland'll never be tethered down, I don't reckon,' Maria had told Jewel. 'Likes the lasses too much, aye. And they like him, though I can't say I blame them. Handsome divil, he is. He's allus off gallivanting with Lord only knows who and coming home at all hours; not until the following day, oftentimes. Mind, his father must be weary of covering for him at the bank – he's away from his work more than he's in. Whether he's tried curtailing his son's antics or no, I can't say. In any case, it don't appear that Mr Roland is for changing his ways any time soon.'

Jewel wasn't overly shocked at hearing any of this. Hadn't she witnessed with her two eyes his flirtatious manner with Maria, and suspected that was his way with women in general? And she herself had seen him slinking home early morning from a night spent goodness knew where. Nor did Maxwell tolerating such behaviour surprise her. He was a kind and decent man, and clearly a dedicated parent. No doubt he disagreed with Roland's antics and hoped he'd soon curb them. However, he'd never cast him out or turn his back on him – Jewel knew this instinctively. She'd never met a father quite like him; he seemed to live and breathe for his children.

Despite what she knew, she couldn't dislike the wayward Birch. She could see it to be a weak and immature trait he possessed rather than intentional badness. It appeared he couldn't help himself where the fairer sex was concerned. Some men were like that, God only knew. Thankfully, he hadn't turned his attentions in her direction. Besides the occasional lingering look and his overfamiliar habit of calling her 'little nightingale', he'd so far left her be. He'd do well to make sure it stayed that way, too.

After supper, when Jewel had tidied and swept the dining room, she closed the door with a thankful sigh. It had been a long and emotive day. She couldn't wait to drop on to the lumpy mattress and rest her body and mind.

Crossing the hall towards the kitchen stairs, she caught sight of Maxwell at the opposite end, busy battening down the hatches for the night. He'd already extinguished the lights, bar the single gas lamp left burning whilst he completed his task, and his tall figure cast its shadow, like a pool of shimmering smoke, across the tiled floor. She watched through the amber glow him reach up to fix the bolt in place then, changing his mind, open the front door wide. His head swung left and right along the street; then, sighing, he stepped back inside and secured the lock in place.

149

He must have been checking if his son was on his way home, Jewel thought; she'd seen Roland exit the house shortly after the evening meal. She'd been right, then, in her assumption that his lifestyle wasn't something his father bore without disapproval.

Anger that his selfishness was causing unnecessary concern for the older man sparked inside her. It was no doubt one more worry Maxwell could do without.

Not wishing to startle him, she cleared her throat softly – nevertheless, he turned sharply and she flashed an apologetic smile. 'Goodnight, God bless, sir.'

'Goodnight.'

Jewel had reached the top of the stairs when she heard him call her name. She glanced back over her shoulder. 'Aye, sir?'

'What you said earlier about Constance ... and myself . . . my abilities as a father . . .'

'I meant it. She's fortunate to have thee. As is Roland,' she hastened to add.

Maxwell's voice was barely above a whisper. 'Thank you.'

'I never really knew my own father. He died afore I'd time to store any real or lasting memories.' She spoke just as quietly, surprised at herself that she was reveal-ing this to him and not knowing why, other than having the strongest urge to reassure him that, as a new wid-ower, he was handling life, his family, just fine. Also, she knew, it was this man's way again, making you want to open up, that sense of trust he exuded. 'But sir,' she added, tone dropping further still, 'if I had known him . . . I'd have wanted him to be just like thee.'

Leaving the admission hanging between them, she smiled, turned and continued on her way to the kitchen.

Snuggled beneath the bedclothes minutes later, Jewel

was on the cusp of unconsciousness when Maxwell's image flitted on the outskirts of her mind. She watched him draw closer, saw herself move forward to meet him. What she pictured next caused a frown to accompany her on her sleep's final journey. For despite what she'd told her employer in the hall, the kiss he gave her – and that she returned with full fervour – was anything but that from a father figure.

Chapter 10

JEWEL HAD CALCULATED that the child would be due in early March. By November, she'd never felt so thankful for anything as she was for the oversized apron.

She'd been steadily loosening her corset for weeks and, only yesterday, the laces had reached their maximum length – she'd known panic at the realisation. She couldn't hide her condition for much longer, and then what would she do? The neat globe was certain to expand significantly over the coming months and no amount of apron material would conceal that. Folk were bound to start noticing any day now. She was done for.

What would happen when the child actually made an appearance, she'd steadfastly refused to dwell upon. Terror of the unknown had seen her bury her head, for it was easier that way. Would she go along with Benji's suggestion that she was attacked by a stranger, hadn't revealed her condition through fear and shame? Would people believe any of it? And if they didn't? If Mam chose to disown her, what then?

She couldn't stay on at the Birch household, that much was clear. What would she do should she find herself destitute? How would she and the child survive with no dwelling, brass or support from a living soul? It would be the workhouse for the both of them, for sure.

And she'd rather be gone from this world, once and for all, than that. Imprisonment in those harsh and heartless institutions was a fate worse than death and she'd make sure she didn't mess up the second attempt.

The time was approaching noon. Though several more hours of daylight remained, already winter's fingers were stroking the light grey sky, and the diluted sun seemed to shiver with the rest of them.

Soon, the frost would come and the town's poorer inhabitants would struggle still more than usual. With little or no money for coal and a daily hot meal, droves wouldn't last through to spring. The sick and weak were particularly susceptible. Friends and neighbours, though having next to nothing themselves, would make it their mission to keep a caring eye to the more vulnerable, sharing what they could, when they could. It was the same year in, year out. The lower class, above all others, looked after their own – an unwritten rule that most adhered to with unshakeable belief.

Ignoring her aching back, Jewel bent again to rinse out her cloth in the pail of water by the front door. She had just reached up on tiptoe to get at the window's corners when hands on her shoulders from behind had her jumping out of her skin – she turned with a squeak.

Maria could barely get her greeting out through her snorts of laughter. 'By, your phizog! I only nipped across to say hello. Did I fricken thee so bad?'

Jewel forced down her annoyance. Building worry and lethargy had of late brought brooding black moods she found increasingly difficult to shake. She gave her friend a rueful smile. 'Aye, you swine. I didn't hear your approach; tha near caused me a mishap there.'

'So I see.' Maria nodded down to Jewel's apron, where

soapy water had splashed when she'd squeezed her wet cloth in her fright. 'Come here, daft ha'porth.'

'Nay! Don't!' Seeing the maid's hand going to her midriff to wipe at the suds, panic filled Jewel and, without thought, she smacked it away fiercely. In the ensuing seconds, as Maria rubbed her stinging fingers, they gazed at one another in shocked silence. Jewel recovered sooner. Swinging her head slowly in horror, she stammered, 'Maria . . . I, I'm sorry—'

'No harm done.' But the maid's tone held a stiff note. 'Well. I'd best get back to my own duties.'

'Please, wait.' Jewel caught her sleeve as she made to leave. 'Eeh, Maria. What am I to do?'

'Do? 'Ere, what's the matter?' she added with concern, seeing that Jewel's eyes had pooled with tears. 'Lass?'

After glancing around, Jewel smoothed her apron against herself, revealing the outline of her bump. 'What am I to *do*?' she repeated in a fearful whisper.

'Mother of God . . .' The words fell from Maria's lips on a sorry sigh. 'You bloody idiot, Jewel. How've you found yourself like that?'

'How d'you think?'

Again, Maria sighed. She scratched her head then her chin. 'Is it Roland Birch's doing?'

Jewel was aghast. 'Nay, nay. It . . . you don't know him. A mistake occurred and . . . I'd rather not talk of it. I need your help,' she finished, a lone tear escaping to splash to her cheek. 'I'm that frightened, Maria.'

'That cousin of yours, him you've spoken on afore. This is his doing, in't it?'

'Aye,' Jewel whispered after some moments, feeling the weight of the crippling secret ease somewhat from her shoulders at the admission.

'Bastard.'

Dropping her gaze, Jewel shook her head. 'Nay, not that. May God forgive me, I consented. I – we – were full of ale. Nonetheless, why I allowed him . . . I'll never know. To top it all, he's denying all involvement.'

'They allus do. Eeh, lass. Does anyone else know about this?'

'Nay. Norra soul.'

'When's it due?'

'Around March. What am I to do?' she beseeched yet again.

Maria's eyes softened. She reached for her friend's hand and Jewel gripped it. 'That depends on thee, lass.'

'What d'you mean?'

'Is tha for keeping the child?'

'What choice have I?'

The maid lowered her voice. 'There's allus a choice, lass.'

For the first time in many months, Jewel knew a stirring of hope. 'There is?'

'Not here. Meet me the morrow at the park. We'll talk on it more then. And Jewel?'

'Aye?'

'You're not to fret no more, you hear? I'm here for thee now. All will be well, you'll see, lass.'

She could barely speak past the lump of relieved emotion in her throat. 'Thank you.'

Maria gave her hand a last supportive squeeze then hurried back to her own residence across the road.

For the remainder of the day, Jewel could think of nothing but their conversation. Had she done the right thing in confessing? she agonised continually. By, but it had felt good to share the burden. What suggestions would her friend come up with tomorrow? Was there

155

really a way out of this hell? Maria had seemed quite convinced there was.

Following that first Sunday off, her afternoons had been incident free. Mercifully, Benji appeared to have got the message – she'd encountered him no more when visiting her mother. It was lovely to spend time with Flora again, just like the old days – albeit for a few short hours and always, at the back of Jewel's mind, with the fear her mother would notice her growing stomach, though she did her utmost to casually conceal it with her shawl. Hopefully, her cousin would continue to steer clear of her; for this, she prayed daily.

What excuse she'd give Mam for missing tomorrow's visit, she hadn't the strength to think on right now, would cross that bridge when she came to it. She must meet Maria, had to hear her apparent solution. Her future – her whole *life* – depended on it.

That night, she took her time completing the last of her duties; anything to prolong the inevitable sleepless hours tossing in bed with worry that she knew were to come.

Maxwell had already locked and bolted the doors, and he and his son had retired to their beds some half an hour before. The house was still, the dying kitchen fire bathing the room in cosy pink light. Forcing her mind on the present – were she to allow it to stray to thoughts of the next day, her heartbeat would quicken painfully – she softly hummed a childhood song.

From its bed of clouds, the arch of silver moon peering through the narrow kitchen window followed her as she pottered about wiping and tidying the already clean and neat space. Though her newly swollen ankles ached, she ignored them – just one more result of her pregnancy that she'd now become adept at pretending wasn't occurring. Gritting her teeth, she trained the cloth on the sink and gave it a thorough wiping. She'd just rinsed it and laid it over the sink's stone rim to dry when she sensed she was being watched. Frowning, she turned towards the stairs leading to the house – and let out a loud gasp to find Maxwell standing staring down at her.

'Jewel—'

'God in heaven above! Sir, tha startled me.' She crossed towards him. 'Is everything all right?'

'Yes, I . . . Forgive me for the lateness of the hour. You must be tired. Would it be too much trouble to ask for a last pot of tea?'

She blinked, surprised. 'Nay, sir. Course not. I'll brew a fresh sup now.'

To her confusion, he didn't instruct her to fetch the beverage to the drawing room or some such then return upstairs. Instead, he remained exactly where he was, saying nothing, whilst she moved around the room seeing to the kettle and fetching a cup and saucer.

Should she enquire after his health? she asked herself, glancing furtively at him once or twice. His behaviour was out of character – never had he sought her out in the kitchen late at night before. He appeared . . . She couldn't put her finger on it. Not ill, in any case. And not so much troubled, more distracted. As though in a world all his own. Before she had the chance to decide, he broke the silence:

'You visit your mother every Sunday afternoon?'

Jewel looked up from the table slowly. His face was unreadable in the dim light and guilt whizzed through her, making her dizzy. Why ask such a thing? What concern was it of his how she chose to spend her days off? Unless . . . Her eyes widened. She swallowed hard. Surely

157

he didn't know, hadn't somehow heard . . . ? Was he aware of her planned meeting with Maria tomorrow instead? And the reason for it? But *how*? Her friend wouldn't have breathed a word to anyone. Would she?

How well did she know the girl across the street? The sudden thought brought panic to her veins. She'd spilled to her her innermost secrets, blindly trusted her in the hope she'd help, when all the time . . . *Dear God!* She'd *kill* her for this! She would, she'd—!

'Jewel?'

'Hm?' She licked her dry lips. 'Sorry . . . Aye, I do. Mostly, aye. Why . . . why d'you ask, sir?' she forced herself to say, her cheeks growing hot with dread.

Maxwell was quiet for a moment, then: 'Tomorrow would have been my wife's birthday.'

'Oh.' *What's that got to do with anything?* she stopped herself from adding just in time, confusion still holding her in its grasp. 'Oh,' she repeated, this time with more feeling, glimpsing the hollow sadness in his eyes. 'You must miss her terribly, sir.'

'Yes.'

Again, silence fell between them. Quickly, she finished making the tea and went to collect a tray. So this was the reason behind his nocturnal wanderings, she realised. Memories of his poor wife were keeping him from his sleep. On significant dates, her absence must, after all, sting especially so. She swallowed a sorry sigh for him and his suffering, couldn't imagine his hurt. Yet why his question as to her habits in her free time? What *had* that to do with his wife?

'Thank you.' Maxwell took the tray she held out to him.

Jewel waited with bated breath but, when no more from him was forthcoming, she murmured, 'Sir?'

'Yes?'

She had to know. 'Why did you ask about my visits to Mam?'

'Ah. Yes. Well.' He cleared his throat. 'It's silly, really. Please forget that I asked.' He flashed a half-smile. 'Well. Goodnight.'

He was walking away. But . . . Wait! She had to know.

'Has Maria said summat?' she blurted to his retreating back. 'Is that it, sir?'

'Maria?' He was staring at her in puzzlement over his shoulder. 'Maria?' he repeated.

'The . . . maid, from across the street. I . . . thought . . .' She rummaged around inside her head for something to fill the agonising silence. To think she'd believed her friend capable of revealing her secret; her paranoia was skewing her judgement. Oh, she was wicked-minded, didn't deserve Maria's kindness. 'I – Maria and me, that is – have planned to meet the morrow, sir, forra walk in the park is what I meant. I'm for giving a visit to Mam's a miss this week.'

'Ah, I see.' Maxwell's face relaxed in understanding, then his brows drew together and, again, he cleared his throat. 'As a matter of fact, the park was the reason I enquired about your plans, I . . . Well . . .'

'Aye, sir?'

He smiled self-consciously and looked away. 'I was going to ask whether you would like to accompany Constance and me tomorrow.'

'To the park?'

'Yes.'

'Me, sir? Really?'

'Yes,' he said again, quieter this time, and Jewel felt a queer warmness flow through her. 'Several hours away from this house and the memories it holds will be beneficial to my daughter and me, I believe,' Maxwell added.

159

'However, please don't give it another thought – like I said, it's silly, really—'

'I'd love to.'

He raised his brows slowly. 'You would? But your plans—?'

'Maria won't mind,' she cut in again, at the same time asking herself what the hell she was playing at. She *had* to see the maid, didn't she? Her friend had vowed to help her, and Lord did she need it. Yet here she was instead, speaking these words to this man, without a clue as to why. What she did know instinctively was that it wasn't out of pity for him that she'd accepted his invitation. Nor was it from a sense of duty.

Then what? her mind asked. The answer that whispered on the outskirts of her mind had her glancing to her feet, for the truth of it she couldn't deny. She wanted to spend time with him. Constance, too. Everything else, even her own trials, paled in comparison. The realisation left her bewildered.

'Well, if you're certain . . . ?'

'I am, sir.'

'Excellent.' A genuine smile spread across Maxwell's face. 'Constance will be pleased. She'll enjoy the excursion infinitely more with you in attendance, I'm sure. You have a knack of keeping her entertained.'

She knew a sensation akin to her guts falling from a height and struggled to keep the disappointment from her face. That was why he'd asked her along: for his daughter's sake. He wanted her there as a nursemaid, to keep an eye to the child. And why should it be anything more? she insisted to herself. *Stupid, stupid.*

'Right, I shall leave you in peace.' He motioned to the tea things in his hands. 'Thank you.'

'No thanks needed, sir.'

'Goodnight.'

'Goodnight.'

She watched him until he disappeared from sight then crossed to the bed. She perched on the edge. Her mind really wasn't her own of late; being with child was warping her common sense, she was certain. The thoughts she found creeping in sometimes shocked and filled her with shame in equal measure. For since her dream, of she and Mr Birch together, their *kiss* . . . Cringing, Jewel heaved another long breath. Was she developing madness on top of everything else? It really wouldn't surprise her, the way her luck was going at present!

Cancelling her plans with Maria was proof that she was losing her grip on reality, surely? Just what was she thinking? What was she going to do now? Would her friend be upset with her for choosing to spend time with the Birches instead? After all, she couldn't very well go back on her agreement with Maxwell now. Would Maria still be willing to help her?

Busy with her thoughts, Jewel at first took the faint flutters and taps in her stomach to be but nervous tension. When another more forceful blow struck beneath her ribs, she glanced down with a mixture of horror and awe.

Over the next few minutes, as the life growing within her made for the first time its presence known, a clogging ball of conflicting emotion built to a ton weight in her breast.

She looked to the heavens through a blur of tears then closed her eyes in despair.

*

Jewel awoke the following morning with a scratchy throat and a head that felt home to a dozen drummers;

161

wincing, she flopped back against the pillows. Illness must have dragged her back to sleep, for the next thing she was aware of was full daylight filtering through the high window – her early starts were in pitch-darkness during winter months – and she dragged herself up with a gasp. Pain speared inside her temples at the movement and nausea rose. 'God above, I feel terrible,' she croaked to what she thought was the empty room.

'Indeed, you look it. No offence.'

Opening one eye, she squinted up in surprise. 'Sir.'

'Forgive my intrusion, but I felt I ought to check in on you, given your absence.'

'I'm sorry, I—'

'You'll do no such thing,' Maxwell instructed her as she attempted to rise. 'You must rest.'

'But sir, the fires haven't been lit.' No doubt it was this which had caused him to seek her out. 'Your breakfast. The house, my duties . . .'

'Your only task today is to remain in your bed. That is an order.' Though he spoke firmly, a hint of concern showed in his eyes.

He was likely worried she'd pass whatever ailed her on to his family, Jewel thought, and who could blame him? Young Constance especially was of an age where severe colds could easily develop into something more serious. Nonetheless: 'But . . . the park, sir,' she couldn't stop herself from saying, unable to hide her disappointment. 'You said yourself, Miss Constance will want me there . . .'

'As do I. Alas, these things cannot be helped. Now, try to get some sleep. It's the body's natural healer and will do you the world of good. I'll check in on you again upon our return.'

162

'Ta, thanks.' Already, her lead-heavy eyelids were drooping. 'Sorry, sir.'

'Shh. Sleep.'

Maxwell's whisper floated on the edges of her consciousness. Then what felt like a hand gently brushing damp hair from her brow seeped through to her and she knew she was sicker than she'd realised. Delirium had her in its grasp, was causing her to imagine things. Groaning, she turned over and fell into a heavy sleep.

She awoke some time later to light tapping coming from above her. Her wooziness was worse than before and the hammering inside her head had spread; it was like a physical thing gnawing on her skull. Assuming she was hallucinating again, she closed her mind to the noise.

'Psst. Lass, it's me. Is tha all right?'

Frowning, Jewel peered up at the window. Beyond it, kneeling on the flagstones in the street, was Maria. Hands cupped around her eyes, she was staring through the pane. Jewel gave her a weak wave then held a hand to her forehead and imitated a cough to show she was unwell. Her frown grew when, catching her meaning, her friend stood and walked away without another word. But Jewel felt too rotten to dwell on it; she closed her eyes once more.

''Ere, lass. Sup up.'

Again, the world came into focus. To Jewel's astonishment, she saw her friend perched on the bottom of her bed. She glanced around the room – yes, this was definitely her kitchen. She hadn't wandered off in her confused state; nor did the smiling woman seem to be an apparition. Then how on earth . . . ? 'Maria? Is it really thee?'

'Aye. I let myself in. Don't fret,' she added when Jewel's eyes widened in horror. 'No one will know – I'll be away afore Mr Birch returns. Lift your head, that's it. Mind now, it's hot.' She supported Jewel as she took sips of the sweetened brew. 'Better?'

'Nay. I feel bloody awful.'

Maria resumed her seat on the bed. 'I spotted your Mr Birch exit with the little 'un earlier. Looked back at the house several times whilst walking away, he did, as though reluctant to leave. I figured summat were afoot.'

'He did?' At Maria's nod, something came back to Jewel that she'd been too poorly earlier to register properly. 'As do I.' That's what Maxwell had said when she'd mentioned that Constance would miss her presence at the park. *As do I.* She allowed herself a small smile.

'And well,' continued Maria, 'when you didn't show at the park . . .' She spread her arms wide. 'I thought it best to check in on thee, guessed you'd been taken ill.'

'Ta, thanks. For the tea, too. Eeh, but Maria, fancy you letting yourself in here.' Despite herself, she couldn't help chuckling when her friend grinned. 'You're a mad bugger, you are.'

'I told thee, don't fret. I'll say I spied you through yon window and that you looked reet bad, that I were afraid you were close to death or some such. No one could punish me for that, now could they?' When their laughter died down, Maria added, quieter now, 'How are . . . things?' She inclined her head to Jewel's stomach. 'All right?'

Jewel nodded. 'I felt it kick for the first time last night.'

'Eeh, lass. Jewel, listen, is there really no way . . . ?'

'Nay. I can't keep it, I can't.'

'Happen you were to speak with your mam, tell her what that cow-son cousin of yourn did. Surely she'd understand—'

'I can't *do* it, Maria. Don't you see? It would stir up a

164

world of trouble. Benji will deny everything and I'd have no means of proving it, now would I? It would tear my family to tatters, and for what? The truth won't change nowt, will it? I'd still be left holding the baby – a bastard at that – alone for ever more. For let's face it, no one would want me, would they? What fella wants to shackle himself to a lass what's been deflowered by another? Who would want to wed a whore?'

'Ay now, don't speak of yourself so—'

'Why not? It's true!' By now, tears were coursing down Jewel's face. 'I lay with the lad, Maria. Willingly.'

Silence hung between them. What else was there to say? She spoke sense and they both knew it.

'Besides, who says I *want* to keep it?' Jewel murmured after some moments.

'Do you?'

She answered with a sigh. The thumping in her head increased and she closed her eyes. Now, however, Jewel accepted the pain almost with gladness. For wasn't this a sign? Was it not strange that she'd been struck down with a head cold today of all days, had been forced to cancel Maxwell's invitation? She was meant to see Maria instead, it was obvious now. Fate had intervened, and had done so for a reason. She must give up the child. 'Will you help me still?' she asked with feeling.

'Happen you're a bit too far along now for gin and hot baths, or to seek out someone handy with a knitting needle.'

Jewel shuddered at the thought of that particular practice. Complications resulting in death at the hands of untold numbers of backstreet butchers were all too common. 'Nay, not that. I couldn't.'

'Aye. Besides, it'd mean a lengthy stretch in prison were you to be found out. Tha can't risk that.'

'Then what, Maria?'

'Well, there's allus adoption. There's wenches aplenty take in unwanteds and find them new guardians; desperate couples what can't produce their own, like. Make a handsome living from it, an' all, I'll bet.'

The article she'd spotted in her uncle's newspaper months before came back to her. She nodded slowly. Hadn't she given this avenue consideration back then? Again, she nodded. Then she was reminded of the reason she'd initially dismissed the idea and her shoulders slumped. 'The prices they ask, though, for taking the child off your hands is sky high. I could never scrape together such an amount.'

The maid stroked her chin. 'Aye, you're right enough there. Unless . . . ?'

'What?'

'You could try blackmailing your cousin into coughing up the brass, threaten to expose him to your family if he don't. You never know, it might work.' She shrugged. 'It's worth a shot, eh?'

'Benji's but a lad; he hasn't that sort of brass neither.'

'Nay, but his parents do.'

'You mean . . . ?' Jewel bit her lip at Maria's solemn nod. 'I couldn't force him into stealing it from the shop. It'd be Uncle Bernard that he'd be taking from – he doesn't deserve to suffer for this.'

'Jewel, lass. You need to turn a deaf ear to that heart of yourn and instead start listening to your head. The situation you're in . . . You need to switch your thinking, aye, begin planning a way to get yourself out of this, for there's no one else to do it for thee. Sod 'em, the lot. Put you and that babby first forra change. You're a good lass, deserve a second chance. As for the mite inside thee . . . Just think, a loving family what'll cherish it all

166

of its days. Don't you at least owe the poor bugger that? It's not to blame, is it, after all? Seek out that cousin. Needs must, lass. To hell with the rest.'

'Eeh, Maria.' She covered her face with her hands. 'How have I let myself get into this mess?'

'Mistakes happen, lass.'

The straightforward answer, spoken without hesitation in that easy tone, brought tears to her eyes. Jewel doubted her friend had a single judgemental bone in her body. Maria was a true treasure and no mistake. She dreaded to imagine life without her now. Still, could she do what the maid had suggested and bribe Benji? Would it even work?

'You could hunker down at a lying-in house until you've given birth. That way, no one you know will be aware of a thing. You hand over the child afore leaving and return home alone; norra soul will be any the wiser.' Suddenly, Maria rose and hurried for the stairs. 'I'll be but a minute; wait here.'

'Where are you . . . ?' But her friend had already disappeared into the house proper and Jewel awaited her return with a frown. 'Eeh, Maria,' she said when the maid reappeared and clattered back down the stairs, a newspaper under her arm. 'That's Mr Birch's—'

'Aye, well, he's not in need of it at this moment, is he? I'll return it to the drawing room exactly as I found it in a minute, don't fret. Sooner we get looking, the better for thee.' She resumed her seat and began flicking through the pages, eyes narrowed, tongue poking out in concentration; it was plain she wasn't a strong reader. ''Ere, look. That there word says "wanted", don't it?' she announced after a time.

Jewel eyed the thick black text Maria was prodding. She nodded. 'Let me see.' Scanning the advertisement, her brows lifted in recognition. It appeared to be the same one she'd spotted months before; the request was identical word for word.

'What's it say, lass?'

'A widow reckons she'd be glad to accept the charge of a child, any age.'

'Aye? How much is she asking for to adopt?'

'Eight pounds.' This, Jewel noticed, was the only change – if she remembered rightly, the price had initially been ten.

'Blooming 'eck.' Maria puffed out air slowly. 'That's a lot of brass.'

That it was, even with the reduction. Benji would never be able to get his mitts on such a sum. Would he?

'Does it state whether hers is a lying-in house as well?'

'Nay. But that's what I'll need, Maria. I can't hide my condition much longer. And if by some miracle I managed to conceal it throughout, what about when my time comes? What will I do? Give birth to it here in the kitchen alone?' The notion terrified her. 'Besides, the household would hear my labour cries for certain.'

Maria nodded agreement. 'One what will only take the child when it's born is no good. Tha must have a lying-in house. If this widow *don't* offer such a service, happen a bit extra would change her mind? Another pound, say.'

'Aye, more likely than not.' But Jewel's glimmer of hope was dashed as a sudden thought occurred. She closed her eyes. 'What am I thinking? It's impossible, Maria, impossible!'

'What is, lass?'

She'd been so caught up in her desperation, her need for somewhere to place the child, that one crucial aspect had escaped her attention entirely. 'How on earth am I to explain away my absence to Mr Birch, to Mam?'

168

Chewing on her thumbnail, Maria thought for a moment. Then her face brightened. 'You could tell your mam that Mr Birch's sister . . . what's her name?'

'Mrs Kirkwood?'

'Aye, that Mrs Kirkwood's sick and you've offered to go and nurse her, and that Mr Birch has agreed.'

'And the man hisself? What tale will I spin him?'

'The same, only that you've been called away to nurse a sick relative at your mam's request.'

'But Maria, disappearing for . . . ?' She did a quick calculation on her fingers. 'Three whole *months*? Mebbe more? That's a hell of a long time to be away. Nay, it's no good. It'd never wash with them.'

'What choice have thee but to try?'

None. She had *none*. She screwed her eyes shut once more.

'I've a sister currently out of work what would willingly take over your position here 'til you return, so Mr Birch can't grumble about a lack of a maid. And surely your mam won't question your story, will she? What reason would she have to?'

Jewel had to admit her friend spoke sense. 'I suppose you're right . . .'

'Mr Birch and your mam ain't likely to seek one another out to ask about thee, are they?'

'Nay, probably not.' At least she prayed so.

'Right, well. That just leaves the babby's father to deal with.'

Maria talked as though this was the easy part. In truth, the prospect made Jewel feel physically sick. Just how would this work out?

Chapter 11

WITH PLANS NOW in place, Maria gave Jewel a supportive hug and left her to get some rest. Going above and beyond further still, she'd offered to call in on Flora to explain her daughter's absence; Jewel was more than a little grateful and had told her so.

Maxwell and Constance returned from their outing not long afterwards and, true to his word, Jewel soon heard his tread on the stairs as he came to check on her.

His footsteps halted before they reached the kitchen and, for a long moment, there was silence. Though Jewel had her eyes closed, she felt his gaze from above but didn't react. She was too wrought with grief from recent developments to endure company, even his, and craved to be left alone. To her relief, feigning sleep worked; seemingly reluctant to disturb her, Maxwell left her be.

The door clicked shut behind him and Jewel opened her eyes to stare unseeing at the ceiling. Body and mind felt weighed down yet empty at the same time. A detachedness had settled within her. She felt lifeless, hollowed out. And things were only set to get worse from here on in.

She could have remained here for ever, cocooned in her misery beneath the sheets, but Maxwell's return late afternoon put paid to it. This time, he came right into the kitchen and, leaning over the bed, spoke to her:

'Jewel? How are you feeling?'

'Better, sir, I think,' she lied. She felt sicker than ever.

'Hm. You have a look of the fever about you still.' Frowning, he studied her more closely. 'Perhaps it would be wise to send for the doctor—'

'Nay. Sir, really, there's no need.' *God above, not that.* The last thing she wanted was the medical man prodding and poking about her person, for he'd be quick to discover she was carrying more than a simple chill. 'See, sir, I'm almost recovered,' she added, ignoring her aching joints and head as, reluctantly, she covered herself with her shawl and dragged herself from her bed.

'If you're sure . . . ?'

'Course I am. Now, you take yourself to the drawing room and put your feet up and I'll fetch you up a sup of tea. I'll bring milk and biscuits for Constance, an' all, shall I, sir?' she asked, doing her best to remain upright and not sag against the wall, as she wanted to. Her limbs seemed void of strength; she felt as weak as a kitten.

'Thank you, we'd welcome that.' He gave a grin. 'She's worn herself out with her games at the park – me, too, for that matter!'

Again, Jewel felt a pang of sadness that she'd missed the outing. 'Sounds like youse had a gradely time, sir. Sorry I missed it.'

'There's always next time.'

Warm pleasure filled her. Before she could respond, Maxwell flashed another smile and was gone. She stood for a moment, a smile of her own touching her lips. It stayed with her as she saw to her duties. In more ways than one, she didn't feel so bad any more.

171

That night, as the Birch household slept, she suppressed her own need for rest and instead reached for her shawl. After padding up the stairs and along the hall, she let herself out of the house, closing the front door quietly behind her.

The chill night was black and eerily still. Glancing about her, it seemed she was the only soul left in the world. At the south end of Mawdsley Street, the darkened spire of St Patrick's Church loomed sharply through the shifting shadows. Mist obscuring the view in the opposite direction slowly closed in on her, swirling about her feet and legs like smoky breath, and she shivered, wishing she was tucked up in her small bed. However, this meeting needed addressing, and the sooner the better. If she left it a day, she just knew her resolve would crumble and it would turn into two, then a week, until eventually she'd talk herself out of it entirely and all the carefully thought out plans would be ruined. Shawl pulled low, head down, she stole through the emptiness towards the square.

By now, the potted shrubs used to adorn the pedestals either side of the town hall steps during the opening ceremony were gone. The long awaited lions had taken their rightful place. Poised gracefully atop their sandstone stages, they guarded their domain with military attention.

Jewel kept a watchful eye on them as she passed. They were but statues, hadn't the power to pounce and wreak havoc, she reminded herself. Nevertheless, she involuntarily quickened her pace.

Only last year, a lion tamer was mauled to death in this very place. The travelling menagerie he belonged to had been in Bolton almost a week when, during a farewell performance before heading to nearby Bury, the unthinkable happened. The tamer, though somewhat the worse for drink, was successfully conducting his show in the den when his five male lions set upon him in a frenzied and prolonged attack. It had taken some moments for the audience to realise this wasn't part of the act, and for applause to give way to screams. Fearing he'd be ripped to pieces, panic ensued.

Like the hundreds of other spectators that fateful evening, Jewel still recalled vividly the smell of blood and gunpowder as, despite his obvious agony, he'd kept his cool and fought back gallantly with his revolver and sword; though the blank cartridges and blunted blade had little impact on the manic animals. Likewise, the sound of crunching bone as a black-maned cat seized the showman's only arm – his other had been but a stump, having been lost in a previous lion attack during an exhibition in Liverpool years earlier – was something she'd never forget.

By the time the townsmen had managed to beat the beasts off with pitchforks and hot pokers through the bars of the cage, and drag the tamer to safety, it was too late. Scalped, gouged and gashed, his costume and the flesh beneath it torn to shreds, he was past all aid.

Benji had clung to Jewel, sobbing, as the man's shattered frame was carried to the nearby infirmary, where he'd died from his horrific injuries on arrival, and she'd comforted him like a big sister might.

When – *why?* – had the lad changed towards her? she asked herself again now with heavy regret. Just how had this night come to this?

Witness to such a dreadful demise, it was little wonder then that folk were wary of the town hall's lifelike additions. Rumour had it that once twilight fell they might come to life and strike down without mercy anyone fool enough to keep such ungodly hours.

'Huh. Silly talk,' Jewel told herself, at the same time breaking into a trot just to be on the safe side.

Oxford Street and the umbrella shop on the corner drew closer and she took a few juddering breaths. As she'd surmised, the premises were in darkness. After searching the ground for a stone, she aimed at Benji's bedroom pane. She knew the noise might alert instead Bernard, or worse, Esther, but was past caring. One way or another, she just wanted this whole thing to be over.

'Down here,' she hissed when the window was lifted and her cousin's tousled head appeared.

'Jewel?'

'Aye, it's me. Come down.'

He disappeared and she moved to the entrance to wait for him. Seconds later, there came the scrape of the bolts being drawn back. The door creaked open several inches. 'Jewel?' he asked again, as if to convince himself he wasn't imagining her. 'What the divil are you—?'

'I need to talk to thee.'

'Aye?' His voice held a note of surprised pleasure. 'You want to come in?'

She struggled to suppress a grimace. What was that smile of his for? Did he honestly think she was here, at this time of night, to boot, for friendly reasons? Lord, he really was deluded. Or blinded by arrogance; one of the two. She shook her head. 'I'll not if it's all the same to you. Look, Benji, I need thee to do summat for me. Well, for *us*, really. You see—?'

'You sure you'll not come in?' he cut in quietly. 'Mam and Father are abed. We'll not be disturbed.'

So *that's* what he's a mind for, Jewel realised, watching his small, dark eyes rake over her breasts. God above, the gall of the foul whelp!

Bubbling rage coursed through her. Grabbing a handful of his shirt front in her fist, she pulled his face close, lip curling in disgust. 'Now you listen to me, yer vicious young swine,' she whispered, voice like ice. 'I'm not here the night on a pleasure visit – Christ, I'd rather be any other place on God's green earth than here with thee.'

'You what?' He tried twisting from her hold, but she held on tighter. 'What the hell's wrong with thee? Why the nastiness? What have I done, like?'

'What have you . . . ? What have you *done*?' She shook her head in disbelief. '*Every*-bleedin'-thing, that's what! But nowt neither, aye. Not yet at least.' He stared back in confusion and she took a deep breath. Her thumping heart felt fit to burst and tears were threatening. 'I need brass. Aye, that's the top and bottom of it. And you're going to help me find it.'

'Brass?'

'That's what I said, in't it?'

'Brass for what?'

With her free hand, she grabbed one of his and placed it on her stomach. His fingers stiffened but he didn't attempt to sever the contact. 'For this. For your bloody child. I'm for getting rid and that don't come cheap.' The words tasted acrid on her tongue; a sob of self-loathing shuddered from her. She sounded like a monster. An evil, unfeeling, heartless devil. And yet it was the truth, all of it. *What had she become?* 'There's people . . . wenches what'll take a babby in forra price. They find them new parents, ones who want and will love them, and you've never to worry about it again. I – we – *must* do it. There's no other way.'

'Aye well, like I've said already, tha don't know it's owt to do with me. It could be anyone's—'

Jewel ended Benji's speech with a back-handed slap across his mouth. Temper had her trembling from head to toe. Nostrils flared, eyes blazing, she shook him until his head wobbled on his neck. '*Bastard*, you're nowt else! Tha knows fair well you've planted this life in me, have from the start. I'm done keeping my trap shut to save blowing up a storm. *Done!* It's time you took a share of responsibility for your part in this, this . . . *hell* on bleedin' earth *I've* been living for months. Nine pounds – find it and fast. For I'm warning you, lad, you'll wish you had once I'm done with thee. If I'm to go down, I'm hauling you every step of the way along with me. Right?'

'How much?' The youth was panic-stricken. 'But Jewel, where . . . ? How . . . ?'

'Beg, borrow or steal. I don't care a fig how you find it. Just do.'

'But *Jewel*—'

'You see them?' She jabbed a finger towards the town hall steps. 'I'll climb to the very top, right here and now, and scream our guilt to the bloody stars unless you agree. I'll waken every man, woman and child – including Uncle Bernard and Aunt Esther – and they'll all hear about it, everyone. You want that, d'you?'

The quaver in his response belied the nonchalant lift of his chin. 'You'd not.'

'Aye? Try me. Take a long look at me – I've nowt left to lose, lad. So just you think on that.'

After a charged silence, Benji's shoulders sagged. He dragged a hand through his hair. 'Right, all bloody right. If you keep quiet 'til April, I'll ask permission to wed thee. I'll be sixteen, then, won't I? Mind, I'm not promising nowt; we'll have to see what Mam makes of it.' He folded his arms with a petulant pout. 'That do thee? Happy now, you spiteful cow, yer?'

Utter incredulousness chased away a response. For a full minute, Jewel could only gaze at him in dumb silence. He was truly demented, had to be. She'd heard it whispered over the years that a well-to-do cousin of his mother's – Caroline, was it? – had been committed to an asylum. Clearly, madness ran through Esther's blood-line and she'd passed it on to her son. Benji *couldn't* be right in the head if he thought for a single moment she desired to wed him. It was almost as if he believed she'd planned this from the off to snare him. Mother of God, surely not? Surely she'd misheard?

'Is it a deal, then?'

'You're serious, ain't yer? I don't want to wed thee. Not now, not ever!'

'Why not?' His voice had risen to a child-like whine. 'And what's up with me, then?'

Feeling her anger resurfacing, she forced her hands to her sides before she lost control and smacked the snivelling sod's face black and blue. In clear, concise terms she hoped he'd understand, she repeated slowly, 'Nine pounds, Benji. Find it, fast, else I'll do for you.' And she meant it, too.

Leaving her threat to sink in, she turned and darted through the darkness back to Mawdsley Street.

Would he comply?

Pray be to God, time would soon tell.

*

To Jewel's great surprise, tell it did – the very next morning, in fact.

'There you are.'

Busy making Roland's bed whilst keeping an eye to Constance playing quietly at her feet, she hadn't heard the knock at the front door, nor Maxwell entering his son's room to deliver the message. She jumped then held a hand to her heart, smiling. However, her employer didn't return the smile. 'Is there a problem, sir?'

'There's a young fellow outside asking to see you.'

He was surveying her with a less than pleased expression and she blushed scarlet. This was totally improper; what must he think? Who on earth . . . ? 'A fella, sir?' she asked.

'He gave his name as Benji.'

The colour drained from her face then rushed back again at a dizzying speed, leaving her light-headed. She nodded. 'Do I have permission to speak with him? Just forra minute or two? Benji's my cousin, sir.'

'Oh. I see.' Maxwell's expression slowly changed. His brow cleared and his mouth softened. He cleared his throat. 'Of course. Take as long as you need.'

'Ta, thanks.' Though relieved he now saw the visit as innocent – he and Bernard were but acquaintances, after all; there was no reason why he should know Benji's identity – still her colour crept up further with shame. *If only you knew.* Avoiding his eye, she slipped from the bedroom and hurried down the stairs.

Benji greeted her with a scowl but, before he could speak, she held a finger to her lips. 'Not here. Come on.' She led him to the end of the street, where, satisfied they wouldn't be overheard, she turned to face him. 'I must say, I didn't expect to see thee so soon. D'you have it? The brass?'

'Nay.'

'But . . .' She frowned in confusion. 'We had a deal—'

'I agreed to nowt. You thought yer could bully me last night but you were wrong. I've told Mam and Father everything, about all your lies – and the rest.' He jerked his head to her stomach. 'You're for it now, our Jewel.'

A whooshing sound filled her ears; she couldn't

think, breathe. She swung her head in horror-filled disbelief. 'Nay . . .'

'Aye. So, you see, this ends here. Just you leave me alone, you hear?'

As she watched him – it was all she could do; her voice had deserted her – she noticed a flicker of something behind his eyes and her every nerve sparked with overwhelming relief. The uncertainty in their dark depths was undeniable. He was lying. *Thank you, Lord . . .* 'Nice try. You're too much of a spineless dog to tell.' She was gratified to see his face fall in disappointment and, again, she thanked God she'd been right. 'This is just your lame attempt to slither out of trouble. Trouble you helped create, remember?'

'It's not. I, I *did* tell—'

'Liar.'

'Bitch!' he shot back, looking as though he might cry and reminding Jewel again how young and immature he was.

'This ain't going away, Benji. Find that bloody brass or so help me . . .' Shaking her head, she let her tone drop to a growl. 'Just find it. Else your mam and yer father *shall* know what's what, all right. Only it'll be me what does the telling – aye, and for real.'

When he'd stormed off, she took some deep breaths to regain her composure then returned to the house. Inside, she found Maxwell waiting for her in the hall with his daughter. Her blush returned instantly – surely he could sense her guilt? – and though it was a struggle, she brought a smile to her face. 'I'll get back to my duties now, sir—'

'He wasn't bearing bad tidings, I hope? Your family are well?'

'Oh, nay. All's fine.' She smiled again whilst in her mind praying he wouldn't probe further.

179

'That's good.' He nodded then asked, 'You and your cousin are quite close?'

'Nay, we ain't.' She cursed herself inwardly, had fired back her response sharper than she'd intended. 'What I mean is . . . Well, not really, sir.'

'It's just that I recall you being in good spirits the last time I saw you both together. I simply assumed . . .'

What?

'Of course,' continued Maxwell, 'I should have recognised him when I opened the door as being the lad in your company at the park – although I didn't realise he was your cousin. Alas, my memory isn't what it was. Cursed old age.'

This time, the word was given life: 'What?' she murmured, cutting off Maxwell's chuckle.

'My age—'

'Not that. What was it you said about the park?'

'The day of the town hall opening. I saw you dancing together at the park.' A small frown creased his brow. 'Jewel, are you all right? Your recent bout of illness hasn't returned?'

She shook her head. It was true. Besides a little muscle achiness and a sore throat, she was back to her normal self. It was another ailment altogether that held her in its grip now: she felt stomach-churningly sick with dread. She thought she'd seen Maxwell there that fateful night – he'd seen them, too? Just how much? *What* exactly had he witnessed? 'Sir, I . . .'

'Yes?'

'I . . .' Her breathing was heavy.

'I think I know what's bothering you, Jewel.' Maxwell's voice, much to her bewilderment, held a hint of laughter. 'Please, don't be embarrassed. It was a special occasion, after all. To be honest, I myself partook of more than I should have that night. The drink,' he explained with a conspicuous wink when she frowned in puzzlement. 'You were somewhat merry.'

She stared hard at her feet. 'Aye. Benji and me . . . We both were.'

'You more so by the night's end, I suspect.'

Jewel's frown returned. She glanced back up questioningly.

'I spotted your cousin discreetly pour his drink on to the grass.' Again, Maxwell winked. 'I believe he probably began to feel the effects before you did and wanted to save face. After all, not many lads would be willing to admit otherwise – particularly when up against a member of the fairer sex – would they?'

The universe seemed to hold its breath. Thoughts crashed and exploded through Jewel's brain. Then: 'Aye. You're likely right there. Daft lad.' She smiled with a roll of her eyes. Then, holding out her arms, she took Constance from him and moved towards the stairs. 'Well, I'd best get on with my work, sir.'

'Yes, of course. I, too, must get going to the bank.'

'I'll see thee this evening, sir.' A last smile at him over her shoulder and she was free to flee.

As with her easy response to her employer's shattering revelation, it took every ounce of will and self-control she possessed to make it back to Roland's room without breaking down. Her legs shook, her chest throbbed, and she wanted nothing more than to howl her throat raw. Instead, she returned the toddler to her games and curled into a ball on the floor beside her.

He poured away the majority all night, I just know it. He wasn't inebriated as he claims. His thinking wasn't muddled by drink like mine at all. He plied me with ale after ale whilst all the time remaining fully conscious himself. He planned it.

181

*He lured me to those trees, knowing exactly what was to come.
He knew I was past refusing. He had me believe it was consensual. He didn't care. He raped me. He raped me. He raped
me . . .*

'Benji raped me.'

Once the words were forced through her lips, the
screams inside her head halted.

'Benji raped me,' she said again to the blue carpet.

Trickling from her scorching brain to her toes, an
arctic calm encased her. She sat up, folded her hands in
her lap.

Dry-eyed, she watched the clock's journey to the elev-
enth hour and the nursemaid's arrival to take over
Constance's care.

Chapter 12

'BY, LASS, I'M pleased to see thee. You're looking well.'

Jewel stared at her uncle without seeing him. Her being was focused on but one thing: 'Where's Benji?'

'He's upstairs. 'Ere, how's your new position going?' added Bernard, smiling. 'Mr Birch and his lot treating thee well, I hope?'

She nodded. Then fixing her gaze on the door behind the counter that led to the Powells' living quarters, she crossed the shop floor.

'Aye, go on. You nip up and see the lad, then. I'd be grateful to thee if you'd brew a pot whilst you're up there, lass. We'll have a sup, eh, afore you leave?'

This time, Jewel didn't respond. Pace and countenance controlled, she ascended the narrow stairs.

At her entrance, Benji looked up from the table. Surprise, swiftly followed by suspicion, passed over his face. He returned the hunk of cake he'd been eating to his plate and swept away crumbs from his chin with his sleeve. Folding his arms, he glared at her. 'What you doing here?'

Jewel closed the door quietly and made her way towards him.

'Well?' Though he tried to mask it with a scowl, worry now shadowed the youth's florid face at her unsettling silence. 'Oi, you deaf or summat?'

She paused in front of him and flattened her palms on the tabletop. Tilting her head, she surveyed him, letting her eyes travel down, down, until they settled on his crotch. Pure disgust rolled through her guts but she kept her tone mild: 'Give it to me, Benji.'

'Eh?'

'Give it to me,' she repeated, reaching down to cup the private area and swallowing bile when he began to harden instantly. 'Let me see.'

He laughed in shock and embarrassment. 'Jewel, what—?'

'Shh.'

'But . . .' A low moan chased away his half-hearted protest as she undid his trousers and extracted his member.

She pulled at it lightly, indicating he should stand, and he obeyed without question. Nor did he say a word when she motioned for him to lie on the rug by the fire. Passive as a lamb, he did as she bid and she straddled him, her hold still fixed on him.

When his hands moved behind her to fondle her buttocks, she avoided eye contact lest he saw the choking loathing she was struggling to contain. Slipping her free hand inside her apron pocket, she closed her fingers around the metal handles and slowly took out the pair of large scissors she'd brought along from the house. Face void of emotion, she held them aloft.

Benji stared at the instrument but his expression didn't change. Dumb with confusion, he stared from them to her and back again in silence.

In one swift movement, Jewel positioned his penis between the scissors' cold blades and tightened just enough that he couldn't move. Finally, she lifted her hate-filled gaze to his. 'You forced yourself on me that night, didn't you?' she asked in a murmur.

The colour had drained from his face. He tried to shift his body but her weight on his legs prevented him. Then she closed the scissors' handles slightly, letting the blades bite into his soft flesh, and he went rigid.

'You have to pay. You understand that, right?'

'Jewel.' His breathing came in short gasps. 'I don't know what you're talking ab—'

'Aye, tha does.'

'I didn't know what I were doing. I were drunk is all—'

'You weren't, though, were yer?' She tightened her hold a little more. 'You lied. You got me skenning on purpose, planned it from the off. You violated me. You *raped* me.'

'Nay—'

'You've ruined my life. Now, I'm going to ruin yours by ensuring you never get to hurt another lass with this thing again.'

Petrified tears were coursing down his face. 'Please, don't. I'm sorry.'

'So.' Her lips drew back in a snarl. 'You admit it?'

On a noisy sob, he nodded. 'I'm sorry,' he blubbered again.

Could she really do it? Her eyes flicked to his imprisoned genital. She'd intended to on the walk here, there was no denying it. Never in her life had her temper been up as much, or her mind filled with such murder as it had been then. However, now, finally vindicated, she didn't know what to feel. Rather than stoke the flames of fury, his admission had quelled them instead and she hadn't a clue what to do, hadn't expected this at all.

'I've got the brass, just like you asked. It's here, in my jacket. Feel.'

Frowning, she patted his pocket. Sure enough, the jingle of coins greeted her.

'I were going to fetch it round to thee later. I were, 'onest.'

'It don't make everything all right, though, does it?' she spat, leaning in close. 'It won't change what you've done, what you've put me through . . .'

'I'll tell you a secret if you let me go.'

The unexpected announcement momentarily threw her. She cocked her head, eyes narrowed.

Seeing he had her attention, Benji's eyes widened with hope. He licked his lips with an eager nod. 'Promise you'll let me be?'

Though aware he was clutching at straws, was desperate to distract her attention from the matter in hand, from his guilt, she could tell he did have knowledge of something she didn't. But what?

'You can't tell a soul I've told you, mind. You must keep it to yourself.'

Curiosity got the better of her. She nodded.

'Your mam ain't your mam.'

'What are you talking about?'

'It's the truth. I've heard whispers of it over the years.'

'Whose whispers?' He didn't answer and she shook her head. He really was grasping at anything to wriggle free from this. But what an absurd thing to make up. How did his warped mind work at all? 'Fool,' she said, releasing him and returning the scissors to her apron before shifting off him and rising to her feet.

Benji clutched his groin protectively. His relief was tangible. He closed his eyes, his breathing heavy.

'The brass.' Jewel held out a hand and her cousin quickly fumbled for the gold sovereigns and dropped them into her palm. She placed them with the scissors and headed for the door, knowing not whence he'd acquired them and caring less. He owed her – more so

186

after today. It was a small price to pay for all he'd done, as well as walking from this with all his body parts intact.

'Jewel?'

She glanced over her shoulder.

'I am sorry, you know.'

'Sorry tha got found out.'

With that, she left the room and made her way back down to the shop. To her relief, her uncle was busy tending to a customer and she was able to slip away without further conversation.

Oddly, she felt lighter of mind on the walk back to Mawdsley Street. It was as if the truth of that horrid night had set her free, though she was incapable of understanding why. Surely the new-found knowledge should have made her feel worse, and yet it didn't. Perhaps it was having proof that she wasn't a loose piece, as she'd grown to view herself over the months, that explained her feelings. She'd berated herself continually, and now that could stop, couldn't it? She was blameless, had been from the start. The relief this carried was like a balm to her soul. She wasn't foul or wicked or wrong. She'd *been* wronged. The realisation was comforting.

Drawing level with Maria's residence, Jewel saw her friend cleaning the inside of the windows and slowed her pace, hoping to catch her attention. She did, and lifting her hand made the money sign by rubbing her index and middle finger against her thumb, then patted her apron pocket. Catching her meaning, Maria gave her a thumbs-up.

Fortunately, her short absence had gone undetected and, slipping inside and back to her kitchen, Jewel busied herself with work. All the while, she rehearsed in her mind the conversation she must have later with her employer regarding her planned departure. Would he be disappointed, angry? Would he agree to Maria's sister taking over her duties until she returned? Would she even have a position to return to afterwards? As for breaking the news to her mother . . . Well. She'd tackle that aspect when the time came.

'Sir? I'd like to speak with thee, if you can spare a minute or two of your time?'

Seated at his desk in the firelit drawing room, Maxwell looked up from his papers. 'Jewel.' A genuine smile touched his mouth. 'Of course. Come in.'

The family had finished the evening meal some time ago. Constance had been put to bed and Roland had gone out; Jewel had been awaiting his departure as her cue to seek out his father. She closed the door and stood facing him, fingers plucking nervously at each other.

'To be honest with you, your presence is a welcome distraction.' Maxwell motioned to the desktop then rubbed his tired eyes. 'Cooped up in a stuffy office all day drawing figures, the last thing I desire of an evening is to do the same at home. Alas, someone has to. As senior bank clerk, that must naturally fall to me.'

Tasked with overseeing the clerks below him, dealing with rich and important clients, the vast sums of money entrusted to his keeping . . . Jewel eyed him with more than a little awe. She couldn't have imagined anything worse, was useless when it came to numbers. What a responsibility he had – and what challenging work that entailed. She bit her lip guiltily, regretting having disturbed him.

'What I have to say can wait, sir, if you're busy—'

Lifting his hand, he cut her off. 'Not at all.'

'Well, it's like this. Mam sent word earlier that an owd aunt of hers has taken ill. She wants me to go to her, nurse her a while.'

'I see. When?'

'Tomorrow, sir.'

'*Tomorrow?*'

She nodded. After all, she didn't see the point of drawing this out. The sooner the matter was dealt with, the better.

'Is this what your cousin came to see you about this morning?'

Benji assaulted her mind. The sickening feel of him, the scissors, his eyes wide with terror ... Swallowing hard, she quickly pushed the images away. 'Aye. Aye, that's right. It didn't seem the right time to tell thee earlier, what with you on your way to work.' She lifted her eyes to gauge his reaction in his, but he'd lowered his gaze, was staring at his steepled hands. 'I'll not leave thee in the lurch, sir. A friend of mine says her sister will take on my duties in my absence – if you're in agreement, of course. She's a respectable lass; trustworthy, hardworking—'

'How long will you be gone?' His words were quiet, flat.

'A few months is likely.'

'A few . . . ? There's no one else?'

'Nay, sir. We're all the wench has. And Mam hasn't the strength for it she once had, would wear herself out and become ill herself should she take on the task.'

'Then of course you must.'

'Aye?'

Maxwell nodded. 'I insist.'

'And my job, sir . . . ?'

'Will be here waiting for you.'

189

His goodness cut her to the quick. Her wretched deceit seared further. Sudden tears filled her eyes. Turning, she made for the door.

'Jewel?'

'Aye, sir?'

'You *will* return . . . won't you?' He'd risen from his chair. Hands hanging loosely by his sides, his stare was full of expectancy.

An overwhelming urge to run to him, to throw her arms about his neck and never let go, filled her. 'Just as soon as I'm able,' she said earnestly. 'You have my word.'

In the ensuing silence, Maxwell took a step towards her. As though by some unspoken instruction, she did likewise.

'I – that is, *we* . . . shall miss you.'

'And I you, sir.'

And she meant it, with every whisper of her heart.

Chapter 13

VOICE CRACKING, MARIA clung to Jewel. 'You send word should you need me, d'you hear?'

'I hear.'

'And don't you fret. That sister of mine shall take sound care of your Mr Birch and his kin.'

'You'll remember to call in on Mam when you can, won't you, Maria? Check she's well?'

'Course, aye.'

Again, the friends embraced tightly.

'Ta, thanks. For everything,' Jewel told her as they drew apart, her own cheeks wet with tears.

'Eeh, lass.' Despite the maid's efforts to keep a brave face, it creased. 'Take care.'

'Oh, Maria, I am frightened,' she admitted, her own resolve wavering in turn. 'What if summat should go wrong—?'

'Now you mustn't think like that.' Reverting to her brusque self, Maria wagged a finger. 'Nowt shall, nay. You'll see. You'll be back home where you belong in no time at all.'

And if I'm not? If something *should* go awry? she wanted to press, fighting the urge to grasp Maria and shake the answers from her. Things could and did. Any number of women the world over died daily from child-bearing. Why should she be different?

Suppose the widow from the newspaper, whose acquaintance she was soon to make, wasn't as capable as they assumed; what, then? On nothing but blind trust, she was putting her life in the hands of a complete stranger. God above, how had it come to this? Could she really go through with it?

I have no choice. The response tapped at her mind in an instant. *I must.*

Lifting her chin bravely, she bid Maria farewell. Forcing herself not to look back at the house she'd come to regard as home, she set off on the fifteen-minute walk to Lum Street where, God willing, she was to hunker down to see this nightmare period through. That it was in quite close proximity didn't unduly worry her. Once settled, she'd be sure not to leave the house under any circumstances so wasn't at risk of encountering anyone she knew.

She'd purposely turned right, taking the side streets to avoid Back Cheapside and Town Hall Square – and further heartache. Reaching Crown Street, she breathed a little more easily. She didn't trust herself not to break down if she had to suffer another goodbye with her mother. Last night's had been difficult enough.

The memory of Flora's sad eyes flashed in her mind afresh and Jewel sighed. After giving his permission, Maxwell had sent her to inform her mother – and so the next round of lies had been spun. She'd put to Jewel the same questions he had: 'When will you go and for how long? Several *months*? Oh, lass, as much as that?' Jewel had done her utmost to play the length of time down, telling her it would pass before they knew it, though it had done little to ease her mother's upset.

'Can't someone else do it? It's nice and all that Mr

192

Birch, insisting he wants someone he knows and trusts to nurse his sister back to health, thought of thee . . . but still . . . Is there really no one else?' Jewel had shaken her head and her mother had done likewise, with dull acceptance. 'Their lot click their fingers and we beneath them jump, aye. I know, lass, I get it – owt forra quiet life. By, but I'll miss thee.'

'And I'll miss you,' Jewel whispered to herself now as she dragged her feet, head down. 'More than you could ever know.'

When Benji flitted into her thoughts she instantly pushed him away. She didn't want to dwell on him; not now, not ever again. With her uncle, she did likewise, though for widely differing reasons. It was clearly his money paying for this – the knowledge fed her guilt by the hour. Bernard was a good man, didn't deserve to suffer any of this.

The next image, on the other hand, refused to leave her. And her attempt to scatter this one was feeble at best.

Maxwell had left for work this morning without saying goodbye. Though he'd wished her well last night before retiring to bed, it wasn't the same and she couldn't help but feel upset. She thought he would have at least sent her on her way with a kind word or two – though his presence alone, just one last look at him, would have been enough, something she could have taken with her to look back on over the coming months. Then again, why would he? How could he know what was in her head? She didn't even understand these feelings of hers herself.

She'd consoled herself instead with a hug from Constance, whom she knew she would miss just as much. Even Roland, who *had* offered a warm farewell, she felt a pang at leaving. She really had taken the Birches to her heart, had come to regard them almost as a second family. Whether that was sensible, however, remained to be seen. What was she to them, after all, but a paid skivvy? And now, not even that.

As Jewel emerged from Bow Street and on to Folds Road, her emotions were once more in disarray – though, now, fear overrode all else. She paused to gather her nerves. Beyond Mill Hill's two mills in the distance lay the sprawling moors and meadows of Tonge and Breight-met, and she was tempted to continue past approaching Lum Street and all that went with it. Yet what could other districts offer her? Where would she go, and to whom? She'd just left all she knew and loved behind her. There was no one else. She forced herself onward.

A light drizzle had started up, dulling further an early sky already shrouded in grey from the multitude of surrounding factories' spewing chimneys. She drew her shawl closer around her. Minutes later, heart hammering, she turned the corner of what would hopefully be her temporary home.

Here, she halted again and glanced along the grim-coloured street, scanning the stretch of beer houses, shops and dwellings for one number in particular. When she spotted it, the corners of her mouth lifted slightly. It appeared half-decent; more so, in fact. The step was scrubbed, the windows and curtains beyond them clean. A tidy-looking abode by all accounts – certainly better than she'd dared hope.

Jewel checked inside the rough canvas bag she carried. Nestled amongst the few items of clothing was a cloth pouch which held the precious coins. She nodded. Everything was set. All that was left to do now was to knock . . .

After building up courage with a few shuddering breaths, she did just that.

'What can I do you for?'

Tall and thin, dark hair pulled back into a tight bun and darker eyes narrowed questioningly, the woman who answered the door folded her arms. Like her home, she, too, was neat and clean. Though the greeting wasn't unfriendly, she possessed an assured, somewhat formidable air. Jewel's anxiety heightened further.

'You left an advertisement in the *Bolton Evening News*,' she stammered. 'I, I'm in need of your services, like.'

'Oh aye?'

Fumbling inside her bag then holding out the pouch, her tone was desperate. 'Will you help me, missis? Please?'

The widow gave her and the pouch a long look. Then her stare fell to Jewel's stomach. 'That the one you want shot of, then? But it ain't even ready. I only normally take in babes in arms—'

'Normally?' Jewel's heart had dropped to her clogged feet but, with that one word, a little hope had returned.

'Eh?'

'You said "normally". That means you *do* sometimes offer lying-in?'

'Well . . . I might consider it, aye. If the price is right, of course.' She plucked the cloth from Jewel's hand and tipped out the contents into her own palm.

'There's a pound extra,' Jewel told her as she counted the sovereigns. 'Would that be enough for me to stay until after the birth?'

The woman flicked her eyes up and down the street. 'I don't discuss business on t' doorstep. Too many nosey divils around. Come inside.'

Hope fluttered once more. Surely if she was unwilling, she'd have turned her away by now? Inviting her in was a good sign, wasn't it? Quick on her heels, Jewel followed her into the house.

Like outside, in here it shone like a new pin. The walls were freshly whitewashed and the scrubbed flagged floor gleamed. Every piece of furniture – some good pieces there were, too, nothing battered or worn – was polished, and the blackleaded fireplace shone in the flames' glow. Jewel allowed herself a pleased smile. This was better than anything she'd imagined. Of course, she'd have given anything not to have to be here. But she did, and it was proving more than adequate.

'Sit down, then.'

'Thanks, Mrs . . . ?'

'Just call me Mater. That'll do.'

Considering this to be a rather queer request, Jewel hid a frown. It was only then that she noticed the silence. She glanced around the space again but saw no signs of there being children beneath this roof. No tiny items of clothing, feeding vessels or the like. 'You're not nursing any babbies at present?'

'Aye. I've five under my care at the moment. They stop upstairs.'

'Oh.' She was both surprised and saddened. So many. And her child was soon to add to the number of the unwanted. Just another throwaway. *Forgive me . . .*

'I've a girl lying in already, an' all. She's further along than you look to be, is due any day. You'll have to share with her if you're for staying. I've only the one bed spare, you see. Take it or leave it.'

'I'll take it,' Jewel responded without hesitation. What choice had she? It was a small price to pay. She just hoped this girl was an agreeable sort, that they would get along. The last thing she wanted was grief, had had enough lately to last her two lifetimes. To burrow herself away in peace was all she craved.

'Right, then. Hang up your shawl and set the kettle to

boil. Tea caddy and cups are in the cupboard – there.'
She jerked her head towards an alcove then sat back in
her chair, arms folded.

Though thinking a 'please' wouldn't have gone amiss,
Jewel smiled and nodded nonetheless and got to her feet.

'I'll have a sup if there's one going begging,' piped a
voice from the stairs.

Jewel turned to see that it belonged to what must be
the other expectant mother she'd be sharing a bed
with. The widow wasn't wrong when stating the girl was
due any day; she was as round as a penny.

'You finished up there?' asked Mater when the girl
had seated herself at the table.

'Aye.'

'I'll be checking to make sure, an' all.'

The girl rolled her eyes to Jewel, who responded with
a puzzled half-smile. Finished what? she wondered.
Perhaps she'd been seeing to the children? Would she
herself be expected to perform such duties whilst dwelling here? She really hoped not. The last thing her fragile
emotions needed right now was for her to be caring for
other babies. The very thought was abhorrent to her,
given that she planned to do no such thing with her own.
Tend to others throughout the coming weeks then aban-
don hers upon its entering the world? No. She couldn't do
it. She just couldn't, and would tell the widow so.

Tea made, the three of them drank in silence. When
a sleepy-sounding cry drifted down, Jewel held her
breath and prayed she wouldn't be asked to see to it. But
though the widow sighed, she didn't turn to her or the
girl; instead, she herself rose and disappeared upstairs.

Alone with Jewel, the girl's lacklustre demeanour
changed. She sat forward and flashed a pouty smile. 'All
right?'

'Aye. Well, you know . . . ?' Jewel motioned to her stomach. 'As well as I can be, at any rate.' Her voice thickened. 'Coming here . . . I had no choice.'

'Do we ever? Never the fellas left to suffer the result of their fun, though, is it?'

Jewel shook her head, whispered, 'Were you forced, too?'

'Me?' The girl's mouth stretched in a slow grin. 'Oh nay. I were willing, all right.'

'Oh. Oh, I . . .' Colour had washed across her face. She eyed the girl with a mixture of disapproval and curiosity. Not knowing how to respond to the shameless declaration, she lifted her cup and sipped at her tea.

'He reckoned he wanted to wed me. Silly bitch that I am, I fell for it. It wasn't 'til I'd been caught with this,' she added, jabbing at her huge bump none too gently, 'that I discovered he were already married to another. Promised me the world, he did. Instead, he were planning on putting me up in a few rooms, where I was expected to dutifully wait for his visits if and when he felt like it. No, thank you. Rent and everything else paid for or no, I'd sooner go it alone than live like that. That's no life, not really. I wanted all of him or nowt at all.' She shrugged. 'It is how it is. His wife's welcome to him, poor cow.'

'The swine, that's awful. Does he know you're here and what you're intending?'

Again, the girl grinned. 'Where d'you think the brass came from to pay the fee? I didn't just have all them pounds lying around doing nowt, you know. Aye well, sod him. Once I've rid my body of this thing, I'm off out of this shit-tip town; to hell with the pair of them.'

Jewel was lost for words once more. This girl's hardness, her apparent sheer dispassionateness, was difficult to fathom. She hadn't spoken with anger or bitterness or even regret, not at all. She was simply matter-of-fact about the whole business, almost unfazed.

'So what's your story?'

'My cousin decided to take what weren't his.' It was Jewel's turn to shrug. 'I couldn't let on to Mam, the family. It'd be harder still now; it's gone too far for that, I reckon. Hopefully, once all this is over with, I can carry on like afore and no one will be any the wiser. The trouble it would cause, the shame ... I can't do it to Mam, I can't.'

The girl took a swig of her tea. 'Louise.'

'Eh? Oh,' she added, smiling, when the girl pointed to herself. 'I'm Jewel.'

'Has that one upstairs told you yet that you're to call her Mater?'

Louise's words had been tinged with amusement. With a curl of her lip and a roll of her eyes, Jewel nodded, and they both chuckled. 'What's the deal with that, then, you reckon?'

'Likes her privacy, don't she? The less we know of her, the better – who can blame her in her line of work?'

Jewel frowned. 'But why the secrecy? She's providing a social service is all.'

'Ho! That's one way of putting it.'

Her confusion grew. As far as she could see, this was beneficial for all concerned. Without such procurers, mothers lacking the support of a husband, family or friends found it nigh on impossible to keep themselves and their child out of the workhouse. Few private charities extended help to fallen women, less so their offspring – English society placed little value on illegitimates. To do so would, they believed, promote bastardy and encourage immoral behaviour. Regardless of circumstances, it was deemed that fault lay with the female.

This blinkered ideology only compounded matters for an already shunned and struggling minority.

In addition, women like the widow, in need of income, got by on the premiums they charged, procuring in return adoptive parents willing and able to offer infants a brighter future. Therefore, surely this route, which provided all with a lifeline, was for the good? Furthermore, it was simple, quick and legal, with few questions asked.

Alternatives were limited. Abandonment was a criminal offence – as, too, was abortion, which commonly resulted in severe haemorrhaging or even death. If the woman survived and was found out, imprisonment awaited her instead.

'Where would I – both of us – be at this minute but for folk like her?' asked Jewel. 'I can't see the bad in it at all. Besides, what they do don't go against the rules of the law, does it?'

'Oh, come on.' As though debating whether Jewel was having her on, Louise ran a hand through hair the colour of spun silk, eyes creased. 'Surely you ain't so green?'

'What d'you mean by that, like?'

'Surely you know . . . ?' Realising she didn't, Louise shook her head slowly. '*Mater* is a baby farmer.'

Jewel stared back blankly. A what?

'Or as I like to think of them,' added the girl, 'an angel maker.'

'I don't . . . What—?'

'Shush,' Louise whispered, cutting off her questions as approaching footsteps from above sounded. As though not a word had passed between them, she picked up her cup and resumed drinking her tea.

Jewel was more mystified than ever. What was going on? What had she meant? What on earth was a baby farmer? She had to know, though now wasn't the time to probe further; the girl clearly didn't want to speak on it in front of the older woman. She'd get it out of Louise later, she determined.

Even so: *baby farmer*. The term swam around her brain as she, too, sipped her drink. *Baby . . . farmer?*

The widow, a brown blanket-wrapped bundle under her arm, descended the stairs then disappeared without a glance at either of them. Moments later, shifting and banging noises drifted up to them from the cellar – peering at the ground, Jewel frowned. 'What's she up to, I wonder?'

Though her gaze had dropped, too, Louise offered no suggestion. Placing her cup on the table, she scraped back her chair. 'I'm going forra lie-down.'

Jewel watched her lumber off up to the bedroom. She looked to the floor again when silence fell then fixed her eyes on the door – however, the widow failed to reappear. Taking her frown with her, she busied herself washing up her and Louise's cups and saucers.

Eventually, still clutching the bundle, Mater emerged from the cellar. Now, she gave Jewel a long look before disappearing once more, this time to the back yard. Dogs' barks sounded then died away. When she re-entered the house, she was empty-handed. Without a word, she resumed her seat at the table, picked up the teapot and refilled her cup.

After putting away the tea things, Jewel, too, made to return to the table. Then, changing her mind, she crossed to a fireside chair. Watching the dancing flames without seeing them, she tried to make sense of what had transpired since her arrival. Louise's words; the widow and her bundle; the queer, unsettling feel of the place . . . But she could fathom none of it.

Have I made a mistake in coming here? she wondered for the first time. And without understanding why, her hand drifted unconsciously to her stomach.

Chapter 14

AS IT TURNED out, Mater didn't expect her lying-in guests to lend a hand in tending to the children in her care at all. In fact, she positively insisted they steered clear of the back bedroom altogether.

Though thankful when Louise revealed this to her, Jewel couldn't shake her curiosity over the unseen scraps of life. Despite this now being her third day here, she'd seen nothing of them at all. A faint cry would ring out now and then but, once the widow had been in to see to them, they wouldn't hear a thing more for hours.

'I'll not be asked to tend to the babbies, will I, Louise?' Jewel had asked her that first night when she'd joined her in bed. The girl had told then how Mater preferred them not to interfere with her charges. The rest of the house, however, was another matter – that's what Louise had been doing when Jewel first arrived: scrubbing her bedroom floor, not seeing to the children, as she'd assumed.

'I may as well tell thee afore she does – we're to pull our weight,' Louise had continued. 'The cleaning, sweeping, washing, cooking . . . that's our job beneath this roof. I'll be glad of the help now you're here, to be honest. I've never toiled so hard as I have these past weeks since I myself happened upon her doorstep. But what can you do, eh? If she says we must see to the chores, then we do it. That or likely get slung on to the street. Aye well, it'll not be for much longer; for me, at least. God above, I can hardly wait to be rid of the child and away from here.'

Looking at the mountainous stomach beneath the bedclothes, Jewel had been shocked. Fancy Louise having to see to the entire household duties this far along in her carrying. How had she coped, particularly given the widow's very high standards? It was a wonder Louise hadn't collapsed through exhaustion. She'd be sure to take on the donkey's share from now on, save the girl from making herself ill, Jewel had resolved. It was only right. She herself wasn't so big yet; she'd manage things much easier.

Though Louise had no qualms about relaying the rules of their stay, when Jewel had brought up their earlier conversation and asked again just what on earth a baby farmer was the girl had immediately clammed up. She'd feigned tiredness and attempted to turn away, but Jewel had been insistent: 'You must tell me, for I can't make head nor tail of its meaning. What is she? What, a farmer of babies? But what does that mean? It don't make no sense.'

'Bloody hell's fire, shurrup about it, will thee?' Louise had eventually groaned, pulling the blankets above her head to drown out the questions. 'I meant nowt by what I told thee. It's nowt, just another name for nurses is all.'

'And what you said about how *you* see them? Angel makers, was it? Aye, that were it. What did that mean, then?'

'Oh, I don't know. Just that, in a way, they *do* make angels out of the devils that sinners like us have created.

Aye, little cherubs what unlike us will go on to live wholesome, holy soddin' lives. All right? Happy? Will you let me get some rotten kip, now?' But though Jewel nodded, Louise had made no attempt to rest. Instead, she'd stared at her for a long moment then added, voice almost kind, 'Look, Jewel. All this business . . . It's the best thing all round. You'll see. Once you're shot of the child, you can begin life over again. That's what you want, in't it?' At her nod, she'd continued. 'And the babby; you don't want it, right?'

'It's impossible.'

'Nor do you want to ever see it again, d'you? Run the risk of it tracking you down one day? Everyone you know and love knowing, judging, turning against thee?'

'It's impossible,' she'd murmured again.

'Well, then, here's the thing. Birth it, walk from this house and put it from your mind for ever. It's the only way.'

Jewel knew she was right. Still, it hadn't stopped her from crying herself to sleep.

Now, the hour was approaching nine. Shortly before, breakfast had been eaten and the dishes washed and put away. Louise had taken herself back to bed, and Mater was tending to her charges. Seated at the scrubbed table, Jewel itched for something to do. Having swept and scoured the place to within an inch of its life yesterday, there was nothing to occupy her now for a few hours until lunch needed preparing. She really wasn't used to this inactivity. The boredom was sending her mad.

Generally, it wasn't so bad during the day. The household chores she was instructed to complete kept both body and mind busy but, as night fell, restlessness would

205

creep up on her and she'd yearn to leave the house, go for a walk, anything to kill the stale monotony.

Of course, venturing beyond the door was an impossibility. What if someone she knew saw her? Or, as she'd begun to fear, what if she was unable to stop herself from seeking them out? For the pain of separation was like a physical thing. Though, obviously, she missed Mam, it wasn't the gut-churning pining she'd felt when she'd first left their home. Time at Mawdsley Street had already dulled that particular loss to a manageable ache; she'd grown used to not seeing her daily. Maria and the Birches were another matter.

The maid had become dear to her over the months and she'd have given anything right now for one of her cheeky grins or warm hugs. Though Louise was similar in age to them both, she wasn't the kind of person you could naturally befriend. Whereas Maria harnessed her worldly-wiseness into helping and advising others, Louise's had had the opposite effect on her personality. Her experiences looked to have not so much hardened but developed in her an apathetic passiveness that was difficult to penetrate. Jewel missed the rapport, the banter, the support; the big sister she'd never had.

Little Constance, even Roland, she also wished to see. Was the child missing her? Were the family's needs being met and the household running as smoothly as it should under the new servant? She fretted about them frequently. As for *him* . . .

Sighing, she rose from the table and made her way to the back yard for some air – and much-needed distraction. The man with chocolate-brown hair and eyes to match lingered on the outskirts of her mind constantly. The longing to see *him* was a gnawing in her guts and her chest – her very bones – that wouldn't leave her, though she prayed the pain would dim with time. Whether he missed her or not, she refused to ponder upon. For the answer she suspected stung more acutely still. Why would he? If her temporary replacement was doing her job well, he probably hadn't noticed she'd even gone.

The widow's two large dogs, tied up with rope, lay snoozing on some old sacks. They lifted their heads from their paws and wagged their tails, and she stroked them in turn. As the minutes ticked by, the stillness soothed her racing thoughts a little. Hugging herself, she closed her eyes.

'Go on in afore you catch your death of cold.'

Mind still elsewhere, Jewel hadn't heard the widow's approach; she almost jumped from her skin. 'Eeh, my heart,' she said on a chuckle.

The woman's expression, however, remained impassive. Holding the door wide, she repeated, 'Go on in.'

As Jewel passed her to return to the house, she caught a whiff of gin on her breath. Not only did this surprise her, given the earliness of the hour, but she hadn't realised the woman was fond of a sup. Should she really be at the bottle with young 'uns to care for? The thought made her frown. It grew when she also noticed that, again, tucked beneath the woman's arm, was a wrapped blanket. Eyeing it, she couldn't hide her curiosity.

Seeing this, the widow was quick to explain. She held it up. 'Grub for t' dogs.'

Indeed, her hounds had leapt to their feet, were panting in hungry anticipation.

Jewel smiled a little, nodded, then headed back indoors. Reaching the kitchen, she saw a thin trail of dark droplets across the flagstone floor – blood. It must have seeped through the bundle without Mater noticing.

No wonder the dogs had been excited; the meat inside it must be as fresh as it came, she thought as she went to fetch hot water and a scrubbing brush. Fancy giving the animals good grub like that when folk around here could only dream of affording such luxury. It was blind broth, named so as it consisted almost entirely of vegetables with next to no meat, for some most days. That woman must have more money than sense.

When a knock sounded at the front door, she abandoned the cleaning and, wiping her hands on her apron, went to answer it. The widow had mentioned last night that a new baby would be arriving today; this must be them.

Before opening it, she fixed in place a small smile of understanding for the mother's benefit, guessing all too well what she must be feeling at this moment. Yet it quickly melted when the visitors were revealed.

'Mrs Bickerstaff?'

Jewel gazed at the tall and grim-faced policemen in turn. 'Who?'

'We're here to speak with Ada Bickerstaff.' The burlier of the two stepped closer. 'Is she present?'

They had to be referring to Mater. What was all this about, then? What had she done? 'I'll just fetch her, sir.'

'No need, I'm here.' The widow had entered the room. She bestowed on the men a sickly smile – the first of any sort Jewel had seen her crack since she'd been here. 'Good morning, constables. What can I do youse for?'

From the corner of her eye, Jewel noticed that Louise had appeared at the top of the stairs. Her normally pink cheeks were ashen. Did she have some inkling as to why the law was here? Curiosity mounting, Jewel focused her attention back on the trio.

'We've received reports of suspicious activity being carried out at this property, Mrs Bickerstaff.'

'Oh?'

'Namely that children regularly appear to be deposited here. A mother arrives, babe in arms, only to leave shortly afterwards alone. Inasmuch, we have sufficient reason to believe you're operating a baby-farming business. Is this indeed the case?'

After some seconds, the widow responded calmly. 'I run a foster service, sir. All proper and above board, I assure thee—'

'That's not quite correct, Mrs Bickerstaff, is it?' He raised an eyebrow. 'Under the Infant Life Protection Act, passed last year to regulate and monitor such practices for the safeguarding of children, all persons boarding more than one infant in return for monetary payment are bound to register their houses with their local authority. According to our recent checks, there is no such record held of either you or your home.'

'Oh, ain't there?' the widow asked. She pulled an apologetic face. 'I could've sworn I put my address down . . .'

'I'm afraid not, Mrs Bickerstaff.'

'Oh, I am sorry. I'll be sure to do that first thing in t' morning.' Smiling, she moved to the door to see them out. 'I hope you'll accept my apologies, constables, for taking up your time.'

But they made no attempt to exit. By now, Louise had joined them – the policeman who had spoken before took in her and Jewel's conditions. 'You provide lying-in, too, I see.'

Though the widow's tone remained light, her throat bobbed in a visible gulp. 'Not as a rule, sir. Hardly ever, in fact. These two, well, they . . . they just happened to need some place to stop on and . . . and well, I—'

'Perhaps this is on a larger scale than we first thought,' he cut in to murmur to his colleague, who nodded. He turned back to the widow, whose unruffled stance was rapidly waning. 'How many children are currently under your care, Mrs Bickerstaff?'

'Three, sir.'

'But—' The word escaped Jewel's mouth before she could stop it. Throughout the discourse, she'd barely grasped what was being said, knew nothing of acts and regulations and legal talk. This last answer from the woman, however, she'd understood loud and clear. Understood, that is, that it was a lie. For hadn't she herself queried that very thing on her arrival, to be told the number was five? And as far as she was aware, no baby had left this house since – and especially not two. Nevertheless, all eyes were now on her and she clamped her lips shut, cursing her tongue and wishing she'd stayed well out of it.

'But . . . ? But what?' asked the constable.

'Nowt, sir. Nothing at all.'

His stare remained on Jewel for a long moment. Then he swung it back around to fix on the widow. 'Mrs Bickerstaff. May we take a look around?'

'A look . . . ? For what?' She tried an easy laugh but failed. Her voice rose. 'But . . . I'm a professional, re*spectable*, procurer, sir!'

'If you could just lead us to your charges, Mrs—'

'But . . . ! There really is no need for this, none at all—!'

The constable's clipped interjection brooked no argument: 'Your charges, Mrs Bickerstaff.'

Slowly, the widow's shoulders sagged. Eyes like huge black smudges in her pasty face, she turned as though in a daze and crossed to the stairs. The men followed close behind. The moment they disappeared on to the landing, Louise grabbed a fistful of Jewel's blouse.

'Run.'

'Eh?'

'*Run.*'

Before Jewel knew what was happening, the girl had ripped wide the front door and dragged her into the street. Too dumbstruck to resist, she allowed her waddling captor to lead her in a half-stumble, half-run.

Crouching out of sight in the shadows of the gasworks, the looming gasometer beyond, they fought to catch their breath.

'Louise, what the *hell* is going—?'

''Tain't safe yet. Come on.'

Again, Jewel found herself hauled along the road. They turned bend after bend, skittering through the maze of grey streets, until eventually emerging into Churchgate. Here, Louise ground to a halt, purple in the face and puffing fit to collapse.

'Are you all right?' Jewel gasped out between pants, touching the girl's shoulder in concern. She herself had struggled with her bump's extra weight – goodness knew how cumbersome Louise, due literally any moment, fared.

'I will be.'

As her breath returned, so too did her senses and Jewel suddenly realised where she was. Bare-headed, with nothing to conceal her face, having left her shawl as well as her other possessions behind at Lum Street in the mad dash, she glanced around with a bite of her lip. Mam's dwelling, her place of work, were worryingly close for comfort. How could this be? What was she even doing here? What the *hell* had just happened back there?

'Right, I'm off. Bye, then.'

'What? Oi, hang bloody on!' Momentarily too shocked to move, Jewel had to run to catch her up. 'Where you going?'

'Home.'

'And where's that?'

'Manchester.'

'*Manchester?* But . . . Well, where am *I* going?' Louise stared back blankly and anger washed through Jewel. 'What the divil is the meaning of all this? You've plucked me from the only place I had left to turn and dumped me but an arrow's flight from where I fled – for what? What did we just witness? Why the police? Mrs Bickerstaff, as we now know her to be, what has she done?'

Louise heaved an exaggerated sigh. 'Does it matter?'

'Course it does! Just tell me, will you?'

'Look, I know nowt, all right? Only it seems she's been up to summat, don't it, the way she were acting? And from the look on their phizogs, those constables thought the same. I weren't for taking no chances; whatever's afoot, they might have thought me privy to it and carted me off to prison along with her. I reckoned it were best to get out whilst the going was good.'

'And dragging me along with thee – you're saying you were doing me a favour?'

'Huh. If you're going to be like this about it, I wish I hadn't bothered.'

'*I* wish you hadn't, an' all! I can't believe I let you do this.' Tears of rage and desperation stung. 'And what if you're wrong? What if the widow's committed no crime and it's all just a misunderstanding? *Where* am I meant to go *now?*'

'Erm . . .' Puffing out air, Louise lifted her arms and let them fall back to her sides.

'Well, that's just bleedin' gradely, that is. Thank you very much for nowt!' Biting back her emotion, Jewel peered in the direction they had come. 'I'll have to return, find out what's occurred, whether it were all a mistake. Happen she'll take me back in—'

'She'll not.'

'She'll have to. I've no place else. Besides, I paid her for my stay fair and square.'

'She'll not,' Louise repeated quietly. 'She can't, for she'll not be there. She'll be on her way to the cells as we speak. Trust me. I just have a feeling about this.'

Sheer hopelessness overcame Jewel. Her legs threatened to give way and she leaned against a butcher's shop wall with a low cry. 'I'm done for.'

'Well . . .' Louise shrugged when Jewel lifted her head slowly to look at her. 'You could come along with me?'

'With you? To Manchester?'

'Aye, why not?'

She opened her mouth but no excuse was forthcoming. Besides, what other option was there? 'You really mean it?'

'I'd not have said, would I?'

A flicker of a smile touched her lips. She wiped her eyes on her sleeve. 'Ta ever so. Truly. I'll not forget this.'

'Come on, then.' With a jerk of her head, the girl set off towards Trinity Street Station.

'Oh, no.' Jewel had fallen into step but paused suddenly as a thought occurred. 'I've no brass for the fare.'

'None?'

Heart dipping, she shook her head. 'Norra single copper coin.'

'Well, that makes two of us.'

'What? Then how . . . ?'

'Fret not. I'll sort it.' Eyes narrowed, Louise scanned their surroundings. Something caught her attention by the Man and Scythe, an ancient hostelry, and her face cleared. 'Wait here. I'll not be long.'

Though Jewel had followed her gaze, she could see nothing in particular that could help with their

213

situation. She watched in puzzlement as Louise walked away. The girl approached an elderly man weaving his way down the street, clearly the worse for drink, and said something. They smiled at one another, a few more words were exchanged, and Louise linked her arm through his. They turned and headed towards a narrow alleyway.

When they disappeared, Jewel scratched her head and frowned. Then realisation dawned and, swearing under her breath, she closed her eyes. Louise was going to rob him. God in heaven, what was she thinking? In her condition, too – anything could happen. She'd clearly targeted him because of his inebriated state, but what if he still had enough wits about him to realise her game? He'd be mad with rage, could turn violent, and what would she do then? How could she be so foolish – not to mention cruel?

Mind you, I'm no better, am I? Didn't I force Benji's hand to steal from his father?

Her chin dropped in remorse. Uncle Bernard hadn't deserved that either, yet she'd had no choice. Desperation had driven her to it – just as Louise felt now. Rightly or wrongly, when it came down to survival, needs must. Turning a deaf ear to her guilt, she awaited Louise's return.

Minutes passed without a sign of them and her anxiety was mounting. Jewel was about to go in search of the girl when suddenly she appeared, thankfully looking none the worse for her escapade. No bloody nose or fat lip, no drunkard close behind yelling out her crime – it would seem she'd been successful in lightening his pockets without detection. Jewel rushed to meet her.

'All right?'

Louise nodded.

214

'Did you . . . ?'

'Aye.'

Sensing from the girl's set mouth and her stare fixed straight ahead that she didn't wish to discuss the matter further – perhaps she did possess a conscience, after all – Jewel kept her quiet.

Once more, they set off to catch the train.

Chapter 15

THEIR TRAVELS PROVED a quiet affair. Throughout the ten-mile journey, Louise mostly snoozed. When she did rouse for brief periods, she barely uttered a word. The moment the train choked and juddered to a halt, however, and they alighted on to her home ground, she suddenly came alive.

Emerging from Victoria Station, the girl tipped back her head and took a long sniff of the sulphurous air. 'Eeh, am I glad to be back.'

As far as Jewel could tell, this was no different from the town they had left behind; albeit here was larger, louder and much, much busier.

As in Bolton, over the past century the Industrial Revolution had swallowed much of Manchester's green and pleasant land. Now, pewter was the uniform of the north. The pace of change was staggering and on still it swept, gobbling up every pocket of empty space it found.

Those desperate for employment clambered upon the towns and cities in their droves, toiling in deplorable conditions in order to survive – and help their masters' purses grow plumper. The social gap between rich and poor had never been wider, though only the one side suffering the effects of this seemed to notice or care.

Hastily built, poor-quality workers' houses, some

crumbling with age, a great deal damp and verminous, almost all bursting at the seams with as many folk as could be squeezed into them, squatted around the multitude of mills and factories. These vast buildings and disease-ridden slums alike, clogging the skyline with their spewing smokestacks, had changed the face of the landscape and its people for ever.

And yet . . . it was home. Despite the inequality, despite the hopelessness and the dankness, the filth, the stench, troubled times brought the struggling masses together. Kinships were formed and nurtured through shared hardship, *cherished*, in ways the more privileged could never begin to understand nor be fortunate enough to belong to. When one fell, they all did. It was the fact they helped each other back to their feet that made the difference.

'Have you allus lived here?' Jewel asked Louise now as they passed down a broad street thronged with carts and people.

'That's right. Eeh,' she repeated fondly, drinking in her surroundings, which brought to Jewel a pang of loss for her own town. 'Come on, this way.'

Gradually, they left the centre of the city behind. Streets of densely packed houses grew narrower, branching off every which way into dark lanes, courtyards and alleyways. When Louise stopped before a door in the heart of the squalid maze, Jewel's heart dropped to her toes.

Rotting refuse, mixed with human waste spilling from the nearby privies, sullied the cobbles and she struggled to hide a grimace. Unconcerned, filthy and ragged children played barefoot, their screeches ringing off the smoke-blackened bricks. Across the road, scowling men lounged against their houses, flat caps pulled low, and women in grubby aprons sat on door-steps gossiping. The misery and poverty were the stuff of nightmares.

Not wanting to offend the now-grinning girl, Jewel smiled back, though dread was coiling her guts.

Please, she prayed. *Please let inside be better.*

It wasn't.

In fact, as she followed Louise into the fetid hall and up a flight of stairs, she wished she'd stayed outside.

The girl made for a room with several fist-sized holes in the door, and Jewel's mood slumped further. When Louise threw it open, this time Jewel couldn't mask her disgust and had to press her nose into her shoulder to block out the stale smell.

Furnished with an unmade bed and two sagging sofas, there was barely space for anything else bar a small, wobbly-looking table in the centre. On this were two quart bottles of dark brandy, one full and one empty, and an uncovered pot of beef dripping, a fat black fly walking along its rim. A grubby sheet had been nailed to the window and no fire burned in the grate; the poor light added to the dinginess.

In short, it was a hovel. What a contrast to the spark-ling house she'd just left, where she'd hoped to have her child.

Lowering herself on to the bed, Louise sprawled out with a contented sigh, obviously pleased to be home – though, for the life of her, Jewel couldn't imagine why. 'Come in, then. Sit down.' She motioned to a sofa and, when Jewel was seated, raised herself on an elbow. 'The others must be out. No matter. They'll be back soon, no doubt.'

'How many do you dwell with?' asked Jewel, aston-ished she hadn't thought to query this until now.

'Only the four of us.'

Only? Four – five now she was to join them – in this one small room? *Dear God . . .*

'You'll have to make yourself up a bed of sorts in front of the fire. We'll figure blankets out later; I'm sure we'll find one or two to spare thee.'

Forcing her gaze not to swivel to the mucky flag-stones, Jewel nodded. 'I don't suppose there's a sup of owt going begging, is there?' she asked, her thirst winning through her unwillingness to partake of anything prepared in this room.

'Erm . . .' Looking around, Louise's eye fell on the strong spirit atop the table. She pointed at it, but Jewel shook her head and she shrugged. 'Please yourself. Happen there's some tea lying about somewhere . . . I don't know. You'll have to look.'

A furtive glance around showed Jewel that her search would be pointless. 'It's all right, it don't matter.'

'Please yourself,' the girl said again. Then she yawned loudly, turned over in the bed and promptly fell asleep.

For the next half an hour or so, not knowing what else to do, Jewel attempted to pass the time with rest, too. She turned and shifted on the sofa but the lumps and scratchy horsehair poking through the numerous holes in the material made it impossible to get comfort-able. Finally admitting defeat, she rose and went to seek out a teapot; her thirst was worse than ever. Not only that, she was now hungry, too. Just how did these people survive? How could they live like this at all?

'*Well.* See what we have here.'

Nose deep in a broken cupboard in the corner, which the dim light had failed to pick out upon her arrival, Jewel sprang around. In the doorway stood three women. Though each gave her a fleeting glance, none

219

spoke to her, instead turning their attention back to the girl snoring in the bed.

The eldest-looking of the trio spoke again: 'She's back, look. By, the size of her.'

'Aye,' a female a year or two older than Louise piped. She reached up to remove her hat, a gaudy-coloured item overly decorated with imitation flowers and stuffed birds, and tossed it on to the table. 'Like a sow, she is,' she added, her disdainful gaze running over Louise once more.

The third woman said nothing. Though her attire was plainer than the tawdry finery of her companions, her cheeks were rouged just the same, and the too-low bustline of her dress showed more than was decent. She crossed to the table and picked up the brandy bottle. Clearly from long practice, she glugged the fiery liquid without wincing. Wiping her mouth on her hand, she took a seat on a sofa.

'Lou?' The elder woman had crossed to the bed. She slapped the sleeping girl's thigh a few times, though without much force. 'Oi, come on, waken.'

'Hm? Oh.' Rubbing her eyes, Louise stretched like a lazy cat. 'Hello, Mam.'

Mam? Jewel's brows rose in surprise. Somehow, she hadn't imagined that Louise lived with her parents. Given her unconcerned attitude at returning home and what reception she'd receive regarding her keeping a lover and the resulting child, she'd assumed she dwelled alone or with friends.

'Hello,' the woman responded cordially, sitting on the edge of the bed. 'All right?'

'Aye. Mind, I'll be glad when this makes its appearance.'

Looking down at her daughter's stomach, she nodded, saying matter-of-factly, 'Can't be much longer, I'd say.'

Jewel had slipped to the other sofa and she viewed the scene with increasing puzzlement. She could see where Louise got her temperament. This woman's lack of any emotion was queer, to say the least. Despite their months of separation, they appeared not to have missed one another in the slightest; no hugs or affection at all, as if they were mere acquaintances who had bumped into one another in the street. That this indifference, from both, still carried when speaking of the baby was the most unnerving aspect of all. Thinking of her own mother, her lovingness and attentiveness, *their* meaningful relationship, Jewel just couldn't fathom these people.

'Didn't take thee long to come scuttling back home, did it, sis? What's up? Your fella grow bored of you, did he?'

Louise looked down at the grinning younger woman now sprawled across the foot of the bed. Like it was all some big lark, her own lips stretched in a chirpy smile. 'Shut it, you. If you must know, I got shot of him.'

'Huh!'

'I did, I tell you. The dirty dog were already wed.'

At the revelation, her sister doubled over, screeching with laughter, whilst their mother rolled her eyes with a chuckle. Even the third woman, still clutching the brandy bottle, shook her head and smiled.

'Hawked him right off, I did. It's all or nowt with me; I ain't being anyone's mistress, no thank you.'

'Ho! Don't knock it, love. All the perks and none of the drudgery? It suits me just fine.'

This, from Louise's sister, had Jewel's mouth falling open in shock. Not that anyone else seemed bothered by the shameless statement.

'Fancy him lying like that, though, eh? Carting me off to Bolton town as he did and for what? Nowt but lies and false promises. Swine.'

221

'Ay well, you weren't to know,' her mother told her with a shrug. 'He even had us fooled. You're home now, anyroad, so no harm done.'

No *harm* done? Was she really witnessing this or was it all some strange dream? Jewel genuinely began to wonder. No harm? A member of their family, barely an adult herself, was due to give birth to a married man's bastard. Could it *get* much worse than that?

'And who is that?' As though she'd just remembered she was there, the mother jabbed a finger towards Jewel.

'Oh, her.' Louise let her shoulders rise and fall. 'She had nowhere else to go.'

All eyes were on Jewel; she turned her attention to the mother, saying, 'I'll leave if you'd rather?' and almost wished that she would.

'Nay, you're all right.'

'Ta, thanks.'

'You're welcome, aye.' She eyed Jewel keenly for a few moments then, nudging Louise, added, ''Ere, she's a bonny 'un, your friend.'

'Lovely hair,' agreed her sister, stretching across to stroke Jewel's plait.

The attention brought pinkness to her cheeks. She smiled and lowered her head, and the three women shared a quiet laugh.

'You got any brass?'

'Not much after train fares.' Louise brought out a few coins and handed them to her mother. 'That's it.'

'Well, you'll have to come out later and earn some more. Us three have barely made a farthing betwixt us today – mind you, work's allus slow mid-week, eh? Happen you'll have more luck with that – get more takers, like.' She prodded her daughter's bump. 'Some have a taste for all sorts, after all.'

222

Releasing a tired sigh, Louise nodded nonetheless. 'Aye, all right.'

'Good. In t' meantime . . .' Her mother quickly counted the money then held it out to the brandy drinker. 'Nip down to the inn, Sarah, and get us each a penny pie. Pick us up a sup, an' all, whilst you're there.'

Putting down the bottle with some reluctance, the woman did as she was bid.

'Move up, our Lou.' Budging her across, her sister snuggled beside her beneath the covers. 'I hope Aunt Sarah ain't gone long; I want to grab some kip after my grub, ready for tonight,' she told them on a loud yawn. 'I'm fagged.'

Louise nodded agreement. 'I'd best do the same. That run earlier has left me spent.'

'What run?'

'Eeh, Julia, it were a close call,' she told her sister. 'Two bobbies, bloody hulking they were. I'd not have stood a chance of fighting them off in my condition.'

'Why, what occurred?'

'I decided I had to be shot of the child upon discovering what it's good-for-nowt father were about. But the baby farmer I sought out got her collar felt, that's what. I weren't for returning to Manchester 'til I'd got shot of the babby but, well . . . Today put paid to that, so here I am. Lucky we got away when we did, an' all, for we'd be languishing in a cell along with her, if you get my meaning.'

'Aye, you *were* fortunate, then. As for the child . . . Not to fret. We'll sort summat out when the time comes.'

Their mother nodded in agreement with Julia then added something to the conversation, but Jewel had already ceased listening. Her head felt muggy and her every muscle was rigid with horror-filled shock. '*Some have a taste for all sorts, after all . . .*'

223

My God. Oh, dear Lord in heaven . . . How had she not realised before?

The memory of Louise escorting that man down the ginnel in Bolton now held devastating clarity. She hadn't picked his pockets at all. He'd handed over his money willingly. And in return she'd . . . Jewel closed her eyes to the truth. *I suspected nothing, hadn't the slightest inkling . . .* Her face burned with foolishness.

These women were streetwalkers, and this their den of vice. She'd been so blind. Just what was she going to do? Leave? Where would she go? She knew nowhere, no one, here. She also hadn't a half-penny to her name, couldn't return to Bolton if she'd wanted – which of course she didn't, because what was there for her either? Oh, it was all such a *mess*!

'All right, Jewel?'

Jolting from her whirring thoughts, she brought her gaze to Louise. 'What? Aye. Aye, yes.'

'Happen you're short of a rest, too. I'll find you them blankets I promised once we've had our pies.'

The sheer hopelessness of her situation brought a choking sob and, before she could stem them, gushing tears broke from her to cascade down her face.

'Eeh. What's to do?' The girls' mother moved to her side and placed an arm across her shoulders, but Jewel couldn't help shrinking from the touch. It was neither cosseting nor comforting; never had she ached for her own mother more than she did now.

'Leave her be, Mam. It's been a fraught day is all. It's nowt a good kip won't remedy, I'll be bound.'

'Louise is right.' Forcing her pain down, Jewel flashed a watery smile – anything to reassure the older woman enough for her to remove her arm. 'I'm just tired, honest.'

'Here. Go on, take it.' Having picked up the bottle

from the table, she waved it under her nose. 'It'll calm your nerves.'

Past caring, Jewel took it from her and took a long draught. She heaved and spluttered, much to the others' amusement, but by the third swig her body got used to it and she closed her eyes, sipping at it now, welcoming the fuzzy warmth it brought.

*

When bone-numbing coldness dragged her from her stupor some time later, she at first hadn't a clue where she was.

Squinting through the darkness, she rose unsteadily from the sofa. The room was empty. She stood for a moment, unsure what to do, then crossed to the door.

Voices and laughter drifted from the adjoining rooms but of Louise and her family there was no sign. Jewel retraced her steps and dropped back on to the sofa, wincing as hammers of pain shot through her temples.

She put her head in her hand. Fancy getting herself into this state; what had she been thinking? How much of that brandy had she consumed? Enough, that's what. Lord, she felt rotten. Guilt added to the mix at movement inside her stomach. Sighing, she sent down a silent apology.

After several more minutes of waiting for the women's return to no avail, she swung her legs up and lay down. Nausea swooped then abated and she fell back into a fitful sleep.

'Nay, not Maxwell, lass. Mick's what I go by.'

Jewel's lips moved again and a frown accompanied the name when a hand stroked her hair.

'All right, then, call me what tha likes. I ain't much mithered, not really. Now, let's see these fresh young titties you've got for me.'

225

The gruff words slowly pulled Jewel back to the present. The clammy hand that sneaked inside her clothing and lifted out one of her breasts had her bolting upright as if she'd been scorched. Rigid with shock and horror and confusion, she could only gaze at the stranger's red, stubbled face.

'I'll not hurt thee. I'll suck them nice like Maxwell does—'

'Get your foul hands off me, you bastard!' Panting with fury, she lashed out with her fist but he caught her wrist before it could reach its mark. 'I said, leave *go* of me!'

'A regular viper, you are. Mebbe you like it rough instead, that it? Well, Mick don't mind that – prefers it, in fact.'

Before she had time to blink, the thickset man was on her, clawing at her chest, rubbery lips and ale-sodden breath on her neck. For a moment, overwhelming terror engulfed her. Then Benji's face, the feel of him on her body, the jumble of devastating emotions she'd suffered since and still did burst from her in a scream of such a pitch that the man jerked up to look at her in surprise. Jewel took her chance. Raising her knee, she struck with all her might.

Like a frozen corpse, he rolled from her, stiff face locked in shock, and crashed to the bare flags. Gasping and crying, she leapt away from him and bolted for the door. It opened as she reached out to grasp the knob and she let out another scream as she collided with Louise's mother. The woman grasped her arm to stop her from falling then, eyes wide, took in the scene before her.

'He . . . he . . . That filthy owd swine there tried . . . he tried to—'

'Sweet baby Jesus – look!' She cut off Jewel's hysterical

226

accusations to squawk to her daughters behind her. Pointing at the prostrate man, she doubled over, laughing, and the others followed suit. 'Bloody daft sod got his stick slapped!'

'Wha—?' Jewel was aghast as they stumbled past her and flopped down on the sofas, tears of mirth running down their faces. 'Did youse hear what I said? He tried—'

'All right, screechy. Bloody hell.' Bleary-eyed, Julia frowned across at her. 'You could waken the dead in their graves with that gob.'

'You gave him what for for his troubles, didn't yer, so no harm done,' added her mother.

Even Louise's voice carried a gin slur: 'Aye, no harm done,' she repeated.

Jewel was lost for words. Still gripped in the throes of shock and fear, she was trembling from head to toe, and now fresh tears of injustice and frustration burned her eyes. She shook her head slowly. 'What is *wrong* with you people?'

'"You people"?' Louise's head jerked up. 'Oh, like that, is it?'

'And what's that meant to mean?'

The girl pushed herself from the sofa and placed her hands on her hips. 'Don't you look down your nose on me and my family, Jewel. Don't you bloody dare. But for us, you'd be sleeping in the gutter the night with the sky pissing on your head!'

Jewel opened her mouth but the retort never came. She pursed her lips and breathed deeply. For as much as she hated to admit it, Louise was right. They *had* come to her rescue, hadn't they? They had taken her in when she'd had nowhere else to go. God help her, she was beholden to them. The truth deflated her. She dropped her gaze to the floor.

'You calmed down now?' asked Louise after some seconds.

She nodded. 'I'm sorry.'

'Forget it. Come on, come and sit down.'

Jewel crossed the space, avoiding looking at the still-prone man as she passed, and took a seat on the sofa furthest from him.

'He weren't meant for thee.' Louise prodded him in the ribs with the toe of her clog. 'He were told to wait up here for our return – bloody landlord pounced on us in the hall demanding late rent, you see. We didn't want this one growing bored and leaving, so sent him up in front. He must have spotted you and thought you were fair game, an' all.'

Jewel hid a shiver. 'Don't the landlord mind, then?'

'Nay, so long as he gets a cut of what we earn on top of the rent.'

'Oh.' It was all she could find in way of response. God above, were there any morally sound people in Manchester? she wondered. Not from what she'd seen so far.

'Right, then.' Louise heaved a sigh then nudged her mother. 'Rouse him, Mam, will thee? Let's get him seen to and on his way, then we can all get some shut-eye.'

'Aye, all right.'

The sisters watched in amusement as the older woman shook him awake. After much groaning and cursing, she'd managed to get him sitting up propped against the sofa. 'What were his name again?' she asked the girls, who both thought for a moment then shrugged.

'*Nay, not Maxwell, lass. Mick's what I go by.*' His words came back to haunt Jewel and she shuddered. However, she also knew a flush of shame, for how had he known the name special only to her unless he'd heard it from her lips? Had she spoken it in her sleep? Must have.

228

She'd clearly been dreaming about him again, though for the life of her she couldn't recall it. She was almost saddened by this. What she wouldn't give right now to see his face . . .

'Were it Rick?' proffered Julia.

'Mick,' Jewel murmured. 'His name's Mick.'

'Aye, that's the one.' Louise's mother nodded then shook his shoulder. 'Come on, Mick, my darling. Up tha gets.'

'Huh, where am I?' Seemingly unaffected by his topple to the hard floor – and, to Jewel's relief, holding no memory of it – he lifted his cap and scratched his head.

'Canal Street, of course.'

Squinting, he tried to focus on her face. 'Eh?'

'It's us, remember? We were supping with thee in t' Colliers Arms on t' corner?'

Slowly, his face cleared. He flashed a slack smile. 'Aye, that's right. 'Ere, the other one . . . Louise, her name were. Where's she, then?'

'I'm here, lovey.' Holding out her hands, she helped him to his feet. 'Let's get thee on t' bed, shall we? It's a sight comfier than this rotten floor.'

'Ay, aye.' A lustful growl escaped him as he pulled her closer. 'I fancy that, lass.'

'You sure you can manage it?' Julia called across with a grin.

Bobbing his head, the man puffed out his chest. 'You'd better believe it. Why, you up for joining us, like?'

Jewel had to swallow down her disgust – and it grew when the sisters turned to each other and shrugged.

'Cost thee double, mind,' piped their mother, eyes coming alive with the prospect of more money, and Jewel turned her face away with a grimace. Her very being was void of even the most basic of maternal instincts, had to be. *Lord, she really was deplorable.*

'There you are.' The man tossed several shillings on to the table. Swaying on the spot, he nodded once at her, and she nodded back. Then he held out his hands to her daughters.

Giggling, they led him to the bed.

After laying him down, Louise pulled across a length of curtain to afford them a modicum of privacy and, before she disappeared, she glanced across the room and her eyes met Jewel's. The ghost of a smile, one of reassurance tinged with dull acceptance, touched the girl's mouth. She broke the stare and returned to her customer.

The sounds that were soon reaching them from beyond the makeshift screen were unendurable – for Jewel, at any rate. Her utter mortification was absolute. In contrast, the older woman appeared totally unfazed.

Unable to bear it a second more, she rose, face ablaze, and took herself off to the landing. Shutting the door on the depravity, she closed her eyes and heaved a long, shuddering sigh.

'How was your pie?'

Jewel turned in surprise at the quiet words to find Louise's aunt sitting on the top stair. 'Sorry, what?'

'Your pie what I fetched thee. You fell asleep. Have you had it yet?'

'Nay, I . . . Nay.'

Sarah surveyed her in silence for a moment as she drank from the bottle she held. Then she asked, almost hesitantly, 'All right?'

'I'm not, as it happens.' Jewel could feel her temper rising to the fore. 'The goings-on in that there room, right now, as we speak . . . I, I just can't . . . !'

'Aye.'

'Do you have children, Sarah?'

The woman took another long swallow of brandy. 'Nay.'

'Would you … could *you* condone … encourage what your sister in there—?'

'Nay.'

Catching the spark of passion in her tone, Jewel felt a stirring of alliance. Studying the woman properly, she decided she was quite attractive. Unlike her sibling, her figure was slim, her hair free from grey and her skin of blemishes. Her eyes, however, could have belonged to someone twice her age. Dull green, as though life had faded from them long ago, they were strife-worn, deep with untold disappointments.

Jewel moved closer and motioned to the space beside her. 'Mind if I join thee?'

Sarah shook her head. When Jewel was seated, she glanced across at her stomach. 'You should eat, you know. For t' babby.'

'Aye. I am clemmed, if I'm honest. And by, what I wouldn't give forra sup of tea.'

'We've nowt to make a brew inside.'

'Nay.'

'Mind you, it'd not be much use if we did – we ain't got a teapot.'

Jewel couldn't help but chuckle. 'Bloody hell.'

They looked at one another and smiled.

Pushing the stopper in the top of her bottle, Sarah rose to her feet. 'Hang about, I'll not be a minute.'

She headed downstairs and Jewel heard her knock at someone's door. Muffled voices followed, then the door was shut and Sarah made her way back to the landing. In her hand, she carried a steaming mug.

Jewel was touched. 'For me?' she asked when Sarah held it out to her.

'Aye. Wench down there's a kind sort. Go on, sup up.'

Savouring every precious sip as though it were liquid gold, Jewel now watched the woman head for her own room. She emerged seconds later with a grease-stained parcel. Sitting back down, she handed it over.

The meat pie inside was hard and cold, the jelly congealed. In her ravenous state, Jewel had never tasted anything as delicious.

'Better?' asked Sarah when she'd finished the feast.

Jewel nodded. On impulse, she reached across and pressed the woman's hand. 'Thanks, Sarah.'

And somehow, Manchester and this whole situation didn't seem so terrible any more.

Chapter 16

LATER, AS A weak dawn was breaking above the city, Louise's pains began.

Woken by her groans, Jewel rose from the rag rug in front of the fire and padded to the bed. 'Louise? Have I to rouse your mam?'

'Nay . . . Aunt Sarah. Fetch Aunt Sarah.'

Over the next few hours, the two of them worked together. Whilst Sarah saw to the physical side of things, Jewel hovered by the head of the bed, dabbing Louise's hot and sweaty face and neck with a wet rag and offering words of comfort and encouragement.

Astonishingly, her mother and sister hadn't stirred – likely owing to their gin comas. They snored on, oblivious to it all.

Finally, on a long, beast-like grunt, Louise gave a last push. A grey-white object slithered from her body and into Sarah's hands. Heavy silence filled the room. The three women glanced at each other.

'Is it . . . ?' whispered Jewel.

Sarah placed her hand on the tiny child's chest. Then, frowning, she put her ear close to its nose. Slowly, her face cleared. She lifted her head and nodded to her niece. 'It breathes, but only just.'

Releasing a relieved sigh, Jewel squeezed Louise's hand. 'Thank God—'

'Pass it to me.' The new mother's interjection was toneless, flat.

Sarah looked from her to the child several times, eyes creased. 'Lass . . .'

'Pass it to me,' Louise repeated, firmer now. She held out her arms.

Lifting the almost pulseless piece of life gently, Sarah gazed down on it then, with a pained expression, turned her face away. Before handing it across, she nodded dully to Louise, and her niece returned it.

Jewel thought the girl would attempt to clear the child's mouth and nostrils, help bring life to its airways. However, Louise simply stared down into the perfectly formed, unmoving face, and tears sprang to Jewel's eyes. Louise believed it useless, that hope was gone, it was clear to see. Jewel's heart contracted for her, for though she hadn't intended on keeping it, Louise had wanted it to have a future, hadn't she? A bright one, aye, with people who would love it – why else had she been at the house in Lum Street? She waited for Louise to hold the child against her chest, soothe its passing as only a mother could but, again, she was wrong – Louise didn't do this either.

Instead, she laid the child on the bed in front of her. Then, looking with dead eyes straight ahead, she placed a hand over the baby's nose and mouth and pressed down.

It took a few seconds for Jewel to understand what was happening. With a cry, she grasped Louise's arm and tried to pull it away, but her hold was iron-strong. '*Louise*, please!'

'Come away, lass.' Taking Jewel by the shoulders,

Sarah tried to guide her from the bed, but she shook her off.

'Nay, I can't! I won't just stand here whilst she ... whilst she—!'

'It's for the best,' Sarah told her, taking hold of her again, and there was a catch in her voice.

'But ... Nay. *Stop*, Louise, *please*.' However, it was as if Jewel's words didn't have the power to touch her. Still staring in front at nothing, Louise remained unresponsive.

The child had put up no resistance. A small, thin leg twitched twice then was still. Louise removed her hand and closed her eyes.

'This is the kindest thing all round – lass, wait!' called Sarah as Jewel pushed her off savagely and ran for the door.

'Nay. Nay! It could have been adopted still, given a better life. She never even gave it a chance!' she shot over her shoulder before bolting from the room.

Blinded by tears, Jewel rushed down the stairs and out of the front door. Her legs took her up the street and around the corner until, overcome with sobs, she crumpled to the step in an inn doorway.

That poor child! How *could* Louise? As for Sarah condoning her actions ... They were all as bad as one another: wicked to the core. She had to get away from here. She wouldn't dwell amongst such evil. She *must* leave today, now. Go somewhere, *any*where!

'Jewel.'

She didn't lift her head from her hands. 'Leave me alone, Sarah.'

'You have to understand. That poor mite ...'

'You shouldn't have followed me. Just go on back, let me be—'

'Will you tell?'

'What?'

235

'What you've witnessed the day . . .' Sarah's voice dropped. 'Will you alert the authorities?'

Jewel's hands dropped slowly into her lap. She gazed up at the woman incredulously. 'That's all you're mithered about, in't it? God above!'

Sighing, Sarah perched on the step beside her. 'Think about it. What else was Louise meant to do?'

'She could have had it adopted out to a kind and caring—'

'Could she hell. You saw it: it were frail, lass. Likely wouldn't have survived the day.'

'So you're saying that smothering your own offspring is for the good, aye?'

'Aye, mebbe,' the woman murmured after a pause. 'For some, aye. I reckon she did that poor mite a kindness.' She sniffed then nodded. 'It were a girl, you know? The child were a girl. If, against all the odds . . . where d'you reckon it could well have finished up, eleven or twelve years from now? You've only to look at Louise and Julia to know.'

'You mean . . . ?' At Sarah's nod, Jewel lowered her head. 'Mother of God.'

'It could have followed the same path as them, its grandmother, *me*. That's no life, lass. No life at all.'

Jewel swivelled her gaze to look at her. Fresh lines scarred the woman's brow and a sea of misery shone from her eyes' depths. 'Why do you do it, Sarah?'

'To eat. To survive.'

'But there's other means of supporting yourself.'

'Not for the likes of me. No respectable employer wants an ale-soaked mess amongst their workforce.'

'Do you . . . enjoy it?'

Sarah released a soft and bitter snort. 'I endure it. That's all we can do.'

'Happen you could knock the bottle on the head, go straight, *find* yourself decent work—'

'And be alone with my demons? Oh nay. Nay, lass. The drink dulls what's in here.' She tapped her temple. 'And in here,' she added, repeating the action at her breast. 'Without it . . . Well. I'd not be on this earth for long, and that's the truth.'

Though tempted to ask what from her past plagued her so much she'd rather die than face the memories raw, Jewel didn't. Sarah would have revealed them if she'd wanted to and, besides, she had enough problems of her own at present to cope with anyone else's. Unsummoned, Louise's face flitted into her thoughts – and now, she saw the emotion behind the empty façade, the pain in the outwardly dead eyes. Jewel realised that everything Sarah had just said, Louise knew it, too. In the girl's mind, she hadn't murdered her child. She'd saved her. She wasn't heartless but hardened, and this life had made her so. Poverty brutalised folk. The sufferings for many of this cruel and unforgiving existence . . . it was just so unfair.

'I'll not tell,' Jewel heard herself say.

Sarah smiled softly with her eyes. 'Will you come back with me or are you for moving on?'

To where? Besides, she felt she owed it to Louise to stick around – for now, at least. She rose. Without another word, the two of them headed back to the house.

When they arrived, the child was gone.

Upon entering the room, Jewel's gaze had gone immediately to the bed but, in her absence, all trace of the birth had been removed. Someone had stripped the soiled sheets – clearly, they were the only ones they possessed, and Louise lay now beneath a few ragged shawls. Julia and their mother, pale faced on the sofa, sat smoking in silence.

Jewel made for the girl staring blankly at the mould-spotted ceiling. 'Louise?' she whispered, and as she'd expected received no response. 'I'm sorry. For everything.'

Slowly, Louise turned her back on Jewel and the room and curled into a ball.

'Leave her be,' said Sarah quietly. She patted the space beside her and, with a heavy heart, Jewel went to sit beside her on the other sofa.

*

That night, the women went out to work as usual.

Louise hadn't stirred once throughout the strained hours and now, alone with her, Jewel attempted to strike up conversation, hoping the girl might open up without the others' presence. She didn't. Though her eyes were closed, Jewel knew she wasn't asleep, and was eventually forced to give up. Nevertheless, she knew, sooner or later, Louise would have to face up to this. Keeping it all locked within would do her no good at all.

Later, as she lay in her hearth bed watching the flames of the low fire lick hypnotically over the coals, Jewel couldn't get the dead child's face from her mind. What had become of it? She'd managed earlier to pull Sarah aside and ask in a whisper of its whereabouts, but the woman had told her not to dwell on that, for it wouldn't change anything nor fetch it back.

Neither, Jewel knew, would there be any repercussions. In an age of high infant mortality, the death of a small child attracted little attention. Even when a baby's body *was* discovered and the circumstances were suspicious, it was often impossible to trace the mother.

Whatever the mite's resting place, Jewel just hoped it had found the peace it deserved.

Before sleep claimed her, something else Louise's aunt had mentioned came back to her, and she nodded in grim determination. If *her* child was to have any fighting chance, she must do all in her power to free it of this hopeless existence and have it placed with decent adoptive parents. To achieve that, but one thing stood in her way:

She would have to find the brass for it all over again, and fast.

Chapter 17

'WHAT, NOW? TODAY?'

'Aye, why not? Lust and loaves wait for no man.'

'But Louise, Christmas Day?'

Putting the finishing touches to her painted cheeks, the girl snorted. 'Oh, what? You reckon Jesus will be upset with me, is that it?'

'Don't talk daft. It's just . . . well, I thought we could spend the night together, relax and have a laugh, like. Wench downstairs lent me the borrow of some cards. There's only two missing from the pack; we could still enjoy a game. Besides, it's bitter out there. Why not stop in, eh? Stay warm by the fire?'

Louise's face softened slightly. She secured her hat in place with a sigh. 'We need the brass. Look, I'll try and be back a bit earlier, all right? 'Ere, and if I make enough, I'll fetch us back some hot chitterlings from the inn to eat whilst we play. That do thee?'

Knowing she would have to be satisfied with the compromise, Jewel nodded.

The festive day had been a long and lonely affair. Since awakening, her mother had dominated Jewel's thoughts, and with the hours the physical pain in her heart had only grown. Was Flora missing her just as much? she'd agonised, wishing so but hating herself for it, too. That she was causing her upset like this killed her inside a little more each day. Mam didn't deserve a daughter like her but one so much better.

The one small consolation was knowing that at least Flora wouldn't have been alone. Each year, her aunt and uncle insisted they spend the special day with them at the shop. And thankfully, she would also have eaten well. The Powells always went all out with the Christmas fare.

Now, at the thought of food, Jewel's stomach growled. The meagre spread of calf's-head broth and half-rotten vegetables that she and the women had had to look forward to this afternoon was barely sufficient to fill a bird. But, she reminded herself, at least she'd had *something* to tuck into, unlike many poor souls out there.

When the women had gone, she busied herself with tidying the frankly unimprovable room – anything to pass the time and distract her mind from those back home in Bolton. Since she'd begun lodging here, the cleaning had become her role – not that she minded. After all, with no income, she was living here rent free; the least she could do was keep the place decent whilst the others went out to work. However, there was only so much that water and a scrubbing brush could achieve.

The discoloured walls and the floor's cracked flags she couldn't improve the appearance of, however hard she worked. But at least now, her dogged determination was keeping the creeping, air-polluting mould at bay. Left unchecked even for a day or two and in it stole, leaving every corner and crevice damp and stinking. And the owner of the house, and millions like him, had the audacity to actually charge desperate folk – some, extortionate amounts, too – for living here in such health-destroying conditions. The despicableness of such blatant exploitation made Jewel's blood boil.

241

Having wiped down the mantel, she then swished her rag at a cobweb above with care, mindful of the crumbling plaster and fearful of an avalanche. One end of the silken thread stretched to the corner of the only picture to adorn the walls: a scuffed depiction of a vase of geraniums. Again, she flicked the duster – then swore quietly when the action dislodged the painting from its nail, sending it clattering to the floor.

Jewel retrieved it, relieved to see no further damage had befallen it. Yet as she made to fix it back into place, she paused. In the lighter-coloured rectangle of wall behind where it had hung was a ball of material, stuffed into a hole in the brickwork. She fingered it in confusion then, after glancing towards the door to check no one would return, she eased it out.

Measuring its weight in her hand, she frowned when its contents released a metallic jingle. Carefully, she pulled back the folds and peered inside.

In the following seconds, her eyes grew rounder and rounder as she counted the pile of coins. *Almost twenty-eight pounds.* What the devil . . . ? She'd never seen such an amount in her life. She staggered to a sofa and sat down heavily, mind spinning.

Again, she prodded in awe at the fortune – and her burning curiosity as to whom this astonishing find could belong was salved. Beneath the money was a small gold band holding a ruby stone. *Julia.*

This morning after breakfast, Louise's sister had donned her best hat and sauntered out for a brief clandestine meeting with her lover at the nearby inn. Her eyes had glowed like stars upon her return and, with a flourish, she'd waved her hand beneath their noses to show off her Christmas gift from the married man – the beautiful ring now sitting in Jewel's palm.

However, that didn't explain the money. Had she stolen it, saved it? Or was this also spoils acquired through being a mistress? Come to think of it, she *had* mentioned the role's perks once before, when Louise spoke derogatorily of the lifestyle . . . Bloody hell. And she'd been keeping it secret from everyone this whole time!

Jewel knew this to be true without question. Given her mother's clear hunger for money, no way would this hoard exist had she been aware of it. Only a few hours ago, after eyeing her daughter's ring for most of the day, she'd hinted at the pretty penny it would fetch at the pawnshop – no doubt why Julia had hidden this, too, behind the picture.

Well! Jewel couldn't help but smile in admiration. The woman had worked for it, she supposed. Though just what she had planned for it was another matter – and one which was really no concern of hers.

'In all sincerity, I wish thee the best of luck,' she murmured, securing everything back inside the material and heading to the wall. Then a sudden, heart-shattering thought crashed through her and she gasped.

Could a portion of this wealth have paid to find adoptive parents and save her niece's life? Happen if Julia had told of this money, given Louise a chink of hope, she wouldn't have felt driven to commit her desperate deed . . . ? But hadn't the child been sickly? And yet . . . Devastatingly, they would never know.

Nevertheless, to Jewel the money now felt tainted and she hurried to return it to its hiding place. The very touch of it against her palm made her flesh crawl with the what-ifs. After poking the bundle back between the bricks, she re-hung the painting and wandered back to her seat.

One thing she knew for certain: she couldn't mention it to Louise. After weeks of silent, inner grieving, she'd finally emerged from the darkness. Discovering something like this could set her progress back and cause her unnecessary further suffering – and besides, what would any of it achieve in the long run? The past couldn't be changed, and circumstances would remain just the same. Best all round she told no one of her find.

Falling and stumbling into the room hours later, laughing raucously, the women were not alone. Though Jewel wasn't surprised, her stomach dropped all the same. What she wouldn't give to climb into bed at a decent time and enjoy a sound and uninterrupted night's sleep for once, she thought, dragging herself into a sitting position on the rag rug.

Often, the streetwalkers would simply slip into the nearest dark ginnel with customers then return to the inns; back and to, back and to, throughout the night. Yet other times, such as now, they would fetch their work home with them, and Jewel was forced to wait out their lascivious exploits on the landing. She was almost always exhausted and was bone-weary of being part of this lifestyle. Something had to give, and soon.

'See, I didn't forget.' Louise wiggled her brows and smiled, waving a paper-wrapped package under her nose. 'Chitterlings. Get them down thee.'

Forcing a smile in return, Jewel took them from her, although she no longer had an appetite. She'd have much preferred the girl's company earlier instead, had felt more alone than usual today, given the occasion. However, she didn't voice her feelings. As much as she disagreed with the way her room fellows made their living, she was, after all, here on their charity – though being kept like this didn't sit well with her and she vowed to herself daily she'd repay their kindness somehow, one day.

244

'No need to run off, is there?' Louise's mother clamped a hand on Jewel's shoulder as she made to head out to the landing. Like her daughters and sister, her speech was slurred and her sight squinting. 'Stay awhile with us, enjoy the party.'

Eyeing the knot of men in the centre of the room, all in a similar state to the women, Jewel shook her head. 'No, ta.'

'Ay, come on. Oh no you don't,' the older woman added on a guffaw as Jewel tried to swerve past her. 'Now I'll not take no for an answer. Sit down here, aye. Well, go on, then!'

Having drawn the attention of the others – all except Sarah, who had slipped away with one of the males to the curtained-off bed – she encouraged them to help her in persuading Jewel, which they did with gusto. Outnumbered and not wishing to appear churlish, Jewel was forced to accept. Suppressing a sigh, she went to sit on a sofa.

Almost immediately, a young man with smouldering good looks and arrogance to match sauntered over and took the space beside her. She returned his slow grin with a tight smile then fixed her attention across the room in the hope he'd get the message and not attempt conversation. No such luck.

He leaned in and nudged her playfully with his shoulder. 'All right?'

Nodding, she discreetly inched away.

'Them smell good.'

She glanced to the food she still held and had forgotten about. 'Here. Have them.' At least if he was busy eating, he wouldn't be talking to her.

'Aye?'

'Yes, go on.'

'Ta very much. You'll have some, mind, won't thee?'

'Nay, I'm not—'

'But you must. I'd not enjoy it else. I can't swipe a lass's supper from her and scran the lot myself, now can I?'

Biting back an irritated retort, she shrugged in defeat. *God above, anything for a quiet life.*

On the next sofa, Julia and her mother sat straddling two men in their middle years. Julia's customer had exposed her breasts and was trying to coax her mother to kiss them – both women were helpless with laughter. Swallowing down her disgust, Jewel scanned the room for Louise. She spotted her and a grey-haired man slouched in the corner, backs against the wall, kissing passionately. When the bedsprings began their rapid squeaking, intermingled with the gruff moans of Sarah's customer, Jewel had had enough. She rose abruptly.

'Where you going?' asked the man beside her. He attempted to catch her hand but she pulled it from his reach.

'I'll not be long,' she lied. She had no intention whatsoever of returning until, lusts spent, the males had all buggered off home where they belonged.

'Scuttling off so soon?' Louise's mother yelled across. 'By, I thought you were enjoying yerself?'

Jewel didn't answer. Head down, she hurried her step. However, the moment she opened the door the man she'd been sat next to pressed it shut again from behind with the flat of his hand. She hadn't heard him follow her and, frowning, she turned to face him. 'What—?'

'Stay awhile,' he said thickly, cutting her off.

'I told thee, I'll not be long.' She pulled at the door

246

knob but it didn't budge; his hand was still there, preventing her from escaping. 'Shift,' she said as calmly as she could, though, inside, panicked anger was rising.

'Sit back down forra bit first,' he wheedled, moving in close to nuzzle her neck.

The slap she delivered to the side of his head had Louise's mother roaring with laughter. It turned into a coughing fit and, gasping for breath, she flapped a hand at Jewel. 'Here, that's it, aye – he's partial to a good spanking.'

Ignoring her, Jewel brought furious eyes back to the unfazed man, who was rubbing the spot she'd struck, smiling. Her words came through gritted teeth: 'Let me go.'

'No.'

'What d'you mean, no? You bleedin' well will or else—' The rest of her speech was smothered in his kiss. Rearing back, she pushed hard against his chest. In the next moment, her feet swept out from under her as he lifted her bodily from the ground and, whistling like this was some big joke, carried her back to the sofa. 'Get *off* me! Nay, leave me be!'

'Calm down, for God's sake,' he said on a chuckle, dropping her down on the seat and climbing on top of her. 'Whores like you should be grateful for a fella like me.'

'Leave go of her.'

Gasping in sheer relief at the sound of Sarah's command, Jewel pleaded with her as she struggled beneath him: 'Oh, Sarah, help me. Please!'

'Keep your snout out, you,' Louise's mother piped up. 'It's fair time that one began paying her way around here, I reckon.'

'Aye, too true,' threw in Julia.

247

Good God, they had set this up? Jewel felt sick with betrayal.

'Nay.' Sarah's voice was firm. 'She ain't rotten like us. And that's how it's staying.'

'Is that so? And what's that, then, growing in her belly? The next Lord and Saviour?'

Ignoring her sister's remark, Sarah turned back to the man. 'Off her. Now!'

Finally, mumbling profanities, he shifted his weight. Jewel could barely breathe with relief as she wriggled out from under him and ran into Sarah's arms. She clung to her, shaking uncontrollably.

'Come on.' Sarah guided her to the door and, now, no one tried to prevent Jewel's exit.

Julia had returned her attention to her customer. Though her mother and the thwarted man shot daggers at Jewel, neither said anything further. As for Louise, in her drunken stupor beneath the man now ravishing her body, she was oblivious to it all.

'Where will I go?'

They had paused on the landing. Sarah gnawed her lip for a moment in thought. Then she nodded. 'Wench downstairs will take thee in the night, don't fret.'

'And the morrow?' Jewel's throat was thick with tears. 'Sarah, what the hell am I going to do?'

'Shh. Come. Things won't seem so bad in t' morning, they never do.'

*

To Jewel's surprise, Sarah's prophecy bore fruit. She awoke in the strange dwelling the next day to find Louise standing over her.

'You all right?'

'Aye.'

'Mam were wrong fetching that fella back for thee.'

248

'Mebbe, but . . .' Jewel shrugged. 'She's right, though, in't she? I should be paying my way.'

'Well, they ain't out of pocket none, are they? I'm the one tipping up extra brass for thee.'

'All right, well, it ain't right *you* keeping me, then.'

'What you saying?'

Jewel held out a hand and, when Louise had helped her to her feet, she nodded determinedly. 'I'm for finding myself employment. I'll pay youse back somehow.'

'Don't be daft. Who'll take you on in your condition?'

'I ain't an invalid, Louise. There's plenty I can manage. Besides, I ain't so big yet, am I?' Looking down at the neat globe of her stomach, she pursed her lips. 'Happen I could still conceal it for now . . .'

'Where will you ask, like?'

Again, Jewel shrugged. 'The inns or shops, see if any require a skivvy. It's worth a try. 'Ere,' she added suddenly, face brightening. 'Happen you could enquire along with me.'

'Me?' The girl was genuinely surprised at the suggestion. 'But I know nowt.'

'You could learn. What have you got to lose? Surely to God, Louise, you can't enjoy what you're doing now.'

A defensive look crossed her face then slowly melted into one of despondency. 'Course I don't. I mean, sometimes it ain't so bad with the sound sorts. It's the others, the dirty buggers with a fancy for filth, who spoil it. Relations with *them* I can't stand.'

'Well, then. I know it's Boxing Day, but there's bound to be a few places open.' The Bank Holidays Act, passed two years before, was designed to ease the pressure on workers. However, some family-run businesses, unwilling to lose a day's earnings, chose to ignore it. 'So?' she pressed. 'You'll come out looking with me?'

There was a long hesitation, then: 'Aye, if you like.'

Jewel smiled, filled with hope. She'd failed to convince Sarah there was another way, but now, just maybe . . . Oh, if only she could help Louise free herself of this life her feckless mother had normalised for her, she'd feel her time here had meant something after all.

'We've got bacon going on t' fire. You coming up?'

With thoughts of facing the others, Jewel's mood dipped. 'What about your mother, Julia?'

'It's all right; there's enough bacon for us all.'

'I weren't talking about the grub, and you know it.'

Louise flashed a grin. 'Forget about all that, now, eh? Mam has.'

How very noble of her – she's the one in the wrong, not I! thought Jewel, bristling. But she kept quiet. Louise was trying to be peacemaker and she wouldn't throw it back in her face. However, if Louise's mam ever pulled another trick like the one last night, Jewel knew she wouldn't be responsible for her actions. No one got to mistreat her like that twice and get away with it.

'Come on, then. I'm clemmed.'

After thanking Sarah's friend for her kindness in putting her up, Jewel followed Louise upstairs. When they entered, neither Julia nor her mother, who were huddled around the fire nursing thick heads from last night's gin, looked up. Nor did they make mention of Jewel's assault, and she was inclined to follow suit, preferring not to converse with them now, anyway, unless necessary.

'All right?' Sarah mouthed across to her as she sat down, then winked softly when Jewel nodded.

'Where you off to, then?' Louise's mother asked her a little after breakfast when she and Jewel donned their shawls – Jewel's being an old one of the girls' given to replace her own left behind in Bolton; she was grateful for it as the weather grew more bitter with the shortened days – and headed for the door.

Louise hesitated before answering. 'Forra walk.'

'A walk?' sniggered Julia. 'Since when did you go for walks?'

'Since now, all right, so shut tha trap,' Louise snapped, and Jewel saw her confidence about their job search begin to wane.

'Come on, then,' she urged before Louise could change her mind. 'Fresh air will do us good.' She waited until they had reached the street before asking, 'Why didn't you tell them the truth about where we're going?'

'I don't know. Happen in case they laughed?'

A wave of sadness for this girl and the horrid lifestyle she had only ever known washed through Jewel. She brought her to a stop and took both her hands in hers. 'You deserve more than this. You're *better* than this – better than the pair of them back there, an' all – and don't you forget it.'

Louise blinked with an expression of slight puzzlement, as though Jewel had spoken another language she hadn't understood. Though Jewel knew she was likely at a loss how to respond. Evidently, she'd severely lacked any form of support or encouragement throughout her life.

'Shall we try there first?' Jewel pointed to a boot mender's up ahead. 'What d'you reckon?'

'Do I look presentable?'

'Aye,' she was able to answer truthfully; Louise spared the rouge and ostentatious headwear during the day. 'You'll be fine,' she encouraged, sensing the girl's nervousness. 'Just be polite. Oh, and don't forget to smile.'

Despite their best efforts, they were no closer to finding employment two hours later. Thirsty and tired, their

251

teeth clacking from the cold, they eventually drew to a halt with simultaneous sighs.

'We could allus try again the morrow,' suggested Jewel, though her words held little enthusiasm.

'Aye, come on. I'm frozzen.'

Each place they had tried either already employed a scrubbing girl or they took one look at Jewel's full stomach and empty ring finger – though she did her best to hide both – and quickly sent them on their way.

'I'm for thinking, Louise, happen you'd be best going out by yourself next time. I'm just hindering your chances with my condition. You'd fare better at finding summat were I not with thee.'

'Nay, I—' But the girl didn't get to finish her sentence, for a voice behind them stole their attention:

'Miss Nightingale?'

Halting in cold shock, Jewel turned slowly.

'Why, it *is* you, Miss Nightingale! Hello!'

Good God in heaven. No . . .

'I believed at first that my eyes were deceiving me, but no. What are you doing here?'

'Well, I . . .' Trying desperately to hide her bump beneath the folds of her shawl, Jewel cleared her throat. 'I didn't know you hailed from Manchester, Mrs Kirkwood.'

'Yes, yes.' She held up the wicker basket she carried, filled to the brim with provisions. 'I'm out delivering alms to the needy. So many poor wretches of this city without even a crust of bread most days . . .' Voice soft with compassion, she shook her head. 'A travesty, oh indeed.'

'That's kind of thee, Mrs Kirkwood.' And Jewel meant it. Not many from the privileged classes gave such consideration to their less fortunate counterparts. Mind you, this lady had shown herself to be sound-hearted since the day they had met, hadn't she? She was certainly a rare breed. 'Oh, I wanted the opportunity to say,' Jewel added suddenly as the thought occurred, 'ta ever so for them pictures you got me back in Mawdsley Street. Reet bonny, they are, and brighten the kitchen walls up no end.'

'Oh, you're most welcome. We must spread happiness where we can.' She motioned to the basket to reiterate her beliefs and smiled. Then: 'So, Miss Nightingale?' she pressed. 'What *are* you doing here?'

'I . . . I'm in Manchester caring for a sick aunt. Aye. Mr Birch, he kindly gave me leave. But he's gorra new lass to tend to his household until I return,' she was quick to reassure her.

'I see. Well, I do hope your aunt regains good health soon,' the lady offered sincerely. Her eyes then flickered to Louise with interest.

'This is . . . my cousin, Mrs Kirkwood. She's seeking new employment and, as my aunt was comfortable and sleeping, I offered to accompany Louise in her search.' Jewel's heart was beating so fast she could barely feel it. The lies were tripping from her tongue and she knew that, unless she cut this astonishing meeting short, and soon, she'd slip up and all would be lost. *Take your leave of us, Mrs Kirkwood. Please, please . . .*

'Do you have experience of being in service?' Mrs Kirkwood had turned her smiling face to Louise. 'It just so happens that friends of mine, who reside not too far from here, are currently an under-housemaid short. I could put you in touch with them if you'd like?'

'Ay, ma'am. You'd do that for me?' The girl's face was alight with amazement.

'Why, of course.'

'Oh. But . . .'

253

'Yes?'

'I've never done maid work afore. Happen they'll want someone what don't require training.'

'Hm, perhaps. But there is no harm in trying. Would you like the address? You may, of course, mention that I recommend you for the position.'

Louise glanced to Jewel, who nodded encouragingly. 'Can I ask, ma'am, d'you know what the wages will be?'

Jewel shot the girl a warning look, but she ignored her. *Fancy asking summat like that of the lady!*

'Oh, I . . . I'm afraid I couldn't say. That would, naturally, be at your employer's discretion—'

'But if you had to hazard a guess?' the girl persisted. 'What's the going rate, like?'

'Louise.' Jewel tried to communicate again with her eyes. 'Mebbe don't put these questions to Mrs Kirk—'

'I need to know is all.'

'I suppose, initially,' intervened the lady, though it was evident she found the topic somewhat unorthodox, 'I would place the figure at around ten pounds per annum.'

Louise did a quick calculation on her fingers. She lifted her head slowly. 'But that's not even a pound a month. Me, toil morning noon and night for less than five shillings a week? Huh! Sorry, but no thank you!'

The ensuing silence was deafening. Mrs Kirkwood had blushed a soft pink. Jewel, on the other hand, was scarlet with mortification. Hand on hip, Louise looked from one to the other with an incredulous arch of her eyebrow.

The ungracious, thankless young . . . ! 'Lou*ise*,' Jewel hissed through the side of her mouth. 'God above—'

'Oh, I meant nowt by it – honest, I'm grateful to thee for wanting to help,' she added to Mrs Kirkwood. 'It's just, well, at the moment, I can earn that in a single shift on a good day.'

Mother of God. Jewel's hand crept up to cover her burning face. *You foolish bloody idiot! Why would you say that? Now she knows . . . she knows . . . !*

'Is that so?' Mrs Kirkwood's lips had stiffened slightly in understanding. 'Then I don't think there is anything further to discuss.' To Jewel, she continued with a small frown, 'Well, I must get on with my house calls. Good day, Miss Nightingale.'

'Goodbye, Mrs . . .' But the lady was already striding up Great Ancoats Street. Cringing, Jewel buried her face in her shawl. 'My *God.*'

'What's the matter with thee?'

'What's the *matter*? That was the sister of my employer back in Bolton. What d'you think she'll say when she sees him next? How d'you think *he'll* react to hear of the company I've been keeping in my absence? He'll dismiss me for this, for certain.'

'I don't see how. I didn't make mention of how exactly I make my living—'

'Oh, wake up, Louise!' Hands bunched into fists, Jewel trembled with anger. 'Someone of your standing – *our* standing – fetching home such a sum as five shillings a day? How else would that be possible?'

The girl thought for a moment then shrugged. 'Aye, all right. Happen I shouldn't have said it.'

'Nay, that's correct, you shouldn't. And your rudeness, to boot! She went out of her way to help you, and what did yer do? You threw it back in her face. I'm so bloody disappointed in thee. I thought you wanted to change things, improve your life?'

'Aye well. Not for a pittance, I don't.'

Jewel closed her mouth. What was the use? However

255

much she could argue the point, it would make no difference. Her advice was falling on deaf ears and she
hadn't the energy for it any more. Sod her. Let her live
a life of debauchery for ever more. She was done.

'Domestic service, mill work, scrubbing shop bleedin'
floors . . . it might pay poorly to your standards, aye. But
d'you know what, Louise?' Her voice shook with quiet
passion. 'You can't put a price on respectability.'

Louise said nothing.

After a last look in the direction Maxwell's sister had
disappeared in, Jewel sighed and headed back towards
Canal Street.

Chapter 18

FEBRUARY WINDS BLOWING in across the River Irwell throttled the house, breathed its dull howl down the chimney and rattled the windows in their rotten frames. On her bed of rags before the long-dead fire, Jewel gritted her teeth against another spasm.

Over the past hour, the dragging ache in her lower back had spread around the front and now, spears of fire were attacking her stomach at regular intervals. Running a hand over the taut mound, she swallowed hard. Then, once more, she began to pray.

'Jewel?'

She blinked through the thick darkness. It couldn't be. Her senses were skewed; she'd imagined it. It *couldn't* be.

'Lass, are you awake?'

'Mam?' The name fluttered through Jewel's lips like a mist on the breeze.

Footfalls sounded, drew nearer, grew still close by. 'Has it started?'

'Mam . . .'

'It's Sarah, lass. Hang about, now, whilst I fetch a candle.'

An amber flash split the air. Squeezing shut her eyes, Jewel turned her face from its luridness.

'You're as pale as tripe. Why didn't you alert one of us? Is the pain bad?'

'I want my mam.'

The woman sighed. Placing on to the table the tin plate holding the candle, to allow the guttering light to illuminate a wider area, she said soothingly, 'You'll have to make do with me, but I'll see you through this, fret not. I'll not stray from your side.'

'It's not . . . time.'

'How early are thee?'

Another pain ripped through Jewel. She panted through it before answering. 'A month. Mebbe six weeks.'

'Well, the babby's not looking like it's for stopping put, so we'll have to make the best of it. Now, I'm just going to lift your skirts and see what's occurring. All right?'

'Aye.'

Kneeling before her, Sarah threw the folds of material back and removed her underclothes. She reached for the candle and brought it near – then let out a short, sharp gasp. 'Oh, hell's teeth!'

'What? What is it?'

The woman rose slowly. The candlelight fell across her face and Jewel saw it was now white with worry.

'Sarah?' she pressed.

'It's like this, lass. The child's coming out in an unnatural position. I just . . . I ain't never seen the like afore, I . . .'

'Unnatural?' Prickles of fear journeyed down Jewel's spine. 'How?'

'An arm, it . . . it's out. There's an arm. I can see it.'

Too stunned to speak, unable to process the statement, Jewel simply stared at her open-mouthed. Then another blade of agony tore through her insides, making her scream, and this seemed to jolt Sarah's senses.

'Right.' She nodded wildly. 'All right, erm . . . Oh God, what to *do* . . . ? Nay, mustn't panic. Ah, I know. I know!'

She leaned in close and, breathing heavily with anxiety, stroked Jewel's hair. 'I'm going to have to leave thee just forra short while—'

'Nay! Sarah, please—!'

'Lass, I *must*. Look see, the others shall keep watch whilst I'm away,' she added, glancing around the room to where the women were sitting up, roused by the ruckus. 'I'll be as quick as I can, I swear it.'

'But where are you going?' whimpered Jewel before yet another contraction gripped her: 'Oh, Mother of *God*, it hurts so much!'

'I know, my lovey. Eeh, I must go!' Scrambling to her feet, Sarah tore towards the door and was gone.

The intensity of the pain was stealing Jewel's faculties. Pins of light popped behind her eyes and all sound faded. She was vaguely aware of Louise and her sister and mother crowding around her but she couldn't talk or move at all. Then an aged face appeared through the dim light. The mouth smiled, and something within the eyes' grey depths brought a whisper of comfort. They spoke of wiseness, life experience and of trust. And somehow, she knew she was in safe hands.

'There were only one person whose professional services I could call upon,' said Sarah, dropping to her knees again by Jewel's side. 'This here's Minnie Maddox, and she's going to help thee through this, God willing. If anyone can, it's her.'

'Lass?' The voice was soft but assured. 'How are you feeling?'

'Please . . . Help me, Mrs Maddox.'

'No hysterics. They'll do no one any good. Deep breaths. Now tell me, how do you feel? Are the pains strong and frequent?'

'Aye.'

259

'And what's the pain like?'

'Knives,' Jewel forced out through her teeth.

'Where?'

'My back and stomach.'

'Between your legs also? Is there much pressure?'

'I don't think so. Nay.'

Minnie nodded. Rolling up her sleeves, she turned to Sarah. 'Pass me my bag, lass. The rest of youse,' she told the other women, 'move back, now. Give the girl some air.'

'Will I die?' whispered Jewel as the wizened woman returned her attention to her.

'I'll do my best for you. You have my word.'

Inexplicable terror gripped Jewel in its jaws. 'And the child?'

'We'll see.'

For the next few minutes, Minnie worked in silence. She examined between Jewel's legs then felt her bump, pressing firmly all over. Finally, she reached inside her bag and brought out a spool of thick twine.

'What's to be done, Minnie?' asked Sarah.

'What we have here is an obstructed labour. As you've seen, the left hand, arm and shoulder are presenting. They need pushing back up, then we rotate the child so as it can be delivered breech. Risky, I grant you, but it's the only way. Left much longer, the shoulder will get lower and the chest will become wedged in the pelvic cavity. If that occurs, the baby will suffocate, and the lass could suffer a rupture.'

'Will tha turn the child by massaging the lass's stomach, then?'

'Nay. It must be an internal rotation.'

Every woman emitted a collective breath, though, in her semi-delirious state, Jewel failed to understand why, couldn't make sense of anything much.

'Oh 'eck,' Sarah murmured shakily. 'Have you performed this afore, Minnie?'

'Not me, but I've witnessed it.'

'And . . . was it successful?'

The woman was silent for a moment. 'Nay.'

'Oh 'eck,' Sarah repeated.

'But, as I vowed to the lass here, I'll do my best. Mind,
if the child does pull through, the trauma will likely
leave it with abnormalities.'

'I don't care a fig about that.' The words left Jewel's lips
of their own accord. 'Just save it. Please save my baby.'

Minnie's eyes creased. Then, squaring her shoulders,
she nodded once. 'You feel to be dilated enough, so . . .
let's get to work.'

'What can I do to help, Minnie?' Sarah asked.

'Fetch some lard.'

Sarah hurried off to borrow from the wench downstairs what Minnie had requested. Meanwhile, Minnie
busied herself making a slip noose with the twine from
her bag.

Sarah returned triumphant, and Minnie liberally
slathered her left arm in the greasy white substance.
Then she grasped the baby's limb and slowly, carefully,
passed it back inside Jewel. This done, she took the
noose and once more inserted her hand. Pursing her
lips, she pushed up inside the uterus to the elbow, and
Jewel's terrible screams rebounded off the walls.

'Be still as you can, lass,' Minnie murmured, face
wreathed in concentration. 'Almost got it . . . There. It's
done.' When finally she extracted her arm, she still held
in her hand a length of the twine. Only, now, the noose
end was inside and had been passed around the baby's
foot and secured around the ankle.

'What's next?' panted Jewel, doing her utmost to

remain brave, though she was convinced she was dying. She had to be; it wasn't humanly possible to experience this level of pain and survive, surely?

'Now comes the internal rotation, lass. You're doing reet well, but I'll need to use two hands for this so brace yourself.'

As Minnie lubricated her other arm, Jewel scrunched her eyes tight shut. In her mind, she prayed to God, and to her earthly father, Fred, to keep and protect her. All the while, she wished with all that she was that her mam was here. She'd have given anything for it to be so. *Anything.*

After taking a long deep breath, Minnie now inserted her right hand. Further, further she continued to push, manoeuvring the child up and around. Then she inserted her left hand still holding the twine again, and tugged the foot downwards.

If Jewel had thought the agony couldn't get worse, she was mistaken. It increased in violence by the second and, though her voice screamed on, she felt herself slipping away. This must be what disembowelment was like. It truly felt as if her viscera were being hacked from her with hot blades. She couldn't keep her lids open, was leaving this place, dying . . .

'Thanks be to God, the other foot has followed.' Minnie's words scratched on the outskirts of Jewel's brain. 'Right, lass. Lass? I know you're exhausted but come, you must wake up.'

Jewel blinked up into her worried face. 'I can't. I'm . . . finished.'

'Nay, you ain't. Now listen. The child is in the breech position. The feet are out already and, when your next pain comes, I want you to push for me. All right?'

'Can't . . .'

'Yes, you *can*. We're nearly there.'

The familiar scorch built and tore through her body. Lifting her knees, Jewel thrashed her head from side to side.

'Push! Push!'

Bearing down with all her might, she released a high-pitched shriek to the ceiling. A gush of warm liquid spilled from her, then the child forced its way out. Crying and laughing in sheer relief, she grasped at the air with hungry hands. 'Give it to me. Give me my baby.'

'It's a girl.' Grinning from ear to ear, Minnie placed the slippery, squawking infant on her chest.

Jewel gazed in open-mouthed infatuation at the miracle in front of her. 'Is she . . . ? Is there anything . . . ?'

'There don't appear to be any damage to the child,' Minnie told her. 'Mind, I'll check her over in a minute. You enjoy her awhile first.'

'Eeh, lass.' Sarah put her cheek, damp with tears, against Jewel's.

'My daughter, Sarah. I have a daughter.'

'Aye, you do.'

Memories reached her of the birth that had taken place in this very room not so long ago, and she glanced around in search of Louise. Their eyes met, and the girl smiled without a hint of bitterness for her own lost child. Jewel returned it then gazed up at the elderly woman to whom she owed so very much.

'Mrs Maddox, I don't know what to say, don't know how I'll ever be able to thank thee—'

'There's none needed. I'm glad I could help, aye.' She motioned to the baby. 'Shall I have a look at her, then, see that she's well?'

Nodding, Jewel handed her over. Though she knew that no matter if something – anything – did ail her,

263

physically or mentally, she couldn't love her less. And love her she did, more than she'd ever dared believe. Benji and all that went with it meant not a thing any more. *Her child, and hers alone . . .*

'Norra thing wrong with her, as far as I can see,' Minnie eventually announced with some amazement. 'You, lass, could do with tending to, mind. Glory be to God, you didn't bleed too heavily; though you tore quite a bit, aye. You'll be tender forra good few weeks, I'm betting.'

'I'll patch her up, Minnie,' said Sarah.

'You sure?'

'Aye, I know what to do. You go on home and get some rest and take my true and honest thanks along with yer. I don't know what we'd have done without thee.'

After seeing the woman out, Sarah reached beneath her skirts into the cloth pouch attached to a length of string around her waist and extracted some coins. She handed them to her sister. 'Here. Youse three go and get a bite and a sup at the inn whilst I clean the girl up, like.'

The women didn't need telling twice and after donning their hats took their leave – though Louise did give Jewel a last small smile before following the others out.

With the help of a little brandy to take the edge off, Jewel bore the stitching. When Sarah was done and had helped her into the bed, Jewel held out her arms eagerly. The child was placed into them and she breathed easier.

'She's a bonny 'un, all right,' murmured Sarah, gazing down at her. 'Do you have a name yet?'

'Nay.' Jewel's tone was quiet but firm. 'Nor will I bestow one. That's summat for her new parents to decide.'

'Oh, I see. That's what you're intending, then?'

'It is. What can I give her? Love just ain't enough, Sarah. It ain't.' Tears thickened her throat. 'She deserves a home, regular food in her belly, decent clothes on her back. A proper family, with a mother *and* a father. She'll not get them from me. What Louise felt she had to do . . . this is me doing the same. Sparing the suffering. Putting my child first.'

'For what it's worth, I agree.'

A little of Jewel's guilt subsided. 'You do?'

'Aye. It's the one, most selfless gift a parent in our position can give. Trust me, you're doing the right thing.'

The love that this life had awakened in Jewel was like nothing she'd known before or would ever have thought possible. Now, she was more determined than ever that her daughter would have the very best future she could deliver. And she'd do everything in her power to see that it happened. Whatever it took.

Her eyes flicked to the painting of the geraniums. She lifted her chin with resolution. *Whatever it took.*

'Sarah? Do you know of anyone who can help?'

'With getting the child adopted?'

'Aye.'

'But where in the world would you find the brass?'

Jewel glanced away as she sought to think up something feasible. But, of course, she couldn't. All the women knew she hadn't two farthings to rub together. The child arriving early had only complicated matters further. She'd still been holding on to the hope that she'd find some mode of employment before it made an appearance, and that she'd be able to put money aside for this very eventuality. Anything would have been better than nothing; she'd have begged the procurers on her knees to consider dropping their fee, to take instead what she would have had to offer. She couldn't do that now, could she? You couldn't barter a deal with nothing.

'I don't know,' she was finally forced to respond. 'But say I did have the means? *Is* there anyone you know of?'

'Aye.'

'Eeh, that's great. Who?'

'Minnie.'

'Mrs Maddox, really?'

'Really,' Sarah murmured.

A sob caught in Jewel's throat. For the first time in a long time, she saw a ray of happiness on the horizon. 'I can think of no one else I'd rather go to. After what that woman did for us the day . . . I know she'd do me – do the baby, here – right.'

Sarah's words were softer still. 'Aye, she would.'

Left alone soon afterwards to get some rest, Jewel allowed herself to dream of the tantalising possibilities not too far from her reach. She envisioned a handsome lady tenderly cradling the child, whilst her husband looked on with an adoring smile. She saw her daughter through the years, shiny-haired and pink-cheeked with health, watched her slip from infant to youth into woman-hood without a moment's want or strife. A future worth the living, as she deserved. And yet . . .

Jewel tried her best to dispel another image that had crept in amongst the rest, but it refused to leave her. It was of herself falling to her knees, hand out-stretched in desperation to the retreating backs of the couple carrying her baby away. No matter how hard or how long she screamed, they didn't seem to hear and continued on, taking their precious cargo out of her life for ever . . .

Throat thick, chest heavy, eyes burning with the

266

searing pain of it all, she shook her head. 'Nay,' she told the room on a shaky growl. Then louder: '*Nay.*'

She wouldn't ruin this for the child. She refused to allow her own selfish yearnings to win through, to dominate her decision, affect her daughter's destiny.

That truly would be a cruelty she'd never recover from.

Chapter 19

AS THE PASSING days slipped into weeks, life in the small, cramped room in Canal Street became intolerable.

Though Jewel hadn't expected the women to cease their drunken, nocturnal antics upon the baby's arrival, she had hoped they would curtail them somewhat. But if anything, things seemed to have grown worse.

At least if they had limited their work to the back-street adjoining the inn, things wouldn't have been so bad. But no. Still almost nightly, once the beer houses had kicked out, they fetched back any number of men, and their 'parties' could go on right into the following morning.

The noise was like a torture device from which she couldn't escape. Laughter, singing, shouting, arguing – they seemed to roll on a continual wheel. Then there were the other sounds, the ones that came with their trade, relentless, day and night. The child was constantly being woken and Jewel barely ever managed to drop off to sleep at all. The stress of it all was beginning to affect her well-being and the end of her tether was growing ever nearer. She *had* to get out of here.

Despite her desperation, Jewel had recognised that she wasn't yet strong enough to be up and about. She'd suffered severely from the extraordinary birth. She was weak, grew fatigued easily. Unable to rest properly in comfort and peace was only delaying her progress.

It was midday on a Saturday towards the end of the month when matters eventually came to a head. Louise and her mother had been sniping at each other since rolling from their beds, and the rowing had intensified as the day wore on. Glad of the curtain around the bed that shut her off from the room, Jewel lay with gritted teeth to wait it out.

Julia hadn't been home for two days and the women blamed each other for her absence. Where had they last seen her, and with whom? This wasn't like her at all, to fail to come home. Their line of work brought them into close contact with all manner of people, some worse than others. Anything could have happened to her and they wouldn't even know until a body turned up, as those of streetwalkers did all too often. And on, and on.

'You should have kept an eye to her,' Louise's mother snapped, sounding more disgruntled than worried about her missing child's welfare. 'Don't I allus say you must stick together on t' nights?'

'You're her mam, not me. Why didn't *you* keep a check on her movements?' shot back the girl.

'Aye well, it's all the harder you'll work, let me tell thee. Until she returns, we're an income down. Mine and Sarah's owd cunnies don't attract the fellas like they used to. It's young ones like yours they prefer – and you'll give it to them, an' all, at double the rate from now on.'

Jewel shook her head. Money. That's all it ever boiled down to with the so-called mother of these girls. She possessed not a single ounce of real love for either of them. She truly was the most grotesque person she'd ever had the misfortune of meeting. No wonder Julia

269

had gone. Chances were she wasn't in any danger but had seen the light at long last.

And yet . . . She saw in her mind's eye the picture – and the money nestled behind it. She'd checked only last night, fearing the worst – her daughter's whole future depended on it, after all – but no, it was still there. If Julia *had* deserted, she'd have surely taken her treasure trove with her.

'There's no way I'm toiling extra hours to keep thee in gin. It ain't happening.'

'You'll do as I bleedin' well *say*.'

'Aye? Watch me!' retorted Louise.

There followed next the sound of scuffling. Then the curtain collapsed inwards as both women fell, clawing and tearing at each other's hair, on to the bed, missing the sleeping baby by inches.

With a scream of horror, Jewel snatched up her child and, caring naught for her stitches, jumped from the bed. Burning fury rapidly replaced her shock and she jabbed a finger in their direction. 'You pair of gutter dog bitches, yer!' But lost in their battle, they didn't hear, and she turned instead to Sarah, who was trying to split the women up. 'Take me to Mrs Maddox's.'

'What, now? But Jewel, your confinement's not over—'

'I'm well enough,' she barked, snatching up her shawl and wrapping it around the baby tightly. 'If I stay here any longer, they'll finish up doing my child a serious mischief – or, God help them, *I'll* end up going at the pair of *them*. Just get us out of here, Sarah. Please.'

A woman with dark hair and small, quick eyes opened the door to Minnie's house minutes later. 'Hello, Sarah.'

'All right, Eliza? Is Minnie home?'

'Aye, come on in.'

Following behind, Jewel took stock of the kitchen

270

they entered. Like the procurer's house in Lum Street, this, too, was clean and tidy. Only here there was a marked difference: it was cosy and welcoming and oozing warmth. A sudden lump came to her throat and she swallowed hard. It was almost like stepping into Mam's house. Yet another difference here was the bed by the fire, upon which lay a row of contented-looking babies sleeping peacefully, not holed away in the back bedroom in the way Mater had operated.

'Hello, Sarah love,' called Minnie from her fireside chair. Then her gaze shifted to Jewel and a wide smile spread across her lined face. 'Lass! By, I see you're progressing well. And is that the young angel you've got with thee? Ay, give us her here, let me have a cuddle of her.'

Smiling back, Jewel placed the baby into her arms. 'It's nice to see thee, Mrs Maddox.'

'And youse, all three.'

'Take the weight off,' Eliza told them, nodding to the table before limping to the fire. 'I'll brew a fresh pot.'

'So,' asked Minnie, pausing in her cooing at the child, when they were seated. 'To what do I owe this fine pleasure?'

'I want the child adopted, Mrs Maddox,' Jewel blurted out before she could stop herself. 'Please, will tha help me?'

Surprised silence filled the room for a moment. Minnie glanced to Sarah then back to Jewel.

'Can I ask why, lass?'

'I can't give her the life she deserves. That's the top and bottom of it.'

The old woman nodded. 'It seems to me this ain't a fresh decision. You've given this matter thought forra good while?'

'I've known I couldn't keep the child since the day I discovered I were carrying it.'

A shadow of understanding crossed Minnie's face, and Jewel knew she sensed Benji's crime. Given her experience, she'd likely witnessed this scenario many times over.

'So will you help me, Mrs Maddox?' she continued on a note of pleading. 'Can you find my daughter a better life?'

'There's no going back, lass, once the deed is done.'

'I understand that. Please, you're my last hope. I did find another baby farmer who promised to help, but she—'

Minnie and Eliza cut her off with a collective gasp.

'What is it?' Jewel glanced from one to the other in puzzlement. 'What did I say?'

'How dare you.' Eliza's voice shook with offence. 'Min here is no bloody baby farmer!'

'Oh. But I thought—'

'You thought wrong, lass.' Folding her arms, Minnie's face was grave. 'I have no part, nor have I ever, in that scandalous practice. If it's *that* you're here seeking, you've come to the wrong place – and shame on you!'

'But . . .' Jewel was miffed. 'Baby farmers are a godsend to women like me. They offer a solution, a haven—'

'*What?*' Eliza gazed at her as if she were mad. 'Them beasts are one of the great plagues of society. How can you condone – *accept* – the slaughtering of innocents? Commercial infanticide, that's what it is!'

Jewel's mouth fell open. 'What the divil are you talking about?'

'Lass,' interrupted Sarah quietly. 'Baby farmers are a whole other breed of procurers – and Minnie ain't one of them. She's decent and respectable. Honest, not callous. To put your little one out to nurse, and to *farm* them out, are two different things.'

Minnie and Eliza nodded their agreement. Still, Jewel was no closer to understanding. She shook her head, and Sarah continued:

'The term "baby farmer" is used as an insult and implies improper treatment. No respectable wench would call herself so. Baby farming is an accusation, not a profession.'

'That's right,' followed up Minnie. 'I care for the mites I'm paid to rear or rehome, I don't abuse and neglect them.'

Jewel's mind spun in her struggle to digest what she was hearing. Then Minnie spoke again, and all the blood drained from her face:

'Take that Bickerstaff piece from Bolton town. A regular hell-dweller, and no mistake.'

'Did you say Bickerstaff? *Ada* Bickerstaff?'

'That's the one.'

'What about her?'

'Do you know the divil?'

'Aye. She's the procurer I went to first, months ago, but the arrangement didn't work out.'

'Then, by God,' breathed Eliza, shaking her head, 'yon babby here must have a guardian angel looking out for her to escape them clutches.'

The police storming Lum Street, the children hidden away upstairs . . . Jewel's breathing quickened. She was almost too afraid to ask. 'How do *youse* know of her?'

The old woman wrinkled her nose as though smelling something unpleasant. 'Her name's been in every newspaper in the land – strikes horror still into the hearts of all good and decent folk it does, an' all. I mean, there's been a few sensational cases regarding this in t' press over the years, but nowt on this scale.'

'What's she done?' Jewel whispered.

273

'Murdered an untold number of babbies, that's what.'

No . . .

'She opened the door one day last November to who she thought would be a customer she were waiting on, only to find two constables standing there.'

Oh, dear God in heaven, it was true . . .

'Top and bottom of it is,' continued Minnie, 'they did a search of the property. That's when the gruesome discoveries were made: body parts wrapped in blankets in the cellar. She'd been dismembering tiny babbies down there, then feeding them to her dogs to get rid of the evidence.'

'*What?*' She was going to be sick.

'Aye, beggars belief. Three infants were found alive still in a back bedroom, all in a pitiable state and weighing half what they should. They were removed to the workhouse but never recovered from her neglect and died soon after.'

She'd been there. She'd lived, ate and slept beneath that roof, when all the time, right above her head, in the next room . . . She'd suspected nothing. *Nothing.* This couldn't be happening. She was stuck in some nightmare, had to be, and would waken soon, surely?

'Them angels were simply left to wilt away and die,' Eliza was saying now, though Jewel barely heard her, with the blood crashing through her ears. 'She deliberately forewent even the most basic of care. They were neither fed, bathed nor shown the slightest attention. It were all about the brass she got from taking them on. That's all she wanted and, once she had it in her sweaty palm, the children were nowt but an inconvenience, for their upkeep would have only ate away at her profits. But a mistreated babby is a noisy babby, so she dosed them with "quietness" – narcotic potions and deadly syrups

274

such as laudanum and Godfrey's Cordial – to render them docile. The little loves didn't stand a chance.'

That's why she'd hardly heard the poor souls' cries. When she had on occasion, they were but sleepy-sounding mews. *I'm so sorry, so sorry . . .*

'Seems likely she'd been carrying on her evil trade for ten years or more, could have murdered hundreds of children in all.'

Jewel swallowed down bile. This just got worse and worse . . . 'Mother of God. How was this allowed to happen?'

'Well, the registration of births, live or dead, ain't compulsory, is it? If the authorities ain't aware of a babby's existence, it can be got rid of without anyone knowing the difference. Besides, she moved on regular to avoid detection, changing addresses and aliases as she went. I just thank the good Lord she's been stopped at last and can do no more poor innocents harm.'

'She admitted to everything?'

'Well, she didn't have much choice, did she? The evidence were there for all to see. She made a full confession whilst in prison. She swore she never murdered them with her two hands, by strangulation, say, couldn't bring herself to. But well, leaving them to slowly rot as she did instead is worse in my eyes. It would have took weeks for them to die. What they must have suffered . . .' Minnie paused to wipe away a tear. 'She were charged with five counts of wilful murder – all they could pin on her with the evidence they had, though she were guilty of many more, I'll be bound – and sentenced to death.

'Her defence tried claiming insanity and she were examined. They found she were sane, all right, just bleedin' wicked to the marrow. She claimed whilst holed in the condemned cell that she'd performed but acts of charity. That the children were unwanted and she'd just sent them on to God to be looked after by Him. Bloody warped bitch. I hope she died with a struggle, an' all, knew then how it felt. I *pray* that noose didn't afford her a quick release.'

With a shuddering sigh, Jewel dropped her head in her hands. 'I had no idea. Truly. She practised so openly, were advertising in the paper. That's why I believed it to be above board.'

'Aye well. Reformers are fighting tooth and nail to stamp it out completely. Hopefully, they one day will.'

'I just can't . . . I suspected *nowt*, believed her to be reputable, that she were doing lasses a kindness, that's all. I didn't realise that to be a baby farmer was a bad thing.'

Louise. She'd been the one to tell her that Ada Bickerstaff was one such. Was she, too, unaware of the meaning behind the title? Had to be. She must see the girl, inform her of what she'd discovered, what an incredibly lucky escape they – their children – had had.

'I must go.' She rose shakily, and Minnie handed her child across. Gazing down at the pure and harmless being in her arms, Jewel wanted to cry. *I've wronged you so many times, little one, but I'll make good in the end. I promise you.* 'Mrs Maddox, Eliza, ta ever so for telling me all you have the day. It's made me see even more that this child here must have summat better than this, than me. Please, will you help with getting her adopted? I'll do anything, *please.*'

Minnie was silent as she looked from mother to baby with sadness. Finally, she patted Jewel's hand and nodded. 'All right, lass, aye. I will.'

'Oh. Oh, thank you, *thank* you, so very much.' *All I need now is the money. And by God, I'll get it,* she thought,

276

determination washing through her. 'I'll be back the morrow, Mrs Maddox. You really . . .' She had to clear the tears from her throat before continuing. 'You really don't know what this means to me, my child. Thank you once again, from the bottom of my heart.'

The old woman rose to see them out and, as Jewel followed her to the door, something on the sideboard against the back wall made her do a double-take. She stepped towards it and her eyebrows lifted.

'My mother has this candlestick.'

'Oh?'

'Aye. Very precious to her, it is. But how . . . ?' She glanced over her shoulder to the old woman in amazement. 'Mam's allus said that hers were a last gift from Father afore he passed away. She said it were 'specially made, that there's none other like it in the whole world.' Turning it this way and that in her hands, Jewel's bemusement grew. Some eight inches tall, with exquisitely cut prisms . . . it could have passed itself off as her mother's without a doubt. 'It's exactly the same. How queer.'

Minnie's brows had reacted, too, only hers did the opposite, dropping into a frown. 'Aye well,' she said. 'Happen the designer made more than one after all.'

'Aye, mebbe.'

After the old woman had waved them off, she and Sarah lowered their heads against the cold and set off back to Canal Street. They were almost at the door when Jewel realised how quiet the other woman was and had been throughout the meeting. When she asked her if she was all right, and received but a nod from Sarah in response, she put it down to the recent shocking revelation concerning that wicked piece Bickerstaff, and left her be. She knew exactly how she felt, could barely wrap her brain around it all herself.

Inside, the fight had ceased at least, and mother and daughter were nowhere to be found.

'Probably taken themselves off to the inn to continue their spat there,' Sarah surmised with a roll of her eyes. 'The state they've left the place in, though.'

After laying the baby on a sofa, Jewel took proper stock of the wrecked space and nodded. It seemed they had thrown in anger, or knocked into during their scuffle, every item in their path. Bottles and dishes littered the floor. The table lay on its side and the makeshift curtains had been torn from the window. Then a sudden wave of dread assaulted her and she turned slowly, almost not daring to check. Yet to her sheer relief, the picture remained where it always had, appeared to be the only item to have evaded the onslaught. *Thank God.*

'Youse are back, then?'

Jewel and Sarah turned to find Louise's mother swaying in the doorway. She, too, glanced around at the carnage and, pulling a face, shrugged. 'And where's that hell cat, then? Slunk off to lick her wounds, has she?'

'Place were empty when we returned,' Sarah told her. 'We thought Louise were with thee.'

'Huh, not likely. Vicious young bitch. She'd do well to keep out of my road forra while if she knows what's good for her.'

'Is there no word as to Julia's whereabouts yet?'

'Nay. Ah, to buggery with the pair of them. Bleedin' ingrates. Anyroad, sod it, I'm going to get some kip,' the woman grumbled, shoving past them and stumbling over the debris-strewn floor towards the bed. She fell across it – shawl, clogs and all – and promptly fell fast asleep.

Jewel and Sarah exchanged a weary look. Without a

word, they rolled up their sleeves and set to tackling the mess.

*

Nightfall rolled around and still there was no sign of either of the sisters. Their mother snored on, oblivious to everything, but Jewel and Sarah had begun to get concerned.

'I'm off to search our usual haunts, see if there's been a sighting,' said Sarah, reaching for her shawl. 'Julia's been gone way longer than what's normal; I'm going to report her missing at the police station the morrow if she still ain't back. Not that the bobbies will offer much help,' she added with a note of bitterness. 'Girls in our trade vanish all the time. What's one more missing slum whore to them? But for Louise to disappear . . . The lass ain't as hardened as her sister, nay. And what with how her mind's been of late since the babby . . .' Biting her lip, she set off to scour the inns.

Alone, Jewel's eyes immediately strayed to the picture. Ashamed, she tore them away, but they soon returned, and her feet itched to go to it. For though she, too, was worried about Louise, and even about the spiky Julia, another thought overrode all else: the future happiness of her child. To her, nothing was more important than that. Unable to fight the urge any longer, she hurried to the wall.

After a quick glance towards the bed and the woman within still lost in her drunken stupor, she nodded, satisfied. Then she lifted the picture from the nail and propped it quietly against the sofa.

For a full minute, she could do nothing but stare at the empty cavity between the bricks as the world slowly shattered around her. The cloth purse and the small fortune it contained were gone.

279

Breaths coming in short spurts, she swung her head. 'Nay. *Nay!*'

The picture had clearly been disturbed after all. Louise must have spotted the secret hoard after her mother had taken herself off to the gin palace following their fight. She'd snatched away the lot, ruby ring and all, and had it away on her toes. Jewel was doubtful anyone would see the girl again. And despite her devastation, she blamed her not one bit. Who wouldn't do the same in her situation; the family, the life, she'd been cursed with? Jewel knew, had it been her, she'd have certainly taken the opportunity of a fresh start far from here.

But God above, where did this leave her child? Just how would she pay Minnie Maddox?

Her last hope now dashed to the wind, the fight within her followed suit. With a moan, she sank to her knees on the cold, flagged floor.

Chapter 20

AS SARAH HAD predicted, the desk sergeant at Kirby Street Station had barely batted an eyelid when she went to report her niece missing.

Despite the previous day's search, she'd had no luck – no one in the inns, including their regular customers, had seen hide nor hair of the sisters. And so, as she'd vowed, Sarah had braced herself to go and ask the police for help. No small task for the majority of their class, to whom the law was rarely a friend.

Jewel had felt it only right to tell her about the money, and her subsequent suspicions regarding Louise's disappearance. Sarah had been in agreement therefore that the younger girl had gone off of her own free will, so there was little point mentioning her absence at the station. Yet it also reinstated the likelihood that Julia, given she'd left all that behind, almost certainly hadn't gone by choice.

'Three days? That's no great length of time, now, is it?' the bewhiskered officer had insisted, waving away her concerns.

'Well, nay, I suppose not. But Julia, she's never afore—'

'She'll turn up, you'll see.' *Like the proverbial bad penny; your kind usually do*, his eyes had seemed to add.

'And if she don't, sir? What then?'

'Has it occurred to you that she might not want to be found?'

'Well . . . nay, but I don't think—'

'Something to consider then. Look,' he'd relented when Sarah showed no signs of budging, 'we have her description and will keep an eye out for her. I'm afraid there's nothing more we can do.'

And that had been that. Many cared little for people, particularly women, who slipped below the line of moral respectability. It was simple in their eyes: choose to live a sinful existence, accept whatever fate befell you. Sarah was certain that whether Julia's bloated corpse washed up in the river, was found broken and beaten in some ginnel, or she turned up healthy and well, it was all the same to him and his ilk.

She'd relayed the brief meeting to Jewel shortly before with a touch of bitterness but no surprise. As she'd pointed out, in their line of work, assault and even murder was an occupational hazard. That the worst could occur with every customer, they acknowledged with grim acceptance.

'Not that me and the girls are particularly close,' Sarah admitted. 'It just felt like the right thing to do, lass, you know? Someone had to at least try summat, for their mam wouldn't get around to it.' Sighing, she shrugged. 'If they return, they return. If not . . . Well, I can but pray that they're safe and wish them both well.'

Despite the earliness of the hour, the girls' mother was already out, propping up the inn's counter, drowning her self-pity in funds she'd begged from Sarah. Jewel's patience with the selfish article was wearing thin, though Sarah, God alone knew why, seemed to take in her stride everything her sister threw at her.

'You still for taking the little 'un to Minnie's today?'

asked Sarah now, and tears immediately sprang to Jewel's eyes. 'Ay, it's all right, lass, if you've changed your mind.'

'It's not that. Oh, Sarah, it's all ruined.'

'Julia's brass? Is that it?'

Jewel raised her head and her face flushed pink. 'I didn't want to steal it, you understand? It was for the child, to buy her a brighter future.'

'You were desperate. I get it, lass, don't fret. You do what you must for your kiddies. That's a mother's job.'

'But what will I do now? Louise has taken the lot. I'm out of work, haven't a penny to my name, will *never* find enough to pay Mrs Maddox's fee—'

'Come on, dry your eyes.'

'But Sarah, it's hopeless. *How* will I—?'

'I'll pay.'

'What?'

'Rather than give Minnie a lump sum, we'll see if she'll allow me to pay weekly for the child's upkeep until new parents are found. I were for putting the self-same notion to Louise but, well, given how frail the poor divil she birthed turned out to be . . .'

'Aye.' Sarah was right, Jewel saw it now. Neither hers nor Julia's money could have made a difference to *that* poor soul.

'Please,' Sarah continued. 'Let me do it for thee.' She extracted some coins and pressed them into Jewel's palm. 'Here. Give her that to be getting along with.'

Jewel was almost too choked to speak. 'You'd do that for me?'

Sarah nodded.

'But why?'

'Because you're a good lass with a golden heart. For despite the pain that's eating away at thee at the thought

283

of parting with your daughter, you're willing to suffer it to put her first. I'd say you're one of the bravest lasses I know.'

Now, when Jewel burst into silent sobs, Sarah let her cry. She put her arms around her and hugged her close, and Jewel clung to her.

'It's *killing* me.'

'Eeh, lass. I know.'

'Will I die from it, this agony?'

'Nay.' Sarah's voice was husky with emotion. 'You'll bear it, somehow.'

'She will be all right, won't she? Mrs Maddox will honour her promise?'

'Fret not over that at least,' answered Sarah without hesitation. 'Minnie shall find her nowt but the very best people.'

'And she'll care for her well until then?'

'That you could even wonder at it. Some, aye, are wholly unqualified for the task of hand-rearing babies – not Minnie. What she don't know ain't worth knowing.'

Ada Bickerstaff entered Jewel's thoughts and she shuddered. 'I almost gave her up to an infant killer, Sarah. She insisted no one but her was to enter their room so as not to disturb them – *how* could I be so blind? Louise told me what she were. *Baby farmer.* But I'd never heard the term afore, and when I questioned her, she insisted—' She broke off suddenly as the memory of their conversation flooded back. She lifted her head to look at Sarah. 'Did Louise know what Bickerstaff was about?' she whispered. Then with dread: 'Please tell me Louise didn't know.'

'I'll not lie to thee, lass, she likely did. Though some mothers, victims like yourself, pay baby farmers believing care will be provided, others know the truth. There's an understanding of sorts that the child's chances of survival will be slim.'

Angel makers. That's how the girl had referred to them. Of course, it was all making sense now.

'Whether her child had been born in Bolton or Manchester, weak or robust . . . she didn't want it,' Sarah continued. 'Adopted out or snuffed out, so long as it were off her hands one way or another, it didn't matter. Mind, she didn't expect the end result to fall to her; that's why she sought out a baby farmer in the first place. To her, it were less personal, like. Luckily for her conscience – and mine, for I were witness to it, weren't I? – the child arrived as it did: at death's door through sheer fate alone. Had Louise not intervened, it still wouldn't have lived. I'm certain of that.'

'How can you speak of it so calmly? You don't agree with it, surely?'

'Course I don't. But what could I have done? She's a grown lass; aye, with a callous streak beneath, to boot, like her mother. Nowt I could have said would have changed her mind.'

'She would have let me send my child to the slaughter, though, too. What say if I'd changed my mind soon after handing her over, gone back to reclaim her, only to find . . .'

'Aye, you're right. And it happens, lass, too: some never hear from their child again. Most are too ashamed or frickened to probe, or take their worries to the police, and so it goes on, with baby farmers continuing their trade undetected.'

'How could Louise risk that? How could she be so wicked?'

'You mebbe deciding you'd made a mistake . . . perhaps she didn't think that far ahead.'

'She still should have *told* me, Sarah.'

'What would you have done had you discovered the truth?'

'Left! Immediately!'

'And gone where?'

Jewel opened her mouth but, to this, she didn't have an answer.

'Happen in her mind, shielding thee from this foulness was her way of doing you a kindness. She knew you couldn't keep your child and mebbe thought you'd be stuck getting rid of it, if not with the Bickerstaff one. Who knows? But she saw thee as a friend, I reckon. She fetched thee here with her, didn't she? Whether she did or not, I think the intention to help thee was there.'

Reluctantly, Jewel knew she couldn't deny that. In her own way, Louise had been there for her. She hadn't had to take her under her wing, had she? And the girl hadn't wanted anything in return, can't have done, for she'd had nothing to give. Louise had done it because she wanted to.

'Now, why don't you go and put my proposal to Minnie?' A sad smile touched Sarah's lips when Jewel's arms tightened instinctively around her daughter. 'If it's what you want, of course.'

'It is. It has to be.'

'Then I think it's time, lass. Prolonging things will only make it harder on the pair of youse.'

Jewel's voice faltered. 'You'll be here when I get back?'

'I'll be here,' Sarah whispered. 'Good luck to thee. Be strong.'

*

If Jewel hadn't willed herself on with every step, she would never have got to Kirby Street.

Her every instinct was telling her to turn tail and run, but she silenced it with the mantra she'd adopted months ago: *I must. There's no other way. I must.*

Eliza welcomed her inside then discreetly took herself

off to make tea to give her and Minnie some privacy. Taking a deep breath, Jewel looked to the older woman, sitting smiling softly by the hearth.

'Hello, lass. Come on in, proper like, and sit yourself down.'

She took the chair opposite. 'Ta, thanks.'

Minnie's voice was gentle. 'You all right?'

'Aye. Nay. I hate myself for this, all of it. How have I got here, Mrs Maddox? *How* did things get to *this*?'

'Don't bottle it up, lass,' insisted Minnie when Jewel attempted to gulp down the tears that hadn't been too far away all morning. 'Let it out and gain some relief. There's no shame in showing emotion.'

For the next few minutes, she did just that. Holding her daughter close, her bitter weeping mingled with the sound of the crackling fire. Finally, she wiped her eyes and nodded. 'You were right. I can breathe a little easier now.'

'I'm glad. Now, drink your tea, there's a good lass.'

Eliza had placed it on a side table by her elbow and, between sips, Jewel explained to Minnie the situation and Sarah's generous offer.

'She's a kind soul. Course I'm in agreement to that, aye.'

'Really?' She closed her eyes in relief. 'Eeh, Mrs Maddox, thank you.'

'And lass?'

'Aye?'

'I'll find the very best parents for the little angel there that I can. Never fret on that. You have my word.'

Tears returned to Jewel's throat, making it impossible to respond. Instead, she conveyed her overwhelming gratitude with her eyes.

'Now, there's just a few things I need to ask of thee, if that's all right?'

'Aye.'

'Has the babby developed any health problems since the birth? The labour, it's not had no effect on her?'

'Nay, none.'

Minnie nodded, satisfied. 'And does she have a name?'

'I thought it best not to. You know?'

'I do, lass. Some prefer it that way.'

'Is there owt else you need to know, Mrs Maddox?'

'Aye, just one more thing.' A small smile deepened the lines around her mouth. 'What's *your* ruddy name? By gum, d'you know, I don't even know?'

'It's Jewel, Mrs Maddox.'

The sharp gasp from Minnie, and the clanking of Eliza's cup as she dropped it on to the table to cover her mouth with her hand, rent the air. Jewel stared at them in puzzlement.

'What is it? What's wrong?'

'Who . . . ?' Minnie was gazing at her open-mouthed. '*Who* did you say?'

'Why Jewel, for that's my name.'

The old woman rose from her chair. 'It can't be, it can't.'

'It's uncommon, I know. Folk allus react in surprise when I introduce myself,' she said, frowning in confusion as Minnie began pacing the floor. 'But Lord, never to this extent . . . Is tha all right?'

Receiving no response, Jewel looked instead to Eliza for help but, like the other woman, she, too, had paled and was wringing her hands. *What was going on?*

'Mrs Maddox?' Jewel crossed the room and touched her shoulder, bringing her to a juddering halt. 'Mrs Maddox, you're not well. Come, sit down.'

'Sorry. I . . . I'm sorry.'

'What made you react so?' she asked when she'd guided her back to her chair. 'Eliza, too. What is it?'

288

Minnie cleared her throat. She stared at her for a long moment then cleared her throat again. 'The night you went into labour, when Sarah called here asking for my services ... she just said that her niece's friend needed help, never mentioned your name. And then again yesterday, I never thought to ask, I ... I never ... could *never* have guessed ...'

'Guessed what? *What*, Mrs Maddox?'

'I once knew someone with the self-same name as yours. But it's *impossible*,' she added, almost to herself. Then she looked past Jewel slowly to stare into space, and her lips mouthed the name of another: *Sarah*. 'Oh my God,' she choked.

Jewel's bafflement had reached fever pitch. 'Sarah? What about her? Will someone please tell me what the divil's going on?'

Eliza settled on her haunches in front of Jewel and took her hand in hers. Her expression was one of fearful expectancy and deep pity. 'Lass?'

'What? What is it?'

'Are you Flora's girl?'

Now, it was Jewel's turn to ask: 'Who did you say?'

'Is your mam Flora Nightingale?'

She glanced away from her to Minnie, who was sitting on the edge of her seat wide-eyed, awaiting her answer. 'Aye. But how ... ?'

'Mother of God, I don't believe it,' Eliza whispered, whilst the older woman promptly burst into tears.

'Who are youse? How do you know my mam?'

'She were my neighbour; oh, the best friend a body could ask for,' sobbed Minnie, holding tight to Eliza, who had hurried to comfort her.

'That can't be. She ain't ever stepped foot in Manchester in her life; least not that I know of.'

'It's the truth. She dwelled right there, beyond yon bricks.' Minnie pointed across to the adjoining wall. 'She moved after Fred's death, when you were but a babby, to be nearer to her brother in Bolton town.'

Jewel's mouth formed an O. Why hadn't Mam ever told her they had lived here in this city? She'd assumed that the town she'd grown up in had always been her home. But if this *was* correct, and this woman and her mam had been such firm friends, why hadn't they stayed in touch? It didn't make sense.

'How is she, lass, Flora?' Tears still streamed down Minnie's lined cheeks. 'She's well?'

'Aye, yes. But, I don't, don't understand what's . . . You clearly felt a lot for her, Mrs Maddox, so what occurred? Why did youse lose contact?'

'I forgot about it, you see.' Moaning softly, Minnie rocked back and fro. 'I dressed thee and watched Flora carry thee home, but I'd forgot.'

'Min, think about this you're saying,' Eliza told her, tone deep with warning.

'I have thought, oh, have I! Long and hard, and round and round, for the past seventeen years. I vowed if I ever got the chance to put this to bed, to confess what I did, I would. They need to know.'

'But Min—'

'Nay, Eliza. I'll speak it. I must.'

Eliza made to protest further; then her shoulders sagged and she nodded. She and the old woman turned to Jewel with what could only be described as pure dread.

Throughout the women's war of wills, she'd simply gazed on in confusion, understanding nothing. Now, fingers of apprehension snaked down her spine. She lifted her brows hesitantly. 'What is it tha must confess?'

'I forgot about it,' repeated Minnie. 'I for*got* about the birthmark on your shoulder.'

Jewel's hand strayed up involuntarily to the distinctive marking stamped there beneath her clothing. 'What d'you mean?'

'Flora entrusted me to mind her child. And I did, barely took my eyes from her, but it were no good. She died anyway. No rhyme nor reason for it, as sometimes happens in life. So peaceful, she looked. So bonny, like a true angel. And I knew it, knew without question that Flora would wither and follow her to the grave with the grief. I believed it were for the best, that I were preventing a cruelty. I removed that dead babe's clothing and I put it . . . I put it . . . on thee. And she looked at you, Flora, upon her return. She looked at you forra long minute and she took you home.

'A child bearing a birthmark that shouldn't have been there. A child she never questioned me about, not once. That she poured into all that love she had and more. Never a murmur from either of us. Just like it hadn't happened. But it did. It did. And in t' end, it came betwixt us, that deed. She left here needing to start afresh. Needed to flee the memories, the truth. Me. What I'd set in motion.

'But I'm making it right; now I am. God's sent you here. He saw, and He knows you must hear it. And now you have. I'm so sorry, so sorry, for everything.'

'I'll tell you a secret if you let me go.'

Jewel's head swayed in denial. 'Nay.'

'You can't tell a soul I've told you, mind. You must keep it to yourself.'

The memory of Benji's lies, which she hadn't given a single thought to since he first spewed them, were like knives in her brain. 'You're wrong.'

291

'*Your mam ain't your mam.*'

Yes, she was. She was. 'She is!'

'*It's the truth. I've heard whispers of it over the years.*'

Everyone knew. All of them. All except her. 'Mam. Mam. Mam!'

'Where you going? Eeh, lass, wait. Please, just let Minnie finish the telling—'

With a swipe of her arm, Jewel sent Eliza stumbling into the wall. Eyes glazed, step unsteady, she laid her daughter with the other babies on the bed and crossed the room.

'But you must know, Jewel. Please. Sarah, she—'

The slam of the door at her back extinguished Minnie's voice. Jewel ground to a halt in the centre of the road, closed her eyes and drew in a long, slow breath. Then she turned and made off at a sprint for Victoria Station.

Chapter 21

JEWEL'S FEET GUIDED her from the train, the fare for which she'd paid with Sarah's money, along the platform and out of the station into Trinity Street. For a full minute, she stood stock-still and, as Louise had done the day they arrived in Manchester, breathed in her own town's smoggy air.

The sky of late afternoon had dulled to sludgy mink and off-white clouds cloaked the mill chimneys in the distance. Once more, her feet set off, and she saw they were taking her towards Town Hall Square.

When next she paused, she was at her mother's front door. Again, she stood unmoving, staring at the paint-chipped wood, mind void of thought. Her hand raised itself to the handle but stopped before it could reach it. Her arm fell back to her side. She turned on her heel and walked away.

Bolton Park seemed to offer a whispered greeting as she passed through it, and dim awareness sparked within her. Then, as quickly, it dissipated, leaving now-familiar emptiness. She sat on a hilly rise, tucked her skirts around her and folded her hands in her lap.

Maria saw the procurer's address in the article I answered – has she yet learned of Bickerstaff's heinous crimes? Was the maid worried sick, been forced to tell someone? And what of

Mrs Kirkwood: has she mentioned our meeting in Manchester to her brother? Has he passed on the information to Mam? Have my lies been exposed? Does everyone know my secret? These worries, amongst the rest, had tormented Jewel incessantly over the weeks. Now, she gave not one of them a single care. Nothing mattered. How could it now, given what she knew? How could anything mean a damn thing ever again?

'Who am I?' she asked of a tree's swaying branches nearby. But, like herself, it didn't have the answer.

A moan broke from her and she tore up fistfuls of damp grass. Her whole life a lie? All of it? Who was her real mam, then? What of her father? Who was he? Did anyone know? Flora? Had Fred before he died? What about her uncle and aunt? They clearly knew she wasn't of Flora's flesh – how else had Benji discovered it otherwise? He had to have overheard it from them. Everyone she'd thought she knew, whispering about her throughout the years, discussing and judging and tittering at her sordid mess of a life. And not one – not *one* – with enough decency to tell her the truth. Apart from Benji. Him, of all people. The irony would be almost laughable if it wasn't lacerating her heart to ribbons.

So why was she here, instead of in Flora's kitchen, demanding an explanation? She hadn't an answer to this either. Nothing at all made the slightest bit of sense.

Some time later – how long, Jewel couldn't say, wasn't aware of anything any more – a burst of giggles caught her attention. She turned her gaze to a cluster of bushes; beyond them, Maria and what must be her sister, given their likeness, walked arm in arm.

Of course, it was Sunday. It should have occurred to her that the maid might be enjoying her day off here. Though her eyes creased to see her friend, she didn't call out or go to her. It was like all life had been sucked from her; she could do nothing and felt even less.

'Jewel? Nay, it can't be her . . .' Spotting her moments later, Maria stared wide-eyed. 'Well, bugger me, it is. Jewel, lass! Over here!'

She tried to lift her hand in greeting but failed. Sighing, she watched the females hurry towards her.

'Eeh, lass. What are you doing *here*? When did yer get back?'

'I don't recall.' Jewel's voice sounded queer to her own ears.

'Are you all right?' Studying her more closely and realising she wasn't, the maid turned to her sister: 'Lass, go on and wait for me by the gate. Look at me,' she added quietly to Jewel when they were alone. She put a finger under her friend's chin and brought her head around to face her. 'Speak, lass. What's occurred? The babby . . . ?'

'I gave birth to a girl.' Jewel's chest tightened in searing loss.

'Was she born well, like?'

'Aye. Perfect.'

''Ere!' Maria exclaimed suddenly, grasping Jewel's wrist, 'I heard about that Bickerstaff one you went to. God above, who'd have thought it? What happened?'

'I weren't aware of owt whilst under her roof. Police came and I left with another lass. She put me up 'til I had the child.'

The maid nodded. 'I figured you would have found another procurer. But by hell . . .' She shook her head. 'I ain't half been worried about thee, lass. I'll be frank, I've been on t' brink of calling to your mam's for weeks and confessing what I knew, just didn't know what to do upon hearing of Bickerstaff's arrest. I didn't, mind,' she added quickly when Jewel turned to look at her.

'Don't fret, no one's aware of owt. I figured I'd give thee a bit longer, see if you showed, and if not then it were time to come clean. Thanks be to God you're here and you're well.'

Jewel looked away. 'Ta for not telling,' she offered, though, underneath, she really couldn't have cared less. Not now. Not any more.

'You found another procurer well enough, then, aye?'

She swallowed hard at the memory of her meeting with Mrs Maddox earlier and all that had gone with it. 'Aye.'

'Eeh, lass.' Maria covered her hand with hers. 'Was it so hard, saying goodbye? To the babby, I mean.'

'Aye,' she whispered.

'I am sorry, Jewel.'

'So am I.'

They were silent for a while until the maid asked, 'Did your mam believe your tale, then? She weren't suspicious at all?'

A ball of something hard and clogging settled in Jewel's guts. She shook her head. 'I ain't seen her yet.'

'What? Why? Did you go straight to Mr Birch's?'

'Nay. I came straight here. I ain't seen none of them.'

'Right, what's afoot?' Though Maria spoke with concern, her tone was firm. 'Come on, out with it. Summat's to do here; you're not yourself at all—'

'My mam's not my mam.'

'Eh? What does that mean?'

'I don't know. I were told ... told summat, and, well . . . Oh, Maria.' She burst into tears and hugged her knees. 'I don't know what the hell is happening!'

'Ay, come here. All right, now. Shh.' The maid rocked her in her arms as one would a child. 'Tell me, what's all this you've heard?'

With stops and starts, intermingled with gasping sobs, Jewel relayed Minnie's confession. 'I mean, what am I meant to do with this, Maria, you tell me that? My head, inside . . . It's like it belongs to another. I don't know who I am, don't know what to think, to feel, to *do*—'

'Shh. Eeh, Jewel love.' But that's all Maria had, not that Jewel blamed her – what on earth else *could* she say? That she was stunned by the revelation was clear to see. 'I just, just don't know what to say, like, I . . .'

'Aye, me neither.'

'Can't you go and see your mam, ask her yourself?'

'I don't . . . I can't. For what if she admits it and makes it real? She's my own mam! Except what if she ain't?'

'Right, well.' Maria thought for a moment then nodded. 'If it were me, I'd do nowt.'

'Aye?'

Maria shrugged. 'For the time being, at least. After all, what if this Maddox wench is lying? Lord knows why someone would about summat so awful, but well . . . You never know, do you? Takes all sorts to make a world – bleedin' mad buggers as well as the rest of us.'

'Nay. She knew too much, about me, Mam . . . Besides, what would she gain from it? It just don't make sense.'

And yet the more she thought about her friend's advice, the better it sounded. She was dimly aware that she was being a coward not confronting this, but she couldn't. *God, give me strength, I just can't bear it.*

'Happen I could sleep on it? What d'you reckon, Maria? Should I wait and see how my mind sits the morrow?'

'If you think that's best, then aye. Will you return to Mawdsley Street?'

'If Mr Birch still wants me.' Jewel bit her lip with thoughts of what he might know, had Mrs Kirkwood decided to get a message to him. 'Has your sister mentioned . . . anything to thee, Maria?' she asked cautiously. She couldn't bear to admit even to her friend where she'd been and with whom. The depravity she'd lived with these past months, the things she'd witnessed . . . The shame of it was crippling. God above, if Maxwell should be aware . . .

'Nay, she ain't said nowt. Mind, he promised your position would be waiting for thee, didn't he? My sister's served the family well, lass, but I'm sure yon master shall be glad to have thee back.'

'I ain't half missed— erm, little Constance,' Jewel corrected herself in time, her breathing quickening at what she'd almost blurted out. Though it was true in part: she did long to see the young miss. 'Well, them all, really. I'll be happy to be back, aye.'

'Shall we walk back? Or d'you need more time to gather your thoughts? Just say the word, lass. I'm here whatever you decide.'

'What did I do to deserve a friend like thee, eh?' Though Jewel nudged her playfully, her lip wobbled and grateful tears glistened on her lashes. 'Thank you,' she whispered.

'Eeh, lass.'

'Come on.' Jewel rose and held out her hands, and when Maria placed hers into them helped her to her feet. 'Let's go.'

And yet the nearer the three of them got to their destination, the worse Jewel's pain grew. Being in such close proximity to Back Cheapside and her mother after so long apart was heart-wrenching. Not wanting to see her for fear of what she might learn was all that kept her from running the short distance at full pelt, though her longing to see the woman she loved with every part of her was nigh on impossible to suppress. By the time they reached Mawdsley Street, she was shaking and once more on the brink of tears. Before approaching the Birches' door, she paused to suck in some deep breaths.

'You certain you're all right, Jewel?' asked Maria gently.

She nodded. 'I'm a big girl with broad shoulders; I'll be fine.' She had to be, didn't she?

'Well, I'd best get back in, else my mistress will be having kittens.'

'You go,' Jewel told her. 'And Maria? Eeh, I've missed thee.'

The maid winked, flashed a grin then scuttled to her own residence across the road.

Looking down at the girl beside her, Jewel pulled an apologetic face. 'Thanks for covering my position whilst I've been . . . away. I am sorry to be leaving thee out of a job, lass.'

'Don't be daft, nay.' Just like her sister in personality, it would seem, as well as looks, she gave a warm smile. 'I knew the score afore you left, didn't I, knew you'd be back, that it were but temporary?'

Jewel smiled then peered towards the house. 'Are the family home, do you know?'

'Mr Roland were out when I left, but the young miss and their father should be present. 'Ere, I reckon Mr Birch shall be happy to see thee. He made mention of you regular in your absence.'

Something fluttered in Jewel's breast. 'He did?'

'Aye. Said as how he'd been sad to see thee go. That you're a fine servant – the best.'

'Oh. Aye, yeah. Well, that were nice of him,' she insisted, whilst inside, the small flare dimmed and died. With a soft sigh, she knocked at the door.

'Hello.' Clearly taken aback to see her, it was a few seconds before Maxwell spoke.

'Hello, Mr Birch.'

'You're returned? Your relative has regained good health?'

'Aye.' She felt herself redden a little, and not just at the deception. Those eyes of his . . . She'd almost forgotten how arresting they were. 'Aye, I'm back.'

Still, he continued to stare at her, his lips slightly parted. Finally, he ran a hand through his dark hair and laughed quietly. 'My apologies, Jewel. Please, come in.'

'Hello there, Miss Constance. By, how you've grown!'

The giggling youngster, who had come toddling down the hall to greet her, held out her arms. Picking her up and holding her close, tears pricked Jewel's eyes. Oh, but it felt good to be back.

'I'll just collect my things, Mr Birch,' announced Maria's sister, smiling, as she headed for the kitchen. 'And I just want to say thanks to thee for being a fair and pleasant master. I've enjoyed working here, really I have.'

As Maxwell offered kind farewells to the girl, Jewel looked on with a smile, though inside, as much as she felt mean about it, she was willing her to make haste and leave. She just wanted things to go back to how they were, to be alone with the family, as she used to be. Normality was what she craved right now more than anything else.

Some time later when her friend's sister had gone and Constance had been taken to the nursery for a nap, Jewel headed downstairs to her haven. The familiar surroundings were like balm for the soul. She ran and threw herself on to the bed. Hugging the bedclothes, she closed her eyes, and for the first time allowed herself to think about her daughter. Crushing emotion slammed home. Her arms ached for the touch of her tiny, warm body, and her milk-heavy breasts, bound tightly as she'd seen Louise do to dry them up more quickly, throbbed with their need to sustain, to nurture.

She hadn't even said goodbye. So consumed had she been with the unfathomable news, she'd simply left the child and fled. Though if she thought about it, perhaps that had been for the best. For had she been forced to speak to her, to look into her baby's perfect little face and tell her she was leaving her, she'd have faltered for certain, wouldn't have been able to see it through. Then what would they have done? She'd have spoiled everything for the child.

'I couldn't keep thee,' Jewel whispered into the sheets. 'But know that I love thee, oh, I do, and that I'll think of thee always, every minute. I don't care how you were begot. That matters not a bit any more. You were perfect, lass, a true angel. Please, forgive me—'

'May I speak with you, Jewel?'

'Oh, sir!'

Maxwell came down the remaining stairs with his hands held high, but his sheepish smile and apology for startling her died to see her tear-streaked face. He lowered his arms slowly, brows knotting in a frown. 'Jewel? You've been crying. What's wrong?'

'Nowt, sir, honest. Really, I'm fine,' she assured him, scrubbing at her eyes and cheeks with her sleeve. 'I'm happy to be back is all.'

'May I?' He motioned to the bed and, when she nodded, sat on the edge. Head lowered, he glanced up at her then looked away again quickly. 'I'd . . . like to ask you something, Jewel.'

'Aye, owt. What is it?'

'Are you ...?' He shifted uncomfortably. 'What I mean is, do you ...?'

'Aye, sir?'

'Forgive me. I'm loath to embarrass or upset you further. However, I must ask.' He dropped his tone. 'Are you in the black place, like before?'

'The black place?' She shook her head. 'Sorry, sir, I don't know what—'

'Do you have the urge again to do yourself harm? Only you don't seem yourself at all. The moment you returned, I detected a sadness about you and I thought—'

'Well, tha thought wrong.' Anger and shame and sorrow and suffocating grief were swirling inside her like a bowl of ingredients taking a thrashing from a wooden spoon. She dug her nails into her palms, terrified she would explode.

'I understand, you know.'

His gentle tone did nothing to quell the flames. 'How could *you* possibly understand?' she murmured with bitter incredulousness.

'I know my sister asked you to look after me.'

A little of her frown melted. She blinked in confusion. 'Did she, or did she not?'

'Aye, but—'

'I attempted self-murder a number of times following my wife's death.'

His confession knocked the wind from her sails. She gasped. 'Sir?'

'I never anticipated finding love again after Roland's mother. Therefore, when Mary was taken from me ... I could think of no way to continue living without her. It was like a darkened shroud had wrapped itself around me, obscuring the light. Nothing and no one could penetrate it for many months, during which I . . .' Maxwell paused to look at her. 'Well. Let's just say I was unsuccessful, and that I thank God on my knees each night for sparing me. So you see, Jewel,' he added, hesitantly reaching out and cupping her face, 'I *do* understand.'

Silent tears were coursing down her face. 'I'm sorry.'

'Talk to me,' he whispered. 'A problem shared is a problem halved.'

'I . . . can't, sir. Though please know I've no intention of doing owt daft to myself. I promise thee, I haven't, I just . . .' She heaved a shuddering breath. 'Please don't fret over me. I'll be all right.'

He was staring at her intently. Though he didn't speak, slowly his thumb moved to caress her cheek.

Jewel's heart tripped over itself in two or three hammering beats. Their heads were no great distance apart and, as she locked eyes with him, she sensed him move closer just a fraction.

'If ever you need to speak to someone, Jewel . . .'

'I know,' she murmured. 'That offer also holds for thee.'

'I'm glad you're back.'

Though the words of Maria's sister from earlier whispered in her mind of him merely having missed her servanting skills, the corners of her mouth lifted nonetheless. 'And me. I . . . missed you, Mr Birch.'

His eyes darkened with feeling. He opened his mouth to speak, but instead it was Roland's voice that broke the silence:

'Father? Are you down there?'

They sprang apart as if they had been scorched.

Maxwell stood quickly and cleared his throat, and there was a definite flush to his neck and jaw. 'Yes, son. I'll be with you in one moment.'

She felt shaky with confusion, embarrassment, *euphoria*; though all emotion seeped from her, leaving her dead cold inside, at Maxwell's next words. Turning to her, it was as though he had to force his eyes to meet hers:

'I'm so sorry, Jewel. I don't know what I was . . . I must go.'

'Sir, wait.' She reached out to touch his sleeve, but he sidestepped her.

'I'm sorry,' he murmured again. 'I can't, I . . . I'm utterly mortified.' With that, he almost sprinted up the stairs.

Jewel stood gazing at the door above for an age. Prickles of heat spread across her body; she thought she would die from the shame. What had just happened? She'd felt something then, between them. And she'd liked it, she had. He was mortified? Humiliation burned. He'd remembered her lowly station too late, was that it? He was angry with himself – with her – that the boundary had been crossed? But she . . . Oh, she really did . . . *I like thee, sir,* she said in her mind. *I care for thee.*

'I . . . love thee,' she said out loud to the emptiness.

God help her, she did.

*

'Your mother must be glad to have you home?' Roland smiled at Jewel across the dining table.

'Aye, sir,' she lied quietly, whilst praying he wouldn't ask her more regarding Flora. Fortunately, he didn't:

'As are we, little nightingale,' he continued instead. 'Isn't that so, Father?'

She glanced up tentatively from the tray she carried when silence greeted them. Maxwell's full attention was on his food, though he hadn't touched a morsel.

'Father?' Roland laughed.

'Hm?'

'Are you with us this evening?'

'Yes, of course. Sorry, I – I'm rather tired.'

Jewel willed him to look at her but his eyes remained firmly on his plate. Biting back hurt, she dragged her feet back downstairs.

Since the incident in the kitchen a few hours ago, she'd mulled over every detail, again and again, until the last of the day's light had scattered from the sky and her head ached. Still, it made little sense to her. What had it meant? The way they had looked at each other. The way it made her feel.

She was no stranger to what she perceived as love. Jem Wicks had awakened the first flush of attraction in her, and she recognised the signs once more now. But this was different, she saw it instinctively. The intensity was crushing, the yearning of her body for Maxwell's like hot gushes through her veins that left her almost mad for the touch of him, his kiss. And her heart, it, too, was experiencing something altogether new, for the depth of her feelings went beyond mere carnal urges.

She cared for him fiercely, wanted only the best for him, his happiness. What he'd revealed to her about his own dangerous melancholy had struck inside her chest like a blade. The thought of him hurt or sad made her want to cry, and she longed to protect him, shield him from the bad things that life had a habit of throwing in your path, never wanted him to know a moment's sorrow ever again. And that's how she knew: it was love. Genuine, pure, cut-glass-clear love. She wanted no one else, either today or any other. It was all him.

Yet he'd been mortified at the slightest prospect, and that was that. Her fantastical thinking was hers alone, and would remain so; must, for both their sakes.

Busying her physical form with her chores did nothing to distract her obsessive brain – and she knew it would only worsen once she retired to bed. The quiet darkness had a way of suspending a troubled soul in relentless, regurgitated thought, broken only by either sleep or the rising of a new sun – she knew which it would be for her tonight – and she was dreading it.

Would she ever know peace of mind again? she wondered fleetingly as she climbed the stairs to the house, to ask of the family if they required anything else for today. Could she cope with these ever-occurring difficulties, and the heartache with which they went hand in hand, for a whole lifetime? The answer came to her immediately. No, she couldn't. She'd already endured enough for anyone – thrice over.

Upon entering the hall, she encountered Roland on his way to bed. Her surprise that he was forgoing his usual late-night rendezvous must have shown, for his handsome face spread in a grin.

'It's old and boring I've become, little nightingale. Ah-ha, but for very good reason. Yes, indeed.'

'Oh?' she allowed herself to enquire, her curiosity winning through.

'It just so happens that, whilst you were away, I met a pretty young filly for whom I've fallen hook, line and sinker.' His delight grew. 'We're engaged to be married.'

'Eeh, Mr Roland, sir. I'm that pleased for thee.' And she meant it. Perhaps now, the strain of his wanton behaviour on his father would lift, and not before time.

Roland continued on his way, whistling merrily, and Jewel was still smiling as she went to knock at the drawing-room door. Receiving no answer and assuming Maxwell had already retired for the night, she entered with the thought of tidying the space before heading back to her kitchen. However, she quickly saw that he wasn't in bed at all but fast asleep at his desk. She paused for a moment. Then, biting her lip, she crossed the floor towards him.

The sleeves of his crisp white shirt were rolled to the elbow, his collar loose. Head on his arms on the desk, he was dead to the world. Jewel's eyes softened.

'You work too hard,' she whispered with a light stroke of his hair. She turned and padded back out.

After undressing and climbing into bed, she lay staring at the ceiling. She pictured Maxwell up there, oblivious to everything, to her and her feelings, and ached to return to him. Of course, she resisted. But his image stayed stubbornly at the forefront of her mind.

Tomorrow, she would go to see her mother. Her guts churned at the prospect. What would she hear? *Was* Minnie Maddox somehow mistaken, as Maria had suggested? She clung to the possibility like her life depended on it, which it did, then quickly evicted the matter from her head.

A porcelain face with rosebud mouth and light blue eyes soon swam in to take her thoughts' place, and she closed her eyes on the sear of pain. 'My own babby,' she told her over the miles. 'Please be well and happy.' *I beg of thee, merciful God, love and keep her in my place, always.*

The last words Sarah had uttered to her before leaving for Minnie's called to her from somewhere far away, and Jewel's lids fluttered open. '*Be strong.*' She smiled sadly. The woman had been a tower of strength over the last few months. Jewel missed her calm, unassuming presence already. Her failure to say goodbye to her at least, she knew she'd always regret.

To Jewel's surprised relief, tiredness descended on her. Before it consumed her completely, the vague memory of Minnie making mention of Sarah before she fled the house came back to her, to linger unclear on her mind's outskirts. A frown accompanied her to sleep.

Chapter 22

'YOU BE GOOD for Lizzie. I'll see thee soon, there's a good lass.' Jewel handed Constance over to her nurse-maid then donned her shawl. 'I shan't be long,' she told the domestic, 'I just have an errand to run.'

Assuming she was off to purchase foodstuff for the family's meal later, Lizzie nodded and waved her on her way, and Jewel reluctantly set out to visit her mother.

Terror-induced sickness washed over her every step of the way and she was forced to stop several times to regain her composure. By the time she reached the house, her nerves were shot to pieces. As she'd done yesterday, she paused outside, unable to knock. And yet at the same time, she longed to see the woman beyond the door. She'd missed her something awful, had yearned for her during those difficult months – none more so than when in the throes of her agonising labour. And now here she was, actively prolonging the separation because of what after all might be one old woman's incorrect rambling. This hope Jewel clung to out of sheer desperation. Though, deep down, she knew the truth of it.

Then, suddenly, another notion occurred to her and her eyes narrowed in thoughtful interest. What if she said nothing? The idea sounded ludicrous at first, but the more she mused on it, the more its appeal grew. Say she simply pretended nothing had happened, erased from her mind all she'd discovered – what then? Everything would stay exactly the same, wouldn't it? Life could return to normal and no one would be any the wiser.

Could she do it? Jewel gnawed her lip in contemplation. Bury down inside the secret she was now privy to and just carry on as before? Was it possible? Would it eat away at her until she spoke out, or could she really try to forget about it? More to the point, did she want to?

'Aye,' she heard herself say. 'I do.'

To live a lie seemed, in her mind at this minute, the lesser of two evils. The reality of what exposing her knowledge of her parentage would mean filled her with such horror it left her gasping for breath. She could lose her mother. It would rip an irreparable hole in their relationship that could never be mended. How *could* something of that magnitude ever be repaired? It was impossible, surely?

'Just say nothing, then?' Jewel asked herself. 'Let the whole thing go?' *For all our sakes*, her inner voice added, and a little of the torment lifted.

She nodded once, twice. Then she grasped the handle and opened the door.

'Lass?'

'Hello, Mam.'

'Oh, my bonny girl, come here!'

Jewel walked into her mother's waiting arms. As she'd feared, a sense of awkwardness marred the overdue embrace; she stiffened slightly at the woman's touch, though she did her best to ignore it.

Flora kissed her brow then motioned to a chair. 'Sit thee down, lass. By, it's blessed I am the day. How've you been?'

'Well and good, ta. You?'

'Not too shabby, aye. Mind, I'm all the better for see-ing thee. We must never be parted again, you hear?' she scolded with mock-sternness. Then, smiling, she passed Jewel a cup of tea and sat down facing her. Her soft gaze lingered about her face. 'You sure you're all right?' she asked, and a slight frown appeared. 'You seem . . . different somehow. I don't know, can't put my finger on it. All the bloom's gone from your cheeks. You sickening for summat?'

'Nay, nay.' Jewel cursed inwardly as heat crept up her neck. 'Mebbe I'm tired is all. You not in work the day?' she added quickly to change the subject.

'This afternoon, aye. 'Ere, why not slip across with me – if you've the time to spare, that is? Your uncle and aunt and young Benji would be pleased to see thee, I bet.'

'Aye, we'll see.' This was a lie. She'd make some excuse later, had no intention of showing her face in that shop again if she could help it. Though she had to ask: 'How is Uncle Bernard?' After all, he was the only member of that family she held any real feeling towards.

'Ah, the usual. Hen-pecked to buggery and none the worse for it, you know?'

Jewel chuckled. 'Aye. He must love her a lot, you know – Aunt Esther.'

'Oh aye. Eeh, but rather him than me. That gob on her . . . talk about bleeding earholes.'

Nodding, Jewel laughed quietly again. A thaw was setting in and she welcomed it wholeheartedly. She'd missed this: her and her mam's easy chatter, putting the world to rights.

Mam.

The warmness dimmed somewhat in remembrance

311

and she beat the thoughts back with a feeling of panic. *Forget it, forget it. It matters not. It doesn't . . .*

'What's to do, lass?'

Flora's words came to her as though from a distance. She couldn't move, speak. For her eyes had strayed to the mantel top and the sight of the familiar piece had seized her in a hypnotic trap.

Following Jewel's gaze to the candlestick, Flora's voice was light with amused puzzlement: 'Lass? You gone daft?'

She couldn't uphold this pretence, had been foolish to think she could. It wouldn't leave her, not for a second, was killing her inside . . . She brought her stare back to her mother, and the name fell from her lips: 'Minnie Maddox.'

'Eh?'

'Minnie Maddox,' Jewel repeated, louder now.

Time seemed to halt in its tracks. Flora's cup slipped slowly from her hand and smashed on the hard, flagged floor. Eyes huge, she shook her head.

'She told me everything,' Jewel murmured. 'I know you're not my mam.'

'Lies. It's all, all lies—!'

'Nay. It ain't. Why didn't you *tell* me?'

The woman released a pent-up sigh. Her shoulders drooped and the corners of her quivering mouth followed. When finally she spoke, her tone was hollow. 'I've allus loved thee.'

'So it is true?'

'You're *my lass*!'

'No, no, no, no, *no*!' Panting with dumbfoundedness, Jewel swung her head. 'I've prayed 'til I ran out of words, convinced myself it were a mistake. But I knew. Deep down, I did. Your child, Flora and Fred Nightingale's long-awaited miracle . . . she died. Mrs Maddox passed me off as her, and you knew. You knew and said nothing.'

Hanging her head, Flora burst into tears.

'Who was I? One of Mrs Maddox's waifs? An unwanted she could do with as she liked, for there was no one to question my true whereabouts, miss me, care? Is that it?'

'I've allus loved thee,' repeated Flora brokenly, then winced when Jewel thumped the tabletop in fury.

'I was second best. I *am* second best. The one whose place I stole, she's from your flesh, the one you wanted. She's your daughter, not I—'

'Stop! I'll not hear that, for it's false, it is!'

'I don't believe you.' Jewel's devastation had reached manic proportions. 'I weren't nowt special. You were just desperate forra child. *Any* child would have done.'

'*You* . . .' Flora's eyes burned with passion. '*You* are Jewel Nightingale. Do you hear me? Well, do yer? You are my child. I am *your mother.* Not you, nor Minnie, nor any swine else can claim different. *Never.* You're my own precious jewel, same as you've allus been. Then, now, always. Right?' She grasped Jewel by her upper arms and shook her hard in desperation. '*Right?*'

'Mam.' She exhaled the word on a tortured breath. 'Oh, Mam!'

'Oh, my lass!'

Sobbing, they hugged tightly. For the next few minutes, neither spoke, simply poured out their grief and pain and love, feeding each other's souls with proof – *truth* – of their unbreakable bond.

'Who am I, Mam? Who am I really?' She felt Flora shake her head against her. 'Please. I have to know.'

'I don't know, and that's the truth.'

Crushing uncertainty left her desolate. She wept anew.

313

'You poor, poor lass.'

'Oh, Mam.'

'I'm so sorry, Jewel. I'd take this hurt off you in a heartbeat if I could. Eeh, dearest daughter.'

' "Dearest daughter",' she repeated in a whisper. In that moment, she thought the pain would kill her. 'Mam, there's summat I've not told thee.'

She must. How could she continue to keep her secret after all she'd just said to Flora? She was a hypocrite of the highest order, wasn't she? Blasting this woman for concealing the truth, when all the time . . . If there was one thing she'd learned this day, it was the importance of trust. Without it, what was the point in anything?

In broken snatches, Jewel told her mother everything. The ale, the trees. Benji. The shame, terror. Her plan to seduce Jem Wicks. The horse and cart and what she'd intended. The bribery and the scissors, the taking of Bernard's money. Bickerstaff. Canal Street and its occupants, the horrific birth. And her precious offspring. Her agony at the parting, and how much she missed her. She left out nothing.

'There's summat else – tha might as well hear it all,' Jewel continued when Flora had stumbled to her chair and was sitting, staring into space. 'I think I'm in love with my master, Mr Birch. He's thrice my age and a gentleman, to boot, and I've fallen for him.' Shrugging, she laughed mirthlessly. 'My life is a shambles. *I'm* a sodding shambles. So there you have it. I bet now you're wishing Mrs Maddox had given you another babby instead of me, ain't yer?'

For an age, Flora seemed incapable of speech. Then, voice flat: 'Come to me, lass.'

Jewel flew to her. Falling to her knees by her feet, she rested her head in her mother's lap. Flora stroked her hair and she closed her eyes. 'I've made a mess of everything.'

'Not thee. He's to blame for this, that foul young dog across the way.'

'What am I going to do, Mam?'

'We, my lass. You ain't alone with this burden any longer.'

'Eeh, Mam. I wish I'd come to thee sooner. I were just . . . so ashamed and . . . I just couldn't find the words—'

'I know, I know.'

'I've been that scared.'

Flora breathed slowly and her next words came through gritted teeth. 'Don't tha fear a thing, not no more.'

'What will happen now, with Benji?'

'Shh. That'll come later.'

'And . . . what I said about Mr Birch?'

To this, Flora made no comment. Instead, she nodded decisively. 'First things first . . .'

'Aye?'

'First things first,' the woman said again, straightening her shoulders. 'We fetch your babby home.'

Jewel's head snapped back to gape at her. 'Mam?'

'Is it what tha wants?'

'Yes! Oh, yes, more than owt, but . . . ? What will folk say?'

'I care naught for that, and nor should thee. You've nowt to be ashamed for.'

'How would I manage, what with work and money; husbandless into the bargain—'

'*We.* Remember?'

Eyes swimming, Jewel crushed a hand to her mouth. 'You really mean it, Mam? *Thank* you. I love thee, I do.

Eeh, Mam, wait 'til you see her. She's an angel from heaven, really. When can we . . . ?'

'There's no time like the present.' Rising, Flora inclined her head across the room. 'Fetch me my shawl, lass.'

Jewel's joy was almost too much. How had she ever doubted this woman her pure and selfless heart? Why hadn't she confessed all to her sooner? She'd been such a coward, *such a fool*. But, God above, was this happening? She was to keep her daughter? The child was coming home? Jewel couldn't believe it, wouldn't until she was safely in her arms again. *Please don't let this all be a dream, sweet Lord.*

'Now I don't want thee fretting but I must say this, so take heed,' announced Flora, pausing by the door.

'What is it?'

'Yon babby might not still be where tha left her. Minnie could have found new parents for her already.'

The terrible prospect turned the blood in her veins to ice. With all the strength she could muster, she nodded bravely. 'I understand, Mam. But we must try.'

'That we must, and the sooner the better. Make haste, lass, come on.'

*

'Mam?'

'I'm all right. Just the memories, Jewel, you know?'

'Nay, I don't,' she answered truthfully – what did she know of anything any more? – and Flora winced.

'Course, aye. Sorry, my lass.' She nodded to the imposing building that she'd halted by. 'This here glassworks was where my Fred toiled many moons ago, along with Minnie's husband. The candlestick back home, it were presented when he passed away for his service to the company. All employees received one. I never mentioned that – Manchester, nor the rest – lest you probed further and my lies tripped me up,' she admitted.

Jewel nodded slowly in understanding. That explained then why Mrs Maddox owned the same one. The old woman, clearly sensing that the facts had been bent regarding how her mother came by hers, had withheld the truth, likely hadn't wanted to involve herself in the matter. All this information only now coming to light . . . What else had she yet to discover?

'Eeh, but I miss him.'

'Mam, did Father know . . . about me?'

'Nay. I think it were for the best, an' all. Now then,' she continued, fixing her stare on Minnie's dwelling. 'Let's do what we came here to.'

'You'll not be angry with her, will you? Mrs Maddox, I mean? She did the right thing in telling me; I did have a right to know. Besides, we'd not be here now, come to take my daughter home, if not for her confessing. I'd likely not ever have plucked up courage to tell thee had we not argued about my beginnings.'

'I'm not angry, lass. Truth be told, I've missed the wench deeply. I just couldn't . . . thought it best to put that part of my life behind me upon arriving in Bolton, didn't want to risk you finding out . . . Aye well. It came out in t' wash in t' end, eh, as things allus do.'

Mother and daughter trained their gazes back on the house. They took a simultaneous breath and crossed the street to Minnie's door.

'Hello, Eliza, love.'

'Flora? By!' Her amazement slipped. 'Will tha come in?' she asked hesitantly.

Flora nodded, and Jewel eagerly followed her inside, eyes darting straight to the bed, desperate for a glimpse of her daughter.

317

Minnie rose slowly from her chair, her dread-filled gaze locking with Flora's. 'Wench . . . Wench, I—'

'Hello, Minnie.' Flora held out her arms. After a long and confused hesitation, a stunned Minnie ambled into them.

'Oh. Eeh, love, I've missed thee. I had to tell Jewel, lass. I had to, for the act has ate away at me each day since. I believed it the right thing to do, I did, I—'

'It's all right, wench. I allus knew it would come out some day. You're right. Jewel deserved the truth. I were just too much of a coward to reveal it myself.'

'Mrs Maddox?' Scanning the infants for a third time, Jewel was becoming frantic. 'Where's my child? She ain't here. Where *is* she?'

Minnie and Eliza exchanged puzzled looks. 'You know where,' remarked the latter. 'You gave your consent, after all.'

Jewel couldn't breathe. 'She's gone?'

'Aye.'

She was too late. *No, no.* 'You've found new parents for her already?'

Minnie was frowning deeply. 'Sit down, lass.'

'Nay! Nay, I have to know where she is, I . . . I want her back. Mam knows everything, has vowed to support me . . . I want my daughter!'

'Sit down,' repeated the old woman. Her expression was serious. She nodded forcefully to a chair at the table. 'Seems I've been hoodwinked, and we need to figure out why . . . Please, Jewel.'

Jewel sat. She grasped one of Flora's hands and the two of them awaited Minnie's explanation with wide-eyed dread.

'Hoodwinked?' asked Flora.

'By who?' Jewel added.

318

'Sarah's sister came and collected your babby last night.'

'What?'

'She said as how you'd agreed, that Sarah was to raise her as her own—'

'That's lies!' Jewel leapt to her feet. 'Why would you believe that drunken mess? What the hell is her game? How could you hand my child over to her, the *state* of her. I must go there. I'll *kill* her!'

'Wait.'

Something in Minnie's tone made Jewel halt by the door. She turned questioningly.

'I'll tell thee why I let that woman take off with the child. It's because I assumed that Sarah, having discovered . . . I thought she wanted to make things right this time. She has a tie there, after all—'

'Tie? Discovered what? Tell me!'

'When your mother—' Minnie paused and shot Flora an apologetic look. 'When your *birth* mother brought you here that day, lass, she were just like you were – hurting. Difference being, she wore an icy mask that never slipped. It's a common front that a lot of women adopt; self-protection, like, to cover up their true feelings and keep at bay the pain of giving up their child. Anyroad, a few short months after Flora moved with thee to Bolton, your birth mother showed up at my door wanting you back.' She nodded sadly. 'I told her you'd gone to a new family already, that it were too late and nowt could be done, that she must believe you'd gone to a good home and to put thee from her mind.

'She bleated in my arms like a newborn lamb but accepted you would be happy and well cared for, and that this was for the best. It brought her some comfort, you know? Well, from that day, she became a regular visitor, and it grew into a friendship, aye. I were keen to keep an eye on her welfare; she liked the bottle too much, and her family were a no-good lot, with the reputation of it, to boot. I felt sorry for her – and guilty, aye. I couldn't have her tracking down Flora and demanding thee back, for that would have benefited no one. But by, she never forgot thee, lass. You allus – *allus* – held a piece of her heart.'

'Oh, wench.' Flora had her face in her hand, her sorrow tangible. 'That poor woman.'

Minnie nodded. 'As much as my own heart hurt for her, I knew Jewel was better off with thee. What was done was done. Uprooting the lass, wrenching her from you, who she saw as her mam, shattering your life in the process . . . It wouldn't have been right, nay. It wouldn't.'

Jewel had flopped back into her chair. Wordless, head bowed, she tried to process this fresh information. One thing, however, needed no extra thought: Mrs Maddox had done the right thing in leaving her in Flora's care. Had her birth mother showed up in Bolton, taken her away from Mam . . . It would have killed Flora, she was certain. Besides, from the little Minnie had just revealed, it was doubtful she'd have fared well in the other woman's care.

Having been raised by Flora had been a blessing, she realised. Although knowing that her real mother had come back for her, had wanted her after all, hadn't simply abandoned her without another thought, did make her feel ever so slightly better. She wasn't the unwanted she'd come to believe she was, not entirely. Oh, but the whole situation was such a sorry bloody *mess*.

'What has all this got to do with Sarah's sister taking

my daughter?' she asked, though, deep down, she already knew the answer.

That Minnie had wanted to tell her something about Sarah the last time she was here . . . How comfortable she herself had felt from the beginning in Sarah's presence, like she somehow knew her, though she couldn't understand why . . . It all made sense. As if, somehow, fate had finally brought them back together.

All this Jewel processed as though through a sheet of thick glass. Reality was muffled, emotions numbed. The truth was the truth, but it couldn't penetrate the clogging shock she was shrouded in.

'Sarah's your birth mother, lass,' confirmed Minnie, and Jewel accepted it with a nod. 'She came here looking for thee that evening after you fled. She'd been expecting thee back, were worried. I revealed who you were – had to – for Sarah deserved the truth, too, once you knew it. She left here promising to find thee, said that she'd put things right. So, when her sister came later for the child, I believed you'd returned to Canal Street, that you and Sarah had talked – though I see now you're only just hearing of her true identity. I thought Sarah had offered to raise her grandchild for thee, that you were in agreement.'

'Nay,' Jewel murmured flatly. 'I left Manchester without saying goodbye to her, haven't seen her since.' She lifted her eyes to Minnie's. 'How did she take the news that I'm her daughter?'

'As you might expect, lass.' A tear dripped to the old woman's cheek. 'She were beside herself.'

'She told me she didn't have children. I asked her once and she said nay.' Jewel shrugged. 'Well, she didn't, did she? She gave up the title of mother the day she left me here with thee.' She wrapped her arms around

321

herself. 'Do I deserve *my* daughter back? Didn't *I* forgo all rights, too, when I walked from this house without mine?'

'Be that as it may – in your mind, at any rate,' said Flora, squeezing her hand, 'but the fact remains, lass: these wenches lied. They took your babby without permission. That, they had no right to do. Just 'cause she gave her own child away, and whatever the reasons for it might have been, it don't give her leave to steal yours. Now I say we go around there and get the mite back.'

Minnie nodded. 'I'll come along with thee, see if I can't talk some sense into her—'

'Nay.' Jewel looked to them both. 'Please. This is summat I must do alone.'

That it wasn't just her getting the child back that she was referring to, both women seemed to understand. They nodded. Jewel gave them each a sad smile in return, then left the house.

When she reached the familiar dwelling in Canal Street, the front door was swinging wide. She entered, closing it quietly behind her, and climbed the stairs to the sisters' room. As she neared, she heard the distant sound of a child's cry – *my baby*. She cleared the landing in a heartbeat and burst inside.

'Well, looky here.'

Jewel took in the scene slowly. On a sofa, the griping child clutched protectively in her arms, was Sarah. Standing before the dead fire was her sister and, as Jewel's gaze settled on the knife in her hand, she swallowed hard.

'Looky here,' the woman repeated, stepping forward. Her lip curled. 'Shut the door. Now.'

Jewel did as she bade. All the while, it took all her strength not to run and snatch up her baby; the crazed

322

look in the slattern's drunken eye deterred her. She moved gingerly into the room.

'Stop there,' the woman snarled, jabbing the blade through the air between them.

'What's all this?' Jewel asked, heart thumping. 'Sarah?'

'Shut it. You talk to me, all right, not her!' Swaying slightly, the woman swished the weapon again. 'So. You've returned, eh? And, by God, you best have fetched along with thee what belongs to me.'

'I have nowt belonging to you—'

'Liar!'

Jewel glanced once more to Sarah, who stared back desperately, tears coursing down her face. 'What does she mean?'

'I had two visitors at yon door on Sunday, not long after you left,' shot Sarah's sister before she could speak. Nodding, she took a swig from a bottle of strong spirits then fixed her murderous glare back on Jewel. 'First 'un were a bobby to say they'd found my Julia. Seems she fell foul to a bad make of customer. Dragged her from the canal, the police did; naked, beaten and lifeless.'

'Mother of God . . .' Jewel covered her mouth with her hand. 'Eeh, I'm sorry.'

To this, the woman didn't respond. Again, she took a long draught of alcohol. 'D'you know who the second visitor were? Go on, guess.'

'I don't . . .' Frowning, Jewel shook her head.

'Mr bleedin' Brown.'

'Who?'

'Julia's lover.' The woman's tone was high, mocking. 'Remember, him what bought her that pretty ring at Christmas?'

'Him who she were mistress to?'

'Aye, that's the one – you catch on quick, don't yer?'

323

she sneered with a roll of her eyes. 'Word soon spread to the inns and alehouses that the police had been here and why, and our Mr Brown heard. Hotfooted it here, he did, broken-hearted. 'Ere, and guess what he told me?'

Clueless still, Jewel shook her head once more.

'Turns out that snidy bitch daughter of mine were saving. Fancy that, eh? She'd told him months afore, reckoned she fancied herself a nest egg, summat forra rainy day. He thought it only right to make mention of it, reckoned it might aid with the cost of the funeral. And yet . . .' Rushing to the painting hanging nearby, she swiped it from the wall, sending it crashing to the ground. 'What do I find? Nowt. Empty. Gone!' Nostrils flared, she crept closer to Jewel, the knife's tip pointed straight at her. 'You had it away, didn't yer? You thieving young *bitch*, yer!'

Jewel's face was void of blood. 'Nay. I didn't.'

'Aye, you did. And you'll give it back, or so help me that brat of yourn will cover the costs for the rest of her life.'

'You what?' Hands beginning to shake with white-hot rage, Jewel stepped closer. 'That was your plan, was it? Snatching her from Mrs Maddox 'cause you think *I* stole that rotten brass?' She looked to Sarah. 'You – *you're* in on this? Mother of God, how could you, given what you've learned—'

'Lass, nay. I've played no part in this, I've not. She collected the child without my knowledge—!'

'What you've learned?' The woman turned narrowed eyes to her sister. 'What's she on about?'

'I wanted to go and find thee in Bolton, had to explain . . . *She* wouldn't let me leave, threatened to harm the child if I tried. Besides, I knew you don't need nor want someone like me, I know, I just . . . I just had to see your face one more time. Oh, lass. Oh, I love thee, have *allus* loved thee.'

Jewel stared back through a film of tears. 'Sarah . . .'

'I couldn't give thee what tha needed, had no choice—'

'What's going on?' demanded her sister. 'Well?'

'Jewel, she . . . She's the child I gave up all those years ago.'

'Ay. Fancy that. So, you're one of us, are yer?'

Jewel lifted her chin. 'You're nowt but a disgusting hussy. I'm nothing like thee, and neither is my daughter.'

'Is that so?'

'Nor, for that matter, is Sarah.'

'Huh! That dried up owd slut? She's had more pricks than a second-hand pincushion.'

Seeing shame colour Sarah's face, anger and an odd sense of protectiveness brought blood rushing back to Jewel's own. 'She's got one thing you ain't, though: a heart. You . . . What I've witnessed with my two eyes . . . To sell the bodies of your own offspring like you did all those years without a shred of conscience? You're the devil's own daughter, you are.'

The woman was nonplussed. 'Aye, well. *They've* gone, the pair, now, ain't they?'

'Not afore time.'

'But you . . . you're here, ain't yer?' Wiggling her eyebrows, she nodded. 'And here you'll stay – the infant along with you – until I get my money back.'

'I've told thee, I didn't take the—'

'You'll stop on here whether I have to tie the pair of youse to that bloody bed, and you'll work your debt.' Her eyes moved to the child. 'Oh, yes. There's fellas aplenty what will pay handsomely to be the first to take her innocence. Likes them young, some do, aye.'

'You foul-tongued *bitch*!' Springing forward, Jewel

325

lunged at the woman – stopping short when metal flashed by her cheek. Gasping, her furious gaze flicked from the blade to the smirking face. In the next moment, her plait was grabbed and her head wrenched back. The cold point dug into her jaw and she closed her eyes.

'You leave Jewel be!' screamed Sarah.

'Where's my brass?'

Beads of perspiration had sprung at Jewel's top lip, and her heart threatened to leap from her chest. After sending out a silent apology to the absconder – and a plea that the girl never returned, if this was what awaited her once the truth was out – she murmured, 'Louise. She took it.'

'Nay. She wouldn't. It's you—'

'Didn't I tell thee? You'd not believe me, would you, but look, *see* the honesty in her eyes. She speaks the truth. Louise has gone, and for good.' Holding the child away from her sister, Sarah rose. Her voice was firm. 'Now let Jewel go.'

'The girl wouldn't do that, not to me.'

'Aye, 'cause you're worthy of her loyalty, ain't yer?'

The venom in Sarah's tone had her sister glancing her way in surprise. It was clear she'd never known her to stand up to her; she was at a loss how to react.

'All these years, I let you convince me I'd not survive without you. I needed you, yer said, for who else did I have? You've ruined me, aye, you have. But d'you know the worst of it? May the Lord forgive me, I've sat back like a bleedin' coward and watched thee destroy them girls of yourn. But listen here. You'll not do the same with these girls – *my* girls. I'll tear your head from your neck for you if you so much as think to. By God, I will. Now, for the last time, let Jewel go.'

326

As though in a daze, the woman obeyed, and Jewel rushed to Sarah's side.

'Come on.' Eyes never leaving her sister, Sarah guided Jewel to the door.

'Please. I can't be alone. I can't!'

Sarah paused on the landing. 'It's what you deserve and more,' she murmured over her shoulder. Then she put an arm around Jewel and they walked from the house without a backward glance.

Outside, Sarah looked down at the child in her arms. 'This cherub, my granddaughter ... And you,' she added, lifting shining eyes to Jewel. 'Always know I love you.'

Jewel could barely speak past the lump in her throat. 'Sarah . . . I—'

'Shh. It's all right, lass. I understand. I'll be all right.' She handed the baby over, gave them each a last, lingering look and walked away.

Watching her retreating back, tears splashed to Jewel's cheeks. She pictured Sarah doing this same thing seventeen years ago, appreciating only too well the strength it had taken. Now, however, must surely sear far more. To meet again the one for whom you never stopped caring, thinking about, yearning for with every fibre of your being, only to face the parting a second time? How did she bear it? Once more, she was putting her own wants, her own pain, aside for what she believed was the good of her child. Here, without doubt, was living proof that a mother's love knows no bounds. Jewel knew that if she'd inherited just an ounce of Sarah's fortitude she wouldn't go far wrong.

The figure up ahead grew smaller. Deep in Jewel's breast, the ache intensified.

Wait.

At the corner, Sarah paused. She made a movement with her head, as if to look back. Then, as though thinking better of it, she picked up her feet and continued on her way.

Wait, please.

When she'd disappeared from sight, Jewel released a soft breath. Then she was running, running, to catch her up:

'Sarah! Sarah! Come back!'

Chapter 23

SHE UTTERED NOTHING when Jewel halted, panting from the exertion, in front of her. Nor did she have to; her eyes said it all.

'I don't want thee to go.'

A solitary tear rolled down Sarah's cheek. She laughed brokenly.

'Flora, the woman who raised me, will allus be my mam. But . . .'

'But?' whispered Sarah.

'I'd like you in my life, an' all. We both would, me and your granddaughter. If you'll have us?'

'Eeh, love. Oh, you don't know what this means, my precious one,' Sarah murmured into Jewel's hair as she enveloped them both in a hug. 'How much and for how long I've dreamed of this moment. I can scarcely believe it's here.'

Jewel smiled softly. 'You'll come to Mrs Maddox's? Meet Mam?'

Her joy visibly waned. 'Happen she won't want me around, though? Not that I could blame her, mind. As you said, she's your mother, lass. Whilst I . . .' Her eyes creased in shame. 'Why would she – why would *you* – want someone such as me in your life? By God, the things you've witnessed in that room back there.' Moaning, she

329

dropped her chin to her chest. 'I'm foul, I am. To have thee see . . . Oh, I can't *bear* it.'

'Sarah.' Jewel took her elbow as she turned to flee. 'I care naught for what's gone afore. It's now and all our tomorrows that matter. Please. Please come.'

Another long embrace and more tears later, they headed arm in arm for Kirby Street.

Flora needed no introductions; she seemed to sense instinctively who the woman with her daughter was. She glanced from one to the other in the doorway, and Jewel felt the foreboding emitting from her. Was Mam worried she'd lose her now Sarah was on the scene? *Oh, Mam. Never, never.*

'All well?' asked Minnie cautiously.

Jewel and Sarah looked at one another then smiled and nodded.

'Eeh, well. Thanks be to God for it.' Eliza patted Minnie's shoulder in shared relief then beckoned them over. 'Sit down, take a sup.'

Flicking her gaze to Flora, Sarah seemed hesitant. Jewel gave her a look of encouragement and, catching it, she perched on a chair. Holding the baby up with tears of pride shining from her eyes, Jewel then crossed to her mother.

'Ay, lass.' Taking her granddaughter into her arms, Flora was entranced. 'By, would you look at her, the little angel. She's your image at that age, Jewel, she is, really.'

'Aye, she is,' agreed Sarah, and lowered her head quickly when Flora glanced up. 'Sorry. I didn't mean . . . What I meant were, it's just—'

'It's all right, Sarah.' Flora's voice was soft. 'All this . . . it's hard for me, an' all. But the fact remains: Jewel were your lass afore she came to me. You've memories of her same as I have. Don't be ashamed or think yourself unworthy of holding them. What happened happened, and it ain't for me nor no one else to judge thee on it. You've a right to know this lass, here, as much as me. You do, aye.'

It was like the sun had come out behind Sarah's eyes; she exhaled what seemed like a lifetime of strife. 'Mrs Nightingale, I—'

'Call me Flora, lass.'

'Flora. Eeh, I were dreading meeting thee. D'you know, I've wondered all these years what the woman who got my daughter might be like, and now . . .' She paused to swallow back a sob. 'Now I see you're all I hoped for. You, Mrs Nightingale – Flora. You're a proper mam, just as the lass needed – *deserved*. I don't know how I'll ever be able to . . .' Taking Flora's hand, she pressed it to her lips and closed her eyes. 'Thank you for being her mother and for raising her with love. Thank you for everything.'

There wasn't a dry eye in the room. In silence, Jewel and the others looked on with sad smiles.

'And thank you, lass.' Flora's voice was just as thick. 'Thanks for the years you gave me with Jewel. There's no ill feelings on my side, nay, and I'm heartened that tha feels the same with myself. Time to put the past behind us, now, eh? Whatever our lass decides is good enough for me.'

The two of them looked to Jewel for an answer, and she breathed deeply. For only now was the full enormity of all that had occurred over the last few days hitting her. Both of these women had a claim to her. Flora would, as she'd stated, always be her mam. Yet a firm bond had already formed with Sarah. Since the night on the top stair of the house in Canal Street, when she'd sat enjoying the cold pie and tea that the closed-off, kind-eyed stranger had given her, she'd felt it. Something. Some tie she hadn't been able to fathom then.

331

But had Flora really spoken the truth? Would it honestly not pain her to have Sarah in their lives? To share her only child with a woman who, in effect, possessed a stronger link – that of blood – with her? Jewel wouldn't have Mam upset, not for the world. Neither did she wish to hurt Sarah. What was she to do?

'Look into your heart, lass.'

Minnie's wisdom reached out to her across the table, as though she sensed her dilemma, and Jewel looked to her in grateful desperation.

'The decision must be yours alone. These women here want only what you want, for your happiness is their happiness. You see?'

She did. She smiled and squeezed Flora's and Sarah's hands in turn. 'I think . . . I need you both. I *want* you both in my life. If that's all right?'

'Ay, of course it is, love,' Flora told her.

'Oh, lass,' cried Sarah softly.

Looking down at her own child, Jewel was struck with such overwhelming love it took her breath away. A feeling of completeness warmed her soul and she sent it out to encompass the others.

For the first time in a long time the future looked promising. And it felt wonderful.

*

On the train journey home, Jewel and her mother discussed what was to be done about Benji. Though Flora spoke in a hushed voice so that the other passengers wouldn't overhear, her eyes couldn't conceal her simmering rage.

'I'll break his face for him. And just let that mother of his try and deny it and, by, I'll rip her limb from limb, an' all.'

Jewel suppressed a sigh. Though understanding absolutely Mam's feelings, this was exactly what she'd wanted to avoid: the family at war. But the truth was, the confrontation to come was not only unavoidable but necessary. The Powells had to know what had occurred – particularly now there was a visible child involved. Besides, Benji deserved punishment. Nevertheless, the knotting in her stomach only intensified with each passing mile that took them closer to Bolton, and the holy storm of upset she just knew awaited her.

Then there was the other issue that was slowly killing her inside.

Maxwell's face struck in her mind and she winced at what it brought to her heart. Whatever brainless designs she'd had were unquestionably dashed for ever. When he discovered . . . and of course he *must* . . . He'd want nothing more to do with her.

Suddenly, her chin lifted. To hell with it. It had been daft dreamings and nothing more anyway. Besides, she had nothing to feel ashamed about. She'd begot this child here through no fault of her own. What's more, she regretted nothing. Not now; how could she? Her daughter – her gift – was *wanted*. Never would she feel otherwise, never, and if others – the man she loved included – saw it differently, that was their problem. And by God, she'd tell them so, too.

'When we arrive, you take yourself home and get the babby settled,' Flora was saying now. '*I'll* confront that lot at the shop.'

'You didn't mention Uncle Bernard.' Jewel turned to face her. 'You said as how Aunt Esther shall likely deny her son of wrongdoing, but not him. He'll not doubt my word, then, you reckon?'

Flora's eyes narrowed. 'Just you leave it all to me.'

333

They lapsed into silence. The train hissed to a stop at Trinity Street Station and they set off on the short distance home, and still neither spoke. What was there to say, after all? Words aplenty would follow soon, all right, though none good. This day was to change everything. Once the Powells heard what Flora had to say, life as they knew it would never be the same, for any of them.

At their door, Jewel paused. 'Happen I should come with thee, Mam—'

'Nay. You and the child go on inside. I'll sort it.'

Though ashamed at herself at not pressing her further, Jewel felt relief. Truth be told, the last thing she wanted was to be present when the details emerged. It would be like reliving it all again and besides, Esther's insistence that it didn't happen – for it was inevitable, wasn't it? – she'd rather not see. The anger and pain of it would be too much. More so should Bernard, too, choose to deny it.

She watched her mother stride away across the cobbles. Then she closed the door quietly behind her. Entering the kitchen, a little of her misery faded. She peered around the familiar space with a quiet smile.

'I can hardly believe you're here, precious one,' she whispered to her daughter, brushing her cheek against hers. 'You're home, my lass.'

Sarah, sitting contentedly by Minnie's hearth, entered her imagination and, again, she smiled. Upon hearing that she'd finally broken free of her sister's clutches, the old woman had insisted Sarah stop on with her and Eliza. Warmth, safety and true companionship were hers now, and not before time. Her demons, along with the drink, she could banish. Sarah deserved nothing less, and Jewel couldn't have been more pleased for her. They had agreed earlier to regular visits, and both knew that nothing would stand in the way. They had been parted for too long but had a lifetime to make up for it.

After taking the baby upstairs to the bedroom, Jewel returned to the kitchen and made for the fire to brew some tea, desperate for the distraction. Despite her best efforts, her thoughts had switched to the drama surely playing out right now in the shop, and dread of the inevitable result returned to torment her. Wringing her hands as she waited for the kettle to boil, she almost leapt out of her skin when a knock came at the door.

She stared at it for a moment, picturing her aunt and uncle's livid faces just waiting beyond, the smug Benji with them, and tried to muster up the strength to hold her nerve at the onslaught to come. A second rap sounded. She sucked in a deep breath and forced herself forward to answer it.

'Jewel. Here you are.'

She stared dumbly at her visitor. This was the very last person she'd expected. 'Sir.'

'May I come in?'

'Aye, yes.' She held the door wide and, when Maxwell stepped inside, pointed to a chair. 'Please, sit.'

'Thank you.'

'Sir, about me abandoning my duties this morning without a by-your-leave—'

'I understand.'

Her speech dying, she frowned. 'Tha does?'

'Jewel . . .' Stare fixed on his hands on the tabletop, Maxwell sighed. 'I can only apologise for my behaviour yesterday. I assure you it will not happen again. Won't you please consider coming back?'

He thought she'd abandoned her position because of the moment they had shared in the kitchen at Mawdsley Street. Oh, if only that were it . . .

'Sir, you misunderstand.' She nodded when he lifted his head in surprise. 'The reason I left ain't because of . . . what you think.'

'But . . . I embarrassed you—'

'Nay, sir, you didn't,' she cut in quietly.

'I didn't make matters between us so awkward that you felt you had no option but to leave?'

'Nay.' *A thousand times, nay.*

'Then what?'

Slipping into the chair opposite his, she gave a brittle laugh. 'What, you ask? Lord, where to start?'

'I find the beginning is usually the best place.'

Despite her heartache, she couldn't help but smile when he winked. 'Oh, sir.'

'Tell me. Please.'

'I . . . have a child.' What easier way was there of saying it? There wasn't. Nor was there any point in dressing the facts up. It was what it was.

'Pardon?'

'Aye. A daughter. I'd planned to have her adopted out but changed my mind. That's where I went to the day: Manchester, fetching her home. It were wrong of me to just take off without your permission, but time was not on our side.'

'But . . .' Eyes dazed, he ran a hand through his hair. 'When? *How?*'

'She were born several weeks past. I lied, sir – there were no ailing aunt. That were an excuse to allow me to go away to have her in secret.'

It was evident that he found the calmness in which she was delivering her responses just as baffling as the revelations themselves; his gaze had narrowed suspiciously. 'All this . . . Jewel, is it some elaborate joke?'

She shook her head. 'That it ain't. As to how . . . My

cousin forced himself upon me the night of the town hall opening. You remember mentioning you'd seen him at the park, pouring away his own drink? He got me skenning and took my innocence.' She swallowed a few times before continuing. 'That day he arrived at your house and you opened the door to him? D'you remember, sir?'

'Yes,' Maxwell whispered.

'It were to speak to me about brass I'd told him he must find to pay the adoption fee.'

He rose and crossed to the fire. Grasping the corner of the mantel, he bowed his head. 'Why didn't you tell me?'

'How could I? I couldn't reveal it to a soul. Mam only discovered the truth this morning. She's round there right now, having it out with him and his parents.'

'I've a good mind to join her this instant and—' He broke off and breathed deeply. 'Your child?'

'Upstairs soundly sleeping.'

He was silent for a long moment. Then he turned to face her. 'The incident with the cart.'

'Aye.'

'This is the reason you wanted to end your life.'

She nodded. 'I could see no other option at the time.'

On another breath, he closed his eyes. 'Oh, Jewel.'

'Yesterday, in the kitchen of your house, when you walked in on me crying . . .' Colour pinched her cheeks at the mention of it. 'I were missing the babby.'

He visibly cringed. 'Oh, Jewel,' he murmured again.

'But, sir?' She rose and made towards him when he continued looking at the floor. 'Sir. Look at me, please.'

'Jewel . . .'

'You helped ease the pain a little. Your kindness, warmth . . . It meant an awful lot.'

'No.'

She frowned. 'Sir?'

'No, Jewel. It wasn't . . . *I shouldn't . . .*'

'What—?'

'I wanted to kiss you.' The words tumbled from him. 'You were upset and I . . . I took advantage of you, I'm sorry.'

Her breath came in short bursts. 'Sir . . .'

'I don't know, cannot explain . . . I was drawn to you, Jewel, from the very start. Your vulnerability . . . I saw something in you I recognised. My feelings, they have deepened for you further this past . . .'

Where Jewel found the courage, she couldn't think – she pressed her lips to his, smothering his rant. After a few stunned moments, Maxwell enveloped her in his arms and kissed her back hungrily.

Dizzying sensations touched every part of her; the only thing that was missing was fear. Her attempted seduction of Jem Wicks and her encounters with the Manchester men had brought back the ordeal like a hammer blow, but not now. This time, with this man, no harrowing memories of Benji's assault crept in to mar it. Even when she felt Maxwell grow hard against her, she didn't blanch. Only peace and light – and the fierce need to explore him further – consumed her, and she matched his furore completely.

'Jewel . . .'

'Please, don't stop,' she begged, drawing his mouth back to hers.

A low growl escaped him as, grasping her buttocks, he drew her body closer. Then, with an obvious struggle, he pulled back once more. 'Wait, Jewel, we—'

Passion blazed through every inch of her. 'What? What?'

'God help me.' His breathing was ragged. 'This is taking every ounce of strength I possess, but we must . . . we must stop. We can't. Not here, not like this.'

Though she knew he spoke sense, frustration had her swinging away from him with a frown.

'Jewel—'

'Sorry. You're right. I just . . .' Feeling tears close by, she blinked desperately. 'I wanted to enjoy this moment, even for just a few seconds longer, before . . . before it all ends. For it has to. This – us – it must stop here, I know it.'

'That is what you want?'

'Nay, never. It's what *must* be.'

'Why, Jewel?'

Her emotions got the better of her and she crumpled. 'Because of all I have told thee, of course. Everything that has happened. My *daughter*, remember? It would have been difficult enough without this; who we are . . . you being you, and me being who I'm not. Now, it's impossible.'

'Says who?'

She lifted wet eyes to his. Something in his expression caused her heart to thump in hopeful disbelief.

'You think I care a jot for convention? Jewel, you disappoint me; I thought you knew me better than that by now.'

Her voice was barely above a whisper. 'What are you saying?'

'Isn't it obvious? I love you. I need you. I want you, body and mind. Us, our children, a marriage, home. To spend together what days we have left on this earth side by side, hand in hand, heart to heart. That's what I'm saying. I want it all. I only have to know that you do too.' He took her hands and lifted them to his chest. 'Say it. I must hear it from your lips.'

Her shoulders heaved with elated sobs. 'I want it,' she mouthed.

'Again.'

'I want it!' Now, it was a raw cry. Laughing, they threw themselves into each other's arms.

'Come with me, back to Mawdsley Street,' said Maxwell when they drew apart.

'This minute?'

'Why not? Collect the child and let's just go, start our life together this *second*. What's stopping us?'

Jewel accepted his kisses with a grin. 'My love . . .'

'Is that a yes?'

'The morrow. I promise,' she added when disappointment creased his eyes. 'Tonight, I must be with Mam. We have much to discuss. I have to tell her about us. And I have to hear what's occurred with the Powells. I need her to be all right with it all. You understand?'

He held her closer. 'I do.'

'I love thee.'

After a lingering goodbye, Jewel closed the door behind him and leaned against it, gazing at the ceiling, a smile caressing her lips. She wanted to bask in this fuzzy haze for ever. It was really *happening*! Maxwell Birch loved her back and, right now, here in this moment, all was magnificent with the world.

She'd have given anything for it to remain so but, all too soon, footsteps outside reached her, heralding her mother's return. Masking her regret, she opened the door to let her in.

'How did it go, Mam?'

'A sup of tea, lass.'

Flora's flat tone said it all. Dread rolling through her stomach, Jewel went to fulfil her request.

340

'Mam?' she pressed quietly when Flora was on her second cup. 'Speak to me.'

'Benji will be gone from here at first light.'

Her eyebrows rose to meet her hairline. 'Gone where?'

'He's to be packed off to Esther's parents', and that's where he's to stay. Mother of God, Bernard's rage ... He's just whipped that boy with his belt to within an inch of his life. But for me – I intervened for my brother's sake, aye, not that swine's – I reckon he'd have done for him. Even Esther didn't try and stop him.'

Jewel derived no satisfaction from hearing this. She felt nothing, was numbed to the whole thing. 'You mean they believe me, the two of them? Benji, he admitted it?'

'Aye, on both counts.'

'And ... the child? Will Uncle Bernard and Aunt Esther accept her?'

Glancing to the stairs, Flora patted her hand. 'They've had a holy shock and a lot to take in. Give them time, love.'

Months of tension rose from her. She released a long, slow sigh.

'It's to the future we must look, now, my lass.'

'Aye, Mam.'

'We'll see this through, me and thee.'

'Mam?'

'Aye?'

'Mr Birch called whilst you were away. He wants to wed me, and I said yes.'

Flora lowered her cup slowly. 'The child ... ?'

'He knows. He still wants me – wants us both. Oh, I'm that happy, Mam! I love him so very much.'

'You do, aye, I see it.' She stood and stroked her daughter's hair. 'I'm away to my bed.'

Jewel was more than a little miffed. That's all she had to say on the matter? 'You're all right, Mam?'

'Aye. Tired, lass. It's been a hell of a day, after all. I'll line a drawer from the chest with a blanket to lay the babby in for tonight.'

Watching the woman walk wearily to the stairs, overpowering love coursed through her. 'Mam?'

Flora turned to look at her.

'You could never lose me, you know. Not to Sarah, nor Maxwell, nor anyone else. You're my number one, allus shall be.'

'Eeh, love.'

'I feel better, you know, Mam. Now the truth of it all is out. Free of mind, aye. No more secrets, eh? No more lies. We must both promise never to keep owt from one another ever again.'

Flora looked as if she'd say something. Then instead she nodded, smiled and continued on her way to bed.

Curling into the familiar chair by the fire, Jewel wrapped her arms around herself with a sense of completeness. She felt whole, at last. The badness appeared to have got bored with her, and good had returned to take its place.

Right now, nothing could touch her. She doubted that anything could go wrong ever again.

Chapter 24

'JUST LOOK AT you.'

Blushing pink, Jewel smiled up at Maxwell shyly.

He drew the bustline of her dress lower still, took her breasts in his slightly shaking hands and pressed his lips to hers.

The nursemaid Lizzie had offered to take Jewel's daughter along with her and Constance on their daily walk. The young miss's perambulator, which she'd recently outgrown, had been brought down and fresh, warm blankets placed inside. The moment Jewel and Maxwell had waved Lizzie and the happy children off and closed the door, they had fallen into each other's arms, right there in the hall. She'd given no protest when Maxwell had swept her up into his arms and carried her to the sofa in the drawing room.

His mouth moved to cover her nipple and the last of her self-consciousness melted. She moaned in rapture. Head back, eyes closed, she ran her hands over his broad, bare shoulders.

The desire he evoked in her amazed her still; she hadn't thought it possible to know such exquisite sensations. The ravenous fire in her veins was building, and she knew that, if not for the fact she wasn't yet healed completely from the birth, she'd have given herself to him in a heartbeat.

As it was, they had to make do for now with caresses and kisses. And though she knew not a scrap of shame for it – nothing had ever felt so right – their union, they had both agreed, they would save for their wedding night. The strength to desist, however, was certain to prove a challenge. It was as though they had been searching for one another their whole lives and, now, their bodies knew instinctively that they had found the missing piece. She let her touch travel . . .

Later, entwined in each other's arms and in between kisses now slow and soft, they were discussing dates for their wedding when the front door rattled open. Like scorched cats, they dived apart and hurriedly corrected their clothing. Maxwell had just finished fastening the last button on his shirt when in breezed Roland.

'Son. Hello.'

Glancing from his father to Jewel, his eyes creased in curiosity. 'Is everything all right?'

'Yes. Fine. All's fine.'

'All's fine,' chipped in Jewel. Her eyes met Maxwell's briefly and, catching the amusement dancing in his, she bit her lip to quell a giggle.

Roland's brow smoothed out and the corner of his mouth twitched knowingly. 'Ah. I see. Well, there's something I need to be getting on with, so if you'll excuse me . . .'

When they were alone once more, Jewel covered her face with a groan. Chuckling, Maxwell removed her hands and kissed her soundly on the lips, and she couldn't contain a laugh. 'Oh, Lord. The shame!'

'That was a close call, hm?' He winked and she laughed again. 'I think the time has come to make it official. We'll announce our union properly, later, over dinner.'

'He will be happy for us, won't he?'

344

'Oh, I'm certain. Roland's an easy-minded lad. He'll offer his blessing, you'll see.'

'Mam knows; I told her last night.'

'How did she take it?'

Jewel frowned slightly in remembrance. 'Surprisingly well. What I mean is, she didn't really say anything.'

'Could it be she's displeased?'

'Nay, nay. I know Mam; she'd have said outright were she not consenting.'

'Then you must invite her to dine with us tonight. Hopefully, I can make her see that my feelings for you are true and that my only mission in life from this day is to make her daughter happy.'

Jewel's breast swelled with love. Then the problem that had nagged her since last night gnawed at her conscience and she lowered her head.

'Jewel? What is it?'

'There's summat you should know, summat I've recently discovered . . .' Would the telling change things? Would he see her differently when it came to light his future wife was born out of wedlock? She took a shaky breath. 'Flora Nightingale ain't my mam. My real mother weren't capable of caring for me and gave me up. Flora raised me instead, as her own.'

'My darling . . .' Maxwell shook his head. 'I don't know what to say. I'm so sorry this has happened to you.'

'I'm illegitimate.'

'Jewel, Jewel. I care naught for that.'

'You don't?'

'No. None of it is your fault.'

Relief washed through her. 'I – I thought you'd view me differently.'

'Dearest love.' He took her in his arms. 'Your father, do you know . . . ?'

345

'Nay.' Her voice dropped. 'A resident, someone passing through . . . he could have been anyone. Sarah has no way of knowing. She . . . was a prostitute.'

Maxwell nodded slowly in understanding.

'But she's vowed to change, she has, and I believe she can. She's free from the foul influences of before and has the support of good friends. So long as she steers clear of her old haunts around Canal Street, she'll do just fine, I know it.'

'Canal Street?'

'That's where she lived. It's in Manchester.'

'Yes, I thought it sounded familiar. I've seen the street name in passing when visiting my sister.' He pulled a guilty face. 'Truth be told, I ought to call on her more often. But what with work and Constance . . . Roland, however, journeys regularly. They are quite close. She's been a great support to him, as well as to me, over the years. His mother's death affected him deeply and he often stayed with his aunt thereafter. The change of scene did him the world of good.'

'When was this?' A terrible, terrible feeling had struck her and, as she awaited his answer, she held her breath, hoping, *praying* . . .

'It shall be twenty years next summer that Roland's mother passed.'

Her heart had begun to thump. 'And how long did his stays with Mrs Kirkwood go on for?'

'Jewel?'

'Please. Tell me.'

'Several years; but I don't see what any of this—'

Dragging a hand across her mouth, she rose to her feet. 'So, say . . . eighteen, nineteen, years ago, he would have been there, in Manchester, around that particular area when . . . when . . .'

346

'When what?'

'When I was conceived,' she whispered.

Maxwell's puzzled frown melted. His mouth fell open. 'Surely you're not suggesting what I think you are. That Roland . . . and this Sarah you mentioned . . . ? No. No, you're wrong, you are—'

'You know what your son's like where women are concerned. He's a thirst for skirt that can't be quenched – no doubt it's been that way most of his life. He'd have been – what? – around my age now at the time that Sarah got caught with me? A young man filled with urges – ones that streetwalkers aplenty would have been only too willing to satisfy . . . ?'

'No. This is madness, it is, it—'

'Ask him. Find out if he ever used the services of the women of Canal Street.' She rushed to Maxwell and clutched his hands when he shook his head. 'I beg of thee. *Please*. Ask him, to be sure.'

'Jewel, I can't just—'

'Please,' she pressed. 'For should there be the slightest possibility, then you know what that means, don't you? Mother of God, you could be . . . *We* . . .'

Sheer horror passed across his face. He sucked in air sharply.

'Seek him out. Go now, Maxwell!'

He made a dash for the door.

The next few torturous minutes seemed like hours. Then the door opened and she lifted her eyes in dread.

The man she loved stood frozen in the doorway. His ashen face confirmed her fears for him.

No . . .

'Roland said yes. He said yes, Jewel.'

*

347

'Tell Lizzie when she returns to fetch the child to Mam's.'

'Wait.'

'I must leave!'

'*Wait,*' Maxwell insisted when Jewel attempted to flee the room. 'Christ's sake, we can't leave things like this. We have to discuss it, sort out what the hell we're to do!'

'What we're to do?' she asked incredulously. Tears streamed down her face. 'I think we've done enough, don't you!' Her arms folded instinctively across her chest and she shuddered. 'My God, what we've done together the day . . . I feel sick!'

'We don't know, can't be *certain*—'

'Aye, but there's the tiniest chance, in't there?'

Maxwell lowered his gaze then dropped his head into his hand.

'And that's enough. It is.'

'I know. I *know.*'

Her voice matched his in devastation completely. 'We've kissed.'

'Jewel—'

'You've known my breasts with your hands, your mouth . . .'

'Jewel, please—'

'I *took* you in my palm. You . . . You—'

'Stop! Stop it!' Grasping her by the shoulders, he shook her sobbing form. 'Listen to me. We'll drive ourselves mad dwelling on . . . things like that. Roland confirmed he used to visit those women, yes, but can't recall them or their names, nor whether one had been called Sarah. Now, I know there's perhaps the slightest possibility, but Jewel . . .' He shook her again in desperation. 'It mightn't be so. It isn't – can't be – surely. I *love* you, God dammit!'

'Don't. Don't utter those words. Not now.'

348

'But I do. *We* do. We love each other.'

She raised tortured eyes to his. Despite it all, her feelings for him, still as absolute, crashed in and she let out an agonised cry. She threw herself against his chest and he held her fiercely.

'I can't give you up, Jewel. God help me, I'd die without you.'

Her head sprang up. Knowing what they shared in their pasts, what, like her, Maxwell had attempted when at his lowest ebb – what he might be capable of again – terror filled her. 'Don't say that. Please.'

'Jewel . . .'

She watched his face draw closer. Though her mind begged her to resist, her breaking heart spoke louder and she knew logic couldn't win, not against something this strong. His lips brushed hers in the softest of kisses.

'I love you,' he breathed, and it reached to her very core. 'Say you still feel the same for me.'

There was no hesitation. 'I do. I allus will. But . . .'

He nodded. 'I know.'

This time, when she headed for the door, he didn't stop her.

She glanced back at him over her shoulder. Simultaneous tears made their lonely way down their cheeks. Dropping her head, she walked from the house.

Chapter 25

'you've scarcely touched your grub again. What's to do with thee, at all?'

Pushing away her plate, Jewel shrugged. 'I've told thee, nowt.'

'Well, it don't favour it to me. Now come on, out with it,' Flora said when her daughter's bottom lip shook. 'I'll not take no for an answer this time, neither. I'm fair worried about thee, lass; you ain't yourself.'

'Oh, Mam.'

'Speak to me. What is it?'

The last few days had been true hell upon earth. Being separated from Maxwell – and the reason behind it – haunted and sickened her equally. Her thoughts were in disarray, totally at odds with each other. One moment, she was filled with horror at the prospect of their being related. The next, half mad with yearning, she was telling herself it didn't matter and could be their secret, that no one need know, that they must be together. Then shame and self-disgust would return tenfold. And on, and on . . .

Overriding everything was the crippling sense of loss, and there were times she genuinely believed she would die from the pain. She should have known it was too good to be true. Her, be happy? Huh! How often did that occur of late? That someone such as he had actually looked her way in the first place was too incredible to be real; she'd known it from the start. Why should this latest development have shocked her? Did she honestly think they – or, more to the point, she – would get a joyous ending?

'Is it your Mr Birch? Has summat occurred betwixt the two of you?'

'He's not my Mr Birch.'

Flora nodded as though she'd solved the mystery. 'Youse crossed swords, then? Eeh, what are you like? All couples have their bickers, lass, especially in t' beginning. You can't let it spoil things, nay. You'll learn as you go that to swallow your pride now and then will make forra quieter life, oh aye. Just so much as he thinks he's in charge, you know?' She chuckled knowingly. 'Some men can be funny about that, like to think their women-folk are the meeker half. In reality, mind, we know the truth!'

'What are you *talking* about?'

'Lass?'

Scraping back her chair, Jewel stood and shook her head. The tears never far away fell unchecked down her face. 'It ain't some daft bloody spat, Mam. Nor can it be rectified, not ever. It's finished with; done afore it even began. And that's that.'

Flora's frown melted. 'Eeh, you're a dramatic bugger. What, pray tell, can be so bad that you'd chuck aside a fine fella such as he? By, you were mad with love for him not a week past, and now this? Well? What is it, then, that's gone and changed your mind?'

'You really want to know, do you?' Jewel's breathing was ragged. 'Have I to tell thee, aye?'

'Go on, spit it out!'

351

'His son might have had relations with Sarah. Aye,' she choked when Flora's mouth fell open. 'The man I love, the man I had planned to wed, could just be my grandfather. That's what, Mam.'

The silence was deafening. Bar her wide eyes, Flora's expression was blank. The seconds ticked by and, after a full minute, she still hadn't spoken. Finally, Jewel threw her arms in the air:

'Well, say summat. *Owt.*'

'Lass . . .'

'Now d'you see?' Weeping softly, she dropped back into her seat. 'Mam, what am I to do? How will I bear this? Lord knows I love that man with every part of me. And it's wrong – *foul* – it is, I know, but . . . I want him!'

'Lass. I don't know . . . I . . .'

'Nay, me neither. What *is* there to say, after all?' Her tone softened at Flora's clear distress. 'I just feel I can't let this be it, Mam. I can't just let him go, not until I know for certain.'

The other woman raised her gaze to hers slowly. 'But how will you . . . ?'

'I'll fetch Sarah here. I'll take her to Mawdsley Street, and I'll make Roland see her, and I'll demand they try to remember. Surely one of them will – well, just *know*, when they come together?'

Face corpse grey, her mother squeezed her eyes shut. 'Oh, love.'

'You see why I must find out, Mam, don't you?'

'I do,' she mouthed.

'I simply cannot give Maxwell up like this. Not without a fight. Being parted from him . . . I've never known agony like it.' A heart-wrenching whimper escaped her. 'Why can't I be allowed to be happy, Mam, like others?

352

Ain't I worthy of it? What's wrong with me? What did I do that was so bad that I'm to suffer like this? Tell me, Mam, please. Make me understand. Why does the Almighty hate me so?'

'Don't think those things. You, you're the kindest most beautiful girl the sun ever shone on. What you've been dealt with, all of it . . . By, you don't deserve this on top. Eeh, nay.' Suddenly, Flora's face cleared. It held a look Jewel had never seen before, something akin to defeat mixed with dull acceptance. 'I must.' She nodded. 'I must.' Dreamlike, she rose and headed for the door.

'Where you going? Mam? *Mam*—' But she took no heed; before Jewel had time to follow, her mother was gone.

Jewel wandered to the drawer by the fire within which her daughter lay sleeping peacefully. Kneeling beside it, she gently traced a finger down the silken cheek.

'Just you and me, lass,' she murmured. 'I thought I'd found thee a father, a proper one like you deserve, but it's all ruined. I keep failing you, don't I?' A sob caught in her throat. 'I vowed when I got you back to be better, that *I'd* give you a good life, that I *could* do it. Turns out it were daft talk, for everything's worse now than I'd have believed it possible. I'm so sorry I keep getting it wrong. I just don't know what to do, love.'

Oblivious to its mother's anguish, the child slept on, and Jewel kissed her brow tenderly. Then she resumed her seat at the table to await Flora's return.

Where was she? Jewel wondered with increasing concern as the minutes wore on. Had she merely gone for a walk to help her process what she'd learned? *Dear God, please don't have gone to see Maxwell*, she prayed fervently. The last thing she could cope with right now was him turning up here. For she knew she'd be unable to send him away. It would be impossible. One word, one look from him, and she'd fall right into his arms, she was in no doubt. And she couldn't do that, couldn't let her heart overrule her head, not in this.

The slight possibility of who he was would be there always, and nothing could change that. Sarah must have had uncountable men over the years, and Roland was little better when it came to his exploits – no way would either be able to recall if the other was one of their experiences. Her plan to get them together and hopefully learn the truth had been a desperate, *brainless* notion. It was all she'd had, but it would never work. She simply had to face facts: the truth of her parentage wouldn't ever be proven. She and Maxwell were no more.

Another glance to the clock showed that twenty minutes had now elapsed. Jewel wiped her tears and went to the window. Still, there was no sign of her mother, and her worry intensified. She plucked down her shawl from the nail and threw it on. Then she crossed back to the fire to get the baby.

Jewel was stooping over her, ready to pick her up, when the door opened behind her. 'Mam,' she said in relief, turning, 'I were just about to come and look for thee – Oh. Hello.'

The man in her mother's company inclined his head. 'Hello, lass.'

Jewel hadn't expected this; she lowered her gaze uncomfortably. Like Esther, Uncle Bernard hadn't been near since the revelation of his son's attack on her. Now, though Flora had insisted he and his wife took her word as truth, she didn't know how to react.

What was he even doing here? she asked herself. Why

would Mam involve her brother in this? What at all good would this do?

Flora heaved a sigh. 'Jewel, love, sit down.'

'But what—?'

'Please,' added Bernard. 'Please just do as your mam asks.'

Frowning, she obeyed. They joined her at the table.

'How to say this . . .'

'Mam?' Jewel reached for her hand. 'You're trembling. What is it?'

Rather than answer her, Flora turned instead to Bernard. 'I can't do it, lad. I can't.'

For a moment, he looked panic-stricken. Then his shoulders sagged and he nodded. 'I should be the one to do the telling, anyroad.'

'What's going on?' Jewel glanced from one to the other with creeping dread. 'What telling? What must I know?'

Bernard swallowed hard. Then, avoiding her eye, he began to undo his waistcoat.

'What's this, Uncle Bernard? Mam, what's he doing?' she asked of them both. Neither offered an answer. She watched on in increasing confusion as he loosened his collar then unbuttoned his shirt. Finally, he raised his gaze to hers. To her great surprise, tears had filled his eyes. 'What?' she asked again. 'Please, tell me!'

Turning sideways in his seat, Bernard looked to Flora, who nodded. Then, slowly, he moved aside the material from his right shoulder.

Jewel's mouth fell agape at what he'd revealed. There, stamped in the same place as her own, was a coffee-coloured birthmark. It was like looking in a mirror. The shape and size were one and the same.

'You see what this means, lass?' murmured Flora.

'Nay,' was her honest reply; her mind was a whirl of shock.

'There's some say they ain't hereditary, aye, but I've heard talk of it afore, of a parent passing such marks on to their offspring . . . What you believe about Mr Birch is wrong. Bernard here is your father.'

'But he can't be. He's my uncle, he . . . *How?*' she rasped.

'It were after a ruckus one night with Esther. They hadn't been wed long, were dwelling in Manchester close to me and Fred. Bernard stormed from home and got blind drunk in a nearby inn. There, he finished up finding comfort in the arms of a streetwalker, but thought no more of it the following day after making up with your aunt. They moved here to Bolton town not long after, and that were that. Or so he thought.'

Shooting her brother a weary look, she continued. 'I'd spotted the mark on *your* shoulder, lass, shortly after fetching thee home from Minnie's, knew she'd switched my child with another and figured why. I also recognised it as being just like the one Bernard bore. When next I saw him, I pointed it out and told him of the facts concerning how you'd come to be at Minnie's in the first place. He confessed to me his adultery, and the pair of us guessed what had happened. The woman he'd briefly known intimately, and the mam who had left you at Minnie's, were the same person.'

Jewel felt as though she was set in stone, could neither move nor speak, even if she'd wanted to.

'Now you know the truth.' Her mother took her limp hand and chafed it. 'You, above all others, deserve some happiness. I couldn't see thee lose the chance of having it through mistaken identity. Mr Birch's son and you 'ain't linked, nay. You're free to be with the fella you love.'

'We said no more secrets,' Jewel whispered. 'You swore to me there were nowt left to tell.'

'I did. But, lass, I believed I were doing the right thing, never dreamed all this would come to light, that you'd get hurt . . . I didn't *want* thee hurt! The time for full truths is now. I'm glad I've finally brought this whole sorry mess to light. Even if it means you hating me, disowning me for good . . . you had to know.'

'Is Aunt Esther aware of who I am?'

For the first time, Bernard spoke. 'I confessed all to her when I realised who you were, lass.'

'That's why she's allus been cold with me, in't it? It's all making sense. She's never liked me, has she?' Who could blame Esther for that? To have this – *her* – always there, tainting their marriage . . . Jewel couldn't help but feel sorry for her now. 'She resents I were ever born.'

'But you were.' He spoke quietly. 'And I, for one, am glad of it. To watch thee grow over the years . . . It's warmed my heart more than I can put words to, it has. I'm so proud of the fine woman you've become.'

'Oh God. Oh *nay*!' she exclaimed suddenly as another realisation slammed home. 'Benji. What he did . . . And he's . . . ?'

'Now you understand why I were more reluctant still to tell thee?' croaked her mother.

'Your lack of a proper response that night when I told you of Maxwell's proposal . . . I know why, now. Your mind were too taken up with this nightmare to think of owt else properly, weren't it?'

'I'm so sorry.'

'I've borne my brother's child.'

357

'Lass, lass . . .'

Jewel shook her head as Flora and Bernard made to comfort her. 'I need some air.'

Outside, it was cold and raining, but she paid no heed. She wandered towards the square. Sitting on the town hall's wide steps, she folded her arms around herself.

She felt no anger. A dull throb of betrayal, perhaps, but nothing more. Nor was she surprised at this. For she understood. All these hidden secrets – and, to be fair, she herself had added enough of her own to the mix – were primarily to protect those they loved. That fact made it all a little easier to bear. Done with malicious intentions would have been unforgivable, but this was far off the mark. In each of their minds, they had thought they were doing what was best. That, she knew, she could live with. Were their birthmarks sheer coincidence? Was mere wishful thinking at play here? Surely not.

Still, the shock had yet to abate, she realised this. Yet, in some way, the latest revelation was less shattering than others that had come before it. Though she would always hold Fred Nightingale dear, she couldn't deny that Bernard being her father held some appeal. She had no recollection of the man who would have brought her up had he lived, no warm memories to help ease the feeling of having missed out. Perhaps, after today, she'd get to experience something akin to a father's love. If truth be told, *hadn't* she always loved Bernard as a father anyway?

Jewel's next thought, however, had her biting her lip: would she feel differently towards her daughter, knowing the lad who had helped create her was a much closer relative than she'd thought? But then again, she reminded herself, that was no blame of the child's. If she'd learned anything lately, it was that a body was blameless of its beginnings. Those were wrought by the actions of others; the matter was entirely out of your control.

Despite everything, a small smile touched her lips. A few short months ago, she'd have been bunching her fists and spitting curses, ready to vent her fury over these changes on all and sundry. What had happened to her? *You've grown up, girl, that's what,* her mind whispered, almost fondly. *You're able to see the world now and those in it for what it is – flawed, just like yourself. That doesn't mean they, like you, deserve to suffer their mistakes for ever.*

She wasn't perfect. She could be hot-headed at times, selfish even, for she was only human, after all. She was a mother now, had matured. Mostly, she was bone weary of all the upset.

The decision was hers. Would she let the past go and look ahead to the bright future that was hers for the taking? Or would she cling on to grievances that wouldn't change things or do anyone any good? Repudiate or forgive?

She knew the answer immediately. She rose and headed back the way she had come.

Instead of continuing for Back Cheapside, she found herself taking the few extra turnings to Mawdsley Street. The lightness in her breast remained all the way and, when she knocked at Maxwell's door, a serene smile had joined it.

'Jewel?'

Her feelings for him, unquestionable and unrestrained, shone in her gaze. She held out her arms and he ran into them. He crushed her to him in a long-awaited embrace.

'Oh, my darling . . .'

'My love,' she whispered, resting her cheek against his chest.

In the fading light they stood as one, never needing again to be anywhere else. And all was well with the world.

Chapter 26

'ANOTHER LEMON CAKE, my lass? Go on, then.'

Grinning and clapping her hands, Constance then helped herself from a check blanket spread on the jade-coloured grass.

Flora smiled as she toddled off. Then her mouth fell open and she pointed, chuckling, to where the youngster had stopped by a cluster of waiting birds. 'Well, now! I worried the child were for making herself sick with all them sweet treats, but nay; that's where my ruddy baking's going!'

Sarah threw her head back and laughed. After dropping a kiss on to her granddaughter's head, she passed her across to the older woman. ''Ere, Flora love, you take little Minerva. Come here, you imp!' she added to Constance, rushing towards her, fingers wiggling with the threat of a tickle, much to the child's delight.

Watching the two at play, the group shared a warm smile.

'You wouldn't think she were the same person, Mam, would you?' murmured Jewel, filled with pride.

'And that's all down to thee.' Flora nodded. 'And the little cherub, here, of course. Her girls gave her summat to start afresh for.'

Jewel blinked back tears, then grinned when Maxwell

nuzzled her neck. She turned to him and their lips met in a feathery kiss.

'Eeh, aye. We picked a fine day for it, anyroad,' announced Maria, squinting up at the cloudless sky. 'Ta for holding this on my day off, lass,' she told Jewel as she helped herself to a beef-and-pickle sandwich. 'Reet thoughtful of thee, that were.'

'As if I'd have it any other way. It wouldn't have been the same without thee.'

It wasn't Jewel's birthday for another five days, but they had chosen to hold the celebration the Sunday before to allow the maid to attend. Well, the date which Jewel had always *recognised* as her birthday, at any rate. Truth be told, from what Sarah had said, she'd actually turned eighteen yesterday.

A confusing but happy mess! she thought with a crooked smile, determined now to see the positives where she could. Not many – bar British monarchs, at least – could lay claim to two birthdays, could they? A lucky circumstance, she'd say!

The delicious picnic, prepared by Flora and Sarah this morning, was a sight to behold. Beneath the leafy canopy of a large tree, and amidst much joviality, cold meats, cakes, fruits, custards and pies – washed down with gooseberry wine, Roland and his fiancée's contribution – had been enjoyed by all. The day, so far, had been one of the best of Jewel's life. She really didn't want it to end.

Now, gazing around at the merry faces of the people she loved, she sighed contentedly. What a contrast to life just a few months ago. So much had happened in this one short year, it was difficult to comprehend. And changes wrought were seen nowhere else more than in some of the folk here today.

Again, her eyes sought out Sarah, sober and healthy and glowing with life, and her heart swelled.

Her thoughts drifted to Roland: calmer, matured and besotted with the pretty young woman he was soon to wed. Though not in attendance, the couple had wished the day well, much to Jewel's gratitude. This had strengthened her hopes that despite his initial surprise that she was to join his family, Roland was gradually coming around to the idea. And to think that someone she'd once supposed might be her father would soon be her stepson. She chuckled inwardly. As she'd just mused, definitely a confusing but happy mess! Nor would she have wanted it any other way.

Maxwell's laughter as he watched Sarah sweep his daughter, overcome with giggles, into the air, brought Jewel back to the present. She motioned for him to join them and, after planting another kiss on her, he headed off across the park.

''Ere, I spoke with that Jem Wicks one yesterday,' Flora told her when Maxwell had gone.

Jewel's smiled slowly slipped. 'Oh?'

'We passed in the square and he said as how he'd heard you were to be wed. He asked if I'd give thee his warmest best wishes. He's norra bad lad, really, eh?'

'Nay,' she murmured, her happiness returning as another bad episode in her past was put to bed. There had been wrongs on both sides; if he was prepared to forgive, then she was more than willing as well. Yet another stepping stone towards her fresh start, she knew. 'Nay, he's not.'

Later, out of puff and pink-cheeked, Sarah fell grinning on to the blanket beside her. 'By, I'm fagged! She's a bundle of energy, that young angel Constance and no mistake.'

363

'And you enjoy every second of it,' Flora told her.

'I do, aye. I look forward to Minerva growing and being able to join in the fun. Eeh, it's in heaven I am,' she finished on a whisper almost to herself. 'Bloody heaven.'

Jewel reached for her hand and squeezed. 'I'm pleased you came today, Sarah.'

'As if I'd of missed it, lass!'

'What time you off back to Manchester?'

'Stop at mine the night if you'd like,' offered Flora, and was rewarded with a huge smile.

'Aye?' Sarah asked.

Flora nodded. 'That way, you'll not have to fret about missing the last train home, can spend more time with Jewel and the kiddies.'

Jewel smiled. That these two had hit it off to the degree they had warmed her heart something lovely. Their relationship may have formed through a shared desire to do what was best for their daughter but had since developed into a solid friendship. She loved the very bones of them both.

'Minnie's well, lass, is she?' Flora was asking now. 'Eliza, too?'

'Oh aye. 'Ere,' Sarah continued, turning to Jewel, 'they were over the moon when I told them what you'd named the child. Minnie cried buckets.'

Taking her baby into her arms, she stroked her cheek. 'Choosing Minerva in homage to Mrs Maddox felt the right thing to do, me and Maxwell both agreed. She did what she did with good in her heart. Without her and the decision she made all those years ago, none of us would be here together today. I see that, and I thank her for it daily. She's enriched all our lives.'

Bright-eyed, the women nodded their agreement.

'I've never been happier than I am now, living with the two of them,' said Sarah. Then her face dimmed a little and she sighed. 'I only wish I could find employment. I've searched and searched, but . . .' She shrugged. 'I hate dwelling on their charity.'

'If it's a position you're after, I reckon Maxwell's sister Mrs Kirkwood would be only too happy to help you, Sarah,' offered Jewel.

'Aye?'

Recalling Mrs Kirkwood's enthusiasm to help Louise last year, she nodded. 'That lady is golden-hearted; it's what her philanthropic soul lives for, I'm sure. I'll introduce you to her, shall I, at the wedding next month?'

'Eeh, aye. Oh, ta, lass,' she cried, beaming.

As the group lapsed into companionable silence, Jewel's thoughts returned to Louise. She'd told Maxwell's sister during their chance meeting that day that the girl was her cousin, little knowing the truth in the statement. Still, there had been no word from her and, in a way, Jewel was glad of this, for hopefully it meant she was settled wherever she'd chosen to go. She was confident that Louise was doing well, had finally found the decent start she deserved. Sadly, it wasn't to be for Julia. A victim of her upbringing, she'd stood little chance. However, Jewel was sure that her sister was making the most of her life, doubly so, for the pair of them.

As for the woman who gave birth to them . . . She shuddered at the memory of her. Sarah hadn't seen hide nor hair of her since, and for that they must all be truly thankful.

'Here's Bernard, look.'

Following her mother's gaze across the park, Jewel

smiled at the man making his way towards them. She knew a throb of disappointment that Esther wasn't with him, but refused to dwell on it. The woman was hurting, in more ways than one. Benji, when all was said and done, and despite his faults, was her only child. She must miss him terribly. Moreover, with Sarah now on the scene, her heart was surely sorer still.

Would they ever be able to get past this, as a family? Jewel certainly hoped so. The past, after all, was where it belonged. Peace, for everyone, and love and togetherness were what she desired more than anything else.

'I'm glad you came,' she told Bernard when he stooped to kiss her cheek. 'Thank you.'

He nodded, smiled. Then, dropping his gaze, he shifted from foot to foot.

'What is it?' Jewel asked.

'Esther.'

'She's here?' She strained her eyes towards the park's entrance. 'Where?'

'By the gates.' His tone held both guilt and hope. 'She told me to go on in front, needed a minute to compose herself, like. But ay, she agreed to coming, eh? That's a good sign, lass, in't it?'

Jewel gave him a small smile of reassurance then, catching sight of her aunt in the distance making her way towards them, she rose from the blanket. Holding Minerva close, she set off to meet her.

'Afternoon,' Esther said quietly with an awkward nod of greeting when she reached her. 'Bernard said it were all right that I came . . .'

'Course, aye. I'm glad you're here.'

Her face showed surprise. 'Aye?'

'Aunt Esther, all that's occurred, what we've learned . . .

366

I just want to be happy, that's all,' she said earnestly. 'It's all one bloody big mess, I know, but well . . . Can't we try to get past it, together? As a family? Please?'

The woman's stare misted. She looked down at her granddaughter and a ghost of a smile appeared at her mouth. She brought her gaze back to Jewel and took a deep breath. 'I hope youse have saved a bit of grub for me, lass, I'm fair clemmed.'

Tears of quiet relief pricked her eyes. She beckoned for Esther to follow, and the two of them made off to the party.

When her aunt was seated between Flora and Bernard, and Maria's sister – who had reprised her role as Maxwell's maid – had handed her a glass of gooseberry wine, Jewel left her to settle in and went in search of Maxwell. She spotted him at the steps by the colourful flowerbeds. Constance on his knee, he was pointing out the different blooms to the enraptured child.

Pausing for a moment unnoticed, Jewel drank in the scene with a full heart. To think that they were her life now, her family. She surely was the luckiest lass in the world.

'Come here, you two.' Spotting her and Minerva, Maxwell held out a hand. 'What are you thinking?' he asked Jewel, putting his arm around her when she snuggled beside him.

'How things could so easily have been very different,' she murmured. 'I never believed I could feel like this, my love, thought happiness weren't meant for me.' A smile crept across her lips. 'I were convinced you only noticed me for my domestic skills.'

He grinned. 'That's what I liked to have you and others believe, never dreamed you'd think to look twice at an old fogey like me. When you left for all those

367

months . . . God, it near killed me. You were with me in mind constantly.'

'And me. Is that why you didn't say goodbye?' she asked suddenly. 'I've allus wondered.'

He nodded. 'I couldn't trust myself not to beg at your feet for you not to go.'

'What are we like, eh? And ay, don't call yourself that again,' she scolded softly.

'What?'

'Old. For you're not.'

'No?'

She shook her head. 'You're mature, experienced. I like that.'

'So I've noticed,' he whispered with a wink, then laughed when she swatted his arm, blushing. He looked towards the picnic and the wicked gleam in his eye deepened. 'What say we run away to some far-off place where no one will ever find us? We'll do nothing but drink champagne in the sun and make love in the moonlight for the rest of our lives. Are you game?'

Playing along, she arched an eyebrow. 'And where would we find the brass to fund this tempting life-style?'

'I'll rob the bank.'

'And when you're caught and prosecuted for embezzlement?'

'Oh, but it would have been worth it!' he growled, pulling her close and kissing her neck.

Laughing, she lifted his chin with her finger. Lips soft and warm found hers and she closed her eyes.

'We had better get back to our guests,' he whispered against her.

She pulled him closer. 'In a minute.'

'I don't have to leave, nay,' she told him when, finally,

they walked arm in arm back to the others. 'I have everything I need right here.'

Things were not perfect yet between them all, it was true, but they were good enough. Besides, the future could only get better. For she had family, friends. She had love.

And, really, what was life without it?

About the Author

Emma Hornby is the author of *A Shilling for a Wife*, *Manchester Moll* and *The Orphans of Ardwick*. Before pursuing a writing career, she had a variety of jobs, from care assistant for the elderly to working in a Blackpool rock factory.

She was inspired to write because of her lifelong love of sagas and after researching her family history; like the characters in her books, many generations of her family eked out life amidst the squalor and poverty of Lancashire's slums.

Emma lives on a tight-knit working-class estate in Bolton with her family.

Discover more about Emma and her books at her website: www.emmahornby.com